3-

AA
BP

STORM SURGE

STORM SURGE

T. J. MacGregor

HYPERION   *New York*

In memory of Frank Rutledge

1914 – 1992

and Fyrne Rutledge Grisinger

1908 – 1992

Special thanks to Diane Cleaver,

who makes all things possible;

to Rob, my first reader always;

to Mom and Dad, for everything;

and to Megan

That pink, that incredible Miami pink.

MICHAEL MANN

Miami has no beginning. It has no middle. But it does have an end—if you're willing to drive far enough to find it.

T. D. ALLMAN
Miami: City of the Future

STORM
SURGE

Prologue

Charlie hears it in the fading dusk, a noise that grips the warm, still air and tightens it until he can barely breathe. Footsteps, punctuating his own.

He walks faster, faster. The muscles in his neck creak like rusted springs when he finally steals a glance behind him. Nothing there. He's alone on the street, alone with the dark shapes of cars standing motionless at curbs, alone in this forgotten neighborhood of crumbling sidewalks, pitted asphalt, and storefronts that are boarded up, sealed like coffins.

Alone.

And yet.

There are alleys between these abandoned buildings, nooks and crannies to duck into, places to hide. He rubs the back of his hand over his mouth, wills his legs to move more quickly. His eyes skip ahead, measuring the distance to the end of the block. He strains to hear the footsteps again, but other sounds reach him, waves breaking on the beach three blocks east, the quickening beat of his heart, the soft click of his shoes against the sidewalk.

Charlie turns off Collins Avenue and onto Fourteenth Street, where a dim light burns at the end of the block. In between lies a wasteland, a casualty of the Deco craze. No pretty pastel buildings here, no wide white beaches, no fancy restaurants. He sees a gas station (closed), a junk shop (closed), a coffee shop (closed), a tattoo parlor (closed), and The Deuce Club, open and crying for business.

Although he doesn't hear anything behind him now, he feels something—a presence, a weight that presses up against him like a strong wind. Sweat dimples his face. His hands are damp. His legs won't cooperate. He wheezes like a failing machine. His bones creak and ache and feel as thin as tissue paper. Bones aren't meant to last eighty-five years.

When he can't stand it anymore, when the enormity of what he imagines overpowers him, he looks back. He isn't sure what he expected to see—a mugger, a vampire, death racing toward him on a silent motorcycle. The darkness is empty.

He hears music as he nears The Deuce Club, a welcome sound even though it is distant and soft, closed up behind windows that won't open, inside air that is always stale. He slips inside the club quickly, furtively, into the irritating twang of country music from the jukebox, the stink of smoke, the gloomy light. Three old-timers are hunched over their drinks at the bar, a couple of young Latinos are playing pool, sunburned tourists occupy a table. Charlie hastens to the left side of the bar, where he can watch the front door, where he can see who enters, who leaves, where his back is to the wall. Heckler, who values punctuality, hasn't arrived yet. Not a good sign, not good at all.

He orders rum over ice. A little rum, a lot of ice. He watches the clock on the wall as though the act of watching time pass will hurry Heckler. The bartender, a pretty young woman with a quick smile, sets down his drink and a bowl of popcorn. "Run a tab, sir?"

"No, thanks. This is it."

He pays her with a five and she strolls off to get change. When he raises the drink to his mouth, his hand shakes. He quickly sets the glass down. Don't, hand, please don't. He rubs it, flexes the fingers, makes a fist and releases it. Now. Try again. He cups both of his hands around the glass when he lifts it this time.

The first sip of rum burns a path down his gullet and pools like spoiled milk in his stomach. Sourness swells in his throat. For a horrifying moment he's certain he's going to vomit. But the feeling passes.

All things pass, he reminds himself: illness, grief, success, triumph, even fear. That most of all. Next week or next month, he'll no longer be able to remember what terrified him so deeply out there on the street. He'll laugh at his certainty that he was being followed.

The door opens and a couple enter. Lovebirds, holding hands. They sit at the table under the clock, a fitting statement of their youth. A part of him envies the years that stretch before them, an undiscovered country.

Tick tock, whispers the clock. Heckler is late.

The last of his rum vanishes. His fingers drum the counter. He wishes Heckler would hurry.

One of the old-timers at the bar swings off his stool and walks over to the jukebox with a drink in hand. He's dressed in baggy trousers, a faded checkered shirt, a khaki raincoat with a huge pocket on either side, and running shoes. An eccentric. This town is filled with them. But there's something familiar about the man, about the way he moves. Then he turns and Charlie's breath catches in his throat.

Heckler, it's Heckler. But the face is all wrong, gaunt, sallow, old. He looks as if he has aged twenty years in the three since Charlie last saw him. His hair isn't just turning gray: it's absolutely white and long, well past the collar of his raincoat. The sunbursts at the corners of his eyes that once seemed charming are now deeply etched, rune marks carved in stone. He smiles, but there's no joy in it. He's sweating profusely, sweating even though the air in here is cool.

"*Fooled you, didn't I, professor?*" *He straddles the stool next to Charlie.* "*It's the hair. Does it every time.*" *He flicks it off the back of his neck, an abrupt, nervous gesture.* "*Who'd expect a fifty-four-year-old man to look like an aging hippie, right?*" *He snorts.* "*A young goon, that's who.*" *Heckler tilts his head toward the door; no one is there.* "*Bastard's been tailing me all the way from the Lincoln Road*

Mall. Five bars, Charlie. But he hasn't touched me. He thinks I'm just drinking my way south. Guess I am at that." He laughs again and signals the bartender for a refill. "*What're you drinking?*"

"*I'm fine. Let's go somewhere else, to my—*"

"*No. No, there isn't time.*" An urgency has entered his voice and from one of his raincoat pockets he brings out a large wrinkled envelope. "*This will take care of everything, Charlie. And me, I'm gone. Switzerland, France, Greece, it doesn't matter.*"

He looks at Charlie then, his dark eyes bright with terror and with something else, something that takes Charlie a moment to define. Drugs, that's it. Heckler is stoned. "*Yeah,*" he says softly, as though Charlie has spoken aloud. "*Morphine.*"

"*Jesus, Steve.*"

A corner of his mouth twitches, then the twitch spreads across the rest of his face, as though the skin is stone that is cracking. "*You never had kids, Charlie. You don't know what it's like when you lose your own kid. That's when my hair went totally white. Woke up one morning and there it was.*"

His daughter, a suicide. Charlie can't remember when it happened. Two years ago? Three? For Heckler it was yesterday.

"*And then the wife left and, well, what the hell. It doesn't matter.*" He drops his gaze to the envelope, pats it once, twice, as though it's a pet. "*There are some things that even men like me can't live with, Charlie.*" He wipes the back of his hand across his mouth. "*Don't keep this stuff, okay? It's not safe. Divvy everything up, send it to people you trust until you're ready to use it. Don't say I never did anything for you, Charlie, huh?*" That sad smile appears briefly, then vanishes as he slides the envelope over in front of Charlie. He drops a ten on the counter for his drink. Too much, Charlie thinks. A dollar bill would do it. "*I'm going to the men's room. Just get up and leave. And, Charlie, thanks.*" Heckler squeezes his shoulder, then he's gone.

Heckler, thanking him, when he's the one who should be giving thanks. Charlie's hand trembles again when he touches the envelope: the torn corners, the coffee stains, the doodles, each detail a cornerstone of Heckler's dark solitude. He quickly folds it, sticks it inside his shirt, zips his windbreaker. Get up and leave, he thinks. Now.

He walks from his stool to the door, but the sensation of movement eludes him. There is only the weight of the envelope inside his jacket, the shape of it against his chest, then the night air against his face.

Outside the bar, he hesitates. His eyes dart here and there. He hunches his shoulders against the dark. Back to Collins, then nine blocks south to Fifth Street. To Woolley's Fine Foods, where he'll buy envelopes, stamps. He'll divide the material into fifths, send out four parts, keep one for himself until—when? When will he be ready? When will it be safe?

He won't think about it right now. He will walk. Right foot, left, right again, good, very good, keep up the great work, Charlie. Keep moving, Charlie, but not too fast. Past this old building and that, past an alley, the silent cars. Now: a hot prickling at the back of his neck, sweat oozing down the undersides of his arms, the envelope stuck like a Band-Aid to his bony chest.

This time he doesn't look back, doesn't have to. He knows someone is back there. He knows. He breaks into a run, a graceless loping. His bones rattle, his lungs beg for air, his muscles shriek for a reprieve. But he doesn't stop. He stumbles through one intersection after another, passing through lights, darkness, lights again. Then he's inside Woolley's, safe inside with other shoppers, in an ordered world of aisles and displays.

He hurries to the front desk to cash a check. The clerk's face is a mirror that reflects his panic: she thinks he's one of the old crazies who walks the streets with grocery carts stuffed with his belongings. She sees him as his own worst nightmare.

A wave of darkness sweeps over him. He wants to grab her by the arms, shake her, scream at her. He isn't one of the crazies, he isn't, he used to teach at Princeton, he used to be someone. But she's already stepping back from the counter, her polite smile straining at the edges.

He pulls a blank check from his wallet, fills it out, shows his check-cashing card. She avoids his eyes, counts out his money. "Stamps," he says. "I need stamps."

"How many stamps, sir?"

Panic. How many. How many will be enough? "Eight stamps, twenty-nine cents each."

She opens a drawer, tears eight stamps from a sheet. He pays her, scoops up the rest of his money, and rushes off.

Stationery, where's the stationery aisle? How can he not remember? He has been up and down that aisle hundreds of times. His eyes bulge, sweat stands out on his face, his heart skitters around in his chest, a dying fish on a hook. His feet save him. His feet remember the way.

His fingers fumble with the flap on the envelope and he pulls out papers, photographs, the pieces of a giant puzzle, just as Heckler promised. Now all he has to do is divide everything, figure out who will get what until he's ready to use it.

The entrance to the stationery aisle is blocked by a long line of people waiting to use the copier. Retirees, all retirees like himself, with stacks of forms: Medicare forms, social security forms, pension forms, bank forms, yes, yes, he knows all about forms. Move, he thinks, please move.

Once he's in the aisle, the choice of merchandise nearly overwhelms him. Quick quick quick. Choose something, choose anything. A packet of manila envelopes, a notepad, a pen. He hastens to the express-checkout register, then has to wait while a woman gets a check approved and a man fishes bills from his wallet. He is nearly crazy with waiting by the time he reaches the area where the grocery carts are parked.

Charlie sets everything on the ledge that runs along the bottom of the window and scans the parking lot. People. Cars. The darkness, rubbing up against the glass like a cat in heat. The reflection of the clerk's face floats in the window, a pickled egg in vinegar; she has stepped out from behind the front desk to watch him. Charlie looks down, pretends he hasn't seen her.

Hurry, just hurry. He begins scribbling his notes, four identical notes. Now. How to divide the material? To whom should it go? Whom does he trust? What should he keep for himself? Panic claws at the back of his throat. He knuckles his eyes. Chess, it's just another chess move, that's how he must think of it.

And just that easily, the names come to him. He addresses the envelopes from memory, eighty-five and his memory is sharp as glass when he needs it. He slaps stamps on the envelopes, drops them in the mailbox outside as he leaves. None of the envelopes contains enough to provide a complete picture without its counterparts.

He zips the original envelope inside his jacket, then calls Will's place from the public phone. It rings and rings and finally the machine kicks in. Charlie leaves a message.

When he finally reaches his street, he's so tired he can barely stand up. It's a bone fatigue, pervasive, cruel. He leans into a rubber tree at the side of the building and presses the heels of his hands against his eyes. He feels Death just off to his right, a cool presence in the warm darkness. It waits for him but isn't quite ready to take him yet.

Go to it, Charlie, Death whispers. Wrap it up.

He climbs the open stairs to his apartment, unlocks the door, and slips inside, into the dark. The dead bolt clicks into place, a sharp, reassuring sound, and he leans into the door, forehead against the wood. Safe now. Safe.

Suddenly the light winks on and Charlie spins around. A figure stands in the dark pool of shadows next to the couch, a man, a woman, he can't tell which. But he can see the gun protruding from the shadows like an animal's snout, a gun aimed at his chest. "I wish it could've been different. I really do. I'll take that envelope."

Charlie opens his mouth to speak but nothing comes out. A white, savage terror grips him. His only thought is how foolish he was not to believe what he felt, that he was being followed, that Death was galloping toward him, disguised, whispering his name. Now Death is here and he has nothing to say.

The first shot strikes him in the chest. He feels it, feels the biting sharpness near his heart, the sudden cruelty of the pain, a rush of something leaving his body. Then he is falling back, back, the ceiling tilting, the window upside down, everything slow, strange, the light winking off and on. Death's arms reach out to catch him before he strikes the floor; he can see the arms, long, narrow shapes emerging from the shadows. He anticipates the embrace, accepts it, and then surrenders to it with a single violent and pathetic shudder.

1

From a distance, the Miami skyline was seductive. Buildings rose dramatically in the excessive light, shooting upward in bold, clean lines as if to support the sky or conquer it, Quin couldn't tell which.

Down here on the ground, though, it was business as usual. The stoplight at the bottom of the exit ramp was stuck on red, traffic was knotted at the intersection, horns blared, cars tried to squeeze into line in front of her. Moonies were hawking flowers, two motorists were shouting at each other through their open windows, and a kid with a roll of paper towels and a bottle of Windex offered to clean her windshield for two bucks. Down here on the ground were all the reasons she and McCleary had left without regrets nearly two years ago.

A Mercedes crept in on her right, trying to cut in front of her. The driver was hunched over his steering wheel, a Kamikaze pilot who pretended she didn't exist. That was one of the rules of Miami roads: if you cut, don't look. In the old days, she would have inched forward until her bumper touched the bumper of the car in front of her so the Mercedes wouldn't be able to sneak in. But no more. Too many Jekylls carried guns in their glove compartments.

Welcome to Miami, paradise flawed, paradise falling, paradise gone.

This wasn't her first visit since they'd moved. But with every visit she realized that, although she didn't miss living here, a part of her still yearned for the city's unique and maddening rhythm, its pulse of heat and light and color, its lunacy. Miami was addictive, and the twenty-seven years she had lived here had marked her as surely as Cain. This was where she'd gone to high school, come of age, where she had met and married McCleary.

Quin had known Miami when there was no skyline, when it was old folks playing shuffleboard in the warm winter sun and rich folks sipping drinks by the swimming pool. She had known it when pink '56 Caddy convertibles cruised Collins Avenue with the tops down, the fading Art Deco hotels in the background.

The city's transformation since those days had been a process, a gradual evolution that wouldn't have happened in Des Moines, for instance, or Bismarck, North Dakota. Its location at the tip of the Florida peninsula made it accessible to immigrants from Latin America and the Caribbean, thus creating a populace that was ethnically mixed. Its climate had begun to lure young families who built homes in surrounding communities—Coconut Grove, Hialeah, Coral Gables, dots on a map that had burgeoned. Then, in 1980, all hell had broken loose.

The Mariel boatlift flooded Miami with more than a hundred thousand refugees; race riots blew Overtown apart; cocaine cowboys ruled their domains like feudal lords. Quin had lived here when the FBI had declared that only Atlantic City had a higher murder rate than Miami, something everyone in town already knew. And when the era of grits, glitz, and guns had given way to Sonny Crockett and Cristo and a vision of Miami as Deco pastels and wet streets, a paradise reclaimed, she had ridden the crest of the boom like everyone else.

Now it was tough to say exactly what Miami was. The old problems still existed, crime and drugs, refugees and racial tensions, much of it worse than before. The blacks in Overtown were still poor. Real estate was in a slump. The schools were a mess. And every year the homeless and the elderly flocked here in greater numbers, overloading the circuits of social services.

Miami Vice, the TV miracle that had neatly divided the city's history into Before and After, was now in reruns. And maybe that was the heart of the problem, Miami drifting in a post-*Vice* trauma, hoping for another miracle, a new identity that would usher it into the nineties.

She turned into the lot behind the Metro-Dade Police Department and scanned it for McCleary's red Miata. He'd driven down here two days ago with the envelope Charlie Potemkin had mailed to them, the envelope postmarked the day after he was shot in his apartment.

Charlie had presumably understood what the grainy photos were all about, but he hadn't bothered explaining to them. For all she knew, they might be nothing more than pictures of former students, something from an old man's collection of memorabilia. As long as she'd known him, he'd saved things with the compulsion of a man who believed his life might otherwise escape him.

They'd become friends after his retirement from Princeton, when he was teaching several criminology courses at the University of Miami and she'd sought his advice on a case. Charlie was already in his seventies then; she was in her late twenties. Contrary to what other people believed at the time, there were never any father-daughter overtones to it. Neither of them was looking for substitutions. They were teacher and student and the roles were interchangeable. He'd learned from her as readily as she'd learned from him.

She could still remember the clutter in his tiny office: files that had bulged with hundreds of newspaper and magazine clippings, shelves crowded with books. You could ask him virtually anything and he probably had a file or a book on it.

The hastily scribbled note he'd included in the envelope might have related to nothing more than the contents of some favorite file. *Hold on to this until you hear from me.* You bet, Charlie. But why all the mystery, Charlie? Because that was how he'd always done things.

She didn't see the Miata. Hardly surprising. Her husband func-tioned according to his own clock, which was usually twenty to thirty minutes behind everyone else's. She found a parking place at the end of the lot and nosed into it. Nosed carefully. The Explorer was still new enough so that she wasn't quite accustomed to parking it yet. Especially in a lot as crammed as Metro-Dade's.

The Metro-Dade PD was responsible for the entire county, ten thousand square miles of the most ethnically diverse population in the state. It was as large and complex as any bureaucracy, divided and subdivided like plots of land in a housing development. When McCleary had resigned from here nine years ago, he'd been at the helm of the Homicide Department, burned out and ready for some-thing new. The new had come about when they'd gone into business together and bought the private detective agency where she'd been working. Somehow, though, the homicide part of it had stuck to him like a shadow. Whenever she remarked on this fact to Benson, his standard reply was straight out of Sonny Crockett's mouth. *Karma, it's his karma.*

Quin supposed that Benson, a cop for twenty years and now head honcho for the entire Metro-Dade, knew a thing or two about murder and karma. You wouldn't think it, though, to look at him. Thin and sinewy, an inch or so shorter than her five feet ten, he seemed as benign as a ladybug.

He was at his desk when she entered his office on the second floor, a room he'd occupied since he'd made lieutenant fourteen years ago. His wire-rim glasses rode low on the bridge of his nose, his dark curly hair had new streaks of gray at the temples, and as always he was surrounded by papers, files, folders, books, computer printouts. Ev-erything was arranged in tall, tidy stacks that formed a barricade between him and the rest of the room. His enthusiasm and energy, though, were as constant and unchanged as the June heat.

He hugged her hello and informed her McCleary had just called to say he was on his way. "He and Will are moving some boxes from Charlie's apartment."

Will was William Boone, Charlie's closest friend and a retired gumshoe buddy of McCleary's. He had found Charlie's body. "What do you think about the photos, Tim?"

He leaned back against the edge of his desk and poked at his glasses. "They were so grainy we decided to make computer enhancements. One of the men is Lawrence Crandall, the brains behind Crandall Development. You heard of him?"

"Isn't he the guy who ushered in Deco Madness?"

"He didn't just usher it in, Quin. He was the primary force behind the revamping of the Deco District. He made a fortune, Miami became paradise found, and everyone was happy. His newest vision is to turn the eleven-hundred block of Ocean Drive into a Deco resort. The three hotels and two restaurants on the block had been having financial problems for a long time. Absentee owners, competition, seasonal business, the usual stuff. Anyway, as each place went under, Crandall bought it.

"But the critical piece of property is an old folks' home in the middle of the block. The county owns it. They agreed to sell it to Crandall, with a shitload of restrictions, naturally, and the sale was supposed to be finalized sometime in July. Then Charlie got into the act."

"I don't remember any nursing home on Ocean Drive."

"It's not a nursing home. It's just a low-rent apartment building that the county's owned for the last twenty years. The Sea Witch, the county's white elephant, a senior citizens' apartment building. The twenty-five residents have been there practically since Flagler built the railroad, and they were going to be out when the sale was final. Charlie became their spokesperson, got the local media into the act, and organized a rally in front of city hall. It got incredible coverage in Dade—two dozen elderly people against city hall and all that. There was a good turnout at the rally but Charlie was going to try again. Bigger numbers, more coverage. He got in touch with some national news shows; *Sixty Minutes* bit. The rally was scheduled for mid-July, several days before the closing on the property."

"And now?"

"All bets are off. Charlie was the mover behind this thing, Quin. With him dead, the residents are facing eviction."

"What about the second photo?"

"A German, Ebo Rau. He owns a string of import-export businesses in Berlin and does a lot of his buying here in Miami."

"Are he and Crandall business partners?"

"They have been. Crandall was the developer for a shopping complex in Berlin that Rau owns." Benson walked over to the coffeepot on a low shelf under the window. "You want some?"

"Yeah, thanks."

"With milk, right?"

"Good memory, Tim."

"You couldn't convince my son of that. He thinks I'm on the road to Alzheimer's." He came back across the room with two mugs. "When they hit thirteen, Quin, they become a weird subspecies and it's all downhill after that. So when it happens to Michelle, don't say I didn't warn you."

She laughed. "She's got a ways to go yet." Her daughter was sixteen months old; Benson's son was almost college bound.

"How's preschool working out?"

"Great. And it beats seven baby-sitters in nine months, I'll tell you that much. Ellie loves it."

Benson didn't sip from his mug; he just kept stirring it, the spoon clicking against the sides. She sensed he was working up to something and suspected she wasn't going to like it, whatever it was.

"Did forensics come up with anything?" she asked.

"Nope. And neither did Doc Smithers." The coroner. "There wasn't any struggle. The place hadn't been broken into. The bullet was from a standard .38, went straight into his heart from a distance of six or seven feet, and he was facing the killer when it happened. No one in the complex heard anything. It was hot that night and everyone's AC was on. Will got a call from Charlie at eight-thirty, but he wasn't home and Charlie left a message on his machine to come over as soon as he could. He got there shortly after ten and found him."

"Was the door unlocked?"

"No, Will had a key. He and Charlie had traded keys a while back."

"I gather Will isn't a suspect."

"It crossed my mind, Quin. Will found him, had a key to the place, knew him better than anyone else. But, hell, he and Charlie were chess partners for ten years and I've known him twice as long. He's eccentric, but Christ, he's no killer."

Eccentric was a polite term for a man who was known as The Conspiracist among people who liked him and as Boone the Loon among people who didn't. Quin, like McCleary, fell into the first category. Benson was somewhere in between.

"Besides," Benson went on, "he didn't have a motive. I mean, we're talking about a couple of antiquities whose friendship made getting old on Miami Beach a little more tolerable."

The way he said it left a bad taste in her mouth for old age and for growing old on Miami Beach in particular. While Miami proper was casting around for a new image, Miami Beach—with the exception of the Deco District—had already found one. For its elderly population, it was a tarnished yellow brick road strewn with broken promises.

"So you're looking at Crandall, who had a motive."

He nodded. "My wife's college roommate, Irene, has been working in Crandall's Miami office for twelve years. She's head of personnel. She doesn't know him very well personally, but knows the business thoroughly enough to recognize inconsistencies when she sees them: accounts that don't balance, unexplained expenditures, unexplained income, that kind of thing. She thinks he's mixed up in something. Although she's nosy, this isn't her line of work and she's the first to admit it. Crandall's personal assistant left three months ago when her husband was relocated, and the slot's still open. Irene suggested we slip a pro into the spot."

Quin held up her hands for him to stop, but he rushed on. "Look, I know all your objections. I know things are different now that you've got Michelle. But I need help on this one. We'd pay for everything, including a furnished apartment on Miami Beach. We'd provide your cover, back it up on computers, whatever needs to be done. You'd still have weekends free. Mac would be at Boone's, working the case from that angle. I need some answers and there's no one else I trust the way I do you and Mac."

"Slide Mac into the spot."

"Can't. Crandall's personal assistants have always been women. Most of his employees are women."

"Tim, I'd like to help, but—"

"I know it's not easy for both of you to get away from the office."

"It's not the office. We have one other investigator working for us now who can take care of things. It's Ellie. I can't just move her down here."

"Would your sister be able to take her for a couple of weeks? Mac mentioned that she's living down here now."

"I'd have to talk to her."

"Great, talk to her, think about it over the weekend." He backed off now, and she knew he was banking on the past, on the many debts that had accrued over the years. How could she blame him? How could she deny him? How?

The point wasn't whether her sister could take Ellie. She would be thrilled to do it. But what would happen next time this came up? And the time after that? Benson didn't understand how it was. His son was older, and besides, it was different for men and women, different and still unequal despite Steinem and Friedan and NOW and everything and everyone else who had followed.

You couldn't have it all unless you hired help—an au pair, a housekeeper, a lawn service, a cook, your life doled out in parcels to other people. But if you did that, you might wake up one day and realize that what had been a cranky whine at one was, at fifteen, a fondness for petty theft or coke.

Quin told Benson she would let him know by Sunday night and he said sure, no problem, just as she'd known he would. Then he left word with his secretary that they were going to lunch at the Colombian restaurant down the street and to send McCleary over when he arrived.

McCleary breezed into the restaurant twenty minutes later. He stood just inside the doorway, a tall, lean man with dark hair paling at the temples and a neatly trimmed beard threaded with gray. He tilted his sunglasses back onto the top of his head; his smoke-blue eyes moved through the room, looking for them.

There were always moments like this, when McCleary was unaware that she was watching him, that her pulse quickened. It was a visceral reaction, a peculiar anticipation of the instant their eyes would connect and their history would slide into place around them. Nearly eight years of marriage, she thought, and his mere presence still possessed the power to transform the air that she breathed.

He smiled when he saw her, a quick, telling smile that said he'd already made up his mind to help Boone regardless of what she decided about Benson's proposition. She'd expected that. McCleary had been as fond of Charlie as she had.

But as he made his way over to the table where she and Benson were sitting, she noticed a quality about McCleary that she hadn't seen since his sister's murder seven months ago. She realized he *needed* to take on this investigation, that he viewed it as a kind of redemption that would mitigate the blame he felt about Cat's death. Mission would replace guilt and eventually guilt would die of inertia. The back door to psychic restoration, she thought. But what the hell, if it worked, she was all for it.

"Sorry I'm so late," he said as he claimed the chair next to Quin. "You wouldn't believe the stuff Charlie's son was going to toss or give to the Salvation Army."

"I thought he'd already left town," Benson said.

"He has. He told Will to pick through what he wanted. Now everything is stacked in the spare bedroom." He accepted the fork Quin proffered and they shared her platter of *arroz con pollo*. "Will thinks there's a lot more to this than just the Sea Witch."

Quin caught the fleeting expression on Benson's face and knew he was thinking the same thing she was: it was almost inevitable that Boone, conspiracist, one-time follower and employee of New Orleans D.A. Jim Garrison, would draw such a conclusion. "I, uh, don't mean to be cynical, Mac," he said. "But Will could probably see a conspiracy in the fluctuation of weather patterns in the country."

McCleary shrugged. "Yeah, probably. But that doesn't necessarily mean he's wrong about this."

"Real-estate developers lose deals all the time," Quin went on. "It's the risk of doing business. It doesn't warrant murder."

"Not on the surface," Benson said. "But there was a lot more to this than just a lost deal. The resort he wants to build could generate millions over the years."

"Greed? That's all?" McCleary sounded disappointed. "C'mon, Tim."

"Well, until we know more, greed is the best place to start."

Silence. They both looked at Quin. She didn't have to be a genius to figure out what it meant. She reached for one of the *arepitas*, a cornmeal delight filled with chunks of meat and vegetables. She broke it in half, ignoring them.

McCleary spoke first. "What do you think of Tim's idea?"

"I'd like to mull it over."

"What's there to mull?"

As though Benson weren't present. "Ellie." She glared at him. "You know, your daughter?"

His jaw tightened, he dug his fork into what remained of the *arroz con pollo,* and didn't reply. Benson squirmed, glancing from one to the other, the man in the middle. "Hey, guys. No big deal, okay? If you decide you don't want to do it, Quin, that's fine. I understand. Really." Then, to McCleary: "Ease up, Mac."

Referee, soothsayer, friend.

And Charlie, she thought. What had Charlie been? Mentor and friend and confidant, a whiz at seeing connections that were invisible to everyone else. She owed him, too, owed him for the dozens of cases he'd helped her with over the years, cases she wouldn't have resolved without him. If she had been the victim, he would have been right in there with McCleary, fitting the pieces together.

Yeah, Charlie and Mac. Christ.

She pushed away from the table and walked off to find a phone to call her sister.

2

"... so Michelle finally gets to the top of the beanstalk, right? And she sees this huge castle and decides to knock on the door and ask for something to drink. It was a long climb and she's thirsty. . . . Hey, El, you listening to this story or not?"

Mike McCleary's daughter, hunkered down in her car seat to his right, glanced at him, grinned and clapped her small, perfect hands. His sunglasses were perched on the tip of her nose, a shield against the morning sun, the early June very hot sun. "Dadda's," she said, and pressed her open hand against the lenses, pushing them farther up on her nose. The gesture reminded him of Benson, forever poking at his wire-rims.

"I've got another story to tell you, okay?" He braked for the red light just ahead. "Some bad people hurt a friend of Mommy and Daddy's, people like the giant in 'Jack in the Beanstalk.' We don't know who the bad guys are, so we need to find them. While we're gone, you'll be staying with your aunt Ellen."

Quin's sister's name was magic to his daughter. She associated it with other kids, a neighborhood of kids who all seemed to congregate at the home of her cousins, a seven-year-old boy named Ricky and a four-year-old girl named Rebecca, otherwise known as Icky and Eka. Her face lit up, she clapped her hands again, and McCleary knew it was going to work out just fine.

"Elchi?" She gazed at him with blue eyes that were clones of her mother's, a pale, ghostly blue in the center, ringed by a darker blue. "Elchi?"

"Elchi, elchi, elchi," he murmured, trying to decipher what it meant.

"Elchi?" Her voice had taken on a whine of frustration because he didn't understand what she was saying.

He repeated the word to himself again and again with a growing sense of panic. The light turned green and he sped through the intersection to the rhythm of *elchi, elchi.* "Does Aunt Ellen have cheese? Is that what you're asking?"

"Yay, Dadda," she said, clapping again.

Saved. "Yes, Aunt Ellen has plenty of cheese. And pasta and coffee yogurt and apple juice, all your favorite stuff." She also had four cats, two dogs, and a parrot. "She'll be taking you to school and picking you up, then your mom and I will be home on the weekend." He pulled into the Tot Stop parking lot, stopped the car. "You understand what I'm saying?"

She looked at him now, pensive and somber. Her face was a perfect amalgam of his and Quin's. Those eyes like her mother's, a bow-shaped mouth like his own, hair that was straight like his and as blond as Quin's had been when she was Michelle's age. But there were nuances that were entirely hers, evidence of a personality that seemed to be sculpted daily, as though she, like Michelangelo, were releasing an image from stone.

Her smile was gone and a slight frown creased her forehead. Then she nodded that she understood what he'd said and held out her arms to be released from the seat. McCleary obliged her, set her down on the ground. He reached into the well in back for her suitcase and the gray teddy bear that was her favorite.

The Fids bear, gray, soft, and huggable, was a gift from a former client whose nickname was Fiddlestix. Recently, though, Michelle had been calling him Darla, who had actually begun as an imaginary friend. A month or so ago, Darla had made the leap to teddy flesh and the real world, a kind of transmigration of the soul. Ever since, Michelle had been holding him more, cooing and patting his back as if to burp him, and insisted that he accompany her everywhere. Even to school.

Tot Stop was a Montessori school with bright, spacious rooms and low windows that had been built with kids in mind. Each age group, the Ones, Twos, Threes, and Fours, had its own room and playground, which was where they found Ellie's class this morning. Kids laughing, whining, gazing off into space, kids on swings, in the sandbox. Ten munchkins in all. Half of them crowded around him and Michelle, saying her name, touching his beard, fussing to be held. He wondered if his daughter wandered up to other parents when they arrived and beseeched them with those big blue eyes. After a few minutes, she dismissed him with a kiss and a hug and hurried off into the sunlight with her friends, the gray bear clutched in the crook of her arm.

McCleary watched, her suitcase still in his hand, and tried to remember her as a newborn. Her pink face. Her hooded eyes. Her tiny, perfect fingernails. But the recollection was all mixed up with his memories of his sister, who had been present for much of Quin's labor and had been there at the birth.

He could still see Catherine and the nurse there toward the end, Cat urging Quin to push, push harder, the nurse gripping one of her hands, McCleary gripping the other. Unlike his sister, the nurse had a soft, calm voice, and between them they'd struck just the right balance. The nurse, Cat, and Quin, an impeccable trinity that, at one point, had made him feel incidental to the entire thing.

Cat, his youngest sister, his favorite, separated from him by twelve years and three other sisters, had been murdered in early November, at her home outside of Gainesville. Seven months ago. Not very long in the grand scheme of things, but it already felt like a lifetime.

In the beginning, his grief had seemed as tall as Jack's beanstalk, an insurmountable hurdle that he climbed, that he fought, that he struggled to conquer. Now it was merely an unpleasant fact of life.

There were moments, though, and this was definitely one of them, when he sensed her presence. It wasn't anything as tangible as the scent of her perfume, which had happened only twice, when he and Quin had been staying at Cat's farmhouse. This was more subjective, a sudden breath of air that stirred the leaves of the banyan under which he stood, a strange certainty that if he squinted and peered into the oblique shadows around him he would glimpse her.

Usually, the impression passed within seconds. But not today. Today it pursued him when he returned to the building. Today the back of his neck tightened, a sensation like a warm breath or butterfly wings brushing the skin. He went into the Ones' room to fill Michelle's cubby with diapers and actually glanced behind him, certain he would see Cat. Or someone. But the room was empty.

"What?" he whispered to the emptiness, rubbing a hand over his neck. "What is it?"

The clock ticked in the silence. Air hissed through an AC vent near the ceiling. The sensation of wings touched his neck again, and was gone.

Not so long ago, this part of Palm Beach County had been farmland, groves, fields of mango trees growing wild. Now it was civilized, domesticated, with more than three hundred homes, a dozen lakes that glinted in the morning light, and a landscaped terrain of flowers, shrubs, trees, and rolling berns blanketed in green. There were bike paths, a school, tennis courts, clubhouses with pools. It was as if the neighborhoods had been grown in Petri dishes and then transported in here fully grown and already inhabited by families. The suburbs, South Florida style.

Twenty years ago, he could not have imagined himself living in a place like this. But then again, twenty years ago he had not imagined himself a father, either. Although he preferred the narrow neighborhood streets of Miami, where there was a *tienda* or *mercado* on every other corner and you heard Spanish spoken more frequently than English, Miami wasn't a place to raise Michelle.

Just the same, he missed its noise, its street vendors, its diversity. The essential difference between West Palm and Miami, in fact, was that one was predictable and the other was not. Here, you knew what to expect. You knew that if you drove north far enough on A-1-A, for instance, you would eventually pass the Kennedy compound, the Trump estate, and a beach as unflawed as the complexions of the people who occupied the mansions. You knew that the peons lived on one side of the bridge and the royalty on the other.

But in Miami, nothing was that clearly delineated. You could never be quite sure who lived where. An accidental turn might lead you into a community of Haitians or Hindus or Central American freedom fighters. You had Coconut Grove with its boutiques and restaurants, its parks and its marina; Little Havana and Calle Ocho; and of course, Miami Beach and Art Deco. Always there were the clash and fusion of cultures, values, religions. And Charlie, he thought, had been killed in the crossfire.

When he swung into the driveway, Quin was outside by the Explorer. She looked tropical, like one of those women you might see in the Caribbean, a woman in a strapless sundress who was fanning herself with a white hat. Although Quin's dress wasn't strapless and she wasn't holding a hat, she seemed exotic, tall and thin. Her umber hair was pulled casually off her shoulders and knotted in the back, with strands that curled loosely around her face.

She was surrounded by things she was loading into the Explorer, items for her apartment. A toaster, a blender, a coffeepot, a bag of groceries, several cardboard boxes. Today, June 9, was her final interview with Crandall; but Benson's contact in the personnel department had already assured her she was a shoo-in for the job.

"The neighbors are going to think the worst," he said as he walked over to help her.

"Really. I can just hear the speculation when the boys get together on the corner this evening."

The boys were five or six men on their block who congregated on the same corner nearly every evening while their kids ran wild outside. They griped about their wives, their jobs, the present homeowners' association. They traded information on water pumps and chiggers and brands of house paint. They also gossiped, although none of them would ever call it that. "We're already suspect," he said, lifting her bag into the back of the Explorer. "This will just confirm it."

"You think Ellie'll be okay with my sister, Mac?"

"She probably won't want to come home."

Quin slid the bag of groceries inside the car and nodded, but he could tell she wasn't entirely convinced. Not about Ellie, not about any of it. There was always a central issue at stake with Quin; it had been like that as long as he had known her. The issues had changed over the years, but usually concerned some essential difference in opinion between them.

"Look," he said. "It's not like we're leaving her with someone we just hired."

Quin flicked at something on her dress. "I know."

"We'll see her on weekends."

"Yeah."

"She won't be at risk this way."

She looked at him, one hand grasping the edge of the open hatch as the other went down to the strap on her left shoe. "She'll be at risk, Mac, as long as we investigate homicides."

"This homicide is a hundred miles from home."

She had adjusted the strap on her shoe and straightened up, so they were nearly eye to eye. It occurred to him that Quin's height, five ten in her bare feet, a shade taller now, was probably one of her best weapons. That and her eyes. When they were narrowed, as they were at the moment, there was something almost menacing about them.

"Distance doesn't make it okay," she said.

Detour, he thought, don't pursue it. "I've got to get my things." He headed past her and through the garage to the utility-room door.

"Coward," she muttered loudly enough for him to hear.

"Where's Flats, anyway?" he called over his shoulder.

"Down by the lake. It won't go away, you know, just because you don't want to deal with it."

"I *did* deal with it, Quin." He let the screen door bang shut behind him. It seemed to echo in the warm stillness as he hurried through the house to the backyard, whistling for Flats.

His sister had rescued the sheepdog from the Gainesville pound when she'd bought her farm. Flats was 140 pounds of hair and muscle, bred for herding on the Scottish highlands. There were no sheep to herd out here, no cattle to bark at, no chickens to chase. But the area around the lake was thick with mice and rabbits that migrated from the mango grove on the other side. On days when the hunt produced nothing, Flats snoozed in the warm shade, as lazy as Ferdinand the bull. She was coming with McCleary to Miami Beach because the kid who fed the cats could not also feed her and walk her three times or four times a day.

She flew toward him, a huge and wonderful beast that had been unable to save his sister's life, but had saved his wife's and daughter's. Her front legs left the ground and landed hard against McCleary's chest, nearly knocking him over. "Okay, girl, down. You ready to hit the road?"

She took off around the side of the house, a black-and-white blur, and was already in the passenger seat when he came out a few minutes later with his bag. Quin was petting Flats through the window, talking to her in that soft voice she reserved for animals and children. She eyed him over the Miata's roof as he opened the door. "That's it? We're just going to leave it like this? Have a nice week and see you next weekend?"

"What do you want me to say?"

"Oh, maybe 'Good luck.' Or 'See you around.' " She rested her elbows on the Miata's roof. "Or maybe that I should stop by Will Boone's place some night for coffee with the boys and the animals. Something like that."

"I'll call you at the apartment." He ducked inside the car and cranked it up. Quin stood there for a moment, her hand motionless on Flats's head, then she turned without another word, walked to the Explorer, climbed in.

Get out and go over there, he thought. Hug her goodbye. Don't leave it like this.

But it was too late, she was revving the Explorer's engine, grinding the gears into reverse, rolling back out of the garage. The message was clear: move or kiss your bumper *adiós*.

"Have it your way." He peeled out of the driveway, leaving patches of rubber on the road that would keep the boys on the corner buzzing for a month.

The official Deco District was one square mile on Miami Beach. It contained more than four hundred buildings that had been deemed historic in 1979 and included hotels, private residences, apartments, even the post office.

McCleary, who had once aspired to become an artist and still dabbled on weekends, considered Deco overrated. Yeah, the pastels and the neon were great, but so much of it was downright tacky. The parapets that rose like periscopes from the tops of many of the buildings, the busy moldings and friezes, the mostly small windows that left the interiors dark. Worst of all were the terrazzo mosaic floorings, so confusing in color and design that they could catapult a reasonably sane man into a hallucinogenic nightmare for a week.

The one building that he liked was the Miami Beach post office. It wasn't cluttered, wasn't vain. The large cylinder that comprised its center and the steps that led up to it made it seem somewhat grand, like an opera house or a presidential palace. It just happened to be located across the street from Boone's place.

His building wasn't Deco. It was merely small and old and somewhat neglected. Boone's two-bedroom apartment was on the second floor and he shared it with a female raccoon named Elvis and a feisty tabby cat named Fox. McCleary wasn't sure where Flats was going to fit into the animal scheme of things, but Boone had assured him it wouldn't be a problem.

Boone, however, was so delighted to have human company McCleary knew he could have brought along a Bengal tiger and the old man would have said, No problem. He had made up the spare room, had fixed a bed for Flats under the window, had put out fresh towels in the bathroom. He had also whipped up a brunch, which they ate out on the tiny terrace as the raccoon, the cat, and the dog hung around for handouts.

"See what I mean about the animals, Mac?" Boone said with a trace of pride in his voice. "They make their own peace if you leave them alone." He tossed a bit of egg to Elvis, who caught it in her front paws, then dropped his checkered hat on the raccoon's head and pulled it down over her bandit eyes. She flicked it off, pounced at it, sniffed it, batted it like a ball, and finally picked it up between her teeth and put it in Boone's lap.

He swatted the cap against his thigh, set his plate on the floor. The raccoon and the cat assumed positions on opposite sides and proceeded to finish off the leftovers. McCleary set his own plate on the floor for Flats, who lacked the grace and subtlety of the raccoon and cat. She sucked up everything and had licked the plate clean in seconds.

"Charlie gave Elvis to me. He comes in here one day with this scrawny little thing in his pocket and says it's me or the pound. He'd found her in Flamingo Park under the baseball bleachers."

Boone tugged the cap down over his thinning white hair and sipped at his coffee as he gazed down into the street. He had once been about McCleary's height and perhaps twenty pounds heavier. But he was in his early seventies now and the erosion of the years showed: a hunch to his shoulders, the shiny baldness at the front of his head, the way he limped when the weather cooled. And yet he wore glasses only when he read, his hearing had remained acute, and age had been kind to his face. When he chose to, he could look as dapper as Cary Grant.

"Why didn't Charlie keep her?"

"I think he figured he was too old, that Elvis would outlive him. You'd never know he thought about being old, what with the Sea Witch business and all. He was like people who seem"—he groped for the right word, his eyes fixed on the street below—"well, invincible.

"But he thought about his age all the time. It's why he'd structured his life like he had. This was a guy, Mac, who had a day set aside for everything. Mondays meant dinner at Wolfie's. Tuesdays were the nights we played chess. Thursdays and Fridays were general roundup days—laundry, grocery shopping, the housing project, like that. Saturdays and Sundays were for friends, for reading, for walks in the park, on the beach."

"And Wednesdays?" McCleary asked.

Boone lifted his feet onto the terrace railing and crossed them at the ankles, his thinker's pose. "I don't know. But from things he said and didn't say, I think he was seeing someone."

Good for you, Charlie, McCleary thought. Eighty-five and undaunted. "You have any idea who she is?"

"Nope. He would have said something eventually. If he'd lived."

He fell silent then, an old man who squinted and watched the passing traffic as if a part of him believed he might spot Charlie somewhere down there.

The friendship between the two men had always struck McCleary as odd. Boone was a high school dropout with a nose for the streets and Charlie had been an erudite professor, a renowned criminologist who had written several classic tomes on the criminal mentality. The very things that Boone distrusted—government, the judicial system, law enforcement—had defined the parameters of Charlie's world. But apparently none of that had made a difference in the twilight of retirement here on the beach, where no one gave a damn about who you had been.

"Did Charlie belong to a chess club?" McCleary asked.

"Not that I know of. He and his wife used to play when she was alive and there's a black kid over at the Sea Witch he was teaching to play. Charlie said R.D. has got talent for the game. Anyway, you'll meet him. He's got himself a new job and is working all kinds of crazy hours, so he's tough to pin down right now."

"I thought the Sea Witch was for the elderly."

"R.D. lives there with his grandmother and sister. Anyhow, he and Charlie played chess over at R.D.'s place the morning of the day he was killed. A short game. Charlie left around noon. Said he was expecting a call."

"From his son?"

Boone's expression made it clear that he didn't like Potemkin's son, a criminal attorney in Philadelphia. "That asshole figured that as long as he helped out with the rent on Charlie's apartment and called once a month or so, he was doing right by his old man. And I think he'd already called in May. I got a call from Charlie that night around eight-thirty, I guess it was. I wasn't home, so he left me a message."

Benson had played the tape for McCleary and Quin after their luncheon last week. He'd been calling from a public phone; the noise of traffic was clearly audible in the background. *You there, Will? Pick up if you are.* When Boone hadn't answered, Charlie had muttered that he was onto something important. *It's going to make a difference. But we've got to talk first. I have to show you this. Come over as soon as you can.* He had sounded excited, breathless, and scared.

"What'd you think he wanted to talk to you about?"

"The Witch, what else? I figured he'd maybe dug up some dirt on Crandall that he was going to use as leverage. Charlie knew that sooner or later the place was going to be sold to *someone;* the county's in deep shit financially and they need the money. He was just trying to stall things for a while. He was getting his ducks lined up."

"What kind of dirt was he looking for? Did he ever say?"

"Anything. I know he was tracking down all the exes in Crandall's life—ex-employees, ex-friends, ex–business associates, an ex-wife. He'd heard that Crandall's ex-wife is living out of her car and figured she might be willing to talk."

"Living out of her *car?*"

"Yeah. She got screwed in the divorce settlement and now she's supposedly piss poor. Charlie had heard she spends a lot of time in the Grove, but I don't think he was ever able to track her down. There might be something on her in that stuff we brought over here."

The "stuff" Boone was referring to was a dozen wooden crates jammed with memorabilia, half a dozen chess sets, and files. They were filled with information about places and topics and people that had fascinated Charlie but not his son, who had emptied the cabinets they'd occupied and given everything to Boone. They were still stacked where McCleary and Boone had put them last week, in a corner of the room where McCleary would be sleeping.

As they started going through the crates, the magnitude of what they contained consumed him and he forgot to look for information on Crandall's ex-wife. This was more than just a collection of newspaper and magazine clippings. It was a history of a man's professional and personal life, eighty-five years of memories fragmented and scattered through appointment books, love letters, lecture notes, correspondence, drawings that his son had made at three, at six, at twelve. Here were the painful junctures of family life—miscarriages, injuries, sorrows, death, as well as the triumphs and successes. Charlie had not been a meticulous chronicler, but he'd certainly been thorough.

Included in the cartons were letters from five former directors of the CIA, congratulating Charlie on the success of his summer workshop at Langley. The first one was dated in 1960 and the last in 1990. From Eisenhower to Reagan, from the cold war to the collapse of the Soviet Union and the Berlin Wall. Even the spooks at Langley had sought Charlie's expertise.

"According to these letters, it looks like Charlie was lecturing at Langley every summer for thirty years, Will."

Boone, sitting against the wall, peered at McCleary over the rims of his granny glasses. He looked—what? Sad? Disappointed? Shaken? McCleary couldn't tell.

"Did you know about it?" McCleary asked.

"He never said anything. But considering my attitude toward the

CIA, that's not too surprising. Thing is, Mac, I knew the guy ten years, we played chess every week, and I'm beginning to realize I never knew the man. I mean, take a look at this."

He handed McCleary a folded sheet of paper from one of the boxes. There was no envelope; the note was written in red ink on a wrinkled sheet of blue paper. It was dated Wednesday two weeks ago:

> *My dearest,*
>   *You have just left and my rooms seem impoverished by your absence. You have made me whole again.*
>
>   *Much love always,*
>   *xxx*

3

The pain. He could feel the pain rolling toward him again, rolling through the mist in his head. Beyond it somewhere was a room, this room, the room he'd inhabited for days, maybe weeks. He didn't know, couldn't remember. Time was no longer measured by the ticks of a clock or squares on a calendar. It was sunlight and darkness and the thickening stink of his unwashed skin.

He moved slightly against the bed, trying to relieve the pressure on his wrist, his left wrist, the wrist that was cuffed to the headboard. But the metal bit into the skin, the bones. A soft, dry rasp fell from his lips. Sweat sprang from his pores. The odor of his sickness washed over him in waves, each worse than the one before it, and he wanted to jerk the stink over his face like a blanket or a quilt until it smothered him.

He yanked on the cuff. The sharp, terrible pain stabbed at him, a hot poker, and he shrieked. The brief, shrill sound slammed against the walls, the ceiling, the heavy curtains that hung over the windows, and seemed to echo in the room's twilight. Then the door suddenly swung open, ending it, and he squeezed his eyes shut.

Footsteps. Quick, purposeful. Kilner's. "I don't know how you stand it so dark in here, Steve. It's a glorious morning. Just look."

Light, flooding the room, pressing against his eyelids. He turned his head to the side. "Don't."

"Hurts, doesn't it, Steve?"

He looked. He looked at Kilner, who was now standing next to the bed, smiling as benignly as a father who intends to impart some small piece of wisdom to his rebellious son. The face, he would always remember this face, long and gaunt, the dark eyes too small, the nose with the bump in the middle, the mouth that tended to pucker at the corners, the high, thin brows, the utterly bald head. He would remember the short solidness of Kilner's body, a body carved from a goddamn block of cement.

Hey, Jerry, imagine meeting you here, you fuck.

"I hear you were impolite to Gracie," Kilner said.

Gracie, the cook. "I wasn't hungry."

"You shouldn't have thrown your breakfast tray at her, Steve. She's just doing her job."

"Like you."

A big smile from Kilner. "Like me. You really should eat something. You won't be allowed to starve yourself. You either eat or we hook you up to IVs."

"Where am I?"

"Long Key."

This seemed correct, but he didn't know why, he couldn't bring it into focus, the pain was approaching too quickly now. "I want my pills. I don't feel well."

"That's what happens in morphine withdrawal, Steve. And it's been—what? Three years? Granted, you were admirably careful about the doses, but the body still craves, doesn't it?" Kilner leaned into his face, leaned so close that Heckler could see himself in the dark mirrors of the man's eyes. "The nausea's going to get worse, the sweats will make you shake, your skin's going to crawl like you're covered in ants. It won't be pleasant." Kilner pulled a chair over to the bed and turned it so the straight back faced Heckler. Then he straddled it like a cowboy in his saddle. "But you already know the rules. Answer the questions and you get a shot."

"I've given you all my fucking answers, Jerry."

"You've given me bullshit. Who were you working with?"

"No one."

"I don't buy it."

"It's the truth." He hated the supplicating tone of his voice, the way it cracked with dryness, with fear, with the first bites of pain. "You know it is. You gave me pentothal, for Christ's sakes, and asked the same questions and you know it's the truth."

"And we both know that pentothal isn't all it's cracked up to be. Don't piss me off, Steve. We know the professor went into the grocery store. We suspect he mailed something in the box outside."

Heckler rubbed his free hand over his damp face. Gritted his teeth against the first assault of pain. When it passed, he said through his teeth, "Then you should've impounded the mailbox."

"The asshole who was tailing you got careless. Who did Charlie mail the material to?"

"How the fuck should I know? I wasn't there. Your goon probably killed him."

Killed Charlie. *Sweet Christ. I'm sorry, Charlie. It was supposed to help you, not kill you.*

"Charlie told you what he was going to do, didn't he?"

"He didn't tell me shit."

The door opened again and another man entered the room and came over to the bed. Heckler had seen this guy before, too. He was Kilner's minion. Dan Pisco of the mismatched eyes, one blue, one brown. Pisco of the powerful physique, the rippling biceps, the thighs like tree trunks. Heckler knew a con when he saw one and Pisco was definitely a con, probably recruited straight out of Huntsville or Attica. Yeah, Kilner was good at finding lackeys.

"Let's back up a little, Steve. Let's talk about what was in the file you gave Charlie."

"I've already told you what . . ."

"Lies," Kilner snapped. "Were there memos? Photographs? Who helped you, Steve?"

Heckler started to laugh, a wild, panicked laughter that suddenly collapsed into a fit of coughing that turned his stomach inside out. He lurched forward, trying to reach the plastic puke pan on the nightstand. He missed it and vomited on the bed, on himself, on Kilner's knees. Kilner leaped up so fast his chair toppled. Heckler was vaguely aware of Kilner's shouting, of hands wrestling him back against the bed, of Pisco jabbing a needle into his arm. Then there was only the silken softness of the drug sliding over him, through him, and carrying him away.

Away.

∎ ∎ ∎

Jerome Kilner stared at Heckler, at the sheets tangled around his skinny legs, at his long silver hair spread across the pillow like bleached seaweed, at the spots of blood in his puke. Then he wrenched his eyes away and looked at Pisco. "How long has he been puking blood?"

"I didn't know he was."

"It's your goddamn job to know."

"Yes, sir."

"Clean him up. A bath. A shave. Clean clothes. I want him to get some sun, see the water, feel the sand under his feet. And for the next few days, he gets anything he wants to eat and a shot every six hours."

"Yes, sir."

"You're there for him around the clock, Dan. You're his friend, his confidant. Got it?"

"No problem, sir."

"I'll assign someone else to your other patients. Heckler's yours. I want to know everything he says and I don't care how ridiculous or fucked-up it sounds."

"Understood, sir."

Sir sir sir. The words echoed in Kilner's head, rising and falling around him as he hurried out to shower, to change clothes, to escape the stink that suffused the very air in Heckler's room.

If Heckler sank into a coma, if he died, *if.* It all came back to that, didn't it, to the fat, glaring question mark of unknowns.

4

The tall man stepped out of the terminal at Miami International at 9:02 A.M. on Wednesday, June 17. The time and date were important. They marked the beginning of the end of his life as Fernando Gabriel.

The air was hot, still, and so clear that it smelled almost sweet. As he waited in line for the Hertz shuttle, he was aware of the constriction in his chest that afflicted him every time he landed in Miami. This was a city he'd fled eleven years ago as John Gabriel Tark.

The events that had precipitated his flight still haunted him. He couldn't escape them anymore than he could change the color of his skin. Ghosts inhabited the very air that he drew into his lungs. An acute heaviness seeped through him like gas. His sense of purpose, the thing that had brought him here, seemed too huge to contemplate. It was a travesty that would be committed by some other man, his other persona, Fernando Gabriel.

He rode the shuttle to the Hertz terminal and picked up his Cherokee. He didn't need the map in the glove compartment. He'd been born and raised in Miami and knew it by heart: the twists of the city, the tricks, the roads that suddenly changed names or ended, the numerous interstates, the maze of highways. In Iquitos, Peru, where he now lived, a city surrounded by jungle, all the roads led nowhere except into the jungle. He supposed both designs corresponded to something in the geography of his own psyche, but he didn't want to think about it. He'd become quite adept at sealing off certain rooms in his head, then building new rooms that he filled in new ways.

It was a mechanism of survival, he thought. A way to continue moving forward when you had cheated death and wished that you hadn't. He should have died eleven years ago with his wife and daughter; that was Miami's lesson.

He drove north to the Julia Tuttle causeway that led to Miami Beach. The tendency in Miami to name places after people who had left their mark was similar to the Latin American custom of naming every plaza after Simón Bolívar. Tuttle hadn't liberated any nation, but she was considered the "mother of Miami."

Like the millions who eventually followed her, Tuttle had been a Northerner, a snowbird from Cleveland, a widow with two children. She had ended up in Florida in 1875 because she'd inherited her father's plantation after his death. She'd eventually given up the plantation and bought six hundred acres on the Miami River, which she pledged as a townsite to whoever built a railroad to Miami.

Henry Flagler had built the railroad, gotten half the land, and inadvertently ushered in the boom-or-bust mentality that had prevailed ever since. He had roads named after him, too. Tark supposed that someday there would be a road named after Don Johnson or Cristo, the Bulgarian artist who had draped eleven islands in Biscayne Bay with six and a half million square feet of pink plastic and called it art.

He turned onto Ocean Drive. Fifth Street marked the southern boundary of the Deco District, which extended west to Lenox Avenue and north to Fifteenth Street. But when people talked about Deco, they usually meant South Beach, SoBe to those in the know.

This long stretch of road was bordered by the Atlantic on one side and the refurbished Deco hotels on the other. It was the Miami that

TV had popularized, a slick pink paradise now populated by international trend setters, models on photo shoots, sunburned tourists, Orthodox Jewish men in their black frock coats and long beards, and retirees. Out of sight, hidden offstage somewhere, were the homeless, the drunks, the vagrants, the people for whom the beach had never been paradise.

He nosed the Cherokee into a parking space on a side street and walked two blocks south to Mango's Tropical Café and Hotel at 900 Ocean Drive. The café part was a courtyard enclosed under a skylight, with a Mexican tile floor inlaid with bright ceramic designs and a profusion of plants. The hotel section was ten rooms on either side on the second floor. A sign just inside the front door announced that psychic readings were available by appointment. The New Age, he mused, had arrived on Miami Beach.

The tables were occupied by European tourists and people who probably spent their winters in St. Moritz and Aspen. Tark walked past them and stopped at the half-moon desk at the far end of the courtyard. He identified himself as Fernando Gabriel, a combination of his father's first name and his own middle name, the name that was on his passport and by which he was best known in the business.

The clerk, a young man with a deep tan and an earring in his left ear, flashed his best public-relations smile and set a package on the counter. A large package, a foot square, was wrapped in Christmas paper and tied with a blue ribbon. In perfect Spanish, he said, *"Bienvenido a Miami Beach, Señor Gabriel."*

Since the kid didn't ask for ID, Tark figured he'd been given a detailed description to work from: that Gabriel stood six four; had a thin scar over his left eye that cut through his left brow; black, curly hair; a salt-and-pepper mustache; that he was in his early forties. At any rate, the kid would know only what he needed to know. "Is my room ready?" he asked in English.

"Yes, sir."

An Aussie, Tark thought. Peru was filled with them, global nomads who possessed an impressive facility for languages.

"Number one at the front on the right. You're already registered and paid in full." He dropped a key and a parking decal on the counter. "We've got a small parking lot in the back."

His room had a marvelous view of the Atlantic and Ocean Drive, a pint-sized fridge, a bathroom built for midgets. Tark double-locked the door, lowered the blinds, and opened the package. Inside were several color photos, numbered on the back; a Smith & Wesson .38 with a box of ammo; typed instructions and background information; and sixty grand in cash. Another sixty had already been wired to his account in the Caicos Islands and, upon completion of the job, a third payment of a hundred and twenty grand would be wired to his account in Switzerland. Though he didn't believe he had been short-changed, he began counting the bills.

There were men and women in the business who worked for less, much less. Maybe they were as good as he was and maybe they weren't; Tark didn't know and didn't care. He had an instinct for the work, a talent, a sixth sense, and the fact remained that his clients believed that the more you paid for something, the better the quality of the job. Tark tried not to disappoint them.

On the rare occasions when he failed, he refunded whatever he'd been paid. He accepted no fewer than two jobs a year and no more than four, and after this job, he would retire. His rules were simple. He didn't work the Mideast, didn't get involved in political assassinations, and refused to touch anything that smelled even remotely of terrorism. His jobs usually came to him by word of mouth and this one was no exception.

Three days ago, he'd gotten a call at his home in Iquitos from the only person in Miami he trusted, Alfonso Ruiz. *This one's pretty straightforward, Gabby. I don't know the specifics except that it involves retrieving stolen information.* Yesterday afternoon, a ticket was waiting for him at the airport. Iquitos to Lima on Fawcett Airlines and Lima to Miami on Avianca. The date on the return ticket was open.

When he had finished counting the money, he put it in a gym bag that he pulled from his suitcase. Then he showered, changed into comfortable clothes, and sat out on the tiny private balcony with the photos and background information.

Seventeen days ago, an intelligence operative, Steven Heckler, had passed classified documents to Charles Potemkin, a retired professor of criminology and former lecturer at Langley. Potemkin was killed by an unknown assailant in his apartment that same night and the documents disappeared. They concerned an arms deal that had been under investigation for two years and Tark's job was to find the original documents. It was believed that Potemkin had mailed them to someone. Anyone who got in the way was expendable.

Simple enough, but why the fuss? Tark wondered. He picked up the photographs. These were the players, the ones who determined the texture of a job. Lawrence Crandall: real-estate developer and suspected arms dealer. William Boone: retired gumshoe and Potemkin's close friend and chess partner. Liz Purcell: Crandall's newest employee, seen with the chief of police of Metro-Dade, believed to be working undercover, real identity unknown. Roger Darren (R.D.) Aikens: a seventeen-year-old black kid who lived with his grandmother and sister at the Sea Witch, the senior citizens' apartment building that Potemkin had been fighting to save and that Crandall was trying to buy.

An equitable representation of humanity on Miami Beach.

Tark read through his instructions. When the file was recovered, he was to leave a note in Locker 14 at the Amtrak terminal in Miami, specifying where the final exchange was to be made, the stolen file for proof that the remainder of his fee had been wired. No problem. He jotted a few notes, then carried everything into the bathroom.

He tore the typed pages into long strips, one page at a time, and flushed them down. He turned the photos over in his hands, so he couldn't see the faces, and shuffled them. He always liked this part, the wheel of chance spinning, then the telling decision about who would be first.

He turned the top photo over. Boone, the old man. He memorized the face, held a match to it, dropped it into the sink as the corners began to blacken, then burn.

Next. The developer. He lit a new match.

The third was the black kid. Another match.

He turned the last picture over and studied the woman's face. He liked what he saw. Her eyes were a strange blue, pale in the center and darker at the rims, the way he imagined the eyes of a witch would be. Her hair was dark, thick, shiny, falling nearly to her shoulders in unruly waves. He guessed she was in her late thirties or early forties, as old as his wife would be now, had she lived.

The thought disturbed him and he shoved it away. But behind it were other thoughts, questions, inconsistencies. If there was a suspicion about Purcell's identity, why hadn't Tark's employer just lifted one of her fingerprints? Or, if the prints yielded nothing, why not her apartment? That would solve the issue mighty fast. And what difference did it make if she was undercover for the cops? Even though the feds generally didn't like working with local yokels, it seemed to Tark that it would be to their advantage to do so in this case.

For that matter, which spook division was he dealing with here? CIA? FBI? NSA? AFI? Someone else? He obviously hadn't been fully informed of the facts, but that was typical. And in all fairness to his employer, he hadn't been hired to ask questions.

He stroked the woman's lovely mouth with his thumb and smiled. "You first," he whispered.

■ ■ ■

It was one thing to visit South Beach, Quin thought, and quite another to work here. In just a week, all the details that made the place attractive had become almost commonplace: the wide white beach, the astonishing blue of the water, even the hotels.

She'd gotten used to seeing the expensive cars, the leggy Ford models, the guys with short bleached hair who swept by in trios, sporting gold jewelry and the latest fashions. Every morning at the News Café, the current hot spot for breakfast and coffee, she knew which faces she would see at which tables.

The Japanese businessman, for instance, always ate alone and read three different newspapers front to back. The knockout black hooker arrived each morning with a new man and ordered the same thing, expresso and the house biscuits. The sunburned couple from Toledo claimed the same table every morning and their chunky son always had his nose buried in a Batman comic book. The playwright usually sat under one of the potted ficus trees, smoking, and editing his screenplay on the Israeli secret police. The celebrities varied but looked basically the same in their dark sunglasses and beach wear that probably cost more than her monthly mortgage payment.

Then there was Dave Petrovsky, the muscle man who favored Italian suits even when the temperature was eighty-five and climbing, as it was this morning. Dave, whose jacket rendered his weapon invisible, was Crandall's bodyguard.

Not that anyone would admit it.

Dave was the first of Crandall's entourage to arrive at the café in the morning. Quin figured he got there at the crack of dawn, when the tables were being moved outside to the sidewalk. He staked out the boss's spot, ordered a pot of Cuban coffee to be delivered as soon as Crandall appeared, and probably checked the place for bugs or something.

In the week she, as Liz Purcell, had worked for the big man, the only thing Dave had said to her was *Excuse me, ma'am,* when he'd bumped into her in a rush to open the car door for Crandall. She had never seen his eyes; they were always hidden behind dark shades. She had never seen him eat, either, and that bothered her more than the gun he toted. The way in which someone ate, the kind of food consumed, the ritual or lack of ritual involved, usually told her more about a person than what he or she said.

Crandall, for instance, was meticulous about everything concerned with food. The coffee and biscuits had to be hot, he didn't like ice in his water, his eggs had to be scrambled without butter and on the dry side, and his utensils better be clean or watch out. A controller. He periodically patted his paunch as he ate, as if to remind himself that he needed to lose fifteen pounds, or smoothed a hand over his balding head. When they sat at one of the sidewalk tables, as they did most mornings, Crandall tended to wear his sunglasses. It wasn't because of the sun, since they were usually in the shade, but to what Quin suspected was a SoBe affliction: the desire to create a mystique about himself. The little Buddha, which he physically resembled, holding morning court with his minions. Like that.

His chauffeur, Cindy Youngston, ate and drank whatever was in front of her, in whatever condition it arrived. The free spirit. Her irreverence for food and ritual, however, didn't extend to her appearance. Her short honey-colored hair was professionally styled, her eyes were carefully made up, and she was fastidious about the way she dressed. Everything matched. Red slacks and a red-and-white-striped shirt were paired with gold-and-red earrings, an expensive gold watch, white sandals, and a red-and-white purse. It was as if Cindy couldn't make up her mind whether she was a student—which she supposedly was, in law school at the University of Miami—or a full-time employee of Crandall Development.

Then there was Ebo Rau, Crandall's German buddy, who was

almost military in his approach to meals. For him, only one way existed to unfold a napkin or hold a glass or a mug. He didn't eat red meat, and coffee had not passed his lips in thirteen years. Every morning he ordered the same thing, a bowl of Cheerios with a sliced banana and fresh strawberries on top. The disciplined soldier. He looked somewhat like a soldier, too, the crew cut, the lean body, the controlled expressions on his pleasant face.

Then there was Betty O'Toole, who pecked at whatever was in front of her. She was a hummingbird, high-strung, nervous, in a perpetual rush to be somewhere other than where she was. She kept Crandall punctual. She'd been promoted from secretary to personal assistant the day before Quin had been hired and Quin had ended up in her former position.

It was Betty who broke Crandall's monologue this morning. She cleared her throat and hooked strands of her short dark hair behind her ears. "Uh, Mr. Crandall, you've got to be at the cable station by eleven. The woman who's going to be interviewing you is known to cancel if a guest is late. I don't think we want that to happen."

"So he's five minutes late," Cindy said with a roll of her baby blues. "So what? He's not running for political office."

"He should be. I think he'd make a terrific mayor," Betty replied with an indignant sniff, as though Crandall weren't even present. "He would get things done."

Crandall thought that was funny and slapped Rau on the back. "You hear that, Ebo? Mayor Crandall."

The German guffawed. The bulbous tip of his nose seemed to glow pink, suggesting that his tea was laced with schnapps. "You, my friend, are not mayoral material. I tell you that many, many times. Besides, the mayor doesn't make enough money to compensate for his many headaches."

"No amount of money would make the job worth it," Cindy remarked.

Betty cleared her throat again and tapped the face of her watch. "Uh, Mr. Crandall, if you're going to be on time, you need to leave right now."

"Okay, okay." He tossed two twenties on the table and asked Betty to take care of the bill. She hastened off and Crandall pushed to his feet. So did Dave. And Cindy. And Rau. And Quin. The entourage took their cues from the Buddha: that was one of the unspoken rules.

"Liz, I'll need that bio you prepared on the talk-show host."

"Got it right here." Quin tapped her briefcase as they crossed the street.

"Ebo, we'll have dinner in the Grove tonight, how's that sound?"

"Fine, my friend. Six-thirty?"

"Make it seven," Quin said. "He's got an eye appointment at five and probably won't be out of there before six."

"Cancel the eye appointment," Crandall said. "Six-thirty's fine. Cindy will pick you up at your hotel."

The entourage stopped at Crandall's mocha-colored Lincoln, parked in its usual spot in front of the Neon Flamingo. Ebo departed with a wave and headed off to his own car. Cindy swung behind the wheel. Dave opened the passenger door for Crandall, who slid in next to Cindy and looked at Quin, who was still on the sidewalk, waiting for instructions. "You joining us, Liz?"

"I thought Betty . . ."

"She's busy this morning. You're coming with us."

She repressed an urge to salute and got into the backseat with Petrovsky.

During the drive, Crandall glanced through the bio Quin had prepared on the hostess for *Look Alive*. It was brief, but included specifics that Crandall had insisted on—the woman's birthdate, where she was from originally, her political leanings, and whether she supported his resort project on Miami Beach (she didn't). That meant Crandall would be going into the interview on the defensive, which made the birthdate information all the more important.

Crandall claimed he didn't subscribe to a belief in astrology. But then again he probably didn't consider himself a superstitious man, either, and he definitely was. This was a guy who refused to open an umbrella indoors, whose license plate was all eights (the number of money), who always requested the same row and seat number on a plane. And despite his professed skepticism about the stars, he invariably paid close attention to anything Cindy, the astrology expert, said on the subject. Which was why he'd requested the birthdate.

"September thirteenth," he said.

Cindy shook her head. "A solid Virgo. Too bad she isn't a Pisces or a Cancer. I would have preferred a water sign."

"Why's that?" Crandall asked.

"Not so critical. We're looking at a woman who's extremely critical, very precise, and has strong opinions on everything. She'll be impressed with numbers and figures, Larry. If you appeal to her vanity, she might not be quite as hostile."

"I happen to like Virgos," Dave piped up.

Cindy laughed. "Yeah, because you're one."

"What else?" Crandall asked.

"Virgos generally have sharp minds. It's that Mercury influence. So this isn't a lady you can bullshit, Larry. But there's one thing that can either work for you or against you. Mercury went retrograde this morning, so she's not going to be at her best. On the other hand, it means communication breakdowns, electrical things going on the fritz, stuff like that."

"So we're looking at technical delays today."

"That'd be my guess."

"Shit," he muttered, and fell silent as they pulled up to the station.

Crandall told Quin to come with him and instructed Cindy and Petrovsky to return in an hour and a half. Good ole Petrovsky didn't like it much, but he conceded with a nod and got back into the car.

It had been clear to Quin from the beginning that Crandall didn't need a chauffeur anymore than he needed a personal assistant or a secretary. It was, in fact, pretty much what he'd said to her when he'd hired her. His exact words were that she was an accouterment of his success. She was like his chauffeured Lincoln, his sprawling Spanish-style home in Coral Gables, his twin-engine Bonanza, his Porsche, his yacht. She was a luxury he could afford and which would help make him look important to other people. In the world according to Crandall, if other people believed he was as successful as he knew himself to be, then that success tended to assume a life of its own. So, aside from a few responsibilities he'd spelled out, her job was mostly window dressing. She was part of the entourage.

Since the point was to discover exactly what Crandall was involved in, she'd sought to win his trust and favor at every opportunity and had been shameless in this pursuit. In the week since she'd started, she had sacrificed lunch hours and coffee breaks and stayed late every night. The problem was that Crandall or Betty or both of them also put in long days, which made it impossible to poke around in his files or search the computer in his office. So far, she'd turned up nothing incriminating on Crandall.

"So we're on time and here we sit," Crandall fumed as they sat in the waiting room.

"Mercury retrograde," Quin quipped.

He smoothed his palm over his shiny head. "I shouldn't have let Betty talk me into this. She thought it would be good for public relations, what with the fallout over Professor Potemkin's murder. But the sale of the Sea Witch will go through regardless of public sentiment. The county needs the money and the hotel association supports the move."

"The professor's murder delayed things somewhat, didn't it?"

He glanced at her, amused. "If I took every delay in this business seriously, Liz, I'd be a fruitcake. I'm sorry about what happened to the professor. But in the long run he didn't make much of a difference to the outcome."

As though the future were already laid out, cast in stone, as inevitable as tomorrow's breakfast at the News Café. Such confidence. Such unbridled arrogance. *Make me gag, Larry.*

She was relieved when he was finally called into the studio and delighted that he'd left his briefcase behind. She picked it up and carried it down the hall and into the ladies' room. She went into one of the stalls, locked the door, set the briefcase on the toilet seat.

It looked like something a drug dealer would carry, solid, rectangular, with a combination lock. Quin removed a ring of keys from her purse. Charlie had given her the keys, eighteen in all. He'd claimed they would fit virtually any lock. She didn't think he'd been referring to *this* kind of lock, but what the hell. The second key fit but didn't open the lock. The sixth key turned it enough to make it click, but didn't open it either. She dug around in it with a bobby pin until she felt the resistance, then pressed and inserted the sixth key again. The lid snapped open and she was in.

Before she touched anything, she noted how things were arranged. The lay of the land. There didn't seem to be any particular order to Crandall's arrangement, but that didn't mean much. One man's chaos, after all, was another's Dewey Decimal System.

The only thing of interest was Crandall's leatherbound appointment book. She expected it to be a duplicate of the twelve-month calendar on his desk that she and Betty used to keep track of his appointments, but this covered eighteen months and the entries were strictly personal. Picnics with his sister and her family, dates for his nephew's Little League games, flowers to be sent on his mother's birthday, that sort of thing.

Two dates were starred, July 3 (Jungle Queen) and July 8 (no entry). The Jungle Queen was a paddlewheel boat that traveled up and down the Intracoastal Canal, strictly tourist stuff, caviar and cocktails beneath a moonlit sky, music from a live band, lights on shore winking through the trees like fallen stars. Hardly what the owner of a ninety-foot yacht would do for pleasure.

Quin replaced the appointment book, snapped the briefcase shut, flushed the toilet. She stepped out into the hall, then crossed it to the producer's office and set the briefcase against the wall. When she turned, Dave Petrovsky was striding toward her, frowning. She was already spinning a tale about the briefcase in the event that he'd seen her with it.

"Where's Larry?" he asked without preface.

"Taping. He'll be a while."

His small, suspicious eyes darted through the office behind her. "What's his briefcase doing in here?"

"I suppose that's where he left it. Excuse me."

She stepped around him and walked over to the water fountain. She felt his eyes on her back until, moments later, he moved past her, clutching the briefcase as though it were a sacred totem.

5

To McCleary, the Sea Witch was straight out of a fading sepia photograph of old Miami Beach. The porthole windows on either side of the door, the terrazzo steps, the busy friezes on the front columns, the elderly people seated on the porch: it was all there, unchanged.

The building stood smack in the middle of the eleven-hundred block on Ocean Drive, a solitary sentinel, a fading bastion of the good ole days. It was four stories, with a column of pale green glass straight up through the center of it and sections on both sides that curved around. It looked, McCleary thought, like a bird shooting upward, wings pressed back.

To either side of the Sea Witch were vast boarded-up ruins, the once bankrupt and now partially reconstructed hotels and restaurants that Crandall owned. The area was sectioned off by wire mesh fences that bore construction signs and NO TRESPASSING warnings. Tractors and bulldozers moved around inside the fences like prehistoric beasts. There was no greenery inside, just dirt that had blown out onto the sidewalk and over the curb. The dirt marred the landscape, impoverished it, made it seem temporary. It was as if the entire block, except for the Sea Witch, existed in some warp outside of time and awaited the touch of Crandall's magic wand to transform it, to place it into a historical context once again.

"You can see why Crandall wants the place so badly," Boone said. "Without the land the Witch sits on, he isn't going to be able to build his goddamn Deco resort."

"How big's the property?"

"An acre. It's got the most land on the block." Boone pointed at the second building to the right. "That used to be the Tuttle Inn. The same guy who built it also built the apartment building where Quin's staying, L. Murray Dixon. He was one of the principal Deco architects. It was the first place I stayed when I got here from New Orleans. It had apartments in those days."

"Crandall's boys really sealed the place up."

"Yeah." Boone gripped the fence. "It was gutted by a fire when the previous owner still had it and was eventually condemned. The word was that the guy had torched it himself for the insurance money because he'd lost his shirt on the place. Crandall picked it up for a song."

The site quivered with heat and brightness. When McCleary skewed his eyes against it, he seemed to detect the vague shape of Crandall's resort, as though the future were already perched at the edge of the present, rising against its horizon, waiting for that final sleight of hand in Crandall's bag of tricks that would bring it all into being. Landscaping. Full-grown trees. Hedges trimmed in tidy geometric shapes. Flaming bougainvillea. Pink-and-blue buildings. Neon. Crandall's version of Club Med, he thought, his profitable little Walden.

"Hey, Mac, you coming?"

Boone and Flats were five or six yards ahead of him, almost to the front of the Sea Witch. A breeze brushed the back of McCleary's neck, that sensation like wings. He glanced around, but no one was there.

McCleary almost whispered her name, Cat's name. But it spooked him. He hadn't consciously been thinking of his sister, it was broad daylight; he didn't know what it meant. Maybe nothing. Maybe everything. Maybe he'd imagined it. He hurried up the sidewalk, rubbing the back of his neck. Was this how the mind broke? Not as swiftly as a bridge that suddenly collapses, but in bits and pieces that fall away like dust and bits of rock from some windy cliff? Was this how it had happened to Boone nearly twelve years ago?

The old man rarely mentioned that period of his life, and McCleary never brought it up. But he knew the details because he'd been around when it happened. He was in Homicide with Benson, the Mariel boatlift was only a few months old at the time, and *Miami Vice* was still just a whisper in Michael Mann's ear. Boone was working a missing-child case in Little Havana and had learned from several supposedly reliable sources that among the refugees were Castro infiltrators. These Fidelistas allegedly intended to wage a not so private battle against anti-Castro sympathizers by blowing up their businesses, their banks, their homes. He eventually came to McCleary with the information, but not before he'd gone to the press.

The massive investigation that was launched involved McCleary only peripherally. But early on he'd suspected that Boone had been set up, fingered as a conduit for publicity about the plight of the Marielitos. When the investigation proved that the rumors of a plot were unfounded, the press dredged up his past association with Jim Garrison, labeled him a nut, and everything began to unravel for him.

His business suffered, he started to drink heavily, spiraled into depression, and within months he suffered a breakdown. He was hospitalized for a while, underwent electroshock, and finally retired here on Miami Beach. And here he had somehow survived on social security, a small pension, and whatever odd jobs he lucked into.

His wounds appeared to have healed, but you could never be sure what went on inside someone else—which rooms had been sealed, which routes to the past had been cut off or left open. Perhaps someday William Boone would wake up with one of those rooms wide open, the suppurations of his old rage pouring out, and he would walk into the hot light with a sawed-off shotgun and blow away whoever was there. The possibility seemed as remote as winning the lottery, but you never knew.

The old-timers on the porch all knew Boone and crowded around him, hungry for news about the murder investigation, the pending sale of the building, and any other morsels of information or gossip he cared to impart. He was the baby of the group, ten or twelve years younger than the youngest among them, and basked in their attention. He introduced McCleary, who hung back, and Flats, who didn't, then drew up an old rocker and brought them all up to date.

There wasn't much to tell, but that didn't daunt Boone. He possessed a storyteller's gift for embellishment and fielded questions with the polish of a seasoned politician. It was easy for McCleary to imagine him as he must have been so many years ago in New Orleans, a man whose convictions had been scrawled all over his face, a man with a mission, a zealot who had probably not been too far from the truth.

McCleary, who was in no particular rush, leaned against the wall of the porch and people-watched. Years ago, Miami Beach was as seasonal as the rest of South Florida, virtually deserted during the summer. Now it was inundated by Europeans, Japanese, and Florida residents lured by the summer's steep discounts in the hotel prices. The area was small enough, though, for him to recognize people: the Cuban woman from Mappy's Café up the street who had waited on them at lunch, the man and woman with the plump kid whose nose was still in a Batman comic book—and his own wife.

His wife, strolling up the street in an outfit he'd never seen before, with a purse he didn't recognize bouncing against her hip as she moved. Her umber hair was pulled away from her face with tortoise-shell combs, her dark shades hid her eyes. He probably wouldn't have noticed her at all if she hadn't been the tallest woman in sight. But then that was the point, wasn't it? Quin zipped into the bones of her other persona, Liz Purcell, the divorcée who had moved here from Gainesville to "start over again" and had lucked into a job with Crandall Development.

Liz, in her flashy clothes, that short skirt, those terrific legs.

She was with a woman who seemed to vibrate as she moved. Hummingbird, he thought, and knew she was Crandall's personal assistant, Betty O'Toole, whom Quin had described in considerable detail this past weekend. They were each carrying two plastic-foam cups, probably coffee from the Cuban market on Fifth and Collins.

McCleary watched her, fascinated by how utterly foreign she seemed to him, how aloof, how utterly unapproachable. During the weekend at home, this other woman, this interloper, had surfaced from time to time in the foods she had eaten, the clothes she had bought, in the way she had touched him, made love.

Like a woman emerging from a long abstinence, she'd been coy, sly, hungry for the whole scene of seduction, physical intimacy, experimentation. Quin but not Quin, his wife as a divorcee from a college town, eager for his mouth, his hands, furtive touches in the garage, the utility room, the kitchen as he made supper and Ellie watched her old friend Pooh on the tube.

As Quin passed the front of the building, Flats suddenly caught her scent and darted, barking, for the steps. McCleary caught the sheepdog's leash, pulled her behind the wall, and turned his back to the street. "Stay, girl, it's okay."

She peered up at him with those big sad eyes and cocked her head as if to say it wasn't okay at all, what was wrong with him, anyway? Then she lifted up her huge front paws, put them on the edge of the wall, and gazed after Quin, whining softly.

Betty had stopped to talk to someone and Quin was looking straight at him. Her smile was quick and sly; to anyone else, it would seem she was smiling at the dog. McCleary raised his fist to his ear: *Call me.* She gave a barely perceptible nod, then she and Betty walked off. He watched her like a curious and appreciative bystander. The curves in all the right places. The muscular calves from running. The way her hair moved as she moved.

"Hey, Mike, c'mon." Boone motioned him over.

"Let's move it, Flats," McCleary said, and they followed Boone around to the side of the building, where an open staircase led to the second-story apartments.

Boone rapped on the door of Apartment 8 and a voice inside shouted, "Yeah, hold on, hold on, I'm coming."

The kid who appeared was the perfect amalgam of Miami's ethnic mix: part black, part Caucasian, part Hispanic. Dreadlocks to his shoulders, dark blue eyes, skin a soft, rich chocolate. He wore faded coveralls with no shirt, Adidas without socks, and held a plate of black beans and rice that were almost gone. He was scooping a piece of Cuban bread through the remains.

"General," he said to Boone. "Good to see you. Sorry we didn't connect before. But I've been working a new job. Eighty, ninety hours a week." Flats barked at him and offered her paw; the kid laughed, shook her paw, then tossed her the rest of the bread. "Hey, this here's one great dog."

"Flats, Mike, this is R.D."

"You're the dude the General here talks about all the time." He swung around, set the plate on a nearby chair just inside the door, grabbed a gym bag off the floor, and slung it over his shoulder. Then he shut and locked the door. "I'm headed out, so let's talk on the way down to the parking lot. What's going on, General? Cops turn up something on the prof's murder?"

"Not yet, R.D. But I've been thinking about that last Sunday when you two played chess."

"What about it?"

"Go over it again. So Mike can hear it."

"We were supposed to go over one of Fischer's strategies, but there wasn't time. The professor said he was expecting a call and had to get home. He didn't say who was calling and I didn't ask. We played a couple of straight games. I could tell right off his head was somewhere else. I told him he was playing like some dude who had himself a new woman and he laughed and asked what did I think about that. About a guy as old as he was with a woman. 'Well, hey,' I says to him, 'just go for it.' And he gets this funny look on his face. And says she doesn't play chess."

Bingo. "Did he mention her name? Tell you anything about her?" McCleary asked.

"Nope, just that she didn't play chess. I knew he was thinking about his old lady. She and the professor played a lot of chess. I told him maybe it'd take three or four ladies to make up for the missus, one for dancing, one for chess, one for sleeping with, like that. He laughed and said he didn't have the time or the energy for so many ladies. Thing is, though, his head worked that way, you get what I'm saying? You could see it when he played chess. This move here, that move there, like nothing was connected. Then bang." R.D. clapped his hands. "It comes together and you see he knew all along exactly what he was doing. He had the whole thing already worked out up here." He tapped his temple.

They had reached the rear parking lot and stopped next to a battered blue pickup with a bumper sticker on the back that read CHECKMATE. R.D. tossed his gym bag through the open window, then turned, his thumb sliding along the inside of the coveralls' straps. "Hey, General, you got any idea what's going to happen to the Witch now that the prof is gone?"

"It looks like everything's on hold for a spell," Boone replied. "But sooner or later the county'll sell. If not to Crandall, then to someone else."

"Yeah, that's what I figured." The car door squeaked as he jerked it open. Flakes of rust rained from the single hinge that held it in place. He climbed inside, slammed the door, poked his head out. "Stay in touch, General."

"You bet, kid."

"Hey, R.D.," McCleary said.

"Yeah?" He had slipped on a pair of reflective sunglasses that now held twin images of a miniature Boone—old, slightly hunched over, checkered cap pulled low over his eyes—and of McCleary, who seemed to be nothing but smoky blue eyes and a beard threaded with gray.

"The day Charlie was killed, he mailed me a couple of photographs and asked me to hold on to them. He didn't explain what they were and I was just wondering if you might know something about them."

"Pictures, huh?" Frowning now, pensive, then a quick shake of his head. "Nope. He didn't say nothing to me about any pictures."

"You know of anyone else who Charlie might've talked to about his personal life?"

"The General . . ."

"Not on this," Boone replied.

"That's how he was. Real private like. Only other person I can think of is a *bruja* who's got a shop over on Collins. They used to have coffee together sometimes."

"A *bruja*?" Boone smiled. "Charlie and a witch?"

"She's not exactly a witch—no broomsticks or shit like that. She's a *santera*. Around here she's known as *La Vieja*. Word is that in the old days, in Cuba, she worked against Castro. Like I said, her shop's over on Collins and Ninth. *Ojo de Dios*. I hear the best way to catch her is early in the morning, like around eight. Gotta split, guys, or I'm late." He touched his fingers to his temple in a mock salute which Boone returned, then peeled out of the lot, smoke belching from the pickup's tailpipe.

"General?" McCleary asked.

Boone shrugged. "His sister thinks I'm a retired general. She inhales too much hair spray or something at her beauty shop. To her we were the general, the professor, and the kid. C'mon, let's head back up Washington."

They started walking, Flats tugging hard on her leash. "You know anything about this *santera?*"

"Nope. I'm not too clear on what *santería* is. I was pretty much off the streets when you started hearing about it back after the Mariel. Some kind of Cuban voodoo, isn't it?"

"Not really."

The comparison to voodoo was a common misconception about *santería*, the result of media hype about blood rituals and animal sacrifices as well as the American need to name, tag, categorize. Both had originated in Africa and used sympathetic magic, but the similarities ended there. *Santería* was based on the worship of *orishas* or saints; that was what the word meant. Its origin lay in Nigeria with the Yoruba people, pagans who revered a vast pantheon of gods. When they were brought to the New World as slaves, many of them ended up in Cuba, where Spanish missionaries attempted to convert them to Catholicism.

Instead, a gradual melding of the two religions occurred in which the traits of the Yoruba gods were assigned to particular Catholic saints. Francis of Assisi, for instance, was known as *Orúnla*, the great diviner. St. Peter was *Oggún*, patron of metals and working people.

"A *santero* is someone who has 'taken a saint' and been initiated into the rituals and secret practices. They're basically mediums who channel their particular *orishas* and when in trance, they heal, tell the future, counsel, you name it and they supposedly do it."

"Christ, this shit's about as far away from Princeton as you can get, Mac. What the hell was Charlie doing having coffee regularly with one of these people?"

"Tomorrow we'll ask the lady herself."

They had reached Washington Avenue. Here the homeless wandered in their tired bones and rotting shoes, snoozed in the deep shade between buildings, sipped furtively from brown paper bags. The homeless, like the tourists, followed seasonal urges.

During the winter they numbered more than ten thousand, swelled shelters beyond their usual capacity, and spilled into public parks. But it was June now, their numbers had fallen. And yet, like the Europeans, the Japanese, and the Florida residents, they stuck around for the deals—the shelters where the rules were more lax, the beaches where the cops might not chase them off, the kindness of strangers, whose blindness during the winter was miraculously healed the Monday after the mass Easter weekend exodus.

"You know, Charlie's greatest fear was that he would become like these people," Boone said. "That his old ticker would keep going so long his pension would be worthless, his social security would dry up, and his idiot son would either be dead or unable to help with his rent. Me, I figure it's one of those fears that just worsens with age. You either get used to it or it drives you nuts. It comes with the territory, you know?"

Yes, McCleary knew, and suspected the fear was as much Boone's as it had been Charlie's. The shape of his own demons had changed over the years, as anyone's did. But since his sister's murder, the nightmares were about the loss of people he loved. The possible forms of this loss were quite specific: that he would outlive Quin or Michelle or both of them, that one or both would end up as victims as his sister had, that he would grow old alone, like Boone.

It had made him overly cautious about Michelle. Just this past weekend, he'd given Quin's sister the name and number of a cop in West Palm and told her to contact him in the event that anything happened. Ellen had regarded him with that disarming equanimity that seemed to be her birthright and asked him to define "anything."

Hangup calls, yard lurkers, deliveries for things she hadn't ordered: his list of suspicious behaviors prompted her to touch the side of his face as though he were a very young boy in need of comforting. *Stop worrying, Mac. She's fine here.* But his sister-in-law lived in a world populated by third graders, where loss was defined as a ball that rolled away during recess. She didn't understand and neither did Quin. His wife's demons were as different from his as his were from Boone's or Charlie's.

No matter how you looked at it, when you hit a certain age your internal battles were waged, for the most part, against ghosts. The ghosts of the past, the ghosts that might be conjured up in the future. It affected every choice you made, even something as simple as coffee with a *santera*.

* * *

Except for the color of his Lincoln, Quin thought, earth tones didn't exist in Crandall's public image. From the clothes he wore to the offices in which he worked, he lived in a world of pastels. Even the ordinary business accouterments were true to the motif: company letterhead was light blue; business cards were baby pink and celery green; every computer was pale yellow; pencils and pens came only in pink and violet. Carried to such extremes, the color scheme had become Crandall's personal symbol, his calling card in the real-estate market, his emblem among his peers.

She had nothing against pastels. They calmed, they soothed, they pacified, they were pretty. But to live among them day after day left her yearning for a splash of burgundy, a burst of royal blue, the richness of forest green. In her office, three of the walls were a bubble-gum pink that matched the pink in the dizzying pattern on the terrazzo floor. On the fourth wall was a mural that typified Art Deco: four pink flamingos standing under an arc of water shooting from a fountain, with a wall of lush tropical foliage behind them. McCleary wouldn't consider it art, but she liked it for the bold green of the plants.

Beneath the mural were six filing cabinets that violated all the color codes: they were wooden, very dark, very scuffed, and Crandall was getting rid of them. Quin and Betty were removing the folders that were in the drawers, old, dusty files that looked as if they'd been in here since the turn of the century.

The dust irritated Betty's sinuses and she sneezed frequently and dramatically, in quick, violent bursts that always seemed to come in threes. Every time she sneezed, she stopped what she was doing and patted her pockets for a hanky or Kleenex so she could blow her nose. Then she used one or the other to wipe the dust off the file she'd been handling and griped about her numerous and mysterious allergies.

The litany was usually accompanied by habitual gestures: a quick pass of her fingers through her short, curly hair; fussing with her glasses; a quick roll of her lips. It all began to grate on Quin.

"I'll do the rest, Betty. Maybe you should get some fresh air or something."

Sniffle, sniffle. "Sometimes it's worse outside. It depends on which way the wind's blowing, you know. If it's coming from the west, the melaleuca pollen gets me. If it's coming from the north, it's the acacia pollen. When I first went to work for Mr. Crandall, he was still married and his wife had cats. He'd come to work with cat hairs on his clothes and I couldn't be around him without sneezing."

"How long have you worked for him?"

"Three years." *Sniffle, blow, wipe.*

"You must like it."

"He's the best." Like a groupie. "I make more money here than I could anywhere else on the beach, the benefits are great, and Mr. Crandall's pretty easy to work for once you understand what he wants. And now that I've got you to help me out, it's even better."

She seemed to be in the mood to gab, so Quin seized the opportunity. "He and Mr. Rau are pretty tight."

"I guess so." She opened a couple of the folders, rifled through papers.

"They in business together or what?"

"They collaborate on some things." Cagey now.

Quin dropped the subject. "What's the ex-Mrs. Crandall like?"

"Haughty. She used to waltz in here like she was better than everyone else. She was always on him about working so much, twelve-hour days, six, sometimes seven days a week. Woman like that can't understand that for someone like Mr. Crandall it isn't just work. It's his life."

This little speech was delivered in the prissy, sanctimonious tone that was the domain of the self-righteous. "Who divorced who?"

Betty sneezed again, blew again, wiped again. "You sure ask a lot of questions."

"Just curious."

"Yeah." Her mouth pursed. "So was his last assistant and she left after ten weeks."

Quin dismissed the remark with a laugh. "That a warning or something, Betty?"

"It's a fact." She dropped the file she'd been holding on Quin's desk. "Before you toss this stuff, you should probably check the labels against the list of Mr. Crandall's projects. If they appear on the list, it means they're already on the computer. I'll get you a copy of the list. Be right back."

Quin wondered if Little Miss Priss's reticence was because she was a jealous guardian of her turf or if she was just covering the boss man's ass.

It took her until five to go through all the files in the drawers and check the labels against the master list. In the past decade, most of the property Crandall had developed, owned, and sold was on Miami Beach. Apartments. Hotels. Houses. Restaurants. The exceptions were several cherry farms and a papaya grove that he'd owned for years in west Dade. Besides the groves, he only had three current projects in the county—two small housing developments in south Dade and The Resort. But three years ago he'd bought a warehouse in an industrial zone in west Dade. He'd sold it less than six months later. A warehouse. Not Crandall's style at all.

Quin started to make a call from her office, thought better of it, and went downstairs. From the pay phone in the lobby, she called an old contact at the county courthouse, an ex-client. She told Joan what she needed and thirty minutes later called her back.

According to the real-estate records, Crandall had bought the warehouse for $103,000 and sold it for half that to a company called Invest, Inc. "The only buyer listed is an attorney who was representing the company. It's a German outfit based in Nassau. The warehouse seems to be the only property they own in Dade. I hope that helps."

"Yeah, it does. Thanks, Joan. I appreciate it."

"You bet. Don't be a stranger, kiddo."

A German company. Owned by Rau? Maybe, but so what? That didn't make him guilty of anything. Only two facts didn't add up: that it was a warehouse and that Crandall had taken a steep loss on the sale.

She returned to her office, stacked the files to be tossed tomorrow, then picked up her purse, her briefcase, and closed up for the night. The second floor was deserted. Her footsteps echoed on the steps as she walked back downstairs. No sign of the night watchman yet. The Lincoln wasn't parked out front. The receptionist's desk was empty. Maybe, just maybe, she'd gotten lucky.

She swung by Crandall's suite of offices on the first floor. The door was partially ajar, she didn't hear anything, so she slipped inside. Silence, as smooth and perfect as a bubble: breathe too hard and she would pop it. She was in the reception area, Betty's desk to her right, a couch and chairs to her left. The doors to the adjoining rooms were shut. She moved toward Crandall's office and stopped dead when she heard something. From the conference room.

Giggling, it was Betty giggling. "That tickles, Larry."

"How about that?" Crandall's voice sounded different, unguarded, soft and loose. "Does that tickle?"

Betty, moaning. It sounded like a cow in pain.

"Tell me what you want, sugar. C'mon, say it. Tell me."

Sugar. Crandall calling Betty sugar.

Quin crept back, a hand over her mouth to stifle her laughter until she hit the sidewalk.

6

The wheelchair whispered through the trees, moving with the languid slowness of a stupid beast. Pisco was pushing it, which suited Heckler just fine. He didn't have the strength yet to negotiate the chair on his own and this gave him the opportunity to learn the geography of the compound and the rhythm of the routine. With each outing, the details grew clearer: the four wooden houses that rose seven feet high on concrete pillars, the fence that surrounded the three-acre compound, the number of employees, who came and went and when, the changing of the guard at the gate, and most important, the texture of Kilner's game.

He didn't know yet what he would do with his small discoveries. Although his strength was returning and he was down to two morphine tablets a day, escaping was out of the question. When he wasn't locked in his room, Pisco was his constant companion and he was incapable of overpowering the man. Even if he managed to escape, he wouldn't get far. Only water and highway lay between here and the nearest town.

The most he could do now, he thought, was to buy time. And the only way he could do that was to lead Pisco—and thus Kilner—to believe he might be persuaded to come clean in return for a deal. He held no illusions about the nature of such a deal. Addiction among operatives was often forgiven; betrayal was not. But exceptions were made to every rule, especially when men like Kilner and his boss, Elliot LeFrank, were involved. After all, power was the name of the game and Heckler knew that his little secret could seriously unhinge the balance of that power.

The wheelchair stopped at the dock. Pisco hit the foot brake, set down the fishing poles, brought out the tackle box, the bait. He whistled as he worked, a disjointed tune that drifted up through the branches of the trees. Heckler gazed across the brilliant blue of the Gulf waters, out toward the horizon, where thunderheads were already forming in the morning sky.

He turned his head and glanced left, into the compound. Other patients were being brought out of the houses now, for breakfast, for exercise, for their daily doses of sunlight and warmth. If his suspicions were correct, then these people were spooks like himself from any number of intelligence agencies who had plunged through the dark spiral of addiction or burnout or whose minds had simply broken. Here on Long Key, within the confines of Kilner's little kingdom, they would be treated, rehabilitated, and patched back together so they were almost as good as new. Those who were beyond treatment would be put out to pasture, retired with full pensions and no fanfare. He supposed that among them were a few like himself, men and women who posed security risks. He didn't know what happened to them. He didn't want to know.

"Hey, man," Pisco said. "What kind of bait you want to use? We got crickets and night crawlers."

"What's a night crawler?"

Pisco laughed and popped the lid on one of the plastic containers. Black dirt: that was all Heckler saw until Pisco dug his thick fingers into the soil and pulled out a wiggling earthworm. "That's what we called these critters when I was a kid."

As he hooked the worm, there was a glint in his eyes, the same malicious glint Heckler had seen in Kilner when he'd slit the throat of a young Indian woman in the jungles of Colombia years ago.

How many years ago? Heckler wondered. When had that happened? Which agency had he been with then? CIA? DEA? Yeah, the drug boys, that was it. And Kilner had been sent to their division to organize and implement a raid on a coke factory. Kilner, a physician by training, playing commando in the Colombian jungles. Yes, Heckler remembered. The memories were still vague, but at least the morphine hadn't emptied his head entirely.

"So what's it going to be?" Pisco asked.

"You hook, I'll cast."

"The trick is making sure they're on the hook real good."

Yeah, in fishing and in life on the compound.

"Mind if I ask you a question, Steve?"

Steve and Dan: like they were old fishing buddies. "If I mind, I'll let you know."

"What was in it for you?"

"Nothing."

Pisco regarded him with those strange eyes, the blue one being slightly narrower than its brown counterpart. "C'mon, man. It's just between us."

Sure it is, Dan.

"I'm curious, okay?" Pisco prodded. "Why steal information?"

"I was just evening up the score."

"Returning a favor to the professor?"

Returning one favor and doing another, he thought. "Yeah."

"And that's it?"

"That's it."

"Mr. Kilner's not buying it."

"So he's said."

"He thinks it may have something to do with Elliot LeFrank."

"Why would he think that?"

"Probably because you were LeFrank's right hand for so long."

"That ended a while back." A long while.

"Only because he ran for the Senate."

And subsequently lost. "You've done your homework, Dan."

"Yeah." Pisco handed him a pole, the earthworm dangling at the end, struggling valiantly. "You got to cover your ass in this business."

His lips pulled away from his teeth in a predatory grin. "But I don't have to tell you that, huh."

Amen, Heckler thought, and cast his line.

. . .

Kilner stood in front of the huge hurricane-tracking map on the wall of his office, studying the latest coordinates of the tropical depression. It had formed to the southwest of the Bahamas more than a week ago and was the second depression since the hurricane season had begun on June 1. If it developed into a tropical storm, it would be dubbed Albert, a fine example of equal rights.

The early Spanish explorers had named hurricanes after the saints on whose special days the storms occurred. Later, they were identified by latitude and longitude, then by alphabet letters—Able for A, Baker for B and so on. In 1953, the Weather Bureau started tagging storms with female names, a practice that was believed to have originated during the Second World War when servicemen named Pacific storms after their wives or girlfriends. By 1978, protests from women had grown so vociferous that the next year every other storm was given a male name, beginning with Hurricane David.

Kilner had ridden out two hurricanes—Cleo in 1964, a direct hit on Miami, and Elena in 1985. She had roared up Florida's west coast, forcing the evacuation of over a million people between St. Pete and Pensacola and causing more than a billion dollars in damage. He had no desire to go through another hurricane. It worried him that the second-lowest barometric reading ever recorded was right here on Long Key. September 2, 1935: The Labor Day Hurricane. Maximum winds weren't recorded because wind-measuring equipment was blown down before the storm ever peaked. Subsequent calculations, though, placed the velocity of the winds between two hundred and two fifty miles per hour.

Under such an assault, particularly if the winds were accompanied by a storm surge, Long Key would sink as surely as Atlantis. And that was a deeply disturbing thought.

The phone on his desk rang, an intrusive, irritating sound. Kilner was tempted to let the machine answer it, just in case it was his son calling to make his usual request for money. His son was twenty-five, a wasted orphan of marriage number one, now wandering around Tibet in search of something: Nirvana, ecstasy, a woman, who the hell knew. His quest was beyond Kilner's comprehension. But he usually called in the middle of the night, so Kilner picked up the receiver.

"Kilner here."

"Jerry, it's Elliot." Old pal, old buddy.

"Yeah, Elliot. What is it?"

"I assume you're keeping an eye on this depression?"

Kilner squeezed the bridge of his nose and stared at the map. LeFrank hadn't called to talk about the weather, he thought. "Of course I am. Why?"

"Well, in the event that the worst happened, I hope you've put together an evacuation plan."

"Don't worry about it, Elliot. What's up?"

"Where do we stand?"

"Gabriel got here two days ago."

"Good, good. How long will it take him to recover the file?"

"He's supposed to be fast and efficient."

LeFrank snorted. Kilner could see him in his head—that salt-and-pepper hair, the trim physique, the brilliant blue eyes, LeFrank and his revolting Midwestern cheerfulness. "He'd better be, considering what we're paying him. I still think our little lady could have handled this."

Our little lady: as though they owned the woman they'd planted in Crandall's operation. "She doesn't know anything about Gabriel and I'd just as soon keep it that way. She's got her hands full."

"Anything new on this Purcell woman?"

"She's being watched. And so far, my Miami team hasn't picked up anything. We got a set of prints, but they were smudged."

"What about phone calls?"

"The phone isn't bugged. But from what the Miami boys have heard of her side of conversations, Purcell doesn't appear to be anyone other than who she says she is."

"Except that she was seen with the chief of police."

Yes, except for that.

"What about lovers? Doesn't she have any lovers?"

"None so far. Look, we're on top of it, Elliot."

"How's Heckler doing?"

Kilner walked over to the window with the phone. He could just make out Heckler and Pisco, fishing from the end of the dock. "I think he's told us everything he knows."

"I'd like to release him, Jerry."

Sure you would, Elliot.

"I'd like to set him up somewhere pleasant. The Adirondacks, the Ozarks, hell, even the Andes. He's always loved mountains."

You oughta know, Elliot.

"He might even do okay for a while. But sooner or later he'd get on this morality kick and blow it."

"Probably."

"That's the problem with these addictive types, Jerry. One week they're cured and the next they're overdosed. But in Heckler's case, I think we should give it a while longer."

How much longer? Kilner wondered. Just how long a reprieve was LeFrank willing to give his old foot soldier? "Whatever you say."

"One other thing. Due to all these cutbacks, there's been some talk about closing up Long Key. The argument is that we have rehab centers closer to D.C. and this is an unnecessary expense."

Kilner's ears rang with the words. He had a sudden vision of himself tethered to a desk in some dreary office in the Pentagon and knew he wouldn't last six months. "VA hospitals don't come close to what we offer here and just what the hell are they going to do about the security risk, Elliot? Cross their collective fingers and pray? What're they going to do with people like Heckler?"

"I know, I know." That smooth, polished voice. Kilner could almost see LeFrank patting the air with his hands. "And we'll present those arguments when the time comes, Jerry. I just wanted you to be apprised of the situation. Frankly, I don't expect it to ever go beyond the talking stage if we pull off this project. They'll realize that the Long Key facility is too valuable to close down."

They and them, we and us, the CIA versus LeFrank's small but powerful coterie of security watchdogs. The battle lines clearly drawn.

If this goes down the tubes, Jerry old buddy, old friend, you're going with it. Yeah, Kilner read him loud and clear.

7

It seemed to Quin that she had heard the shriek of sirens most of the night. Sometimes the sounds had been distant, like background noises in a dream, and sometimes the sirens sounded as if they were coming from inside her apartment. Even with the windows closed and the air conditioner on, she could hear them, muted wails that echoed through the dark streets, ushering in a Friday of tainted, troubled air.

Her first thought when she hauled herself out of bed was that something had happened to Michelle, an accident, a fall, that she'd choked on Cheerios. Quin started to dial her sister's place, then remembered the routine.

Benson's play-it-safe routine.

It was okay for McCleary or Ellen to leave her a coded message on her answering machine, but she had to call them from the pay phone in the courtyard. McCleary was not to visit her; they had to meet elsewhere. Whenever she was home, she should have the TV or a radio on, just in case the place was bugged. So she slipped out into the courtyard in her nightshirt and a pair of jeans, her hair unbrushed, her teeth unbrushed, and called her sister with an AT&T card.

Ellen was awake, naturally. With three kids in the house she had probably been awake since the crack of dawn. Michelle was doing just fine, of course of course, and was eating breakfast and watching cartoons with Ricky and Rebecca.

"Nothing's changed since you called last night, Quin."

Translated: you're being paranoid.

So what. Motherhood entitled her to a certain degree of paranoia. "What's she having for breakfast?"

"A soft-boiled egg, Cheerios, toast, juice."

Quin balked. Her daughter never ate like that at home. "You sure we're talking about the same kid?"

"She eats whatever Rebecca eats. I'm telling you, Quin. It's a cinch when you've got more than one."

Sure. "Let me say hi."

Michelle got on the phone, giggled when she heard Quin's voice, and squealed, "Mama!"

"Mommy misses you, El."

"Uh-huh."

"You being a good girl?"

"Uh-huh."

"Mommy loves you."

She laughed and dropped the phone and Ellen got back on. "You've been preempted by Chip and Dale, Quin. Listen, would you and Mac mind if we took Ellie with us to Disney World? Hank got some discount tickets from a guy at work and now that Ricky's out of school we thought it'd make a nice vacation."

Disney World. Her daughter at Disney World. Quin had wanted to take her. "For how long?"

"Probably a week or so."

"A *week*? A whole week?"

"You'd be down there anyway, Quin, and Ellie would love it."

Of course she would love it. What kid wouldn't? But that wasn't the point. "I'll talk to Mac, but I'm sure it'll be fine. When would you be leaving?"

"Next week sometime. You coming home tonight?"

"Not until tomorrow evening. Crandall asked me to work tomorrow." On a Saturday, a free day.

"How's the investigation going?"

"Okay."

"Look, I've got to run. Don't worry about Ellie, Quin. She loves it here."

Loves it here. The words bounced around inside her skull as she went back into the apartment. Liz Purcell's apartment. Cathedral ceilings, a tile fireplace, spacious, and old, so goddamn old. Leaky faucets, cracks and fissures in the paint, the tile, the bathroom floor. There were different linoleum patterns in every room, the furniture shouted other people's histories every time she sat on it, the kitchen appliances were flawed. What was she doing here, anyway?

She fixed herself a huge breakfast, eggs and bacon, toast and hash browns, slices of mangos and papayas, and ate to chase away the blues. But by the time she stepped out into the heat of the courtyard, she was ready to tell Benson to find someone else for the job, that she was returning to the life she'd abandoned. To the daughter she'd surrendered to her sister. Ready and yet unable to make the call, unable to walk away from something she'd started until it was finished. It was her greatest strength and her greatest weakness, a professional asset and a personal failing, the single most perplexing dichotomy she'd discovered in herself.

It had prevented her from despairing when, several years ago, McCleary had come to one morning in a motel room with a dead woman in the next bed and twenty years of memories on ice. It had kept her from filing for divorce when they'd been separated for seven months, had kept her from hating him when he'd had an affair with a woman he'd known before they had married.

Charlie Potemkin had known all that because she'd told him one night over drinks in a Cuban restaurant in Little Havana. He had been that kind of man, a good listener with wise, quiet eyes, an almost archetypal figure, like an alchemist or a medieval magician.

"Everyone," he'd said, "has a breaking point. It's different for all of us, but when you reach it, you act, and the consequences be damned. The bull's rush, that's what the cons call it." Then he laughed and confided that he'd borrowed the term from the con who'd told him and used it in one of his books. "You just haven't reached your breaking point yet, Quin."

Did you, Charlie? Were those photos about his breaking point? His bull's rush?

She stopped at the Explorer, then decided to walk off the blues. It was something Liz Purcell, new to town, would do. Besides, she needed the exercise. She hadn't gone running since she'd moved here.

The temperature was in the low eighties and it wasn't too humid yet. Cumulus clouds were stacked against the sky like huge clusters of cauliflower; the acacia trees burned with crimson blossoms; bright yellow flowers adorned the pui trees; marigolds and Mexican heather, the survivors of summer heat, had replaced beds of impatiens; and the daily showers had turned everything a deep, rich green. In another few weeks, the real heat would begin, the kind that left you weighted, leaden, the kind that sucked you dry. Most noticeable, though, was the absence of tourists.

Snowbirds complained that Florida lacked seasons, but it simply wasn't true. The seasons were subtle. Fall arrived when the debilitating September heat finally broke. Bougainvillea bloomed, the green began to fade, the acacia trees lost their buds, and the early crops of grapefruit hit the stores.

Winter started around Thanksgiving, with the first cold spell and the arrival of the tourists. Tangelos and pink grapefruit spilled from produce bins, mango trees began to flower, the acacia trees shed their leaves, rainfall diminished. In a bad year, winter was the time when water restrictions went into effect. The level in Lake Okeechobee, the state's lifeline, the blood of the Everglades, was monitored more closely than the President's health.

Spring always crept in through a backdoor, it seemed, with the rains picking up, the skies turning gradually bluer and hotter, and the tourists heading back where they'd come from. It lasted until the fierce heat started and air conditioners came on.

She paused at the corner of Washington Avenue and Fifteenth Street, waiting for the light to turn, then darted across the road, headed east toward Ocean Drive. That was when she first noticed it, the black Jeep Cherokee turning as she turned. Never mind that other cars were turning as well. The Cherokee hung back, didn't speed up to make the next light, didn't jump lanes, didn't play the Miami road game. Granted, she'd been born with paranoid tendencies that fifteen years as a PI had exacerbated, but this had all the makings of a tail.

Just to be sure, she walked north two blocks along Washington to the Cameo Theater, one of the monuments of the Deco District. Its billboard announced TWO BIG HITS AT ALL TIMES. Today's hits were vintage Hitchcock, *Vertigo* and *Psycho*.

"One, please." She pushed a five through the window.

The woman in the booth cracked her gum and glanced up from the tabloid she'd been reading. She looked as if she'd spent her entire adult life in this tiny cage. "For which movie, hon?"

"It doesn't matter." The Cherokee was now moving up the street. "Just hurry."

"You got to pick one or the other. For the records, you know."

"*Vertigo*."

"You've already missed half of it, but *Psycho* just started."

"Fine, that's fine."

"For *Psycho*?"

This was what life in a tiny cage did to the mind. "Yes, for *Psycho*. That's what I just said."

"No, you said . . ."

"Just give me a ticket."

The woman made a strange little sound, a snort, a burp, it was difficult to tell, and slid the ticket and three bucks through the window. Best deal in town, Quin thought, and hastened through the double doors.

The Cherokee now idled at the curb on the other side of the street. *So what's it going to be, guy? You going to sit there or come on in?*

She ordered a box of popcorn and a lemonade at the refreshment counter and glanced into the street. A tall man climbed out of the Cherokee, a very tall man, six-four, maybe six-five. He wore jeans, a checkered blue shirt, a brown windbreaker, and a blue baseball cap tugged low over his sunglasses. The only detail of his face that she could make out was a mustache. He put money into the meter and started across the street.

In the event that he belonged to that peculiar subspecies of psychotics that breed like mosquitoes in South Florida, she would be forced to second-guess him if she stayed where she was. Would he or would he not pull an automatic weapon out of that windbreaker as soon as he walked through the door? She slapped a five onto the counter to cover her order and made a beeline for the theater.

Psycho had already started. In the thin wash of light from the screen, she counted four people in the theater. Four. That was it. No

ﻭﻟﻛﻥ لا

safety in numbers here. But at nine in the morning, what did she expect? Quin hastened down the left aisle toward the glowing red EXIT sign, popcorn and lemonade still in hand, and pushed on the horizontal metal bar. Nothing happened.

She pushed again. Nothing.

A wedge of light fell into the dark at the other end of the theater. She didn't know whether it was the tall man entering or someone else; it had ceased to matter. She threw her weight against the bar. The door gave with a horrendous screech that suggested it hadn't been opened since the sixteenth century. She stumbled out into the bright light, heard someone shout, "Hey, shut the door!"

Quin kicked it shut, glanced left, right, trying to orient herself. Stay off Washington, she thought. The Cherokee was on Washington. She dropped the popcorn and lemonade and ran right, toward Ocean Drive. Ran with her arms pumping at her sides, her new skirt flapping at her knees, her new sandals clicking against the worn alley, her new turquoise blouse dampening with perspiration.

Sorry I'm late, Mr. Crandall. Sorry I don't look quite up to snuff. Sorry, sorry, but you wouldn't know anything about this tall guy in the Cherokee, would you, Mr. Crandall?

If the man had entered the theater as she'd left, if he had figured out that she was the person flying through the rear exit, and if he had followed, then she had only seconds before he appeared in the alley. Seconds. But suppose he'd gone back out the front instead of following her? Then he would be waiting for her when she emerged from the alley.

Her head snapped around.

Empty, the alley behind her was empty.

She could see Collins Avenue just ahead, cars and pedestrians, but not the tall man. She slowed. Stopped. Backed up to the wall between a pair of metal trash cans. She dropped to a crouch, wrapped her arms around her knees, pressed her face into her skirt. Heart pounding, she waited.

Minutes ticked by. Three, four, five. Quin finally raised her head, heard music drifting through an open window in the building in front of her. She stepped out, arms clutched at her waist. He was gone, she was sure of it. She was equally sure that she hadn't seen the last of him, of the tall man in the black Jeep Cherokee.

■ ■ ■

A pro, Tark thought. Only a pro would have noticed. Only a pro would bait him as she had done, detouring into the theater, then slipping out the rear exit. He could have followed her, but why bother? He knew what he needed to know. Now all he had to do was confirm it.

He drove back to Mango's, paid for another week just to keep the room, shaved off his mustache, packed his bags, and left by the rear door. He drove to Hertz and exchanged the Cherokee for a Honda, a car that Liz Purcell or whoever she was wouldn't associate with him, then swung by her apartment on Fifteenth Street, between Washington and Drexel.

Merle's Bed & Breakfast. Like it was some neat little European inn instead of the tired, aging structure that it was.

He pulled into a spot at the corner of the parking lot, shrugged off his windbreaker, removed his baseball cap, combed his fingers through his curly black hair. He walked through the courtyard, looking for the manager's apartment. He found it easily enough. There were only seven apartments in the building and hers was at the corner, marked by a weathered sign that read MANAGER, J. LINK. He knocked, heard the drone of a TV through the open jalousie windows. A movie. J. Link was a hard-core addict. Even in Iquitos, a city of a quarter million enclosed entirely by jungle, there were TV addicts. Christ only knew what they watched; the choices were hardly comparable to what was available in this country. But it was Tark's experience that TV addicts were usually addicted to something else as well. Food, booze, drugs, sex, money, take your pick. And the woman who answered the door was probably no exception.

J. Link looked like a refugee from the Bronx who had come here with high expectations that hadn't panned out. She was plump, wore baggy shorts and a T-shirt that was a size too large, and in the unforgiving morning light her face was a road map of bad choices and indiscretions. "Yes?" she asked, holding on to the edge of the door and lifting her bare left foot to scratch at her right calf. "What can I do for you?"

"Do you have any vacancies?"

"Sure. It's summer. What'd you have in mind?"

"I'd like to rent an apartment."

■ ■ ■

In uncertain times, the hocus-pocus business flourished, McCleary thought. Housewives channeled spirits older than the known universe; Christ performed miracles on television through loyal minions who were later indicted for fraud or some sexual perversion; the faithful moved to Seattle and Oregon on the advice of their psychics. And judging by the line of people outside of *Ojo de Dios,* no one was busier in the Hispanic community than the local *santera.*

"We're in the wrong business, Mike," Boone remarked as they got in line.

"Definitely."

A young man moved down the line, asking people if they were here to shop or to see Señora Villa. Shoppers were allowed inside. Everyone else was given a number and told to go around the side of the house to the courtyard.

The courtyard was no larger than a postage stamp. It was enclosed by tall oolite walls that were a faded, dirty pink and draped in crimson bougainvillea. The brick floor had long since worn away to dirt, and the fountain in the center didn't look as though it had contained water since the turn of the century. Chickens clucked and pecked through the dirt, a goat nibbled at the dying leaves of a croton, cats snoozed in patches of sunlight and shade. At the side of an aluminum storage shack were half a dozen cages that contained doves. And everywhere there were people.

They clustered at the walls, occupied foldup chairs, sat on the back steps and along the walls of the fountain: Latinos, Anglos, Haitians, a Hindu, Europeans. Twenty-two people in all; McCleary counted twice just to be sure. And each of them waited for the moment when the door of the aluminum shack would open and their number would be called.

"Jesus," Boone muttered. "What country we in?"

"The Land of Weird. C'mon, I see a vacant spot over by the fence."

They waited for an hour and a half, waited while the goat chewed and the chickens pecked and the shack's AC unit dripped and coughed and the number of people dwindled. Twice someone emerged from the shack, opened one of the cages that held the doves, removed one, and went back inside. The doves didn't reappear.

"Those doves flying around inside that shack or what?" Boone asked.

"I doubt it."

Boone stopped pacing and looked at McCleary, his bushy brows sliding together as his eyes narrowed with suspicion. "What the hell does that mean?"

"I think they're used in some sort of ritual."

"A ritual." Boone stared at the shack as though he believed the walls would suddenly part like the Red Sea. Then he shook his head. "I think the kid's mistaken. Charlie never would have been part of something like this."

"All he said, Will, was that Charlie and the woman had coffee sometimes. That doesn't make him a *part* of anything."

Boone snorted and continued his pacing. He'd awakened this morning in a cantankerous mood that showed no sign of improving. Over breakfast, he'd announced that today was June 19 and just where the hell were they in the investigation? His mood had not improved since. He grumbled about the wait, the dust that made him sneeze, the chicken shit he stepped in. He needed coffee, he needed to use the can, he needed to get home and feed Elvis. He had become the ugly American you sometimes ran into overseas, the guy who, stripped of everything familiar, griped and complained his way across whatever country he happened to be in.

Even though McCleary understood it had more to do with Boone's changing perceptions about his old chess buddy than it did with the place itself, the old man's behavior irritated him. He finally handed Boone the keys to the Miata. "No sense both of us wasting the morning. I'll meet you back at the apartment later."

"I'll drive down to the Grove and see if I can get a lead on the ex-Mrs. C."

"Great."

He dropped the keys into his cap, tugged the cap down over his head, and managed a tired smile. "I'm an obnoxious old fart, huh."

"Irascible, I think that's the word, Will."

"Now you sound like Charlie. Catch you later."

McCleary watched him shuffle out of the courtyard, his shoulders hunched as if against a strong wind.

The courtyard continued to fill with new arrivals, shadows shrank, the sun grew uncomfortably warm. His number was finally called and he stepped into the shack. It was like a repository for religious artifacts in a country where religion was forbidden. It was cool and dimly lit by flickering candles arranged on a square wooden table to his right. The table, covered with a white cloth, contained a bowl with pieces of fresh coconut in it, colored beads, a deck of cards, a bottle of cheap rum, a box of cigars, matches, and a bottle of Florida water, a type of cologne that was a staple in *santería*. There was also a Mason jar stuffed with bills.

Crowded around the table like an audience were numerous religious statues of varying heights and colors. An umbrella stand contained dozens of freshly cut lilies and roses. Petals covered the floor, muting the noise of the air conditioner on the other side of a huge Guatemalan blanket that divided the room. The Land of Weird for sure, he thought.

"*Señora* Villa?" he called.

"*Sí, sí, ya vengo*," replied a soft, husky voice on the other side of the curtain. "*Siéntase, por favor.*"

He sat down on one of the hard wooden chairs at the table, and a moment later a woman emerged from behind the blanket. She was maybe five feet tall, slender but not thin, and wore white pedal pushers, a loose white shirt, a string of red-and-white beads around her neck. She was barefoot. Her toenails and fingernails were painted a bright red. Her hair was white and long, like a witch's, and seemed to flow behind her as she moved. He guessed she was at least sixty, and yet her dark eyes seemed much older.

"*Es americano*," she said, sitting down and reaching for the cards.

"*Sí, pero hablo español.*"

"*Ah, bueno. Es más fácil.* My English it is not too good." She shuffled the cards with the deftness of a dealer at Vegas and switched back to Spanish when she spoke again. "Is there anything in particular you want to know?"

He started to tell her why he'd come, but sensed she might be more amenable to talking about Charlie if she read for him first. "No, nothing special."

She tapped the cards against the table and handed the deck to him. "Just hold them between both hands for a moment."

The cards weren't Tarot or ordinary playing cards and were smaller than both. The flowered designs on the back were worn and faded, and when he held them between his hands, they felt as old as they looked. "What kind of cards are these?"

"Brisca. It's a Cuban card game." She lit a stogie and blew smoke over the table and toward the statues. "That deck belonged to my *madrina*. She worked on my father's sugar plantation in Cuba and gave them to me when I was initiated. They belonged to her grandmother, a former slave, and are well over a century old."

She set the cigar in the bowl with the pieces of coconut, opened the bottle of Florida water, and poured some into her hand. She flicked it around the immediate area, her mouth moving as if in silent prayer. Then she opened the bottle of rum, drank from it but didn't swallow, and blew the rum in a fine spray across the table.

"Your beads," McCleary said. "Which *orisha* do they represent?"

"Red and white belong to Changó."

"Is the coconut for him?"

"No, for Eleggúa. He opens the doors." She smiled and asked for the deck. "Most Americans I have read for do not ask as many questions as you do."

"It's a bad habit of mine."

"No, no, quite the contrary. It is the kind of thing that should happen more often between Hispanics and Anglos."

She laid the cards out in an arc, like a rainbow, three rows with seven cards each. She puffed on the cigar as she studied the layout, and was quiet for what seemed a long time but probably wasn't. She set the cigar again in the bowl with the bits of coconut and began to speak, her voice so soft he had to lean forward to hear what she said.

"There is much violence in your past, *señor*. And many injuries to the heart because of it. I see people in uniform, people who carried guns, blood that was spilled. The military, perhaps, or . . ." She raised her eyes. "Were you a policeman?"

Impressive. "Yes."

"That was many years ago."

"Nearly a decade."

She frowned. Her finger glided through the air over the bottom row of cards and landed, finally, on the last one to the right. "But the violence has followed you. This person died violently. A woman, someone close to you, a lov—no, a sister. This was your sister."

Jesus.

"Is this correct, *señor?* Please tell me if it is not and we will shuffle and deal the cards again. On days when I see many people there are sometimes confusions."

"It's correct. Go on."

Her finger moved to the middle row. "Your present." She frowned again and shook her head. "This isn't clear, *señor.* There's a woman here with dark hair and a young child who is blonde, a girl. Your wife? Yes, yes, your wife and daughter. You live with them sometimes, but not now. The woman is looking for something, for papers. She has two faces, two names, two separate lives. She is surrounded by duplicity, by people who are not what they appear to be." A pulse beat hard and fast at her temple now and although it was cool in the shack, her face glistened with perspiration. She spoke more quickly, as though she couldn't get rid of the words fast enough. "There is danger around her, danger from these two men." She tapped two more cards. "They stand on either side of her. The one who is closest to her has come from a great distance, from another country. He . . . he *breathes* violence and lives in the darkness of terrible pain."

Her hand trembled as she reached for the bottle of rum. This time she swallowed what she drank, then swept up the middle and bottom rows of cards. She leaned close to the seven that remained. The future. "A man in a wheelchair. A second man who has no hair. A third man, a man of power. Stalking. Darkness. Violence. Death."

She suddenly slammed her fists over the cards. The table shook, candles toppled, the bottle of rum was knocked to the floor and shattered. She stumbled to her feet, shuddering violently, her teeth clenched, her arms clutched against her. Then her eyes rolled up into her head and she fell back, arms pinwheeling.

McCleary caught her before she struck the floor. Dry, rasping noises issued from her mouth, noises like nothing he'd ever heard in his life, the sounds man might have made before he had language. Her eyes rolled and slid around in their sockets like a pair of loose marbles, only the milky whites visible now. She was still shuddering as he kicked open the door of the shack and tore through the courtyard toward the shop, shouting for help, the woman lighter than clouds in his arms.

In a back room of the *botánica,* Clara Villa lay motionless on a couch under the window, her face as pale and perfect as marble. Her hands rested against her chest, her eyes were shut; she looked, McCleary thought, like a corpse laid out for viewing in a funeral home.

Two women—one in her twenties and the other older and wearing a uniform—fussed over her as he waited in the doorway. They elevated her head, loosened her shirt, drew a light blanket over her. The younger woman told the cook or the maid or whatever she was to get the *señora* some tea. Then she hurried over to McCleary with her hands fixed to her plump hips and addressed him in English that was better than his own.

"I'm Clara's granddaughter, Margarita Ordóñez." She held out her hand; it was cool and dry.

"Mike McCleary."

"Thank you for bringing her over here so quickly, Mr. McCleary. There's so much junk in that shack she could have hurt herself. This happens sometimes. She'll be okay in a little while."

"Was it a seizure?"

"In a sense. It signals the onset of a deep trance state in which her guide or one of the *orishas* speaks through her. But it usually happens during our religious celebrations, when there's music and ritual. It's rare that she allows herself to go so deeply during a reading in the shack."

"Look, I actually came here to talk to her about something else."

Margarita combed her fingers back through her black hair. She was attractive in the way so many Latin women were, with the smooth, flawless skin that seemed to be their birthright. She wore just a touch of makeup and had a fondness for gold. Half a dozen bracelets climbed her right arm and jingled when she moved. A delicate gold cross hung from a chain at her throat. There was gold on most of her fingers.

"Maybe I can help you."

"I understand she was friends with Charles Potemkin."

"Potemkin?" Margarita rolled her lower lip against her white teeth. "No, I don't know the name."

"He was recently murdered."

Recognition flickered like light across her features, recognition, he thought, and something else. Evasion? Fear? Sadness? He couldn't tell. "Oh, Don Carlos. Yes, they were friends. His death was a tremendous loss for her. Ever since it happened, she's been working very long hours, trying to lose herself in work."

"How long were they friends?"

She shrugged. "I don't know, Mr. McCleary. A year, maybe more, I'm not sure. I think he came to her originally as a client."

An impulse prompted him to ask: "Did your grandmother receive anything in the mail from him after he died?"

"I don't know, Mr. McCleary. I just come in to help out from time to time. My grandmother lives alone above the shop, so I don't know about all the particulars in her life. Look, why don't you leave a number where she can call you when she's up and about again?"

He would prefer to stick around and wait for her to return from the soft, dark place where she had taken refuge. But there was a strident quality in Margarita's voice now that made him feel like the gringo interloper who had overstayed his welcome. So he jotted Boone's phone number on a scrap of paper. It vanished in the hip pocket of Margarita's skirt, where it would probably remain.

He left through the courtyard, which was empty now. Even the chickens and the goats had taken sanctuary elsewhere. A breeze blew through, rustling the branches of the thirsty crotons and knocking blossoms off the bougainvillea. Little dust devils whirled around the fountain. The door of the shack swung open and shut, creaking softly. The place struck him as bleak and forlorn, like some forbidding landscape in a dream where your only salvation is death.

You have just left and my rooms seem impoverished by your absence. . . .

The words drifted through him with an almost languid slowness, like a refrain from a song he'd heard long ago.

You have made me whole again. . . .

Charlie's lady friend? Possible.

He turned to look back at the shop. Clara Villa's face was framed briefly in the window, the breeze combing her long white hair behind her. Then she was gone.

8

J. Link was the kind of woman who would drive a man to all the clichés, Tark thought, booze and drugs and homicidal madness. She had insisted on walking him through the apartment—number five, right next door to Purcell's—had returned with a supply of fresh linens and made the bed, then returned again with extra dishes, and again with a spare key. Her chatter was an endless loop of non-sequiturs, and he tolerated her presence only because he didn't want to alienate a potential source of information.

When she left for the last time, he locked the door, pulled the blinds, proceeded to hide most of the money. He carried the rest in a money belt that hung along his right thigh. Then he set out on foot.

Miami Beach hadn't changed much since the days he had lived here. Yes, there were more people, more cars, more refurbished buildings, but the basics were still intact. The landmarks still existed: Wolfie's Cafeteria, the post office, the library, Flamingo Park, Ocean Drive.

He walked into the lobby of the Sea Witch, where men and women older than time sat around watching TV, playing cards, reading newspapers. Several shuffled by in walkers or moved with the aid of canes. He inquired at the desk about vacancies—for his mother, he said. The young clerk, who wore a tag that identified him as a county employee, said there were no vacancies.

"Is there a waiting list?"

"Not anymore. The property may be sold, so right now everything's on hold."

"What'll happen to the residents if the sale goes through?"

The young man shrugged. "I guess they'll be evicted. We really haven't heard, sir."

Evicted.

Outside of Iquitos, there was a kind of suburb in the Amazon River that consisted of shacks on stilts. Hundreds of them. They were slapped together from pieces of rotting wood and rusted tin, one or two rooms that sometimes accommodated generations of families. They had no plumbing, no running water. People bathed, drank, and defecated in the river, their primary food source. To any of the unfortunate souls who lived in the town on stilts, he thought, the Sea Witch would be paradise. Although the river people weren't facing eviction, their way of life, like that of the residents of the Sea Witch, was threatened with extinction as the old was subsumed by the new.

He left the Sea Witch and, following the information his employer had provided, retraced Heckler's path the day he had passed the file to Charlie Potemkin. There were five bars in all that twisted from the Lincoln Road Mall to the north and south to Eighth Street. He talked to bartenders, waiters, waitresses, and learned virtually nothing. In Miami time, May 31 was a lifetime ago.

His final stop was a dive called The Deuce Club, Heckler's last watering hole. He sat at the bar nursing a Campari and soda and tried not to think about obligations, the phone call he should make, the visit that was expected of him. He was tempted to just sit here and drink himself stupid, but knew he would wake up with Little Havana beckoning, as it was now.

Get it over with, he thought. Just do it and be done with it.

Tark rubbed his eyes and forced his thoughts in other directions. Heckler. The file. Charles Potemkin. Liz Purcell. The money that had been paid for this, his last job.

The future, he would think about the future, about where he would go when he was finished here. He liked Iquitos okay, but had enough in the bank to live anywhere he wanted.

Switzerland?

Too cold.

The Caicos?

Too laid back.

Manhattan, sure, a man could lose himself in the Big Apple.

Too frenzied, too congested, too excessive in every way.

Florida.

Christ, it always came back to Florida, didn't it? Back to the place where he had cheated death and lost everything that had held meaning for him.

He dropped a five on the counter and walked back to the apartment for the car, the heat beating down on him. He drove into Little Havana and meandered among the narrow, twisted streets of small homes and *tiendas* that all looked the same. He hadn't brought along a map. He hadn't thought he would need one. It had only been two years. But Calle Flores was the kind of road that remained invisible when you were looking for it. Magic, Teresita used to say. Like something in a fairy tale.

When he finally found it, he realized he'd already crossed it several times. He couldn't quite shake the feeling that the street had simply chosen to show itself and was now laughing at him.

Un Paso was exactly where he remembered it, wedged between a used bookstore and a *botánica*. He parked across the street, and for moments, he just gazed at it, certain if he blinked, if he looked away, it would vanish.

He had a bad moment when he climbed out of the Honda. A wall of sweat moved across his back and his hands grew so damp he had to rub them against his jeans. Eleven years, he thought. His daughter had been dead for eleven years and he had become the expatriate American in the Jimmy Buffett song. Now here he was in front of the bar and restaurant where his old life had ended.

Turn around, Tark. Don't do it, whispered the niggling voice in his head. He shook it away and pushed open the door.

Nothing had changed inside. Nothing. The S-shaped bar curved from one end of the room to the other, the floor still sagged in the middle, Julio Iglesias crooned from the jukebox. Four old-timers were playing dominoes at a back table, and the rest of the booths and tables were filled with American and Cuban businessmen, bureaucrats, politicians. They came for the food, which was delicious, plentiful, and cheap, and they came for information.

It was exchanged over platters of *arroz con pollo*, over cold draft beers, over poker games in the back room. At times, this information seemed like an entity unto itself, floating through the air and there for the plucking if you knew the right questions to ask and if Alfonso liked you.

The hostess asked if he would like a table. She was new since he'd been here last, but he guessed she was the daughter or the niece of one of Alfonso's friends. "I'm looking for Alfie. Is he in?"

"Your name, *señor?*"

"Gabriel."

"*Un momentito, por favor.*" She moved through the noise, a lovely vision in blue and red, and vanished through the door on the far side of the room. To the right of that door, midway up the wall, was a line of stained-glass windows. In his worst nightmares, those windows shattered again and again, the spray of colored glass hurling into the room, slivers transformed into lethal missiles. In his nightmares he never heard the explosion that blew out most of the wall. But he heard his daughter's shrieks, heard his wife screaming his name, heard the collapse of his world.

When the quiet had finally descended, he'd been sprawled under an overturned table, water from a broken vase dripping steadily onto the back of his hand. Before he'd even lifted his head, he'd known that Teresita was dead, he could feel the absence inside himself, the *void.*

His wife, Carmen, had lingered for two months in a coma, her neck broken, one side of her face crushed. Had she lived, she would not have walked again. In all, eighteen people were killed that day in August eleven years ago and one of them was a Colombian kingpin, the intended victim. Tark had spent most of the next year in a blur that he could barely remember even now. Then one day the blur had begun to clear and he'd started selling everything he owned—the house, his plane, his chartering business—and a month later he fled the country.

He went first to Venezuela, a country where he'd lived in his youth as the only child of American diplomats. He renewed old acquaintances, found that he possessed a certain flair for bullshit that made people believe he was something he wasn't. At a cocktail party in Caracas, he met a German diplomat whose son was missing. Tark convinced the man he could find the boy and tracked him with an obsession that had grown from his own grief, as though he were searching for Teresita, as though she were still alive. He'd found the boy in Mérida, a mountain town outside of Caracas, where his governess had taken him.

His reputation as a tracker had begun then, burgeoning by word of mouth. He could no longer remember exactly when it had become something else, something darker. Perhaps he'd been born with the darkness already inside him, like a genetic flaw that lies dormant until something triggers it.

Whatever its source, it had manifested one winter in Manhattan, when he had killed for money, killed a man he didn't know who had double-crossed his client in a business deal. As he'd crumpled, he'd become the man responsible for the deaths of Tark's wife and daughter. A sense of power had filled him then that was both marvelous and terrifying, an intoxication of the soul, and he knew he had found his calling.

Now he stood here, where his life had ended and begun, eleven years older and tired, tired of it all.

Alfie suddenly appeared in the doorway at the other end of the room, a short, obese man, a Humpty-Dumpty with a grin as huge as Texas, moving as quickly as his considerable girth would allow. "Gabriel!" he boomed.

Emotion swelled in Tark's throat as Alfie hugged him fiercely. His head barely reached to Tark's chest, the crown as round and smooth as a bowling ball, with wisps of hair sticking out like whiskers just above his ears. Like the back of his shirt, the top of his head was damp with sweat just from the short walk. This and the faint stink of sickness that radiated from his skin told Tark all that he needed to know about the state of Alfie's health.

Alfie stepped back, his dark eyes damp, his plump, dimpled hands gripping Tark's forearms. "Two *years*, you son of a bitch," he snapped in flawless English, the seams of his jaw tightening with anger.

"And it's just like yesterday, Alfie."

His jaw went slack, then he guffawed, released Tark's forearms and dabbed at his face with a handkerchief. "Over here, let's sit over here. You want something to drink? Eat?"

"A beer. A beer would taste great."

He signaled the bartender, held up his index and middle fingers, then the pinky; it meant they were drinking Coronas and make it fast. They slid into a booth under the stained-glass windows, which Alfie had replaced a week after the explosion. He ran the handkerchief over his face once more, stuffed it into the pocket of his shirt, and raised his eyes toward the windows. "Does it bother you to sit here, Gabby?"

His dead wife's father was the one person in the world he had never lied to. "Yes."

"I sit here to tempt God."

"I doubt that God gives a shit, Alfie."

When Alfie laughed, it created dimples like craters at the corners of his mouth and deepened the cleft in his chin. "Probably not." The bartender brought their beers and Alfie lifted his. "A toast, Gabby. To our long friendship."

They clicked bottles and drank. Then Alfie got right to the point. "I heard you were in town."

Tark didn't bother asking who he'd heard it from. "I need to know who hired me, Alfie. And I need some particulars."

"I don't know who. Like I told you on the phone, the request was supposedly filtered down to me through several other people. The man who actually came to me was Ramón Lamadero. He runs a racket at Jai Alai, the dogs, at Calder. He's got contacts, some money, the luck of a saint. When I told him the fee, he said, No problem. I figured you might be able to use the cash, so I called." He turned his hands upward, palms toward the ceiling. "That's all I know, *amigo*."

"You know who Lawrence Crandall is?"

"The Miami Beach developer?"

"Right."

"What about him?"

"Is he running arms? Have you heard anything like that?"

"No way. There're two groups in Miami who run arms and he isn't a part of either of them."

As Tark explained what he'd been told about the missing file and the people involved, Alfie polished off his beer and ordered two more. Tark had barely touched the first, but to refuse the second would insult Alfie, who preferred company when he drank.

"So you were hired by some spook at the CIA?" Alfie asked when Tark had finished.

"I don't know if it's CIA, but yeah, it's definitely some spook organization. And I'd like to know why. It's one thing to find a missing file, Alfie. But if I'm going to eliminate some of the players, I need to know why I'm doing it."

"Since when?" Alfie's dark eyes scrutinized Tark with unapologetic directness. "Since when do you need to know anything other than the type of weapon you're going to use, Gabby?"

Fair question, but Tark didn't have an answer. He shrugged. "Things change, people change, Alfie. You heard anything about Crandall from the cops?"

Beads of sweat kept erupting on Alfie's forehead and he kept wiping them away. That faint odor of ill-health drifted toward Tark now and then. "Sure. They think he's up to his eyeballs in shit. But they can't prove it. They think drugs, the spooks want you to think it's arms, but I say the man is involved in something else altogether. He's been seen around town with an Iraqi whose total net worth could pay off half this country's debt and a German who has got some heavy-duty business interests in the Middle East.

"Nearly three years ago, Crandall sold the German a shitty old warehouse in west Dade. He turned it into a cherry-flavoring factory that Crandall oversees in his absence. Friend of mine wired the place for security. Got four hundred grand for the job. This guy's been putting in alarms for nearly twenty years, Gabby, and he's never gotten a request for the kind of hardware Crandall requested."

"Four hundred grand to wire a factory? Christ, I'm definitely in the wrong line of work."

"The security system wasn't to detect intruders, Gabby. It was designed to watch employees."

"Why?"

"*Quién sabe.* We sure as hell don't run in the same crowd, although you might say we have friends in common."

Political friends. The mayor. Congressmen. The governor. Alfie's business was people. "So what's the story on Lamadero?"

"Small-time. He's cagey, but I myself believe he can be persuaded to tell you what you want to know. Assuming, of course, that he knows anything."

"I don't want it to come back on you, Alfie."

"It cannot." He smiled sadly and supplicated the stained-glass windows with his eyes. "We have been sitting here for—what? Forty minutes? An hour? Nothing's happened, Gabby. God was perhaps tempted but He chose not to act today. That's a good sign." His eyes dropped to the bottle of beer, which he gripped with both hands. His thumbnail tore through the label. "One night some weeks ago, before I called you, Carmen visited me as I slept." He whispered the words, like a confession. "She told me you would come. She told me, Gabby."

And then he squeezed his eyes shut and the tears seeped through his lids and Tark touched his arm, just touched it and didn't speak. There was nothing to say. They were simply two men who had lost their daughters and their wives in an explosion one hot August night eleven years ago. And no matter what else happened, this loss would bind them, always.

■ ■ ■

"When the great white Buddha tells you to shop, Liz, that's what he means. So let's do it." Cindy Youngston swung the Lincoln into a small shopping center in downtown Marathon and pulled up in front of a store called Eve's Delights. "This is the best lingerie shop in the Keys," she announced as they got out.

Quin was more interested in the gourmet deli next door. But with an hour and a half to kill before they picked up Crandall from his meeting at a resort over on the beach, they had plenty of time to shop, eat, and take in the town. Not that there was much to see. Marathon, in the upper Keys, was mostly a concrete wasteland, an embarrassment of fast-food restaurants and tacky souvenir shops, the kind that sold conch shells and paintings of Elvis rendered on black velvet.

Eve's Delights was geared for the affluent female tourist who didn't mind blowing a hundred bucks on a sexy nightgown or twice that on a tennis outfit. Even the sales rack, where she and Cindy were looking, boasted a conspicuous absence of cheaper styles.

"Hey, how's this?" Cindy asked, holding up a thin black nightgown. Delicate lace swirled across the breasts, with translucent circles the color of pearls in the center. "Only a hundred and five."

Only. "For a hundred and five we could stuff ourselves next door for a week."

"Hmm." Food obviously wasn't high on Cindy's agenda at the moment. She stood in front of the full-length mirror now, holding the nightie up against her. "You think I look okay in black?"

"You'd look okay in puke green, Cindy."

She laughed. "Your Honor, I'd like to present this puke-green nightgown as evidence. They'd love you in court, Liz."

"I'm having enough trouble as Crandall's secretary."

"Hey, you're doing just fine."

The opportunity for information wasn't going to get much better than this. She started going through the clothes on the rack in earnest, hoping to prolong the conversation. "So what's the deal on this time-sharing resort where Larry is? You think he'll buy it?"

"I doubt it. He's still got his sights on the Sea Witch. I doubt if he's going to invest in anything until that whole thing's resolved."

"You think the sale will still go through?"

"I'm just the chauffeur." She shrugged and turned away from the mirror, the nightgown draped over her arm. "C'mon, let's find you something so I don't feel so guilty about this."

When they left the shop twenty minutes later, Quin had a snazzy beach outfit that only Liz Purcell would wear, Cindy had her nightgown and a silk robe, and Crandall was $222.58 poorer. They walked over to the gourmet deli and ordered lunch—gazpacho, conch fritters, cappuccinos—and sat at a table that overlooked a lagoon with a dilapidated dock.

They talked about men. The men in Cindy's law-school class, the men in Miami, the men you met when you were single, over thirty-five, and looking. Cindy did most of the talking initially, which suited Quin; she was busy concocting comparable tales for when it was her turn. And the lies came easily when Cindy said, "So what about you?"

Liz Purcell, she realized, was a *what if* creation. What if she and McCleary had gotten divorced at any one of those junctures back when, what if Ellie hadn't been born, what if. She said there had been a few men since her divorce, but no one special, that she was feeling somewhat disenchanted and wasn't really looking.

"All women are looking." Cindy lit a cigarette and blew the smoke off to one side. "Especially the ones who say they aren't. Take Betty."

Yeah, let's hear about Betty, who moans like a wounded cow, Quin thought.

"I practically had to drag her out to a bar one night, but once we got there, you should've seen her. She went home with someone and I didn't."

"Was that before she started screwing Crandall?"

"Betty?" she whispered, aghast. "Really?"

"I thought you probably knew."

"I figured Larry had something going on with someone, he usually does, but goddamn, Betty didn't even cross my mind. How do you know?"

Ah, yes, well. "I was working late the other night and went into his office to leave something on Betty's desk. I heard them in the conference room."

"She's the sixth or seventh in the three years I've worked for him. They usually leave when the affair falls apart. That's what happened to Betty's predecessor. He came on to me about a month after I started working for him and I told him flat-out no way."

"How'd he react?"

"He laughed. He said he thought I'd do just fine as his chauffeur. It was strange, but that's how he is."

"I don't see what the attraction is."

"Money."

"Oh, c'mon." There were some things that even money couldn't compensate for.

"And I hear he's great in the sack."

Quin laughed. "Please. Crandall looks about as sensuous as a mosquito coming off a hunger strike."

"Yeah." Cindy smiled and stabbed out her cigarette. "But Betty probably doesn't know the difference. What's strange is that Larry really values her opinion. She's sharp when it comes to business."

"So she's the business advisor and you're the company astrologer."

"Something like that. He's got this superstitious side to him. You've probably noticed."

Quin nodded.

"All his major business decisions are made on days with an eight in them. He was born on an eighth day. Eight is the number of money. The symbol for infinity."

And July 8, Quin thought, was starred in his appointment book.

"On planes, he always sits in the eighth row. If there's no seat available in the eighth row, he won't take that flight. Like that. Odd, huh."

"He must not have followed the eight rule when he bid on the Sea Witch."

"Hell, the county got cold feet when *Sixty Minutes* bit at the story. But now that the professor's dead and the county boys are fighting over the new budget and need money, they'll sell. They have to. And then Larry's resort will get built and SoBe will be paradise found again."

"And the beach won't ever look the same."

Cindy shrugged. "That's the cycle on Miami Beach. And the cycle here is that the secretary picks up the tab and gets reimbursed later by the boss." She smiled and pushed the bill toward Quin. "Time to retrieve the Buddha." She got up and walked outside, swinging the bag that contained her black nightie.

A receipt for lunch, but not for the clothes. Why not? Quin paid and went next door to Eve's Delights. The clerk who had waited on Cindy was an aging matron who wore a pound of costume jewelry and had the leathery skin of a woman who has spent her entire adult life baking in the island sun.

"Excuse me," Quin said. "I was in here a little while ago and my friend forgot to get our receipts."

"Those purchases were charged to Mr. Crandall's account. The receipts are sent directly to him."

"Oh. No one told me. I'm new."

"Yes, I thought so. It's none of my business, but if you want to keep the job you'd better be careful about what you charge. Last time that gal was in here, she walked out with five hundred dollars' worth of merchandise. Mr. Crandall called a couple of days later when he got the receipts and demanded to know who had charged it. I didn't have a name; we never do on accounts like this, so I described her."

"What'd he say?"

"He apologized. He said he'd been having problems with his ex. She'd been showing up at shops where he had accounts and charging them to the hilt. He told me what she looked like and asked me to give him a call if she showed up. The next day, he sent me roses."

"Well, I'm not the ex," Quin said.

The woman's face creased deeply when she smiled. "Oh, I know that. She's a short little thing, weighs maybe ninety pounds. Anyway, Mr. Crandall put a ceiling of two-fifty on that other gal's purchases."

Which explained how Cindy, law student, was able to afford such pretty clothes. "So you've met the ex?"

"Uh-huh. She pulled up front one morning in a maroon Volvo that looked about as bad as a car can get and still run. But let me tell you, she was dressed like nobody's business. She comes up to the counter with about eight hundred dollars' worth of clothes and toiletries, and in this very cultured voice says she wants to charge everything to Mr. Crandall's account.

"As soon as I told her the account was closed and called her by name, she started to cry. She stood there for fifteen minutes telling me what her life was like. She was getting by on what she made by selling these clothes and whatnot, showered every morning at the Grove Marina, and was living out of her car. Can you imagine? I felt for her, I really did, but I can't afford to lose customers like Mr. Crandall."

"What'd you do?"

"I gave her some of the clothes and told her if she didn't leave I'd have to call the police. I've never seen her again."

The Lincoln's horn blared. "I'd better get going, but thanks for the tip." And the information.

"Don't mention it."

"What's the holdup?" Cindy asked when Quin slipped into the car.

"I thought I'd lost my keys."

Cindy backed out of the parking spot without speaking.

Crandall was waiting outside the sales office of the time-share resort when Cindy drove up. His soft moon face was damp with perspiration and he didn't bother hiding his annoyance that they were late.

"I don't pay you to keep me waiting, Cynthia."

"Sorry." Those baby blues glared at Quin in the rearview mirror, but she didn't pass the buck. "Where to?"

"Just drive around." Crandall dabbed at his face with a handkerchief. "You ever been here before, Liz?" he asked once they were under way.

"I've gone through on my way to Key West, but that's about it."

"What's your impression?"

"In terms of what?"

He looked at her then. She didn't like his eyes; they were small, the color of India ink, the eyes of a man whose internal landscapes were perpetually in shadow. His mouth, smiling slightly, wasn't much better. It was arrogant without apology. "In terms of a resort."

"It'd have to have something really terrific going for it," Cindy opined.

"I don't think it'd make any difference one way or another," Quin remarked. "Marathon doesn't have a soul."

"A soul." Crandall seemed to find the phrase amusing.

"The only thing that could possibly work here would have to be something totally unique for Florida. An environmental prototype, for instance. Solar energy, a self-contained recycling system, a restoration of beaches, homes that are close enough to where people work so they don't have to drive. A community, not just another resort."

"Like Seaside."

"Yes." Seaside was a development in northern Florida that was being hailed as the prototypical community of the future. "But larger. More comprehensive."

Numbers scrolled through Crandall's eyes, columns of figures, the cost, the potential profits and losses. He grinned, his lips pulling away from his teeth as though he intended to bite her. "Rebuild Marathon, that's what you're saying."

"Yeah." Quin nodded. "I guess that's what it would take."

He slapped his hand against his thigh and laughed. "Hit it, Cynthia. Get us out of here."

"You got it." The Lincoln shot through the bright light, a sleek and silent creature that had just sprouted wings.

"Rebuild Marathon," he repeated with a chuckle and shook his head.

Quin sat back against the leather seats, unsure whether she had just passed the test or failed.

Groceries, dinner, bath, bed, Quin thought as she hurried into Woolley's Fine Foods. She hustled up and down aisles, selecting the usual staples, then loaded up on things from the deli. It was a mistake to shop when she was hungry, but if she didn't do it now she wouldn't have a chance until Sunday evening when she got back here. And she wouldn't feel like doing it then, not after the drive from West Palm, not with the week looming ahead of her and the brevity of her time with Michelle so close behind her. Sunday night she, like the old man in the nursery rhyme, would feel like pulling the covers over her head and not getting up till morning.

When she emerged from the store a while later, it was dusk. Tremendous thunderheads climbed the darkening sky to the east. Their gargoyle shapes were shot through with flashes of lightning that made them glow like lanterns. The air that closed around her was thick, humid, weighted with the smell of rain. The storm, she thought, would be a humdinger, an offspring of the tropical depression. She stopped her cart at the phone and called Boone's place.

She hadn't talked to McCleary since Wednesday evening, the night before last. But it seemed longer, like weeks, like months, like half a lifetime. He wasn't home, though, so she left a message for him to call her tonight regardless of what time he got in. In the event that they missed each other, she said she'd see him tomorrow night at home and could he pick up Michelle?

Her orphaned daughter.

It started to rain before she reached Fifteenth Street, plump, heavy drops that dotted the dust on the windshield like tears. A block later, the sky opened up and rain swept across the road, a pale, shimmering wall. She could barely make out the shape of the apartment building when she turned in to the lot. The umbrella that was supposed to be under the front seat wasn't there. She didn't have a raincoat with her. She removed her shoes and panty hose, pushed them down inside one of the grocery bags, and put her purse and the package from Eve's

Delights into the other. She pulled both bags across the front seat toward her, opened the door, and stepped down into a puddle of water.

What the hell. All or nothing. She picked up both bags, kicked the door shut with her foot, and darted toward the pale glow of the courtyard lights. The rain poured over her, the wind gasped at her legs, wet strands of hair slapped her cheeks. It occurred to her that somewhere between childhood and middle age she'd misplaced the simple joy that comes from standing in a warm rain, your arms thrown out, your mouth wide open to catch the drops.

Midway across the courtyard she slipped and went down with all the gracelessness of a newborn colt. Food was strewn around her, a clump of broccoli, a soggy loaf of bread, yolks like jaundiced eyes that quivered in the wind, apples and grapefruit and containers of yogurt. Her shoes—her new shoes, her fifty-dollar Liz Purcell shoes—lay upside down near a bottle of cranberry juice that had shattered. Her purse, also new, had landed on a bed of leaves and flower petals that had clogged the courtyard's drain.

A fine end to an imperfect day. She got up, her wet clothes clinging to her, weighting her, and began scooping up the fallen food, piling everything into her arms.

"I have days like this all the time."

The man who'd spoken materialized like an apparition in the rain. He was barefoot, wore a yellow raincoat with a hood, and handed her an umbrella. "Thanks," she said. "Thanks very much."

He opened a green garbage bag that flapped like a flag in the wind. "We can put the stuff in here. I'm John Tark in five." As if "five" were part of his name.

"Liz Purcell. I'm in six."

They crouched and started picking up the fallen food. "The bread's shot," he said. "And most of the eggs are broken, but some of it will be salvaged."

"Optimist."

He swung the garbage bag over his shoulder, Santa with a load of toys. En route, Quin rescued her shoes, her purse, her soggy panty hose, while Tark explained that he'd just moved in yesterday, J. Link hovering around him like an overprotective mother. Quin laughed and said she knew exactly what he meant.

They dripped their way through her apartment, Quin turning on lights as they went, and stopped in the kitchen. It was then that she got a good look at him and realized he seemed vaguely familiar. It wasn't his face; she would have remembered the thin scar that burrowed into his left eyebrow like a bone-white worm. And she would have remembered these hazel eyes, the color a perfect swirl of pale blues and greens that were oddly fluid, as though they were changing even as they stood there. No, not his face. Not even his black, curly hair. Something else, but what?

Well, it would come to her.

As they unloaded the garbage bag, she found the package from Eve's Delights, wet and ripped. She tossed it on the microwave. They lined the other things up on the counter and speculated about what the "J." in J. Link stood for. "Probably 'Jailbird,' " he said.

"Or joke."

"Jerk."

"Jabber."

"Jekyll."

"Jive."

"Jinx."

"Joust."

He started to laugh then, his eyes bright with amusement, beads of rainwater rolling down the bridge of his nose. "Jesus."

"That counts. It's a J word. Jonah."

"Jubilee."

"June."

"July."

She drew a blank, then snapped her fingers. "Jerboa."

"Doesn't count. It has to be a real word."

"You calling me on it?"

"What happens if I do?"

Making up rules, she said, "If it's an actual word, you lose."

"Jerboa, jerboa." He repeated the word several times to himself as he removed soggy slices of bread from the loaf and lined them up on the counter to dry. Tark, the good Samaritan next door. "I say it's not a word."

Quin whooped. "I win. A jerboa is a nocturnal rodent with long hind legs and a long tail."

"Never heard of it."

"Trust me. It's a word. I used it in Scrabble once."

"All right, all right." He grinned. "But I challenge you to a rematch."

"Fair enough."

The air between them was different after that, awkward, a little self-conscious, mixed up with the chemistry of mutual attraction. No wonder he'd seemed familiar to her. In life before marriage, Tark was exactly the kind of man she'd been attracted to, the character from a Ray Bradbury story who blew into town with bad weather, turned lives upside down, then skipped out, untouched by the chaos he'd created.

"I think the bread will make it if you toast it," he said finally, stepping back from the counter. "You have a broom?"

"A broom?"

"To sweep up the broken glass outside."

She'd forgotten all about the mess outside and realized she didn't have a broom. "I forgot to buy one when I moved in."

"Well, never mind. I've got one. I'll sweep it up."

"Let Jerboa do it."

He laughed and she walked him to the door, thanking him again. He paused on the porch, slipped the hood over his head. "Rematch within forty-eight hours. Those are the rules. And in the meantime, I'm going to check my dictionary for 'jerboa.'" Then he turned and sprinted off into the rain, a dark figure as tall and lanky as a scarecrow.

. . .

Tark dreamed that night, as he did most nights, about the stained glass. How one moment it was flat, solid, beautiful, and how the next it was shattering, the splinters raining down in utter silence, as though his world had been vacuumed clean of sound. He woke before he heard the shriek of his wife's voice, before he saw his daughter bleeding on the floor, before any of that. He woke sweating, shaking, his heart thudding, tears burning the backs of his eyes.

He stumbled into the bathroom, jerked on the faucet, held a wash cloth under the rush of cold water, and pressed it to his face. He sensed, then, a kind of shifting inside himself, as though the tectonic plates of his life had just slid apart and slammed back together in some new way. And he saw—that was the only word for it, saw—himself and Liz Purcell standing at a window, his hand on her arm. Then suddenly they were hurled back and fell through the window. He could feel it, the sensation of falling, the sour taste of his own fear, and he knew Alfie was dead.

Tark dropped the wash cloth, turned off the water, stood there staring at himself in the mirror. Bloodshot eyes. The ugly scar. He pressed the heels of his hands against his eyes. Vision? Premonition? Or just fallout from the dream? He went into the bedroom and heard, for the first time, the rain. He sat down, reached for the phone, pulled his hand back, then reached again and punched out Alfie's number. He rubbed his aching temple as the phone rang and rang and rang.

Please, he thought. Please answer. Please.

Then, finally, the old man's voice, hoarse with sleep, slurred from booze, said: *"Sí, sí, estoy aquí."*

Tark was unable to speak, to breathe.

"Alo? Alo?"

"Alfie. Sorry to wake you."

"Gabby? What the hell . . ." Rustling sounds. "What time is it?"

"Late. I dreamed . . ." *That you were dead.* "Alfie, the first time you met me, when Carmen brought me to the house, what did you think of me?"

"Jesus, Gabby. Let's talk about it in the morning, okay?"

"I need to know."

He made a soft, pained noise. "I knew she would never find a better man."

"And now? If she brought me home now and you knew what you know about me? What would you say now, Alfie?"

"The same."

"The truth, Alfie."

"I just told you the truth, my friend."

"But—"

"Listen to me, Gabby. When I drink, when I'm slopping drunk, what do you think?"

"It's not the same thing."

"Oh, but it is. It is. Eleven years ago, we should have died, you and me, and we didn't. And since then, we've been living with our chosen poisons. I with mine, you with yours. But we're still like father and son. That hasn't ever changed. We talk tomorrow, eh? I need to sleep."

He hung up without another word and Tark replaced the receiver. He sat in the dark for a long while, listening to the rain, and watching the movie in his head, the stained-glass window shattering, then himself and Liz Purcell falling back, back through an ordinary window at some undetermined point in time.

9

Quin came to suddenly, her heart slamming against her ribs, her nightmare as bright as a full moon. The inbreds. She'd been dreaming of the inbreds who had taken her captive during a camping trip in the Everglades more than two years ago. Weston and Opal and their slobbering brood and the crazy old man who had ruled them.

The stink of that shack where they'd kept her had spilled out of the nightmare. The excessive lushness of swamp and water, the decay of rotting wood, the odor of unwashed bodies: it tightened around her, filled her nostrils, threatened to smother her. She tore the sheet away from her body and made her way into the kitchen. She opened the fridge, spun the cap on the container of orange juice, gulped at it.

The stink receded and the vividness of the nightmare faded. She heard the storm now, the thunder, the wind whistling through the crack of a window somewhere that wasn't shut all the way. It had stormed that weekend in the Glades, too, a three-day deluge that had ended a long drought.

She and McCleary had been separated at the time. She'd consented to the trip because a married couple they'd known for years was in town and wanted to go camping and because a part of her had hoped that it would resolve things one way or another. It had, but not quite the way she'd expected. Ellie was conceived on that trip, on a spit of beach during a storm.

Quin went into the living room to shut the window. On her way back to the bedroom, she turned the AC lower. To sixty-five. If she were at home, McCleary would be grumbling about it. He might wake up enough to cite the amount of the last electric bill and they might even argue about it, one of those dead-of-night arguments that would end badly. It was always the petty things that triggered arguments that quickly escalated to encompass everything that had ever gone wrong in the marriage.

As she got back into bed, she heard something. A sharp click. The door, she thought, the click of the door as it closed. And now wet shoes squeaked against the floor. She leaped up, trying to remember where she had put her purse. Her gun was in it.

Think, think, c'mon.

Nightstand. Yes, okay. Easy now, easy. The drawer creaked when she opened it. She groped inside for her Browning, grabbed it, slipped into the closet. She left the door cracked enough so she could see, flicked off the safety, and waited.

Enough light from the courtyard seeped through the Levalors for her to make out the dark figure of the man who entered the room less than a minute later. He stopped at the foot of the bed, his back to her. She nudged the door open with her toes. "Hands up, fucker, or I blow you away and ask questions later."

His hands locked on top of his head and Quin stepped out, hit the wall switch. The lamp on the nightstand cast dim, buttery circles of light; all she could see was his wet poncho and dark hair.

"Turn around real slowly."

He turned, grinning, then touched a finger to his mouth. "You called?" McCleary whispered.

"Christ." She lowered the gun, incensed. "You could have said something."

He walked over to the radio, turned it on, tuned in a rock station.

It wasn't loud enough to wake her neighbors, but it would drown out their voices in the event that the apartment was bugged. McCleary stepped into the bathroom, motioned her in, shut the door, turned on the shower to mask their voices.

"I thought you were asleep," he said, still speaking softly, pulling the dripping poncho over his head. "I was going to crawl in with you." He held up the spare key she'd given him over the weekend. "At least we know this sucker works."

She snatched the poncho away from him and tossed it over the shower rod. "You're getting water all over the floor."

McCleary took a towel from the rack and rubbed his hair with it. "From now on, I wouldn't call an intruder 'fucker' if I were you. It might give him the wrong idea, assuming he didn't have the idea to begin with."

"Uh-huh. You have any other tidbits of cop wisdom to impart?"

"Nope, that's it."

"Well, thank whoever for small favors."

He rocked back on his heels, holding the wadded towel like a football, and they started to laugh.

■ ■ ■

They sat at the round table on the tiny screened porch off the kitchen, doing what they had always done best together, McCleary thought, figuring the angles.

He suspected the porch was the safest spot in the entire apartment. Even if there were bugs out here, they wouldn't pick up very much, not with the noise of the rain and the wind strumming the screen. But they still whispered as they exchanged information.

Quin had fixed mugs of steaming herbal tea and a platter of rabbit food, carrots and celery and slices of apple. Now and then she went inside for something else and his eyes followed her, limning those long legs that her nightshirt didn't begin to cover, the calves tight and hard from running; the curve of her slender hips.

He didn't like the idea of another man in her kitchen, this guy Tark the friendly neighbor moving around in here, laying out the soggy slices of bread, the two of them making small talk. He didn't like it at all. The obvious dangers seemed to have escaped her entirely. This was Miami, after all, the city where the affable meter reader might be a freak looking for kicks. You didn't let strangers into your house regardless of how nice they seemed to be.

But more than that, it disturbed him on a personal level. It was easy to imagine Tark coming on to her, and Quin had probably flirted back, playing her part exactly the way it should be played, the recently divorced woman starting over again in Miami.

And maybe a day or two from now they would run into each other again and—what? She would sleep with him? Doubtful. Women didn't come any more monogamous than Quin. And yet. As he watched her refilling the platter with food, watched the way she moved, she seemed different to him somehow, changed in some essential way by the role she'd slipped into. The cadence of her speech, the types of clothes she had bought last weekend at home, belonged to the woman she had created, to Liz Purcell, not to Quin, his wife.

He came up behind her as she stood at the pass-through window, a new plate of munchies in her hands, and slipped his arms around her waist. He nuzzled her neck, inhaling the fragrance of soap that lingered on her skin, pears or papaya, something that smelled good enough to taste. "I've missed you," he said.

She laughed softly and pulled her head to the side. "Your beard tickles, Mac." Then: "You're not supposed to come here. What if Cindy or Crandall or someone from the office dropped by?"

"At three in the morning?" He nibbled at her ear. His hands slipped under the nightshirt at the back. The skin was cooler and softer than he remembered, as though it had been months since he'd touched her. "Then they deserve to stand out in the rain."

"You know what I mean." She had set the plate down but hadn't turned around, and talked as though he weren't behind her, his fingers tracing the steps of her spine. "I just don't think it's worth the risk."

Risk. It always came back to risk of one kind or another. The risk, for instance, that someone—Tark?—was watching them right now, watching their silhouettes against the screen, watching as McCleary lifted her hair and kissed the skin at the back of her neck, as his hands found her breasts, her tummy, watching as she turned in his arms.

McCleary reached through the pass-through window and flicked the switch on the wall in the kitchen. No lights now.

The utter darkness brought the noise of the rain closer, as though it were on the porch with them, and in some inexplicable way this changed everything for him. The texture of her hair as he drew his fingers through it, the taste of her mouth when she kissed him, the slow burn of her tongue as it traveled across his lower lip, teasing. She fumbled with the zipper on his jeans, he rolled her panties down over her hips, stroked her, eased his fingers inside of her. She breathed into him, filling his lungs, his senses, with a scent that was not hers, and touched him with hands that were urgent, quick, hands not like those he remembered.

They stumbled, laughing, over to the couch on the far side of the porch, and fell onto the damp cushions, into the spray of the rain, into the noise of the distant thunder. There she whispered things that excited him in a voice that was low, husky, not like Quin's at all. The geography of bones and skin that should have been as familiar to him as the streets of Miami had suddenly become another country. Her breasts seemed fuller and softer than he remembered, her arms were longer, her hips less sharp.

When her hands pressed down on his shoulders, they were hard, insistent, eager, urging him lower, and then tightened against the sides of his head like a vise. Her taste was so exquisite, so different from what he remembered, it dizzied him. The sounds that rolled out of her were foreign to him, unlike any sound that Quin had ever made, and her lips moved in a way hers never had, moved so that his mouth was forced to roam.

A twilight filled his head. He felt the muscles in her thighs tightening, felt her hips lifting slightly, shifting the balance again so that his tongue slipped into her, out again. For seconds, it seemed he was suspended in a space between breaths, between punctuation marks on a page, that he was some other man, a man who had met this woman only tonight, through a mutual friend, perhaps, or in a bar or on the highway when her car had broken down and he'd stopped to help her.

Neither of them spoke as they rolled, as she straddled him, lowered herself slowly against him. She leaned forward, her hair falling at the sides of his head as her mouth fastened over his. She guided his hands to her breasts, her hips, and between them. Then everything happened very fast, movements that matched the rhythm of the storm, soft explosions of air, shudders that seemed to alter the very molecules of the air, then stillness.

She moved first, rolling away from him. McCleary raised up. Quin but not Quin, he thought.

He swung his legs over the side of the couch. He needed to stand, to move around, to do something. "I'd better put that food in the kitchen away."

"Mmmm." She groped for her nightshirt, covered herself with it, seemed oblivious of the rain.

In the kitchen, he turned on the light, went into the living room. He parted the blinds with his hand, but the only thing he saw was rain. He let the blinds fall back into place, returned to the kitchen and puttered around, putting the food away, rinsing the dishes, wiping down the counter. He was disturbed by something he was unable to name until he found the package that had gotten shoved between the microwave and the wall.

Inside was a black silk nightgown. The pale circles of silk at either breast were the size of fifty-cent pieces and, thanks to Velcro, peeled open. Peek-a-boo windows. Not exactly Frederick's of Hollywood, but it might as well have been. Quin had never owned a black nightgown in her life; her sleepwear was strictly T-shirts. But apparently Liz Purcell had a fondness for nightgowns.

He slung it over his shoulder, jerked open the sliding glass door, stepped out, shut the door again. "The Velcro's a nice touch," he said, still speaking softly.

"What?" Quin lifted up on her elbows, blinking against the spill of light from the kitchen.

"The Velcro." He stuck his fingers through one of the circles.

Quin didn't chuckle or laugh; she *giggled*. A Liz affectation. "Jesus, a hundred bucks for Velcro. I was wondering what happened to that package."

He balked. "You spent that on a *nightgown*?"

"Me?" She looked at him like he'd lost his mind, swung her legs over the side of the couch. "Cindy and I got our packages switched yesterday. I bought shorts and a shirt."

"It sort of reminds me of Liz Purcell." He tossed it on the couch and turned to go back into the kitchen.

"Meaning what?"

He ignored the edge in her voice. "Liz Purcell, single woman, inviting John Tark, friendly neighbor, in out of the rain."

"I didn't invite him in. He was helping me with the groceries and—" She stopped. "My God, I can't believe it. You're jealous."

"Jealous? Of what?"

"Of Tark."

"Don't be ridiculous. I just think you might be carrying this Purcell stuff a little far."

She burst out laughing. "It's not my nightgown, I told you. Crandall sent us off shopping during his meeting at the time-share place. The clerk in the store is the one who told me about the ex-Mrs. Crandall living in her Volvo."

"Look, I'm just saying—"

She interrupted him, her voice darker now. "I know what you're saying. But infidelity is your thing, not mine."

Of course. He should have known it would end with this veiled reference to his affair with Sylvia Callahan. Never mind that it had happened five years ago or that Callahan had been killed during the investigation that had brought her back into McCleary's life. Never mind any of that. In Quin's mind, their affair continued. Hell, in her mind, the affair had probably burgeoned into marriage; he was a bigamist with a double life.

McCleary started to say something in his own defense, but decided against it. "Maybe it'd be better if I left."

"Yeah." Her voice cold. "Maybe it would."

Fuck it. He grabbed his clothes off the floor and dressed in the kitchen. He walked back to her bathroom, retrieved his poncho, and headed for the front door.

The water in the courtyard was now ankle deep, the rubber trees and dracenas bent in the wind, the rain drummed the hood of his poncho. A light burned in Apartment 5, Tark's apartment, as he hurried by.

■ ■ ■

Mercury retrograde meant communication failures: okay, she believed, she'd been converted. Sort of.

Quin had almost gone after him. But that would be as good as an apology and why should *she* apologize for something *he* had imagined? So she crawled into bed and listened to the rain, and in her head she tracked McCleary across the courtyard and out into the parking lot, where he got into his Miata and drove off.

Nearly two years ago during emergency surgery for a gunshot wound, McCleary had died for twelve seconds. There had been no dark tunnel for him, no blinding white light, none of that. Instead, he had found himself on an emerald-green hill, where he and Sylvia Callahan had talked, where she had explained his choices. Sylvia, tour guide of the afterlife.

The truth, though, was that Sylvia probably haunted her more than she did McCleary. Quin had actually liked the woman. In some maddening and inexplicable way, she had even understood McCleary's need to complete what had begun between him and Sylvia long before she had entered the picture. But just the same, her tolerance, her faculty for being able to see both sides, disgusted her. It came back to that breaking point Charlie had mentioned, the bull's rush she had never reached.

The marriage sometimes seemed to possess a life, a consciousness all its own, and it exhausted her to dwell on it, the twists, the sudden angles, the intimacies and distances, the folds and multiple layers. It was easier to think about Charlie courting a *santera*, about the enigma of Larry Crandall, about the things she was sure Cindy Youngston knew but wasn't telling. She thought about all of it and moved the pieces around in her head as she lay there. But she couldn't keep track of the details.

Quin turned on the lamp and pulled a notebook out of the bottom drawer in the nightstand. She tore out four pages and taped them together, creating a single sheet large enough to scrawl on. Then she began to plot it out, Crandall here, Cindy there, Charlie over here, and so on.

At home, she and McCleary used the blackboard in his den for this. In Gainesville, while investigating his sister's murder, they had improvised, building their visual cues around the crime-scene photos. Although Benson had shown her the photos from Charlie's apartment, she didn't have them now. She suspected they wouldn't be much help, anyway. The answers to his murder weren't going to be found in how he had died, but in how he had lived.

By the time light oozed into the bedroom, she had covered four huge sheets with notes. A housecleaning, she thought, a kind of left-brain purging with right-brain connections. One of the first leads she listed was something the clerk at Eve's Delights had said, which had slipped her mind. How every morning the ex-Mrs. Crandall showered at the Coconut Grove Marina.

It didn't mean she still showered there, and for all Quin knew, morning to the ex-Mrs. C. might be the middle of the afternoon. But it was worth a try. She wasn't due in to work until ten, which gave her plenty of time.

On her way out, she called her sister's from the pay phone in the courtyard. Michelle was fine, naturally, still sound asleep, sleeping straight through the night (as she never did at home), and had Quin had a chance to talk to Mac about Disney World?

"It's fine with him. I think his exact words were that you and Hank are courageous for daring it with three kids."

Ellen laughed. "Courageous or crazy. I'm not sure of the dates yet. Hank has to check the vacation schedules at work and request the time."

Bosses, Quin thought. They had bosses to contend with. But they didn't have to work nights and weekends to make ends meet. If they called in sick, they got paid. If they took vacations, they still drew salaries. They didn't pay for their health insurance or life insurance and put out a pittance for Rebecca's day care because Hank's company had on-site child care. But despite the benefits and advantages, Quin had no desire to work for anyone else. It was just that right now, right this second, she felt cheated by the choices she had made. She felt incompetent as a mother.

She told Ellen she'd see her that evening. As she hurried toward the parking lot, she thought of Michelle on the Dumbo ride at Disney World, of some rusted screw or bolt giving way, of Dumbo flying off into the blue skies over Orlando with her baby still inside.

■ ■ ■

He was no longer handcuffed to the bed, he now had a television in his room with fifty-two stations, and no one entered without knocking first. Small strides, Heckler thought as he stretched out on the bed. But the message was clear: good behavior is rewarded.

The TV was on, tuned to the weather channel, the volume too low to be heard anywhere else in the house. Heckler wasn't particularly interested in the weather, but Kilner was. Kilner, in fact, seemed almost paranoid about the depression's upgrade to a tropical storm, and that alone made it worthy of study. Anything that might influence Kilner's decisions was important. He'd even given Heckler a hurricane-tracking chart yesterday afternoon, *presented* it to him like a gift for a job well done. Then he'd talked at great length about the 1926 hurricane that had devastated Miami, killed more than four hundred people, and turned Belle Glade into a farming community.

Three miles of dike along Lake Okeechobee collapsed under twelve-foot floodwaters, dumping mud and silt for miles, and you know what grows there today, Steve? Sugar cane. Forty-two thousand fucking acres of sugar cane.

He had sat here listening to Kilner's discourse and thinking, So what? If they were going to pretend they were friends, why not speculate about who killed Charlie? Or, at the very least, talk about Crandall and what had thrown them all together to begin with.

Odd how you could know a man as long as he'd known Kilner and yet not know him at all. Heckler still wasn't sure what had prompted Kilner to treat him like a member of the compound's little family. But he was grateful for the insight into Kilner's phobias and now included it in his notes.

The entries were scrawled in a chubby notebook that he'd found in a hole in the mattress, squirreled away with a few other items that had probably belonged to a former patient. It had become his most vital link to himself and to the events that had resulted in his imprisonment here. In it, he was recording everything he knew or suspected, and thanks to Pisco's gradually loosening tongue, he now knew a great deal more.

Pisco, recruited when he was on parole for armed robbery, had a few gripes of his own and no one but Heckler to talk to.

He wrote until he heard footsteps downstairs, then quickly hid the notebook and waited for whoever it was to come up here. But the footsteps receded. Frowning, he went over to the window, parted the curtains, peered outside.

A light drizzle was still falling. Pale light seeped through the wet palms and nibbled at the long shadows beneath them. Two figures in hooded ponchos emerged from the space under the house and walked toward the cars parked near the fence.

Heckler recognized Kilner from the way he moved, that arrogant strut, the quickness of his gait. He couldn't tell who the other person was. They stopped at a car, Kilner opened the door, then the second figure turned. A woman. Her hood had slipped off her head and Kilner was touching her hair, kissing her, embracing her. Kilner, who didn't look like he had a passionate bone in his entire fucking body, was pressed up against the woman as if he hoped to melt into her, to zip himself into her very bones.

It didn't last long, a few seconds at the most. They broke apart quickly and Kilner glanced around nervously, uneasily, like a man who was cheating on his wife and was afraid he might be seen by a family friend. Heckler stepped back from the window and let the curtain fall into place.

Kilner and a woman. But not just any woman. Heckler knew (courtesy of Pisco) that the visitors' log at the guardhouse was reviewed every week by Elliot LeFrank. So this woman had to be someone whose name wouldn't prompt LeFrank to question it. Someone on the inside who was working elsewhere. Working undercover? Working, perhaps, in Crandall's organization?

Now *that*, he thought, was a mighty interesting possibility.

10

A string of brass bells tinkled as McCleary opened the door to the *botánica* and stepped inside. The room was longer than it was wide, with three narrow aisles crowded with religious statues similar to the ones he'd seen in the aluminum shack yesterday.

The shelves were jammed with merchandise that ranged from the mundane to the exotic, herbs to snake oil. One shelf contained nothing but cigars, Florida water, and candles in every conceivable color, size, and shape. On another was a display of beaded necklaces in a variety of colors and combinations of colors, one for every major *orisha*. Bolts of bright, colorful fabric stood upright against a wall like giant packs of chewing gum. The air was sweet, redolent of flowers, incense, strangeness. Latin music pumped from a radio.

He didn't see her until he was nearly at the back of the store. She was seated on a stool behind the glass display case, a newspaper open in front of her, her white hair pulled back in a ponytail. She was already watching him.

"*Buenos días, señora,*" he said.

She gave a small nod and replied in English, making it clear that they weren't equals. "Thank you for your help the other day."

"I'm glad to see you're feeling better. I realized I left without paying you. How much do I owe you for the reading?"

"Ten dollars."

He slipped a ten from his wallet and set it down. "Did your granddaughter tell you I wanted to talk to you about Charles Potemkin?"

"Yes." She folded the newspaper, laced her fingers together on top of it. Her eyes, huge and liquid and dark, revealed nothing. "We were friends."

"When did you see him last?"

She switched to Spanish. "A few days before he was killed. We met for coffee at Wolfie's."

"Did he seem preoccupied? Worried about anything?"

"Don Carlos was always preoccupied with something." She fingered the red beads at her throat. "But he seemed no different than usual."

"What day was that, do you remember?"

"On the Thursday or Friday before he was killed."

"Did you receive any mail from him after his death?"

"No, nothing."

McCleary reached into the back pocket of his jeans and brought out a copy of the letter he and Boone had found among Charlie's things. He unfolded it and began to read: "*My dearest. You have just left and my rooms seem impoverished by your absence . . .*"

The music on the radio had ended and the announcer was talking. McCleary's voice seemed abnormally loud, an intrusion, a violation. He looked up once as he was reading, but her face was a blank wall onto which he could project anything he wanted. "Do you know anything about who this woman might be, Mrs. Villa?"

"No, *señor.* Don Carlos and I were friends who had coffee from time to time. We talked about ideas. If there was a woman in his life, he did not tell me about her."

McCleary creased the letter and dropped it on the counter. "I don't believe you. And unless this letter was also a lie, there was more between you and Charlie than coffee at Wolfie's. I'll hold on to the original. I think the police might be interested in taking a look at it. Have a fine day, Mrs. Villa. If you change your mind about things, you know where to contact me."

He felt the burn of her eyes all the way to the door.

■ ■ ■

No groves remained in Coconut Grove. The tall, graceful palms that rose above neighborhoods and lined Bayshore Drive had probably been hauled in full grown. That was the South Florida way, Quin mused, bulldoze everything, then replant and landscape. But just the same, the Grove was romantic in a sense that the rest of Miami wasn't. Shops, art galleries, outdoor cafés, bike paths, parks, a marina. The scale was human.

Several months after she and McCleary had met, they'd driven over here with their bicycles one Saturday morning and had seen the Grove the way it was supposed to be seen. They'd ended up at the spot he considered the most bizarre example of Miami's numerous idiosyncrasies. It was right next to the front steps of the Coconut Grove Library, marked by a wrought-iron fence. Inside of it was the oldest marked grave in Dade County, where a woman named Eva Amelia was buried. She had died of tuberculosis in 1882 at the age of twenty-six. Her only contribution to Miami history was her grave or, more specifically, the story of how it had ended up next to the steps of the library.

The story, at least the way McCleary had told it, was straight out of a Gothic novel. Eva Amelia's husband was Commodore Ralph Munroe, a transplant from Staten Island who founded the Biscayne Bay Yacht Club and was its first commodore. He'd brought his wife south because of her tuberculosis, traveling by steamship and then sailboat through the Florida Keys and into Biscayne Bay and the Miami River. In 1882, they pitched their tents on a spit of land where the entrance to the Dupont Plaza Hotel was now located.

Eva died while they were there and was buried near the campsite, probably close to where one of the hotel parking lots was now located.

Thirteen years later, after Munroe had remarried and bought land in the Grove, he learned that Henry Flagler planned to build a resort on or near the place where Eva was buried. He decided to move her remains. But there was no cemetery in the Grove then, so he remedied the situation by giving land on McFarlane Road for a church and a cemetery. Her remains were removed, a community grew up around the church, but no other burials were ever made. And there it had stood ever since, the grave that one historian had called "the loneliest in Miami."

It seemed fitting that she would think of it on this particular morning, when it was all too easy to imagine herself living out the rest of her life in the solitude that had followed Eva Amelia into eternity. Easy and depressing.

She turned off McFarlane onto South Bayshore Drive and half a block later pulled into the marina's parking lot. The breeze off the bay swelled with the scent of salt and fish and the easy life Jimmy Buffett sang about. Sloops and ketches and catamarans, yachts and dive boats and fishing vessels. A city of masts rose against the curve of sweet blue sky.

Along the south pier, where Quin headed, were the chartering outfits, dive shops, a market, public phones, and the restrooms and showers. Some of the boats were lived on and a fair number of these people were out and about, working on deck, having breakfast, walking dogs, conducting whatever business you conduct when you live aboard. Quin liked the way they looked, tan and sinewy, with the gleam of exotic places in their eyes.

She walked into the ladies' room and glanced at the women who stood at the sinks. None of them fit the description the clerk at Eve's Delights had given her of the ex-Mrs. Crandall. Of course not. Too easy. The universe enjoyed making her work for a living.

Three of the five showers were occupied, though, so she hung around at a vacant sink to see who would come out. She washed her face and fussed with lipstick and a comb, lingering until she drew attention from several other women. No telling what they thought she might be, a mugger, a thief, a perv in drag. She quickly finished up and walked back outside and sat on one of the benches. She pulled an apple and a book on Deco architecture from her purse. The book was actually a history of Deco on Miami Beach, complete with photographs of a hundred of the most prominent buildings, barely a quarter of the total number in the Deco district.

The Sea Witch was included in the tome and cited primarily because it was the only senior citizens' housing left on Ocean Drive. Constructed in 1940 by Henry Hohauser, it was originally a privately owned hotel. But it failed to compete with the larger hotels on Collins, and by the early fifties the owner was facing bankruptcy. He hanged himself in one of the second-story rooms. The county impounded the building for back taxes and then did nothing with it until 1964, when it was refurbished, divided into small apartments, and rented to the elderly at greatly reduced rates.

The Tuttle Inn, up the street from the Sea Witch, a place Crandall already owned, had also been constructed by Hohauser, and named after the woman who was considered the mother of Miami. The inn's best years were the three seasons that *Miami Vice* was on the air. All the hotels on Ocean Drive had flourished during that period, but the inn was particularly fortunate because it was included in at least a dozen episodes, which made it recognizable to tourists. In 1988, it was gutted by a fire of unknown cause. There were the usual rumors about arson because the owner was in dire financial trouble, but the insurance investigation uncovered no such evidence. The owner was paid off, the building was condemned, and a year later, Larry Crandall had bought it.

That was around the same time Crandall had bought and sold the warehouse to his German buddy, Quin thought. She knew there was a connection, but didn't know what it was. Not yet.

She glanced up as several women emerged from the restroom carrying towels and toiletries, and walked off toward the slips. The shops were open now and the dock bustled with business. She went into the market, bought a cup of coffee, then returned to the bench.

And that was when Quin saw her, a short woman coming toward her from the parking lot. She moved quickly, purposefully, her eyes fixed on the ground, everything about her shouting, *Don't bother me, I'm in a hurry, I have every right to be here.* She carried a gym bag slung over her shoulder and dressed the way the other women from the boats did, in shorts, a T-shirt, thongs. She was tanned, too, the way most of them were, and her hair was pulled back into a careless ponytail.

"Excuse me," Quin said, walking over to her, blocking her way so she had to stop. She raised her eyes; Quin could just barely make them out behind her sunglasses. "I need to speak to you, Mrs. Crandall."

Her smile was brief and cold. "I'm afraid you're mistaken." With that, she stepped around Quin and started toward the restroom. Quin went after her, caught her by the arm. The woman stammered, "Just what do you think—"

"The sign says the showers are for boat customers only. Either you talk to me or I talk to the business office about your unauthorized use of the facilities."

Although she made a point of shaking off Quin's hand, some of the fire had gone out of her. "It's not *Mrs.* anything. And I don't talk to the press for free."

"I'm not the press."

She tilted her sunglasses back onto the top of her head. Her large eyes were a faded denim blue and creased deeply at the corners, as though she'd spent much of her life squinting into the sun. Now that Quin saw her eyes, she realized the ex-Mrs. C. was older than she'd first thought, probably closer in age to Crandall, late forties.

"Then who the hell are you?"

Good question. Was she Liz Purcell or Quin? "I'm a private investigator and I'd like to ask you a few questions about your ex-husband's activities."

"Well, I don't know squat about his activities."

"Fine, just let me ask you some questions. I'll buy you breakfast."

"You have ID?"

Quin fished her PI license from her wallet and the ex-Mrs. C. glanced at her, at her photo, then handed it back. "Quin? That's your name?"

She sort of laughed as she said it and Quin, wired from too little sleep, felt like slugging her. "Right. You want that breakfast or not?"

"Breakfast. Oh, what the hell. Great, let's go have breakfast. And please don't call me Mrs. Crandall. The name's Tiffany."

How fitting.

But as it turned out, she lacked the dazzle and flash that her name implied. At the sidewalk café where they settled, she ordered enough food for four people, then proceeded to consume the entire basket of warm biscuits the waitress had brought to the table. She ate quickly yet delicately, dabbing at her mouth, flicking at the crumbs that fell to the table, her impeccable manners telling as much about her past as her hunger told about her present circumstances.

When the waitress refilled the basket, Tiffany helped herself to several more biscuits, wrapped them carefully in a napkin, and slipped them into her gym bag. Other items followed: containers of jam, packets of sugar and salt, wads of napkins from the dispensers. She was a squirrel preparing for bleaker times ahead. And when she was finished, she sat back, brought out a crumpled pack of generic cigarettes, lit one. "So. What do you want to know about Larry?"

"He may be involved somehow in the murder of a friend of mine and I need some answers."

"If the friend you're referring to is Charlie Potemkin, then you're really off base."

"Why's that?"

"Because the deal's been Larry's since the beginning. The county came to him, not the other way around. They've wanted to unload that place for years; every month it puts them deeper into the hole. All the rest is just a formality." She crushed her cigarette in the ashtray. "You watch. By fall, they'll start construction on the resort and no one will even remember Potemkin."

"I will."

"Memory's a bitch. Don't I know it."

"How's the German fit?"

"Who?"

"Ebo Rau."

"Oh. Ebo." She blew a cloud of smoke into the air above Quin's head. "He doesn't fit."

The waitress brought their breakfasts and Tiffany lit into hers, her appetite apparently unblunted by the biscuits she'd put away. "What's your husband's connection with him?"

"Ex-husband," she murmured around a mouthful of food.

"Whatever."

"Whatever?" She laughed. "Listen, I was forty-one years old and divorced when I married Larry. I was desperate enough to sign a prenuptial agreement that entitled me to seventy-five grand, my car, and my personal belongings if we got divorced. That was it. But I figured there wasn't going to be any divorce. And by the time it happened, I'd gotten used to living a certain way. So I took my money and lived the way I'd been living and it was gone in a year."

"Who filed?"

"I did."

"Why?"

The question made her uneasy. She shifted around in her chair, her gaze dropped to her plate, she pushed food around with her fork, then set the fork down. "He beat me up once too often."

Quin tried to imagine this, the short little Buddha beating up on her, using his fists. That part fit okay, but nothing else did. "Did you report it?"

"No."

"Why not?"

"There just didn't seem to be any point in it."

"Did it come out in the divorce?"

"No way."

"So now you get even with him by charging clothes to his accounts."

She smiled. "I'm the thorn in his side. I like that. I like knowing how much it bugs him every time I do it."

"If he presses charges, you'll end up in jail."

"They'd have to find me first."

"That shouldn't be too hard. I found you."

"You got lucky."

She finished her breakfast, pushed the plate away, lit another cigarette. "Look, the divorce was pretty straightforward. There was a prenuptial agreement and he didn't contest it when I filed. I just wanted out. I never even told my attorney about the abuse. We filed under the great catchall of irreconcilable differences and that was the end of it."

Sure. And that was why she racked up credit charges on Crandall's accounts. That was why she got a kick out of being a thorn in his side. But before Quin could tell her that none of that fit the pattern of abused women, at least no pattern that she knew of, Tiffany went on. She leaned forward, her voice soft, confidential, smoke from the cigarette curling into the air between them.

"Look, what I just said, about your being off base, that's not exactly true. It's possible that Larry was involved somehow with Charlie Potemkin's murder. The publicity scared the county and they backed off. Or at least made a show of backing off. Maybe Larry felt the project was threatened. I don't know. But if that's how it was, then he would have the professor killed and not think twice about it. And it's not the money. That resort has been a dream of his since he was . . . I don't know, fifteen or sixteen, and now that Larry's so close to it, nothing's going to get in the way. Nothing. He'd do anything to see it built, sell everything he owns."

"There're hundreds of resorts in Florida. What's so important about this one?"

"Like I said, a kid's dream. Larry's gift is that he sees potential where other people see nothing but a pain in the ass."

"Is the German bankrolling this project?"

"I don't know."

"What's Crandall's association with him?"

"They do business from time to time."

"What kind of business?"

"I don't know."

"What about this warehouse he sold to Invest, Inc. You know anything about that? Or about the company? Isn't it Rau's company?"

"I don't know."

"You're a lousy liar, Tiffany." Quin scribbled her number and address on a napkin and dropped it in front of her as she got up. "And you're wasting my time. I don't believe Larry ever beat you up, although he's probably capable of it. I think you divorced him because he was screwing someone else, probably several someones. Betty O'Toole, for instance. So when you're ready to get even with him in a way that'll make a difference, give me a call."

She was on the sidewalk when Tiffany came up behind her. "You're in over your head and you don't have the sense to know it."

Quin laughed. "You're absolutely right." She kept walking; Tiffany fell into step beside her.

"And for the record, it wasn't just Betty. There were Cindy and Isabel and Maria, to name a few. He acts like AIDS doesn't exist."

"Cindy Youngston?"

"Yeah. Some were one-nighters, others were longer." She shrugged. "But none of that broke the marriage."

"Then what did?"

"Look, I'm going to give you two bits of information and that's it, so listen real closely. That factory produces cherry flavoring. Check it out. A woman named Helga might talk to you, if she hasn't been sent home. And that's my contribution to the fall of the Crandall empire."

With that, she turned and hastened off in the opposite direction.

11

McCleary heard it before he saw it, the battered blue pickup coughing and sputtering its way up Washington Avenue, smoke spewing from its tailpipe. It coasted to a stop at the curb in front of Boone's building and died with a pathetic shudder.

R.D., the kid from the Sea Witch, climbed out, dressed in his valet threads—black trousers, a white shirt, and black shoes that looked like they were killing his feet. He had a brown manila envelope tucked under his arm and limped over to where McCleary was loading the Miata for the drive home. "Hi, R.D., what's going on?"

"Mr. McCleary." He wagged the envelope. "Got something for you and the General. He around?"

"Yeah, he's upstairs fixing lunch. What is it?"

"Something from the professor. My sister Concha's really bad about the mail. She gets it outta the box every day and if it's not addressed to her, it gets tossed on the kitchen table. And the pile grows, huh? It like grows and mutates there on the table until I get around to sorting through it. This was at the bottom of the pile. It's postmarked the day after the professor was killed."

Impulses, McCleary thought. They were like the dancing ball in the old singalongs, bright orbs of light directing you to do this, to ask that. He had asked the *santera's* granddaughter if she'd received anything in the mail from Charlie, but it was R.D. he should have asked. R.D., himself and Quin, and who else? Were there others?

He whistled for Flats and they went upstairs. Boone was in the kitchen preparing lunch and set an extra place on the terrace table for R.D., then the three of them sat down, surrounded by the raccoon, the cat, and the dog. With a certain degree of fanfare, R.D. opened the envelope and spread the contents in the center of the table.

There were two five-by-seven photographs. The first was of Crandall and another man, dark-haired, swarthy, coming out of the Neon Flamingo at night, taken from some distance away. The second was also a night shot and depicted a dilapidated building. The note Charlie had included was identical in content to the one McCleary and Quin had received.

"So what's this mean, General?" R.D. asked.

"I don't know, kid." Boone angled one of the photos to the light. "There's a magnifying glass in the kitchen, drawer next to the fridge. Would you get it?"

"Yeah, sure." His dark eyes lingered on Boone; he obviously suspected he was going to be excluded from something important. "Don't cut me outta this, Mr. B. I got a right to know."

Boone regarded him with obvious affection. "I never doubted it, kid. You have my word on that."

"C'mon, Elvis," R.D. said, draping the raccoon around his neck like a shawl. "Let's go find you some real coon food, huh?"

When they'd left, Boone's eyes came alive with some of the old fire. "This building, Mike." He tapped the photograph. "Can you make out what that street sign says?"

McCleary studied it. "Southwest something. The first number's definitely a one. I can't make out the other two."

"One and a three, that's what I see."

"The three could be a five," R.D. said as he returned. He dropped the magnifying glass on the table.

"Or a seven." Boone ran his palm over his head. "Christ, it could be a nine, what the hell do I know? Where'd Charlie get this shit?"

"My guess is that it had something to do with the call he was expecting the day he was killed."

"I don't get it." Boone flexed his fingers around his mug. "He sends something to you and Quin. He sends something to R.D. Why didn't he just send the whole goddamn package to me?" He raised his soft, gray eyes, and in them McCleary recognized all of the questions he'd wanted to ask his sister. Questions the dead couldn't answer.

"Because you were the most visible person in his life, Will. He wasn't going to put you at risk."

"I agree," R.D. said, nodding.

"Shit, he shoulda known better."

Yeah, McCleary thought, and his sister should have known better than to make some of the decisions that had led to her murder. Maybe she had. Maybe Charlie had. But some actions you took in spite of yourself, took because your very nature impelled you in a particular direction. Like with Charlie.

"R.D. pegged it the other night, Will, when he was talking about how Charlie played chess." McCleary pushed his juice glass to the center of the table. "This move here." He slid his coffee mug to his left. "That move there. Like they aren't connected. Then bang. 'It comes together.' Isn't that how you put it, R.D.? It comes together and you realize Charlie knew all along what he was doing."

"R.D., you and Quin, and who else? There had to be someone else, Mike. The things we've gotten so far are just parts of a whole."

"Maybe the *santera*. Who else was important in Charlie's life but not very visible?"

He was leaning forward now, elbows on his knees as he tapped his cap against his palm. "Christ, I don't know." He tossed the cap on top of the photos. "Someone at the Sea Witch, someone at Wolfie's." He shook his head. "It could've been anyone, Mac. Charlie knew a lot of people."

But he hadn't known all of them well. "How about his son?"

"I doubt it."

"When's he due back in town?"

"He got back yesterday to close up Charlie's apartment. I talked to him about having a memorial service for Charlie, and you know what the asshole tells me? That the service is going to be in Philly. Charlie didn't know anyone in Philly. His friends were *here*, Mac. But asshole doesn't want to hear it."

"Give him a call and let's see what he knows."

"I can't stand talking to him."

"Give me the number. I'll talk to him."

Boone waved this suggestion away. "I'll do it."

"Now?"

"Yeah, yeah," he muttered. "Now."

The phone rang and R.D. went inside to answer it. Moments later, he poked his head out the door, the magnifying glass held to one eye. "Mr. M., phone for you. Some lady named Liz."

Liz, not Quin. McCleary took the call in the kitchen. "What's up?"

"Who answered the phone?"

"R.D. The kid from the Sea Witch I told you about. Where are you?"

"En route. Listen, Mac, I tracked down Tiffany Crandall. You know that warehouse he sold to Invest, Inc.? Well, according to Tiffany, it's a cherry-flavoring factory. I think you should check it out. I got the address from the real-estate records. One eight seven seven Southwest Thirteenth Street."

The spavined building in the photograph, he thought. If memory served him correctly, the address put the warehouse west of the Florida International University campus in an industrial area.

"The other lead is someone named Helga who works there. Tiffany seemed to think she might be willing to talk. I'll handle that one on Monday. Anything on your end?"

"Some serendipity." He told her about the envelope R.D. had brought over. "I'll drop it by Benson's on my way back to West Palm."

"See you around seven. You'll have to pick up Ellie. They're going to Disney World sometime next week."

"She'll love it."

"Yeah."

But he heard the things she didn't say, felt the tension of her peculiar conflict. "We'll have plenty of chances to take Ellie to Disney World." He believed it, but she didn't.

"When she's eighteen, Mac, she isn't going to be interested in going to Disney World with us."

"Then quit the case."

"No." Flat, unequivocal.

Silence. Neither of them hung up. Now it was last night that loomed between them, a gulf, a sea, a distance that begged to be bridged by an apology. She was waiting for him to speak first, but he didn't know what to say. That he was sorry he'd left? Sorry he'd gone over there? Sorry he'd thought of her and Tark together?

And if she, on the other hand, apologized for her crack about infidelity, he would feel obligated to make some reference to Sylvia Callahan and what was the point? He couldn't rectify the affair, couldn't change it, couldn't pretend it had never happened. And he damn sure wasn't going to spend the next twenty years apologizing to Quin and feeling guilty about it.

"I've got to get off the phone," he said. "Will needs to make a call."

"Okay, see you tonight." And just like that, she disconnected.

Women, he thought, and replaced the receiver.

■ ■ ■

Tark supposed the Miami Amtrak station was as busy as it could be in a state where the preferred mode of transportation was the car. There were maybe two dozen people in all, waiting on benches, in the coffee shop, milling around the newsstand. Two cops patrolled the station, one young, restless, and obviously bored, the other pushing sixty and pleased to be here.

The walls were covered with posters from the Chamber of Commerce. These touted Miami as a mecca with everything except mountains. Sun, beaches, boats, Deco and art, the state's largest book fair, a zoo that rivaled San Diego's, the annual Calle Ocho street festival, even a $2 million transit system, MetroRail.

The lockers where he was supposed to leave a message concerning the final exchange were at the back of the station, against the wall. Number 14 was at the end of the second row. The door was wide open and there was no key in the lock. How was he supposed to leave anything inside if he couldn't lock the damn thing?

Tark went up to the window. A middle-aged guy as skinny as a stick of bamboo was perched on a stool at the counter, paging through a skin magazine. He wore glasses with black frames and thick lenses that magnified his eyes.

"Excuse me. I'd like to put something in Locker fourteen, but there isn't a key."

Those huge eyes blinked; he flicked the magazine shut, with a finger marking the page. "There's plenty of other lockers. Use one of them."

"It's got to be fourteen."

"Look, if the key's not in it, that means it's reserved."

"Yeah, for me."

"Christ," he muttered, reaching for a clipboard. "I dunno why they gotta make things so difficult. I mean, if the lockers are losing money at five bucks a day, then jack up the price, right? Wouldn't that make sense? But, oh no, my supervisor says they can't raise the price. People got these superstitions about numbers, though, and I figure we should double the cost if someone wants his own number. But he doesn't see it that way."

Especially when the extra cash probably went into the supervisor's pocket, Tark thought.

"What's your name?"

"Gabriel."

"Gabriel, Gabriel." His thin index finger slipped out of the magazine and traveled down the list. "We got two reserve systems, see. One by name, one with stars and phone numbers. If it's starred, that means I rent to the first person who requests a certain locker and then I call the number and tell whoever answers that the locker's been rented." The tip of his tongue moved slowly across his lower lip, a gleaming pink bud. "I mean, man, for all I know, it's some drug scam going on."

Tark laughed. "My ex-wife doesn't want me to know where she lives. So this is how I pay our alimony. You know how women are."

"Ain't it the truth," agreed Bamboo, an expert on women. "No Gabriel here. Lemme check the other list." Papers rustled, then: "Okay. Fourteen is starred." He reached above his head and slapped a key on the counter. "Fourteen's all yours, sir."

"May I see the phone number?"

"Oh, I'm not allowed to—" He stopped, eyeing the pair of fifties

Tark set on the counter. "Well, I guess it'd be okay." He slipped the fifties inside the magazine and turned the clipboard so Tark could see it.

A local number. "Thanks, thanks very much. How's she supposed to open the locker if I've got the key?"

"My supervisor's got spares to the reserves."

How convenient. "Do me a favor, would you? Don't call that number for a week or so." He dropped another pair of fifties in front of the guy. "I want her to sweat it out a little. You know how it is."

He grinned, flashing a mouth full of silver fillings. "No problem." The fifties vanished.

"Thanks again."

Tark returned to the locker, pretended to put something inside it in case Bamboo was watching, then locked it. From a phone near the front door, he dialed the number, and the moment it started to ring, so did a phone nearby. Tark turned around to locate it and saw a frail black man in the newsstand shuffle over to a phone. When he picked up, the ringing on Tark's end stopped.

He disconnected and walked over. The man had turned away from the phone and was lighting a cigarette. He coughed, puffed, coughed again. Tark picked up a copy of the Miami *Herald* and dropped a buck on the counter. The old guy counted out Tark's change, his cigarette still sticking from a corner of his mouth.

"Name's Franco," Tark said. "Detective Franco, Metro-Dade."

The man's bloodshot eyes darted to Tark's face. He drew from the cigarette, removed it from his mouth; smoke drifted from his nostrils. "Whoever you're looking for probably took a bus."

Tark smiled. "Business that bad, huh?"

"Ain't been good for a long spell."

"What's your name?"

"Lukas."

"Well, Lukas, it's like this. Locker fourteen. A guy comes up, asks for the key to Locker fourteen, then the skinny guy at the locker counter calls a number on his clipboard and that number rings here in your newsstand to let you know the locker's been rented. What I'd like to know, my friend, is who you call."

He stared at Tark for a moment, then stepped back from the

counter, dropped his cigarette butt to the floor, stepped on it. "Don't know nothin bout no numbers."

"It'd be a real waste of time, both yours and mine, Lukas, if I have to run you in for questioning."

The old man's bloodshot eyes regarded Tark with the disdain that you saw in the eyes of all oppressed people. Without a word, he opened a drawer, rummaged around in it and produced a piece of paper with several years' worth of coffee stains and cigarette burns on it. He ran his finger down the row of names and numbers, copied a number on the inside of a matchbook cover, slid it across the counter. "Don't like him nohow. Name's Ramón Lamadero."

So. It came back to Lamadero, the man with some answers.

■ ■ ■

There were some people, McCleary thought, whose faces revealed so little about them it was as if life had barely touched them. But there were others whose faces told you more than you wanted or needed to know. Allen Potemkin, Charlie's son, was one of those.

He was a burly fellow in his early fifties who looked as if he'd been on the fast track of two-martini lunches and fried foods since the day he was born. He was dressed like the criminal attorney he was, in an expensive suit minus the tie, and shoes that had probably cost nearly as much. His short hair was chocolate brown, tinted, McCleary guessed, and professionally styled. The thin, graying mustache that he sported was a postscript to his tired face.

"I told him right from the start that it was foolish to get involved in this whole business," Potemkin said, referring to the Sea Witch. He paced back and forth across the nearly empty living room of his father's apartment, wearing a track in the rug. "But my old man was a stubborn idealist, Mr. McCleary. Once he'd made up his mind about something, that was it. So look what happened." He stopped in the middle of the room, arms open, as if to embrace the void in the room. "Jesus, just look." His dark eyes misted, then his arms dropped to his sides. He seemed lost, a kid who has gotten separated from a parent in the Christmas rush in a department store.

"Did Charlie ever mention people he was close to here on the beach?"

"Not really. He didn't talk much about his life here. I knew about Will, of course, I'd see him whenever I was visiting Dad, but other than that he was pretty circumspect."

Potemkin walked over to a window and peered out, as if he expected his father to arrive home any second now. Then he turned and leaned back against the sill. "Dad and I differed on a lot of things, Mr. McCleary. I'd been trying to convince him for years to live with my wife and me in Philly; he refused. It became a real sore spot between us. Now it seems so . . . so petty."

The sore spot, as Potemkin put it, was probably the reason Boone disliked Charlie's son. It was easy to imagine this man arguing with Charlie about where he should live, bludgeoning him with his opinions, and doing it because he believed he knew what was best for his father. It was equally easy to visualize Charlie telling his son to pound sand.

"He seemed to be doing okay for himself here," McCleary remarked.

"Sure, he was doing okay. He'd do okay just about anywhere. But let's face it, Mr. McCleary. The beach is a pretty depressing place to live these days if you're elderly. And on top of it, Dad's closest friend is an ex-mental patient and conspiracy nut. Now don't get me wrong. I like Will just fine and I'm glad he and Dad were so tight, but that doesn't change what he is."

"You're confusing what he is with events that have happened to him."

"I'm not confusing anything. I'm giving you my opinion. My dad's fondness for the man didn't diminish his contempt for some of his theories. And if I'm not mistaken, it was a bone of contention between them on more than one occasion."

He was sounding more and more like a defense attorney. McCleary dropped the subject and told Potemkin about the envelopes Charlie had mailed to himself and Quin and to R.D. He'd come here in the hope that Potemkin had received one as well or, at the very least, that he knew something about them. But the bewilderment in his face was utterly sincere.

"And they concern the Sea Witch?" Potemkin asked.

"They're connected to Larry Crandall somehow."

"You think this information is why Dad was killed?"

"Could be. Both envelopes were postmarked the day after his

murder. If he dropped them in a box on Sunday, the day he was killed, they wouldn't have been picked up until the next morning. But what we have so far doesn't give us the whole picture. I think Charlie may have mailed similar envelopes of information to other people, and I think he intended to use the information as leverage to convince Crandall to drop his bid."

"Blackmail?"

"I'm sure that isn't how Charlie saw it, but yes, I guess that's what we're talking about."

"Dad wouldn't have had access to damning information like that."

"He might through his association with the CIA."

A light winked on in Potemkin's eyes. "It wasn't the CIA." He paused. "Dad didn't tell you about that, did he?"

"No. We found some correspondence in one of those boxes you gave Will. He didn't know about it, either."

"Of course not. Will's the last person he would ever discuss it with. He never talked about it much even with Mom. She used to joke that they'd made him sign a vow of secrecy or something." He jammed his hands into his pockets and resumed his relentless pacing, back and forth, back and forth, a tiger in a cage. "It started back in 1960, when one of Dad's books on the criminal mentality became a textbook at Langley. They invited him to teach the course and he went back every summer for four to six weeks. He kept it up after his retirement from Princeton, after my mom died, after he moved down here. He loved it. It kept him current. And the pay was great. It wasn't just CIA people, either, and I think that was one of the things he really enjoyed about it."

And it kept him relatively independent, McCleary thought. "I thought Langley was strictly CIA."

"It's their training facility, but he was lecturing to people from the NSA, FBI, military intelligence, Department of Defense, Air Force Intelligence, career diplomats, agencies I've never heard of. Dad used to say that half the government came to Langley for refresher courses. Or at least that's how it was for a lot of years. I don't know what it's like now."

"Did he keep in touch with any of those people? Maybe someone he was close to but who wasn't visible in his life?"

Potemkin stopped at a stack of cardboard boxes against the wall that held the last of Charlie's belongings. He picked up the phone that rested on top, set it on the floor, and sat down. "There were a lot of people in Dad's life, Mr. McCleary. Students, faculty, reporters, editors he'd worked with on his books, cops he'd advised on cases, other criminologists. I had a hard time keeping track of who was who."

"It might've been someone he'd mentioned recently."

He rubbed his palms over his thighs, thinking. "A month or so ago, I got a call from Dad real late one night. I was half asleep when I talked to him, but I remember him saying that a fellow who'd been in one of his classes at Langley years ago was in town or was going to be in town. He sounded excited about it and it irritated me that he could get so worked up over that and barely show any emotion at all whenever my wife or I visited."

"Did he tell you the man's name?"

"Haskle, Heller, something like that. Dad insisted I'd met the man when he'd stayed at our house one weekend, but I couldn't remember him. There were always people at the house when I was growing up."

"You remember his first name?"

Frowning, his hands still moving over his thighs, the sound of sandpaper against fabric. "Steve, that was it. Steve Heckler."

"Did he say anything else about him?"

"No, not really. It was just part of a conversation and, like I said, it was late and I wasn't paying that much attention."

"Was Heckler CIA?"

He frowned and rubbed his jaw. "He may have been at one time, but I got the impression from Dad that he'd been around for a long time, in and out of different agencies, in and out of the diplomatic corps, like that. I remember Dad mentioning something called the Hereafter, but I don't know what that was. Maybe a joke." He shrugged. "Like I said, I was half asleep."

"Have you run across an address book?"

"Dad never kept one. He prided himself on that. On his memory. He had an incredible memory for minutia."

So much for trying to track down Heckler on his own. He would run the name by Benson.

"What else did you find in those boxes?" Allen Potemkin asked.

"We're still sorting through it, but one of the things was a love letter."

He brightened. "From my mother? To her?"

"Uh, no. We think it's from whoever Charlie was seeing."

"Seeing?" He cocked his head to one side and mouthed the word silently to himself, like someone learning the language. "Dad was *seeing* someone?" His tight, fussy mouth gave way to a sudden burst of laughter. "Don't be ludicrous, Mr. McCleary. He was eighty-five years old, for Christ's sakes."

"Since when is there an age limit on love?"

"Love?" He nearly choked on the word. Color rushed into his cheeks, his fingers curled into tight fists against his thighs, he shook his head vehemently. He looked to be on the verge of apoplexy. "You're wrong. I'm sorry, but you're wrong, dead wrong, Mr. McCleary. Dad was devastated when my mother died eleven years ago. Devastated. He never would have . . . have . . ."

His voice broke, his face crumpled like used wrapping paper, and his gaze dropped quickly to his fists. McCleary looked away, out the window, embarrassed for this man he barely knew. He wanted to offer something comforting, but knew it would sound like a platitude. Besides, what was there to say? Eleven years was a long time to live without companionship, without love, and if Charlie had found a little of both with the *santera,* then McCleary was happy for him.

"I'd better get going," McCleary said. "I apologize for any distress I've caused you, Mr. Potemkin."

The other man nodded, wiped surreptitiously at his eyes, but didn't look up, didn't stand. So McCleary left with nearly as many questions as he'd had when he arrived and drove north with his dog to pick up his daughter and the threads of his own life.

12

Heckler picked his way through the hot sand outside the compound on Long Key. He stepped around the dead Portuguese men-of-war that littered the beach. From a distance, they looked like deflated blue balloons, their tentacles tangled around pieces of driftwood, shells, clumps of seaweed. But close up, they struck him as throwbacks to some earlier, simpler time.

Like me. And that was the bottom line, wasn't it? That he was a throwback to the days before the Berlin Wall had fallen, before the Soviet Union had dissolved, when the enemy was *them*. Now the enemy resided in the Mideast, and Americans like Crandall—and Kilner, he thought, don't forget that asshole—were contributing to the mayhem.

"One of the other guys is going to be with you for the next day or two," Pisco said, impaling a dead man-of-war on the end of a stick and hurling it toward the water. It was the first thing he'd uttered since they'd hit the beach twenty minutes ago. "Kilner's got a bug up his ass, so I've got to head to Miami."

"You sound real happy about it."

"Yeah." Pisco kicked at the sand like a kid contemplating a temper tantrum, tossed the stick aside, and jammed his hands into the pockets of his shorts. They walked another three hundred feet before he spoke again. "That guy we hired, Gabriel, is nosing around, asking questions."

The tracker. Gabriel was the tracker. "Oh." Heckler didn't press for more information, didn't ask questions. He'd discovered that Pisco talked most freely when he acted like he didn't give a shit.

"Kilner's pissed."

"Yeah, he gets like that," Heckler agreed.

"He's taking chances."

"Uh-huh."

"He's ordered the Miami team to bug Purcell's phone," said Pisco.

"I thought it was already bugged."

"Her apartment is. But the Miami team picked up something at her place last night that's made Kilner real nervous. She's apparently got a guy and Kilner wants more information."

Purcell was one of the bloated question marks in Kilner's equation. "Sounds like Jerry's nervous about everything."

"Yeah. And when he gets nervous, he takes risks and makes bad decisions. Then I get stuck cleaning up after him."

"That's the way he's always operated."

"You were in Colombia together, right?" Pisco asked.

"Years ago. Working with the DEA on a job."

"How'd you meet Professor Potemkin?"

"Same way Kilner did. Charlie was one of the visiting lecturers in our training class. He and Kilner never saw eye to eye on anything, but I didn't think Kilner disliked him enough to have him killed."

Pisco glanced at him, his blue eye soft, almost liquid, the brown eye hard and angry. "Christ, we didn't have anything to do with that. If we'd killed him, we'd have the file you gave him, man. His murder's caused us so many problems it'll be a miracle if we ever get anything solid on Crandall and his buddies."

It was suddenly clear to him that Pisco didn't know the full story. Heckler was tempted to lay it all out, to dump the cards he held, to give him the notebook, and hope Pisco was bright enough to keep it to himself. But it occurred to him that perhaps he didn't have the complete picture, either. The woman he'd seen with Kilner, whoever she was, hinted at a private agenda that even LeFrank didn't know about.

"If you people didn't kill Charlie, then who did?"

Pisco shrugged. "I don't know. For a while, Kilner thought it was someone in Crandall's outfit. But if that's true, then Crandall would know about the file, the feds would have him under investigation, and he would have backed off on this deal with the Iraqi."

The Iraqi. Another bloated question mark. Even Crandall was a yawning chasm of unknowns. There was no second-guessing a man like that. Or, for that matter, a man like Kilner.

"Kilner's getting fed up with you, Steve."

Heckler found it difficult to swallow. "It isn't the first time."

"Really fed up." Pisco stopped. Heckler stopped. The blue of the sky seemed to fill the space between them like some thick, viscous liquid. "The kind of fed up he gets when he starts making decisions without talking to LeFrank first."

He wanted to ask what sort of decision, but the words scratched against the back of his throat and the only thing he could do was stare at Pisco. His head throbbed from the heat, the exertion of walking, his need to hear Pisco say what he already suspected about the truth of Kilner's private little world here on Long Key. "What kind of decisions are you talking about?"

He hated the way his voice quivered and hoped Pisco didn't hear it.

"You know." Pisco shrugged and started walking again.

Heckler hurried after him, caught up to him, grabbed his arm. "No, I don't know."

"Bullshit, man, you've been in the game long enough to know what this place is about." Pisco shook away Heckler's hand and began walking again, faster now, his strides long and purposeful, as though he hoped to lose Heckler in the dust.

Heckler struggled to keep up, his lungs constricting, his heart hammering. "Spell it out, Dan."

"Fuck it." Pisco shook his head; his arms swung at his sides like an ape's. "You know what happens to security risks, Steve? They disappear. Two or three a year, vanished. Gone. *Adiós*. That's part of my job. Take care of the security risks. Then Heckler and LeFrank make it look right on paper. So-and-so bit the dust when the old ticker gave up. So-and-so did himself in. You get it now?"

Heckler's throat had closed up; the most he managed was a nod.

"Some higher-up comes to LeFrank. They have a conversation about a guy who's a risk. It's never spelled out that the guy is marked, but when the higher-up leaves LeFrank's office, they both know how the guy's going to end up. LeFrank passes the word on to Kilner, then he tells me. A few days or weeks later, the guy shows up here for rehab and he never leaves." Pisco shrugged and jammed his hands in his pockets. "That's how it is, okay? I mean, c'mon, you've been in this business long enough to have heard about the Hereafter, right?"

Yes, Heckler had heard. The Hereafter was grapevine fodder, a rumor, a kind of myth that had circulated for years within intelligence circles. It was the black hole into which over-the-hill operatives sometimes vanished, a Bermuda triangle. And here he was.

"That's how LeFrank gets just about everything he wants, okay? You get it now?" Pisco went on. "All the big guys owe him. But now LeFrank tells Kilner that the big guys want to close this place down, right? I don't believe it. I think LeFrank's trying to pull something, I don't know what it is, but I'm sick of all of it.

"I do my job, okay? I take orders, I don't ask questions. Kilner tells me to be your buddy, to win your trust, to get you to talk, fine, no problem. But it didn't turn out that way. *I'm* the one who's been doing all the talking. But that's not going to count for shit if the order comes down."

The sun burned a path to the backs of Heckler's eyes. When he spoke, his voice sounded soft. And scared. Yes, that most of all. *Scared.* "The order," he repeated quietly.

Pisco had already moved away, hurrying down the beach toward the gate in the fence. For the briefest of moments, Heckler considered making a break for it, hitting the water at a full run and swimming until they caught him or he drowned. But that would make it too easy for Kilner, too convenient. Heckler could hear him telling LeFrank they'd had no choice, that he'd been shot during an escape attempt. And LeFrank would probably just shake his head and say something about the tragedy of Heckler's life—the daughter who committed suicide, the wife who left him, the drugs. Yeah, he knew how it would be.

But the truth of it, the goddamn truth of it, was that he wasn't ready to die. And so he kept walking toward Pisco, who was at the gate now, waiting for him, watching him as though he'd guessed what had been going through Heckler's mind.

■ ■ ■

Five hours, Quin thought, glancing at the pink-and-blue clock on the wall of Crandall's office. The surroundings were pleasant enough—the Deco touches, the sweeping view of the beach, the numerous photographs of luminaries whom Crandall knew: TV celebrities, politicians, writers, artists, movie stars.

But please. For five long and excruciating hours she'd been sitting here listening to the many versions of a speech the Buddha was supposed to deliver at a Chamber of Commerce breakfast next week. As each paragraph was revised again and again, he read it aloud to Betty and Quin, who made suggestions on content and delivery. It was boring, tedious, and she resented Crandall for requesting that she surrender a Saturday for this.

Betty's disposition wasn't much better, but Quin suspected it didn't have anything to do with working on a Saturday. It was Quin's presence that she didn't like, that she hadn't expected. It was obvious from the way she was dressed that she'd thought it would just be her and Crandall, thick as thieves here in the office, with the couch in the conference room as the prize at the end of the day. Her shorts were very short, setting off her tan and slender legs, and she was braless beneath her sleeveless tank top. Every time she leaned forward, so the strap of her tank top strained, Quin could see the butterfly tattoo on the back of her shoulder.

Now Betty pouted, sinking into long, dark silences that Crandall tried to ignore. She occasionally sniffled and sneezed, par for the course, but it was anyone's guess what triggered it: Quin's presence, Crandall's indifference, Betty's own anger. No telling. When her brooding became impossible to ignore, when her hostility radiated so thickly it was like a fourth presence, Crandall finally asked her to run down the street for coffee.

"I don't want any coffee," she snapped, glaring at him.

"Well, I do." He patted his paunch as if to emphasize the point, and pulled out a five. "And Liz does. Try Salgado's Market. They've got the best. You can get a couple of empanadas, too."

"Liz can go. She speaks Spanish."

"Not very well," Quin said with a laugh.

"Go on, Betty. Be a good girl."

Betty, humiliated and close to tears, grabbed the five and slammed the door as she left.

"Christ," Crandall muttered, running his palm over his shiny bald head. "She's getting to be more trouble than she's worth."

Although Quin didn't particularly like Betty, she felt sorry for her, and Crandall's callous remark irritated her. She spoke without thinking. "Only because you're screwing her."

He looked at her, astonishment widening his eyes, playing havoc with his odd mouth, then he exploded with laughter. "Beautiful. I like that directness, Liz, I like it very much. Cynthia's the same way. It's what I look for in people. Unfortunately, Betty is . . ."

"Young," Quin said.

"Twenty-eight. It's not *that* young."

You wish. "Ask her where she was when Kennedy was assassinated."

His blank expression indicated that he either wasn't the whiz with numbers that she'd believed or that he'd never thought about Betty's age in a historical perspective. "She wasn't born, Larry."

He smiled then, a quick, almost sheepish smile. "Okay, okay, you made your point."

Good, may I leave now? She started to say it, that she needed to knock off early, but suddenly he pushed away from his desk. "C'mere, Liz, I'd like to show you something."

He walked over to a closet, opened the door, and pulled out a long, low table on wheels. On it was a miniature exhibit of Crandall's future resort, rendered in exquisite detail: pastel buildings, trees, shrubbery, lawns, lakes, horse trails, bike paths, restaurants, shops, even playgrounds equipped with tiny jungle gyms, slides, and swings.

When he hit a switch on the side, windows glowed, the trails and paths were lit up, and street lamps burned along a single street that was a perfect replica of Miami Beach during the late thirties and early forties.

It was utterly magnificent, visionary, the kind of project that would transform the face of the beach forever. This was life after *Vice*, the miracle that would usher in the next boom, perhaps a permanent boom. It was also the very thing that would end everything on Miami Beach that was traditional, historical, old. It literally left her speechless.

"I like to think of it as the community on the eleven-hundred block. The buildings will rise along Ocean Drive and Collins, Eleventh Street and Twelfth, with the lake and parks and whatnot in the center. There'll be hotel rooms, cottages, restaurants, cafés, swimming pools, horses, child care, shops. Everything will be Deco. The same lines, colors, friezes, windows, floors.

"It'll create a minimum of two thousand new jobs, permanent jobs, and that doesn't include the spillovers into the local economy. Interior designers to decorate, suppliers for food and beverages, cleaning services, musicians, public-relations people, and so on. Solar power will provide hot water and heat the pools. Showers and toilets will be regulated so water isn't wasted. Everything will be recycled and only recycled items will be used—the stationery in the rooms, toilet paper, paper towels."

"And it's going to cost an unimaginable fortune," she blurted.

His expression darkened briefly; it was like watching a cloud pass over the face of the sun. "Yes."

Give me a figure, Larry.

But he didn't. He just stood there staring at his future, a Lilliputian village.

"Will banks supply that much financing?"

He laughed. "Banks have been falling all over me ever since this was first proposed. But the bulk of it will be privately financed."

"By you?"

"Hardly. I've already invested a fortune in buying up the property." His small eyes flicked from her face to the exhibit. "I have investors."

Like the German? The man to whom he had sold a warehouse for a loss? And what the hell did cherry flavoring have to do with any of this?

Maybe nothing.

Maybe everything.

Betty returned ten minutes later, while Crandall was in the midst of explaining the resort's layout. She had three cups of Cuban coffee and a bag of empanadas. Her mood hadn't improved, but Crandall seemed oblivious. He walked around his exhibit as he sipped at his coffee, peering into the tiny windows, touching the little trees, pressing a fingertip against the lake, blowing dust from the miniature playgrounds.

It was as if he had withdrawn from the room, from them, and was caught up in the whirlwind of his own mind. Betty watched him for a moment, damp strands of her short dark hair curled against her cheeks. Then she brushed past Quin without looking at her, as though she weren't there, and plopped down on the couch. She swung her legs over the armrest, picked up a magazine, and drank her coffee, making it abundantly clear that she could outwait Quin or any other woman who happened to drop by.

Quin left shortly afterward, wondering just how far a woman like Betty would go to protect her interests.

The thought followed her through dinner with her daughter, her husband, her sister and her family. It was there when she bathed Michelle, when she read her bedtime stories, when she slipped back into the routine of her old life as though it had been here waiting for her in a kind of suspended animation. Much later, when she and McCleary were in bed, the three cats crowded at the foot, she voiced the thought, giving it a credence it had lacked until then.

Playing devil's advocate, McCleary said: "If Betty killed Charlie, then how'd she get into his apartment? Tim said the place showed no signs of a forced entry."

"I don't know. Maybe she knew his routine and met a locksmith at his place one day when he wasn't there. Maybe she got in through a window or something. You can jimmy the windows in some of those old places with just a kitchen knife."

"Maybe."

One of the cats strolled up from the foot of the bed. It was Merlin, the black cat, the eldest, her cat since before McCleary. He settled down between them and licked the back of her hand, announcing that it was great to have someone home again, thank you. They both stroked him, their hands occasionally touching.

"What about the *santera?*" she asked. "I'd say she's a fairly solid suspect."

"It's crossed my mind."

"But what was her motive?"

"I don't know."

"We don't have to whisper, you know. This room isn't bugged."

"Ellie."

"The door's closed. Did you give the photos R.D. received to Benson?"

"Yeah, he'll try to have some answers by Monday. I told him about my conversation with Allen Potemkin. Heckler, too. He's going to see what he can find out about Steve Heckler through a contact in the CIA. But . . ."

The big but: It would be easier to arrange a private audience with the Pope than to get straight information on an intelligence spook. Quin turned on her side. "What's your theory?"

"Who said I had a theory?"

"C'mon, Mac."

He sat up and adjusted the pillows against the headboard. "Hypothetical. An intelligence organization has Crandall under surveillance for something. Maybe it's the CIA, maybe it isn't. Heckler knew it and for whatever reason passed the information to Charlie, who was looking for dirt on Crandall that would convince him or the county to stop the sale of the Sea Witch. Charlie got the information, decided to send it out to some people for safekeeping until he was ready to use it. But that raises some questions."

"Yeah, like why the feds would have Crandall under surveillance."

"And what happened to Heckler?"

"And what prompted him to give the information to Charlie?"

"And who else knew about the exchange? And was Charlie killed because of the information or because he was creating public scrutiny that Crandall didn't want?"

"Crandall's the key, Mac, but I don't think he killed Charlie."

"He stood to benefit from it."

"But so did Betty. If Crandall goes down the tubes, so does the affair."

"C'mon, it's not that simple."

"It never is." She rubbed her eyes, which begged to shut. "I've got to get some sleep."

"Me, too." Then: "Quin?" His voice sounded disembodied in the dark.

"Hmm?"

"Are you attracted to Tark?"

This was the first reference either of them had made to Tark since McCleary had left in a huff last night, and she could feel the tightness around them breaking up. But why couldn't he have asked over breakfast? Why did these conversations always take place after midnight? "I don't even know him."

"I'm just talking about gut-level attraction. Like if you were single."

"If I were single and what?" She lifted up on an elbow. "Would I want to sleep with him? Is that what you're asking?"

He hesitated. "Yeah. Yeah, I guess that's what I'm asking."

She repressed an urge to be flippant. "It would depend."

"On what?"

"On what he was like when I got to know him."

"We hardly knew each other when we first slept together."

She laughed and sat all the way up. "I knew it. I knew you thought I was easy. Nine years I have to wait to hear you say it."

He started to laugh then and pretty soon they were both laughing into their pillows so they wouldn't wake Ellie. Just like that, the vestiges of last night's tensions died and it didn't matter that she was attracted to Tark because she wouldn't act on it.

There were junctures in your life where the possible avenues of your future shot away from you like spokes in a wheel. Step here, choose this, and one possibility would become concrete, real. The others would dissolve like aspirin in water. Or perhaps they went on to fulfill themselves in some other way. More often than not, these junctures were the result of people you met, men and women who were, in ways Quin barely understood, like markers in your life.

McCleary had been one of those markers.

Charlie had, too.

And Tark was another. She didn't know why, she couldn't even speculate about what the connection was, she was simply certain that it existed. But suppose that connection had something to do with Charlie's murder? What then?

If she chose to continue with her charade as Liz Purcell, as she probably would, then perhaps she was also, inadvertently, choosing whatever path Tark represented. And that prospect frightened her, frightened her deeply.

13

The beauty of Alfie's world, Tark thought, was that it was populated by a vast extended family. Besides the usual brothers and sister, aunts and uncles and cousins, there were second cousins, friends of cousins, and friends of friends three times removed. This Cuban network ran from Key West to Palm Beach like veins in the human body, and its blood was information.

The son of one of these distant friends or cousins worked at the popcorn stand at the dog track to put himself through college. His name was Diego, and when Tark introduced himself Sunday morning the kid's eyes widened with what looked suspiciously like awe. "You're *the* Gabriel? Carmen's husband? Teresita's father?"

He uttered the names as though he'd known Tark's dead wife and daughter all of his life and yet he couldn't have been more than seven or eight when the explosion had happened. "Uh, yeah, right. Alfie's son-in-law. He said you know everyone out here. I'm looking for Ramón Lamadero."

The kid made a hasty sign of the cross on his forehead, as if warding off the *mal ojo*—the evil eye—then closed up his popcorn stand. "He's here. I'll show you, c'mon."

As they walked past the ticket counters toward the bleachers, the kid kept glancing at Tark. "Tío Alfonso talks about you constantly: Gabriel this, Gabriel that, Gabriel called, Gabriel sent money, Gabriel the legend. Sometimes he mentions his wife, but he hardly ever speaks of Carmen or Teresita. Every Christmas he lights candles for them."

To pacify his God, Tark thought.

They stopped at the top of the bleachers and the kid pointed below, into the bright, hot light. "There he is. The man in the pink *guayabera* shirt. It's his trademark."

Tark tipped his shades back onto the top of his head. "Who's the guy in the suit to his right?"

"His bodyguard. Lamadero has a lot of enemies. *Con cuidado, me entiende?* He's a nasty man."

Tark threaded his way down through the bleachers. As he neared Lamadero, he decided he didn't look nasty at all. He bore a faint resemblance to a mole, that same pointed face, the small, compact body, the quickness with which he burrowed through the crowd at the wall, jockeying for a good view of the track.

It occurred to Tark—and not for the first time—that there was something irrational about the way he was conducting business, that he was not, in fact, conducting business at all. This should have been a straightforward job: find the missing information, eliminate anyone who gets in the way, collect his fee, go home, retire. Instead, he was attempting to track down the person or organization that had hired him. And for what? What difference did it make as long as he was paid? Why bother?

Because he was no longer the man who had left Iquitos. Because Gabriel was dying.

He reached the wall as the greyhounds charged from their cages, chasing the fake electronically controlled rabbits that zipped along just ahead of them. People cheered for this number and that.

Lamadero's fists beat against the warm morning air. His companion, leaning against the wall several yards away, cleaned his fingernails with a toothpick and didn't even look up when Tark slipped in between them.

Lamadero shouted for number three, the second dog; Tark inched closer to him, shades in place again. He addressed the other man in perfect Spanish. "I have eighty thousand American dollars to place on tonight's races and I understand you're the man who can double my money." Tark watched the track as he spoke, but felt Lamadero's gaze against his cheek, warm and damp, like a hand.

"I don't know you, *señor*," Lamadero replied, also in Spanish.

"You don't have to. All you have to know is which dogs are going to place, show, and win. Then you advise me, take my money, and do your thing, *amigo*."

He pretended to think about it, studying Tark the way a gull often studies some dead thing on the beach to determine whether it's still edible. Then he said: "Let's talk where it's quiet." He signaled the bodyguard with his eyes and the man followed them up through the bleachers.

"We do business alone," Tark said.

"My fee is a quarter of your bet."

"Fine."

Without turning, Lamadero held up his hand. When Tark glanced back, the man in the suit was moving away from them. "Do you have the cash with you?"

"In my car."

"Then lead the way."

They walked out into the bright, warm parking lot, a black asphalt sea that glinted with chrome and glass. Tark unlocked the Honda's trunk and removed the gym bag. He suggested they sit in the car, but Lamadero was a cautious man and asked him to unzip the bag first. "Just to be sure, *compadre*. In this business, one meets many talkers, *me entiende?*"

"Of course." Tark unzipped the bag and lifted the towels he'd used to cover the bills. It was a long way from what Lamadero wanted up front, but the little man's glimpse was so brief and his greed was so profound he saw what he wanted to see. He nodded, started to turn away, but Tark said, "Wait."

"Yes?"

"Please put your gun in the trunk. I don't do business in my car when a man's armed and I'm not."

Lamadero looked at him like he was out of his mind and laughed. It was a shade too loud, too hearty. "Fair enough, *compadre.*" He pulled the weapon out from under his *guayabera* shirt and placed it carefully inside the trunk.

It was a fine piece, an automatic with an eleven-shot clip. Tark picked it up and turned it over in his hand, admiring it. Lamadero tensed beside him. Tark smiled and pointed the gun at him. "Never assume the other guy is bound by a gentleman's agreement," he said in English, glancing around to make sure no one was close enough to see them. "Get in the trunk."

He blanched. "*Señor*, I am sure we can reach an agreement about—"

"Get. In." He cocked the gun. Lamadero scrambled into the trunk, his eyes wide, darkening with alarm, his face glistening with perspiration. "Lie down."

"Please. If you would just tell me what you want, *señor*. I'm sure—"

"I just told you what I want. Get the fuck down."

"Jesus, please," he whispered, curling up on his side in a fetal position.

"It's nothing personal, *amigo*. Just business. You know how it is. This will be a short ride. You won't suffocate. If you scream, I'll stop and tape your mouth shut and handcuff you to the spare tire. Understood?"

"The . . . the heat, *señor*. The heat."

"We aren't going that far." Tark slammed the lid and locked it. Moments later, he pulled out of the huge parking lot and headed west toward the Everglades.

Alfie's voice haunted him. *Since when do you need to know anything other than the type of weapon you're going to use, Gabby?*

Since he'd left Peru. Since he'd walked into Un Paso and felt Alfie's arms tighten around him. Since his premonition. But he knew the darkness in him had not been transformed so quickly. It had been gradual, an accretion of moments when he'd felt some deep dissatisfaction with what his life had become. But he'd been reluctant to examine the emotion too closely.

Grief, he thought. It's the demon that twists you, perverts you, becomes your consort, your companion, as familiar to you as your own arms and legs. Then one day you wake up and realize you don't hurt like you did last week or last month. The darkness inside you isn't as thick, as oppressive; it's a receding tide that has left a ton of silt and debris in its wake. And one way or another, you claw your way through it.

He was clawing now.

He sped west along Alligator Alley until scrubby Florida pines and mangroves appeared on either side of him, the bright green walls of Big Cypress Swamp. He turned onto a dirt road, turned again when it forked. He followed it to a hummock of land posted with NO TRES-PASSING signs, where the ground was scarred from old campfires. He stopped and killed the engine.

The noises of the Glades drifted through the open window with the warm air: crickets crying for more rain, birds busy with the advent of summer, the rustling sounds of lizards, mice, Key deer. Deeper in the green were panthers, alligators, herons, flamingos, fish, insects. Here was an entire self-contained universe that didn't give a shit who he was or what he had suffered or what he had done or was about to do.

Tark picked up the gun from the floor between his feet where he'd placed it and got out. He unlocked the trunk. As the lid swung open, he stepped back just in case Lamadero was more enterprising than he appeared to be. But the man was still on his side, hands sandwiched between his knees, his pink *guayabera* shirt damp with sweat, his face slick with it. He squinted and blinked against the light; the tip of his pink tongue moved slowly across his lower lip.

"Get out, Mr. Lamadero."

He rolled onto his hands and knees and panted like a dog. Then he slowly climbed out of the trunk. Streaks of grease stained his shirt. "Jesus, *señor*. Let's talk first, let's . . ."

"Lock your hands on your head and move away from the car."

Terror flooded his eyes. He took one step, another, baby steps. And right then, Tark experienced the old exhilaration, the power, the grandeur of the ubiquitous darkness. "I'm going to ask you a question, Mr. Lamadero. If you bullshit me, if you tell me you don't know, I'll blow off your kneecap or your elbow or maybe an ear. It'll hurt like a son of a bitch, but you won't die. Then I'll ask you the question again. Eleven shots can do a lot of damage, and at the end of it you'll wish you were dead. Do I make myself clear, Mr. Lamadero?"

Tears coursed down his cheeks. He bit at his lower lip and nodded.

"I want to know who hired you to find a tracker and act as middle man."

Blink, blink, went his small, stupid eyes as sweat rolled into them. "Please, you have the wrong man, I know nothing of—"

Tark aimed at Lamadero's foot and fired. His shriek frightened birds from the nearby mangroves, flocks of birds that lifted, squawking, into the warm blue sky, their wings beating against the stillness. Lamadero sank to the spongy ground on his knees, weeping, gasping, pathetic. "Oops, I missed," Tark said. "Guess I'm not close enough."

"Pisco, his name's Pisco. He places bets with me sometimes. Ten, fifteen grand a couple times a year. I don't know who he works for. I swear I don't know."

"How much did he pay you?"

Lamadero wiped the back of his hand across his nose, streaking his cheek with dirt. "Fifteen. Fifteen to get the right man and do the setup and then I was out of it."

"Except for the locker."

"Yes, except for the locker. An old man at the train station. I pay him to watch the locker. If someone rents it, he calls me. Every day Mr. Pisco calls me and I give him a report. Yes or no."

"Where's Pisco live?"

"I don't know."

Tark lifted the gun, aimed at a point just to the right of Lamadero's ear, and sighted down the barrel. "Say again, Mr. Lamadero. I didn't hear you."

"Oh Jesus, oh Christ, it's the truth, I don't know where he lives, I don't even have a number for him. He calls me, I see him at the track, like that."

Tark went over to him, grabbed him by the hair, jerked his head back, and jammed the gun up against his throat. He leaned into the stink of Lamadero's fear, leaned close enough to lick the sweat from his forehead. "I don't believe you, *amigo.* So think fast."

He stuttered, he wept, but in the end he spilled what he knew, which wasn't much. Pisco had called him one night and asked Lamadero to meet him at the Green Turtle Inn in Marathon. He'd told Lamadero what he needed, Lamadero asked around, was given

Alfie's name, then he went to him and Alfie called Tark. When Tark said yes, Alfie called Lamadero back, Lamadero told Pisco, Pisco met him at the track, paid him, and arranged for Tark's ticket.

"Suppose there's an emergency and you need to talk to Pisco right away? What do you do?"

"I . . . I call the Green Turtle Inn. I talk to Estelle. She gets in touch with him, he calls me."

"What's Pisco look like?" Tark asked.

Lamadero described him. "And that's all I know, *señor*. I swear."

Squeeze the trigger, whispered the voice of darkness.

Tark released Lamadero's hair, stepped back from him. "Run, Mr. Lamadero."

His pointed face was raised as if to catch the light. He blinked, his fingers dug into his thighs, but he didn't move.

"I said, *Run!*" And he fired twice at the ground in front of Lamadero. The little man stumbled to his feet and backed away, his face wild with terror, his arms clutched against his filthy pink shirt, the front of his slacks wet with his own urine. Then he spun and charged toward the mangroves, his short arms pumping at his sides, his feet stumbling, his head pivoting on his shoulders.

The voice of the darkness pounded against the walls of Tark's skull, *No loose ends do it do it now now now*, and he raised the gun, aimed at Lamadero's back, aimed as the voice shouted, *do it, do it*. He squeezed back on the trigger and fired again and again, emptying the clip into the ground.

The curve of blue sky above him exploded with birds. But in Tark's mind it was that window in the past shattering again, the shards of glass hurtling toward him as his daughter screamed, as his wife shouted his name, as his world ended. His knees buckled and his body folded up like a beach chair.

The Green Turtle Inn was a landmark in Marathon, one of those joints that flourish regardless of the season. The air was redolent of a spicy richness that guaranteed indigestion as soon as you walked out the door, and today it was busy busy busy. Family day, Tark thought.

He waited in line behind a couple with two kids. They looked like potential sunstroke victims, bright pink faces, thirsty eyes, cranky voices. He stared at the back of the woman's head and wished his own head would stop pounding. It felt like nails were being driven into his skull. The heat, he thought.

He willed the line to move ahead. Christ, he didn't want to eat here, didn't need a table. He was just looking for Estelle. Tark rubbed his temple. His eyes were fixed on the back of the woman's sunburned leg. Her right leg. He suddenly knew that she walked with a limp, that there was something wrong with her hip. And the man, what was it about the man? Tark could feel a darkness in him, an emotional black hole.

He smacks the kids and wife around, that's how her hip was injured.

The thought went on but Tark refused to follow it. He stepped quickly out of line, head still pounding, and spoke to the hostess. "I'm looking for Estelle."

"In the bar."

"Thanks."

He glanced back just before he reached the bar, back at the man and the woman. She was limping along behind her husband and children, a hand rubbing absently at her hip.

He hurried into the bar, not wanting to think about it, not wanting to think at all. A lucky guess, body language, coincidence, there were a dozen reasonable explanations. Maybe several dozen. But none was true. He knew what this was: the instinct, the talent, the peculiar sixth sense that had enabled him to track trails that were cold, to find what other people couldn't. And now, turned inside out like a pocket, it attached itself randomly to targets. To Alfie. To strangers in line. And farther back, to Liz Purcell, to that moment when he'd first seen her picture.

"Sir? You okay?"

He was seated at the bar and the woman behind it had just spoken to him. Was he okay? No, not okay. She looked as though she hailed from somewhere in the Mediterranean, Italy or Greece. Short black hair, brows like thick brush strokes above startling black eyes, tanned skin as smooth and brown as chocolate.

"It's the heat," she said when he didn't speak. "Must be ninety out there and not a breath of air."

She set a glass in front of him. Ice water with a twist of orange and a soft pink straw sticking up out of it. Tark sucked. The terrible pounding in his head eased. The cool air in the dimly lit bar licked at his damp cheeks. "Thanks."

"Can't have you passing out on my bar." She smiled. "Bad for business, you know." She was wearing white shorts and a red halter top that fit snugly across her breasts, with a white shirt thrown over it that was unbuttoned and tied at the waist. "Haven't seen you around before. You just passing through or what?"

Passing through. Yes, he was just passing through. But from where and to where was anyone's guess. "I'm looking for Estelle."

"Estelle, huh." She twirled a finger in one of her gold hoop earrings. "What do you want with her?"

"We have a mutual friend."

"Yeah?" A corner of her mouth dimpling now: she was enjoying the game. "And who would that be?"

"Dan Pisco."

The dimple sank back into the smoothness of her skin, a vanished island. "Oh." She stepped back, removed his empty glass from the bar, washed it out. "You want anything else?"

"Just Estelle."

She fixed a hand to her shapely hip. "You're looking at her, buddy, and she's got nothing to say about any Dan Pisco, okay?"

"I need to know where he lives."

"And I need a winning lottery ticket. So what? Needing and wishing don't count for shit down here in the Keys."

With that, she turned to walk off, then stopped when Tark said, "Wait a second."

"Make it snappy. I'm outta here in five minutes and I've still got a bar to wipe down."

"I'll make it worth your while."

"Yeah, you and the President."

Tark set five hundreds on the bar. She looked at the money, at him, then down at the bar as he added another three hundred bucks. She didn't pick it up. "What's your business with a slime like Pisco?"

Slime. He'd get farther with this woman by eliminating the bullshit. "He has some information I want."

"Yeah?" Something changed in her eyes. "You a cop?"

"No."

"A private investigator?"

"No. Nothing like that."

"Then what?"

"Look, it's a long story. Just take the money and talk to me about Pisco, okay?"

"Keep your moola, and sit tight. I'll be done in five minutes."

She didn't want to stick around the restaurant; Pisco was in the habit of dropping in on Saturday and Sunday nights, she said. So Tark followed her rusted Mazda to a lopsided little house on the edge of town. The place looked as if it had been slapped together with driftwood and old banana leaves. The long side porch sagged. The floor inside sagged. The torn screens in the windows had been patched with squares of cardboard. No air-conditioning, no ceiling fans, no phone. The television was a white elephant from the early sixties with a twisted hanger for an antenna. Fruit and vegetables were jammed in wire mesh baskets that hung from nails around the kitchen.

"Welcome to chaos." She tossed her bag into a nearby chair and kicked off her sandals. "How about a cold beer?"

"Great." He looked around for a place to sit, but the two chairs and the couch were occupied by books—stacks of books and most of them appeared to be travel books. He was still standing when she returned with a can of Coors Lite tucked under her arm and another in her hand. She popped it, handed it to him, then popped her own and drank deeply.

"Let's sit on the porch. I never talk about Pisco in the rooms where I live."

They settled on an old wooden swing surrounded by junk. It creaked as it swung, one of those familiar noises he associated with warm summer nights on the porch of his home in Iquitos. She lifted her bare feet onto the edge of an old wooden crate that served as a coffee table, combed her fingers back through her thick hair, and stared out into the jungle of plants in front of the house. Insects buzzed in the still afternoon heat. A blackbird swooped into Tark's line of vision.

"Pisco," she said. "That's the name of a drink in Peru."

"Pisco sours."

She looked at him. "Even drunks don't know that."

"Peruvian drunks do."

She slapped her thigh as she laughed. She had peasant's hands with short, square, unpolished nails. No rings. No jewelry at all except for the hoop earrings. "So what's your name?"

"Gabriel."

"Your mother must've been Catholic, huh."

"Lapsed."

"Well, I'm Estelle. My mother was Greek Orthodox and I should've had an exotic name. But my old man was American, Navy, and thought Estelle was exotic enough. What the hell. So what's the deal with Pisco? He owe you money? Screw your wife? Fuck you over or what?"

Tark laughed. "All of the above."

That dimple appeared in a corner of her mouth again as she smiled. "Yeah, sure, and all at once, right?" She drank from the can, then held it in both hands against her thigh. "C'mon, for real."

"I think Pisco hired me, through several intermediaries, for a job and I want to know more about the organization he works for before I get involved."

"Take it from me, Gabriel. You don't want to get anywhere near a job that Pisco's offering."

"That bad, huh?"

"Yeah, that bad."

"How'd you meet him?"

"Oh, he came into the bar one night three or four years ago. I hadn't been here very long, was feeling blue like you get when you're in a new place, and we came back here. I had a few too many beers, ran at the mouth, misplaced my better judgment." She shrugged. "Eventually I became his switchboard, okay? Someone calls, leaves a message for him, I call him and relay the message. His bookie, his wife, his buddies, who the fuck knows. I don't ask questions. He pays me five hundred a month to do it and not ask questions."

"What kind of messages has Ramón Lamadero left?"

"Usually he just tells me to have Dan call him. Dan, right? Like they've known each other since kindergarten. But when he does leave a message, it's vague. Could mean anything. Lamadero thinks I don't know that Pisco's a spy." She laughed. "Shit, even Pisco doesn't know I know it.

"So anyway, see, this goes on for a couple two, three years. About eight months ago, I told him I'm sick of being his receptionist. He offered to pay me more. I told him what he could do with his moola. He didn't like that, and two days later he shows up here with some stuff and says if I don't work for him, I'll be going to jail if I'm lucky and dead if I'm not. So hey, fine, I'm scared, I admit it. No problem, Dan."

"What kind of stuff?"

She rubbed the back of her hand over her mouth. "Before I ended up in the Keys I was the middle person in a drug deal in Broward and made off with some cash. Quite a large amount of cash, actually. The dealer turned state's evidence, the buyer's doing ten to fifteen, and here I am. I could've just split, probably should have, but bullies piss me off. So I decided to find out what Pisco's about.

"He works at a Navy research station on Long Key and lives there most of the time, too. But the place doesn't have anything to do with the Navy. My old man's been in the Navy nearly forty years and oughta know."

Maybe, Tark thought, but listened to everything she said before interrupting. According to her old man, the place was a detox clinic for spies and was known as the Hereafter. A little gallows humor the burned-out cases probably wouldn't appreciate, he mused.

The Hereafter supposedly wasn't funded by any particular intelligence agency and took burnouts from every agency. The guy in charge was Jerome Kilner, an M.D. who had never practiced medicine. "He went straight into the CIA out of medical school, spent some time in Southeast Asia, Colombia and Peru, Central America," she said, polishing off her beer. She tossed the can into a large trash bin to her right. "Before he ended up on Long Key, he worked for the Department of Defense, running a detox clinic in D.C. Your turn, Gabriel. What'd Pisco hire you for?"

"To find a missing file and eliminate anyone who gets in the way."

Those black eyes pinned him, seemed to probe around inside him, then released him as she pushed to her feet. "I think I need another beer."

Much later. A six-pack later. They were inside now, seated on cushions on the sagging floor, beers between them. She was showing him the map where she'd marked out her next trip, down to the tip of South America and back. That was how she lived, from trip to trip. She saved, she blew it, then she came home again and dipped into her rip-off money until she got on her feet again.

Tark watched her mouth as she talked and thought of Liz Purcell's mouth. He watched her hands and thought of Purcell's hands. And then he touched her face, Estelle's face, and lifted her chin and kissed her. Her mouth was soft, cool, a piece of summer fruit flavored with beer, and when it opened against his, he tasted hunger and caution in almost equal measures. For seconds, the only thing that existed for him was the sensation of her mouth, its pressure, its shape, its *reality*. Then she pulled back a little, those black eyes searching his face.

Black eyes, he thought, like his wife's.

"What was that for?" she asked.

"Thanks for the help."

She grinned and rocked toward him. "Thank me again," she said softly.

And he did.

14

Quin was barely awake when she walked into the Neon Flamingo Monday morning and Crandall tossed her the keys to the Lincoln. "Cynthia's tied up, you'll have to drive."

"Drive where?"

"To the Biltmore to pick up Mr. Rau, then to Boca and Palm Beach."

Palm Beach. Terrific. A hundred miles up the coast and she hadn't even had coffee yet. But Crandall was already on his way down the stairs, barking orders. "Buzz Betty and tell her I need those new figures on the Sea Witch in an hour. She can fax them to me in the car. And tell her to call my sister and cancel dinner tonight. Where's Dave? I want him downstairs on the double. I'll meet you out back."

Quin clicked her heels and saluted as he flew down the stairs. No time for breakfast at the News Café this morning.

When she slipped behind the wheel of the Lincoln ten minutes later, Dave Petrovsky, bodyguard, was in the passenger seat and didn't bother looking at her. Crandall was busy in the back, his stubby fingers playing his calculator until it sang. No one spoke. She drove south on Ocean Drive, turned onto Fifth, and stopped in front of Salgado's Market.

Dave looked at her, muscles flexing. "What're we doing here?"

"I need coffee," she announced. "You want anything?"

"Nope."

"Larry?"

"Coffee's fine."

At the sidewalk window, she ordered two coffees with milk to go and an empanada for herself, the Cuban version of Mexican tortillas, stuffed with chunks of meat and vegetables. As she waited for her order, someone stepped into line behind her.

"We need to stop meeting like this," McCleary said quietly.

Quin smiled but didn't turn around. "What're you doing here?"

"I'm on my way to meet Tim and Joe Bean so we can go over the routine for the Jungle Queen tomorrow night. Bean's going with me." Bean was an investigator who had worked with them for years in their Miami firm and now headed it. "You playing chauffeur today?"

"Yup. The Biltmore, Boca, and Palm Beach."

"What for?"

"To pick up the German. Beyond that, I don't know." She moved to the side, making room for him at the window. "You going by the factory?"

"Later. Did you call Helga?"

"I haven't had a chance."

A woman returned with Quin's order and change and took McCleary's order. She lingered, plucking napkins from the dispenser, pocketing her money, wanting to touch him. "I'll call you sometime tonight."

"We could meet in Boone's parking garage." He turned those smoke-blue eyes on her. "Or something."

She laughed. "You're a horny lecher, Mac. Talk to you later."

When she returned to the car, Petrovsky was cleaning his nails with the tip of a pocket knife and Crandall was still slumped over his calculator. "Step on it, Liz. I don't want to be late."

Ebo Rau was waiting outside the Biltmore when they drove up, Rau in a suit, his crew cut still damp from the shower, his briefcase large enough to accommodate an infant. "Good morning, good morning," he said cheerfully as he slid into the backseat with Crandall. "I predict it may be a very important morning, my friend."

"Let's hope so. Boca airport, Liz."

"Yes, sir."

He raised the privacy window and she wondered if it was closed when Cindy was chauffeuring. She headed for the interstate, delighted that Petrovsky was wearing a headset; she didn't feel like talking to him. She switched on the radio for the latest advisory on tropical storm Albert.

He was presently approaching Turks Island, seven hundred miles off the Florida coast. Top winds were fifty-two miles an hour. He was moving at a steady twenty, but was expected to slow down as he passed over Turks Island and approached Great Inagua Island. It was uncertain at this point whether he would veer north toward the Bahamas or maintain a more southerly course toward Cuba. A tropical storm watch was in effect for the northern coast of Cuba, Acklins Island, and Long Island.

He was still too distant to worry about, but she worried just the same. With seven hundred miles of ocean to cross and only specks of land in between, Albert would surely intensify. His barometric pressure would drop. His winds would pick up. When they hit seventy-four miles an hour, he would be upgraded to a hurricane and sweep across the warm Atlantic waters like a sentient, conscious being, gathering speed and momentum and fury.

When she'd seen the satellite photos of Hurricane Gilbert in 1989, it had looked like some sort of terrible beast spawned from the primal soup. Those white counterclockwise swirls spinning around the dark, ubiquitous eye in its center. Its breadth. Its magnitude.

It had been a category-five hurricane, with its highest gusts clocked at 218 miles per hour, the lowest barometric reading ever recorded, and the worst storm of the century. It had caused several billion dollars' worth of damage and killed more than three hundred people in seven countries. It would have leveled South Florida.

The doomsayers, with whom she happened to agree when it came to hurricanes, predicted that South Florida was due for a blow. Due, in fact, for The Big One. But even a category-three storm like Cleo in 1964 would do considerable damage; the peninsula, after all, was nothing like it had been nearly thirty years ago. There were too many glass buildings, too much beach erosion, too many people.

According to the experts, the major threat to the coast was a storm surge, a tremendous dome of water caused when high, swirling winds combined with low atmospheric pressure and raised the level of the sea. For a city that stood barely twelve feet above sea level, a six-foot storm surge would put most of Miami Beach underwater.

Over the years, she'd become convinced that weather possessed a kind of rudimentary consciousness, that in some way she couldn't quite comprehend it was a reflection of man's own consciousness. If she picked a spot in the world, any spot, and studied the pattern of its weather and geographic phenomena for the past five or ten years, she was pretty sure she would have a fairly accurate picture of the collective mentality of its populace.

Typhoons, for instance. Was it a coincidence that they plagued countries like the Philippines where violence had become a way of life? And what about the droughts that afflicted parts of Africa, where life, at best, was already a struggle against starvation? Or take earthquakes: California, China, Chile, Colombia. The four Cs, as she thought of them, were rife with change, unrest, eruptions of the spirit.

Then there was South Florida, where most of the populace hailed from somewhere else and "community" rarely extended beyond the end of the street where you lived. South Florida and crime, guns, drugs, racial tension, greed, the continual struggle between the old and the new: a collective consciousness swirling in chaos. A magnet for Albert, that was how she thought of it.

The privacy window whispered open. Petrovsky immediately removed his headset and gave Crandall his full attention. But the Buddha's question was directed to Quin. "What's the latest on Albert, Liz?"

She told him. In the rearview mirror, Rau's face creased with worry, which seemed odd. He didn't impress her as the type to fret about a storm. Crandall was the one who should have been worrying; he had a small fortune invested in Ocean Drive.

"I heard there's a high-pressure system up north that's probably going to keep Albert well south," Petrovsky offered.

"It's too soon to tell," Quin said.

Crandall nodded in agreement. "Pick up a hurricane-tracking chart, Liz, and start plotting Albert. I'll want an update every six hours." Then, as the window was rising again, she heard him say: "Look, Ebo, if it looks like it's going to hit, we'll take precautions that—" The window cut off the rest of the sentence.

Precautions: Crandall wasn't as tranquil about things as he looked.

She exited on Yamato Road and a moment later turned in to the Boca airport. This was strictly a general aviation facility, no commercial traffic, no tower, runways long enough to accommodate the corporate jets that flew in and out of here. Quin could still remember when Boca Raton had three stoplights and a downtown that was about four blocks long. Then IBM had built a plant here and suddenly the town with the unpleasant name ("Rat's Mouth" was the literal translation) had become one of the prime spots to live in Palm Beach County.

Crandall lowered the privacy window again and asked her to park in front of the general aviation building. Like the walk from the parking lot would kill him, she thought. But he was as zealous in his avoidance of exercise as he was of walking under ladders or opening umbrellas indoors. She supposed there was some dark superstition underlying the whole thing. Maybe his old man had died of cardiac arrest while exercising.

When he and Petrovsky went inside, Rau leaned forward. "Tell me, Liz, have you ever been through a hurricane?"

"Yes," she replied without thinking. Then she remembered Purcell was from Gainesville. She shifted around to look at him, his soft eyes like a child's, expectant, waiting for her story. "I was visiting a friend in Coral Gables when Cleo hit."

"What was it like?"

"Scary. The house had hurricane shutters, but we had a peephole on one side where we could watch the storm. Horizontal rain, the trees whipping around like pieces of straw, water rising in the backyard, leaks in the roof. I've never seen anything like it and hope I never do again."

"What was Miami Beach like afterward?"

"I only saw pictures. The beach had washed away and Ocean Drive was under about two feet of water. Most of the hotels had been flooded."

"Flooded," Rau repeated, his forehead creasing as he frowned.

He started to say something else, but a Mercedes pulled up behind them and Cindy Youngston hopped out. She came over to the Lincoln, a bounce to her walk, her hair almost white in the bright light. She flashed a smile of perfect teeth. "Hey, you and I got our packages switched the other day, Liz."

Yeah, tell McCleary about it, she thought. "I've got yours in my car. Who owns the Mercedes?"

She gestured toward the row of hangars beyond the terminal. "Haisar keeps it in his hangar down there."

As if Quin knew who Haisar was.

"Where are they, anyway, Ebo?" Cindy asked.

"Inside. You know how Haisar gets with the soda machines."

"Yeah."

They both laughed, a private joke they didn't bother sharing. Crandall and Petrovsky appeared a few moments later, a third man between them, two other men following them. Haisar, she guessed. And his bodyguards?

Rau got out and greeted Haisar like an old friend, then Cindy hugged him hello. Home week, Quin thought. Haisar was about Rau's height, five nine or so, but that was where the similarity ended. He had a thick chest, broad shoulders, dark hair, skin, and eyes. *Swarthy.* Suddenly she knew he was the man in one of the photos that Charlie had sent to R.D.

He wasn't introduced to her, and as soon as the three were in the backseat, the privacy window went up again and Petrovsky asked, "You know how to get to the Ritz-Carlton?"

Testing her. "No."

"Get back on the interstate," he said. "I'll give you directions from there." He adjusted his side mirror and watched two men getting into the plum-colored Mercedes. A sleek sixty-grand job that Haisar kept in his hangar. Uh-huh. "Okay, we're ready. Stay to the speed limit."

"I always do, Dave. Is Haisar staying at the Ritz?"

"Yeah."

It was the best news Quin had gotten since starting this case.

The Ritz-Carlton, built for a cool $100 million eighteen months ago, was the newest glitz in Palm Beach. Technically, it wasn't even in Palm Beach, but in neighboring Manalapan. There were 270 rooms, all with private balconies and marble-finished bathrooms, which were serviced twice a day. The top suites went for $2,400 a night. The lobby featured art and antiques worth $2 million and the ballroom boasted six chandeliers worth ten grand apiece, each with eight hundred pieces of hand-strung crystal.

There were three Ritz-Carltons in Florida and service was their buzzword. Part of that service included giving guests exactly what they wanted. To accomplish this, the Ritz employed people who did nothing but study individual guests and maintain histories on each of them in a systemwide reservations system.

The person in charge of this operation was a black woman named Kiara, whose daughter was in Michelle's class at Tot Stop. A year ago, her younger brother had been arrested for breaking and entering in Miami and Quin had asked Benson to intercede. The charge was eventually reduced to a misdemeanor and the brother got two hundred hours of community service instead of jail time. Maybe, just maybe, that would get her what she needed.

As soon as the men had gone inside the hotel, she told Cindy she was going to take a look around. "One look's all you'll need," the other woman replied. "You'll come out feeling like you got short-changed in life."

Quin laughed. "Thanks for the warning."

She spent a few minutes in the lobby, checking for Crandall and his group, but didn't see any of them, not even faithful Petrovsky. She took the elevator to the second floor, where Kiara's offices were, gave her name to the secretary, and started to sit down. But Kiara sailed out almost immediately, a slender, striking woman dressed in vivid tropical colors. She wore silver-and-turquoise jewelry that contrasted beautifully with her dark skin.

"Quin. I can't believe it. I thought my secretary had the name wrong. What a pleasant surprise."

"Good to see you, Kiara. Do you have a few minutes?"

"Sure. C'mon in." Her office was as bright and colorful as she was, decorated with Caribbean art that she had picked up on her travels. She shut the door. "How about coffee or something cold to drink?"

"No, thanks, I'm fine. I need a favor, Kiara. If it's an imposition, just say so, and I'll understand." Quin explained.

Kiara bit at her lower lip. "I could get fired for something like that, Quin."

"You have my word that no one is going to know where the information came from. It's between you and me."

"A homicide case?"

"That's how it started, yeah, but I think there's a lot more to it than that. And I need some background on Haisar to fill in what I don't know."

"A Dade case?"

Quin nodded. "For Benson."

The magic name. "Okay. But . . ."

"Between us. I promise."

Kiara flashed a quick, apologetic smile, then swiveled around in her chair, tapping the keyboard. "Haisar? That's his last name?"

"First name."

"Haisar, Haisar. Hey, wait a minute. I know who you mean. Haisar Haddan. Yeah, here he is. Forty-eight years old. Hometown, Baghdad, but he spends most of the year traveling. Has homes in New York, Paris, and Berlin. He always rents a suite with us; his longest stay has been two months."

"At twenty-four hundred bucks a night?"

"Loose change, kiddo, for a guy worth about a hundred million."

"You have his net worth on there, too?"

"Approximate worth."

Impressive. "What else can you tell me about him?"

"Well, he usually has at least two men with him, sometimes more. His wife and daughter were with us only once. He likes blue silk sheets on his bed. The fridge in his room is always stocked with at least two dozen bottles of Perrier on the day he checks in and a box of American chocolates. No booze, no pork, no air-conditioning except in the room that has the office equipment. We stock his room daily with fresh fruit. He particularly likes mangos and papayas. He uses only Dove or Pears soap and is passionate about old American movies. More?"

"Whatever you've got."

She hit another key. "We provide him with a fax, a laptop with a modem, and a private phone line. He places and receives calls from all over the world and his phone bill runs between three and five hundred a day. His Lear is housed in hangar ten at the Boca airport. One of the men who nearly always accompanies him is his pilot. He's never requested that we pick him up or take him to the airport; he has his own transportation. A Mercedes.

"We had the weather channel disconnected from the cable in his room because his religion prohibits any kind of prognostication. This is his third visit in six months and the third time he's met with Ebo Rau and Lawrence Crandall in as many months. How's that?"

"Damn. You have that much on every guest?"

"Only on the repeats. And of course with every visit the data base expands."

"You have any indication what his business is with Crandall and the German?"

"No."

"What about Rau? Has he ever stayed here?"

"Only once when we first opened. He's not in the same league, Quin. Neither is Crandall. I do know one thing about Haddan, though." She lowered her voice and leaned forward. "In the late eighties, he built a tremendous pharmaceutical factory in the middle of the Libyan desert. I assume that pharmaceuticals are one facet of his business."

Haddan's pharmaceuticals, Rau's import-export business, Crandall's hotels and future resort, and a cherry-flavoring factory. Somewhere, she thought, there was a connection.

She thanked Kiara for her help and promised to call as soon as things were back to normal so their girls could get together. As soon as she said it, she realized that the longer she remained on this case, inside the bones of her fictive creation, the less recognizable "normal" became.

■ ■ ■

Joe Bean was already in Benson's office when McCleary arrived, a stringbean of a man who seemed incapable of standing still. He was always moving, bopping, snapping or drumming his fingers as if to some internal beat. Like the black cop with whom McCleary worked in West Palm, Bean was straight out of Liberty City, born and raised.

"M'man," he said, grinning as he pumped McCleary's arm. "It's about time we pulled some shit together. Tim's in the staff room with a lady who walked in ten, fifteen minutes ago. Got me a feeling she might be a lead." He snapped his fingers and McCleary laughed.

"You never change, Bean."

"Hell, m'man, I change by the second. Been seeing this new lady, you know? She's got me hopping. It's embarrassing."

"Tim fill you in?"

"All the way."

Benson and a young woman were seated at a table. She wore a uniform with WOOLLEY's monogrammed across the pocket; her pale hands were clutching a can of Coke. She had a mane of hair, blond curls so thick, so profuse, they swallowed her neck and made her face seem very small.

"Sally's head cashier at Woolley's Fine Foods over on the beach," Benson said. "She was working the desk on the evening of May thirty-first and waited on Professor Potemkin." He introduced McCleary and Bean, and when they pulled up chairs, Benson went on. "Sally, would you mind going through your story again? I'd like these two guys to hear it."

"Yeah, sure. There isn't all that much to tell, though. It was around eight when this old guy blows through the front door and comes up to the desk. His face was sweaty, like he'd been running or was sick or something, and he was sort of, I don't know, wild looking."

Wild looking? Charlie? "What do you mean exactly?"

"He looked like he was going to give me trouble. These old guys do that sometimes. They come in and want us to cash their social security checks and when I tell them we don't take third-party checks, they make a scene, you know? And this guy had a big envelope with him. So anyway, I guess I like stepped back and I could see it made him mad. But he pulls out his check-cashing card and a blank check, so I cashed it for him. Fifty dollars. Then he buys eight stamps, that was all, just eight lousy stamps and pays me with a twenty.

"Then he zips off toward the other end of the store and I like, well, kept an eye on him. I thought maybe he was going to lift something. He heads down the stationery aisle, and after a while, he hurries back out with some stuff, no cart, just the stuff in his hand, and gets into the express line. Once he'd paid, he went over to the place where the carts are and stood there at the window, scribbling. When he finally left, I saw him put some things in the mailbox outside.

"Well, I didn't think anything more of it until I got back from vacation yesterday and was going through my newspapers and saw his picture on the front page of the *Herald*."

"You're sure about the eight stamps?" Benson asked.

"Positive."

"How many stamps did your envelope have on it, Mac?"

"Two."

"And the kid's?"

"Two."

Benson grinned. "Two envelopes down and two to go."

"How did Professor Potemkin seem when he was over by the carts?" Bean asked.

She sipped from her can of Coke, considering the question carefully. "Scared. He kept looking out the window, glancing around behind him. Scared, yeah, I'd have to say he seemed scared."

The sequence of events ran through McCleary's head like a movie. Charlie rushes into the store with an envelope that contains photographs and perhaps other items about Larry Crandall. He's scared because he's being followed. He divides the contents four ways and mails them to people who aren't visible in his life but whom he trusts. But where was he coming from? Who gave him the photos? Maybe one of Crandall's enemies? Maybe his spook buddy Heckler, who, according to Charlie's son, was in town? If so, how were the feds involved?

The coroner estimated that Charlie had been dead at least an hour when Boone found him at ten that evening. He'd arrived at Woolley's around eight and had called Boone's half an hour later, probably on his way home. McCleary tried to imagine that last thirty minutes of Charlie's life, the rush to get inside the apartment, the taste of fear in his mouth, the way he'd dead-bolted the door as soon as he was inside.

Wrong, back up.

If he had rushed inside the apartment and thrown the dead bolt, how had the killer gotten to him? Charlie wouldn't have opened the door to a stranger, not if he'd believed he had been followed. That left only two options—that he opened the door to someone he knew or that the killer had been waiting inside the apartment.

"I've really got to get going," Sally York said, "or I'll be late for work."

A few minutes later, they were settled in Benson's office. "So what'd you think about her story?"

"Someone was tailing Charlie," Bean said.

"Yeah, that was my guess. It's time you pay the *santera* another visit, Mac. Seems to me she fits the profile of someone Charlie might've sent one of the envelopes to."

"I'd like to give her another day to call me. Anything turn up on Heckler?"

"Nope, nothing on the computers. But if he's actually a spook, that's not surprising. I've got another call in to a guy with connections in intelligence circles." He opened his desk drawer and brought out several objects that he lined up on his desk. The only thing McCleary recognized was the electronic bug. "For Crandall's car. Joe, maybe you can attach it before you guys board the Jungle Queen. It's standard."

Bean pocketed the device. "No problem."

Benson picked up the second item, a black pen. "A directional mike. The range is limited, ten or fifteen yards under good conditions." He explained how it worked, set it aside, picked up the last object. It was black, as round as a pancake, and fit perfectly against Benson's palm. "The receiver. Its range is forty to fifty yards. You hook it up to this." He plugged one end of a dark cord into the back of the receiver and fitted the other end into his ear. "If we'd never gone to the moon, guys, none of this would be here. It's possible this is just going to be a family ride on the Jungle Queen, but I doubt it. A man who owns a yacht isn't going to do the Jungle Queen for the fun of it. So find me a reasonable cause to get this fucker."

In more than twenty years, McCleary had never heard Benson speak in quite this way and wondered what he knew that he wasn't telling and why he wasn't sharing what he knew.

Yes, that most of all.

15

Around eleven Monday morning, Tark and Estelle drove over to Long Key. It was so small that if you blinked twice it was gone.

"Don't slow down too much," Estelle said. "The guys at the gate get nervous. It's coming up on the right."

He saw the sign that read NAVAL RESEARCH STATION, saw the guards with their automatic rifles slung over their shoulders, and the fence beyond it. "Doesn't look like much from here."

"There are four houses on the compound. White, blue, pink, and yellow, all on stilts. About two dozen people work there."

His eyes shifted from the compound to her, tan legs pulled up against her on the seat, bare feet hooked over the edge of it, her bare arms resting on her knees, her head turned away from him, toward the compound. Her black hair was swept back from her face, exposing her long neck and the graceful curve where it melted into her shoulder. He reached out and drew his finger along the underside of her arm, where the skin was soft and cool.

She turned her head and peered at him over the rims of her shades. "You keep doing that, Gabby, and we'll have to pull off into the bushes and those Navy boys or whatever they are might get real upset."

He laughed, took his hand away, and shifted into second. When they were well past the compound property, he swung onto the shoulder and into the scrubs and pines. "Hey, I was just kidding," she said.

"Let's play tourist."

"Telephone receptionist to decoy. I love it."

Tark unlocked the trunk, grabbed one of the beach towels next to the gym bag at the back, and slung it over his shoulder. The trunk reminded him of Lamadero. Tark was suddenly certain he hadn't seen the last of him and wished he'd shot the bastard. He shut the lid, locked it, took her hand.

High tide had narrowed the beach to a thin, pale strip of sand, a Band-Aid strewn with seaweed, driftwood, and the debris of man. He didn't intend to venture too close; all he needed was a sense of the layout and a few specifics. Was the fence tied into a security alarm? Where was it most vulnerable? Where could it best be approached by water?

"You going to do what I think you are?" Estelle asked.

"I don't know yet."

"Ahead a ways there's a gate in the fence. Padlocked and everything. I don't want to go up that far, just in case Pisco's around."

The shrubs along the fence thinned and he could see into the compound now. The houses on stilts. A sidewalk that twisted through the trees. He stopped, spread the towel in the sand, and they sat down.

"Now what?" she asked.

"We wait."

She dug a hand into the warm sand, glanced back through the shrubs, then out at the water. "See the mangroves that jut out over there?"

Tark nodded.

"Good place for a boat to hide out until dark. Then you leave the boat and bring a Zodiac raft to shore."

"You've done it?"

She shrugged. "I got as far as the mangroves one night. Just to watch the place. See what was going on."

"Do all the people who work there also live there?"

"No. I watched two nights running, during the week." Sand poured out of her hand as she tilted it. "Besides the two guards, there were only three or four other people who seemed to live there also."

Tark extended his own hand and caught the sand as it left hers. Over her shoulder, he saw a man jog up to the gate, unlock it, and jog through. He was watching something on the water and hadn't seen them yet. Tark cupped Estelle's face in his hand, kissing her, moving her back against the towel. "A jogger, coming this way," he whispered.

"What's he look like?"

"He's too far away to tell for sure."

"Let's get out of here."

"I'd rather he not get a good look at us."

"Then I guess we'll have to scare him off, huh." She brought one of her legs in between his and slipped her hands down inside his shorts to the small of his back, holding him against her.

The sun beat down. His mouth glided between her ear and her throat, where her skin smelled of soap, sand, sea. He turned his head slightly, peering through the brush, and saw the jogger's legs, much closer now.

Turn back, guy.

"He still coming?" she whispered.

"Yes."

"He won't for long." She took his hand, guided it between her thighs, slid her feet back toward her body until her legs were bent at the knees. Tark pressed his face against her shoulder, head turned just enough to see that the jogger had stopped.

"He's watching. Doesn't seem to know what to do."

"So let's make up his mind for him." She shifted her hips against the sand so his hand moved higher on her thigh, under the leg of her shorts, and found only skin, soft, warm, slightly damp.

"You forgot something," he said.

She smiled, kissing him, kneading his back with her hands, murmuring that she never wore panties in the summer. He thought of her in the bar yesterday, waiting on people, waiting on him, and wearing nothing under her shorts. His fingers slipped into her, into the unimaginable warmth, a sea, a dark tide unchanged since last night, since this morning, unchanged, waiting. She made soft rolling noises, almost like purrs.

He forgot about the jogger, no longer cared about where they were. He rocked back onto his heels, rolled her shorts down over her hips, freed himself, and pulled the huge beach towel over them as he sank against her, entering her. He lost himself in the heat of the sun, the sand, her body. They moved against each other as if swimming upstream against some hard, terrible current, the pressure of the past, his, hers, their singular isolation. As she came, suddenly, violently, he thought briefly of Liz Purcell, and then felt himself flung out into the heat, the sun. There he burned, burned the way paper burns, fast, furiously, completely.

When there was nothing left of him, he collapsed against her. Gradually, he became aware of her hands, stroking his hair. He had sand on his tongue, the taste of salt in the back of his throat. He rocked back, away from her. Her eyes were open, fathomless. A sheen of perspiration covered her face. He started to say something; anticipating the words she touched a finger to his mouth. "None of that, okay? If you're around, great. If you're not, that's fine, too. Just let me know before you leave the country, Gabby." Then she grinned. "So we can do more of this."

He laughed, helped her up. "I've got to head back to Miami."

"And I should get ready for work."

They walked back down the beach, back into their ordinary lives, the jogger nowhere in sight now. During the long ride back to Miami, he thought about the fence, the mangroves, the darkness of her eyes.

■ ■ ■

Kilner kept seeing them in his head, the couple on the beach, the man's hand between the woman's legs. Disgusting, he thought. It was disgusting what people did in public, pushing the boundaries of decency to the limit. It didn't matter that they were hidden within the shrubs, that there had been no boats within sight on the water. *He* had seen them.

And stopped.

He could have alerted the guards, called the local cops, made a scene. But he didn't want to draw attention to the compound just now, not with Heckler here. So he had waded into the water instead and swum along the shore, watching them until the man was inside her, fascinated and repelled by his own arousal. And when he'd gotten beyond them, he'd left the water and run hard along the beach, trying not to think about it.

Now he sat at the desk in his office, his head aching, the phone glued to his ear, his son's voice a choppy tide, ebbing, flowing, broken up by static. Kilner wondered what had happened to the pink-faced infant a nurse had placed in his arms a quarter of a century ago. Where had it gone? What had his life amounted to? Two ex-wives, a son drifting around the world, and his work, his little compound, now threatened by LeFrank and forces much larger than he was, more powerful.

Kilner rubbed his thumb and index finger along the bridge of his nose. His son was saying, "Dad? You there? Can you hear me?" Kilner hung up, just like that he replaced the receiver, and felt an enormous relief wash through him.

"Mr. K.? You got a minute?" Gracie stuck her head into the room.

"Sure, Gracie."

She waddled in, a corpulent Jamaican woman wearing a colorful housedress. For fifteen years she'd been the compound's cook and the one person whom Kilner trusted absolutely. She handed him a Fed Ex package. "This just came for you."

"Thanks, Gracie." His heart beat a little faster when he saw the return address.

"You okay, sir?"

"Remind me not to run when it's so hot out, Gracie."

"Told you that plenty of times, Mr. K. Hard on the heart, knees, the whole body. I'll bring you some cold tea."

She left and Kilner looked at the package. It was from a man in Maryland whom he'd hired right after LeFrank's last call. A man who specialized in a particular kind of work and who owed Kilner a favor.

He tore open the package. Two pieces of cardboard covered whatever the man had sent and were bound with a rubber band. The note clipped to the cardboard read:

> *This should put us square, Jerry. If LeFrank ever*
> *makes it to the house on the hill, we're all fucked.*

Kilner removed the rubber band, slid aside the cardboard. Photographs. Four photographs of the true Elliot LeFrank, the monster hidden in the flesh of a man. He quickly locked them in the safe.

■ ■ ■

The industrial area west of Miami was as bleak as the surface of the moon. Washed in the Halloween glow of sodium-vapor lights, the concrete warehouses looked forbidding and strange, McCleary thought, their identical shapes jutting up from the flatness, row after row of them, like tract housing.

The majority of the warehouses were wholesale businesses that sold a particular type of merchandise, Persian rugs, patio furniture, oriental items, shoes. Customers were long gone for the day; the cars in the lots undoubtedly belonged to employees.

There were four warehouses on this street, all of them backing up to a grove of mango trees, the only greenery within miles. Chique Cherries was at the end.

"Sounds like a title for a porn movie," Boone remarked, fanning himself with his cap as McCleary slowed but didn't stop.

"No windows that I can see."

"Nope."

"We'll check for a rear door."

"We'll need a lot more than a rear door. That bastard's solid concrete, Mike, and if there's something going on in there that they don't want anyone to know about, you can bet your ass it's wired."

"I've never known a security system to keep you out of a place, Will, if you wanted in badly enough."

Boone laughed. "You got that right. But I was fifteen years younger, too."

"Shit. You hear that, Flats? You hear what this man just said to me?"

Flats, sitting in the well behind the seats, barked, licked Boone's face, then rested her snout on McCleary's shoulder, pleased to be included. He drove on past the building, swung around in the cul-de-sac at the end, and headed back up the street.

"Let's stick around and keep an eye on the place for a while," McCleary suggested.

"In the mango grove?"

"It looked thick enough to me. We'll head into it from the main road."

Flats barked, a unanimous vote.

The grove of mango trees covered an acre or so behind the warehouses, and was surrounded on three sides by four-lane roads. To the west, the grove continued for perhaps another acre. McCleary hoped the land belonged to some stubborn old codger who refused to sell just on principle. But more than likely it was owned by a family or a small corporation that was holding out for the highest bidder.

A chain-link fence enclosed the grove. But on one side a section had been crumpled inward and flattened. The opening was large enough for the Miata to squeeze through. There was a road of sorts, more of a footpath, really, where the weeds had been trampled into the dirt. He followed it east toward the warehouses, under trees that were older than the roads that surrounded them. Their branches, sagging with age, were filled with mangos that would be ready for harvesting in the next couple of weeks.

Once they were ready to drop, kids from nearby neighborhoods would sneak in here and pluck the trees bare. The fruit would end up in makeshift roadside stands the next day, where it would be sold for an obscenely cheap price—eight or twelve mangos for a buck. Every place he had lived, every country he had visited, had its particular commodity\ that entrepreneurial twelve-year-olds claimed as their own. In South Florida it was mangos.

The trees thinned just short of the fence. He parked under the umbrageous folds of a Haydyn mango tree, the best hybrid around, in a spot where they had a good view of the factory parking lot. He snapped Flats's leash to her collar, the six-foot leash, the one that allowed her to roam without getting into trouble, and opened his

door. She bounded out, delighted to be free of the car, and he tied the
end of the leash to the steering wheel.

"You hungry?" he asked Boone.

"And thirsty. A cold beer would taste damn fine."

"Coming up."

McCleary unlocked the trunk. He brought out a pair of binoculars
and the cooler he'd packed before they'd left the apartment. Over the
years, he'd spent enough long hours on surveillance with Quin and
her insatiable appetite so that now he automatically prepared a cooler
whenever surveillance was a possibility.

He hooked the binocular strap around his neck and joined Boone
on the Miata's hood, the cooler between them. The Coors was cold
and the turkey sandwiches were loaded. He'd packed extra turkey for
Flats, who came around when she had finished checking out the
immediate area.

Between eight-thirty and nine, people trickled out of the building,
one or two at a time until only a few cars remained in the lot. The
night shift, McCleary guessed. Shadows thickened. A breeze kicked
up. Crickets chirred. The leaves rustled.

"Tell me about when you died," Boone said suddenly, without
looking at McCleary. He was leaning forward, forearms propped
against his thighs as he cut slices from an apple and peeled them. A
spill of illumination from the parking-lot lights washed over one side
of his face; the other was deep in shadow. "Tell me what happened."

"Ask me something easy, Will."

"I'm not asking you to interpret it. Just tell me how it was. ABC.
That's all."

So McCleary told him: about the case, the investigation that had
led to a desolate area around Lake Okeechobee known as the "death
flats," about the bullet with his name on it and what he'd experienced
during his twelve seconds as a flatliner. The part about Callahan drew
a nonplussed look from Boone but no verbal comment. When
McCleary went on, though, talking about his sister because it seemed
to fit, Boone's demeanor changed.

"You telling me she's haunting you, Mac?" He tipped the bottle of
Coors to his mouth, polishing it off. "Is that what you're saying?"

"Not haunts, exactly. But sometimes I feel her around."

"Heartburn," Boone mumbled. "That's all it is."

"No. This is different."

"Different from what?"

"Just different."

"It worries me when you talk like this."

"It worried me, too, for a while. Now, I don't know, I find the whole thing sort of comforting."

"Comforting," Boone repeated, setting his empty beer bottle back inside the cooler. "Comforting, the man says. You got some strange ideas about comfort. The whole thing spooks the shit outta me."

"What whole thing?"

Boone held up his hands against the wash of light, fingers splayed, and studied them with an inordinate interest. "Sometimes I think I sense Charlie around. The other day, right before you and the kid showed up and I was fixing lunch, I suddenly knew Charlie was standing behind me. I knew it. It was the strangest thing. I knew if I turned around I'd see him."

McCleary thought of the afternoon when he'd been sitting in his sister's den at the farmhouse and the fragrance of her perfume had suddenly permeated the air. It had preceded the delivery of a letter that had provided him with a vital lead. "Maybe he was trying to tell you something, Will."

His hands dropped to his thighs. "Yeah, that I'm an old fart who should stick to being retired. Hey, look." He pointed toward the factory parking lot. A Lincoln was pulling into a parking space under the light in the far corner. "Crandall's wheels."

McCleary lifted the binoculars to his eyes, focused. He somehow knew Quin wasn't driving. Sure enough, a woman with short blond hair hopped out the driver's side and opened the passenger door. Cindy Youngston, chauffeur. Betty O'Toole, Crandall's personal assistant, emerged next, followed by Crandall and Ebo Rau. The three of them rounded the side of the building and passed out of McCleary's sight.

Cindy of black-nightgown fame, McCleary thought wryly, leaned against the Lincoln's hood in a spill of light from the building. She lit a cigarette, combed her fingers through her hair, gazed off toward the road. A souped-up Camaro cruised into the lot and stopped.

A husky guy got out the passenger side and strolled over, hiking up his slacks and smoothing a hand over his hair. McCleary studied him with the binoculars, a Schwarzenegger clone in expensive clothes. Dave Petrovsky, McCleary guessed, Crandall's bodyguard.

"I say he's carrying, Will." He handed the binoculars to Boone.

"Big guy. Who's the knockout?"

"A lady with a fondness for black nighties."

Boone chuckled and held the binoculars to his eyes again. "You can tell that, can you? Black lace and leather at Chique Cherries. What's she doing working for Crandall?"

"Money. Or so she tells Quin."

"The big guy's interested, but she isn't."

After a few minutes, the man walked back to the Camaro and it sped out of the lot.

When Crandall, Rau, and Betty appeared a while later, Boone suggested they tail the Lincoln, which sounded good to McCleary. He coaxed Flats back into the car with a slice of turkey, the surest way to keep her from barking, and unsnapped her leash. She rode with her front paws draped over McCleary's shoulder and every so often licked the side of his face.

He switched on the Miata's headlights when they hit the main road, then turned east, headed for Thirteenth Street. Just after they'd passed it, Boone stabbed at the window. "There. I saw it. Three cars ahead."

McCleary swung into the left-hand lane, sped up, sighted the Lincoln. Its right blinker was on and an intersection was coming up. He cut sharply between two cars in the right lane and turned seconds after the Lincoln did, onto Tamiami Trail. He was directly behind the car now, where two heads were visible in the rear window.

The Lincoln switched into the left lane, gathered speed. McCleary kept pace, tailing close in case the car turned again, but not too close. Although they were camouflaged by traffic and not as visible as they would have been during the day, the Miata's bright red was hardly subtle.

They turned south, following an older road that was sandwiched between the western perimeter of the FIU campus on the right and the Florida turnpike on the left. McCleary could still remember what the area had looked like twenty-five years ago, before the university had been built. Fields, trees, wildlife, and a deserted military airfield. Now the airfield was all that remained of the old days.

At Southwest Seventeenth Street, the Lincoln hung a right onto the campus. "These turkeys going to school or what?" Boone mumbled. "Only as a shortcut across town."

The recent fiscal cutbacks in education had essentially eliminated night classes during the summer, so there was a scarcity of traffic, either vehicular or otherwise. Many of the buildings were dark and some of the street lamps didn't work. This absence of light, of humanity, gave the place a haunted feel, as if they'd stumbled upon some enclave or town where the residents were mysteriously vanishing.

The lack of light also made it more difficult to tail the Lincoln without being noticed. McCleary dropped back and shifted into third. Headlights struck the side mirror as a car came up behind them, its brights blazing. Flats lifted her head, then slipped away into her space behind the seat, growling softly.

Up ahead, the Lincoln made a sudden left turn and shot away. "What the hell." McCleary sped up, took the turn, shifted into fourth.

The car behind them also turned, its headlights exploding in the rearview mirror. Then it bore down on them, a hungry beast that had suddenly decided they were easy prey, and slammed into the Miata's rear end. The impact hurled McCleary and Boone forward, their seat belts snapped them back, and in the space behind them, Flats alternately snarled and barked. McCleary swerved to the right and floored the accelerator. But up ahead, the Lincoln had slowed and angled across the road, blocking them in, leaving him only one choice. He sped for the curb and the landscaped green beyond it.

The Miata struck the curb, the tires bounced over it, a hubcap was knocked loose and clattered away. They tore through a bed of flowers and ferns and Christ knew what else, and the car charged after them. It was the souped-up Camaro, a blue Camaro; McCleary got a glimpse of it in the mirror before one of the men inside it opened fire.

The first two shots missed. The third shattered the side mirror. He zigzagged to make the Miata a more difficult target, raced between a pair of palm trees, and shouted at Boone to grab the Magnum from the glove compartment. But the old man was already armed, leaning out the window, taking aim with his .38.

The first explosion from the gun reverberated through the darkness but missed its mark entirely. The second destroyed one of the Camaro's headlights. Then the continent of green ended and the

Miata slammed down onto the pavement again. The rear end fish-tailed, Flats howled, Boone squeezed off another shot. But the Camaro kept on coming, a relentless cyclops that swerved as the Miata swerved, turned as it turned, steadily narrowing the gap between them.

Just ahead, the road emptied into the old airfield and the single runway, a straight shot south that would take them into Tamiami Park, into trees, into a maze of roads and footpaths, into darkness. He skidded onto the runway and opened the Miata as wide as she would go.

Something clacked and knocked in her undercarriage, but she didn't falter, didn't fail him. Boone kept firing, Flats kept snarling and whimpering, the Camaro kept gaining on them, the steering wheel shook, the speedometer needle leaped past eighty. "The fucker's still coming!" Boone shouted.

McCleary swung the wheel savagely to the right. The Miata flew off the runway, plunged into the trees, bounced over ruts, potholes. If he could somehow get to Coral Way, they could lose themselves quickly in traffic. But the darkness disoriented him. He couldn't tell which direction he was going, couldn't remember where the nearest exit was.

But Boone remembered. He directed McCleary left, then left again, left where there were no roads, no paths, nothing but grass and flowers. Moments later, the Miata shot out of the park and into the traffic on Coral Way. He hopped from lane to lane to the first intersection, ran a yellow light, a red light, and turned in to the first gas station he saw.

McCleary backed into the space at the side of the building, parallel to the restrooms, and there, in the safety of the shadows, they waited for the Camaro. It appeared less than three minutes later and right behind it was the Lincoln, both cars charging toward the city limits.

16

Six A.M. The pale canvas of the sky was filling quickly with colors, brush strokes of pink and violet, thicker streaks of gold, long spills of rust that arched from one end of Miami to the other. The air was warm and breezy, swollen with the scent of ocean, salt, dead fish that had rotted in yesterday's sun. Waves crashed against the beach as Quin ran, foam hissing around her ankles. As each wave ebbed, it left behind a residue of seaweed and silt in which tiny crabs scurried around.

Albert, she thought, the crabs were acting odd because of Albert. It was as if they sensed what sophisticated instruments could not and knew what the experts couldn't predict, the when, the where, the details. Albert's winds were just shy of hurricane strength, and once he made the leap over that crucial seventy-four-miles-an-hour, his barometric pressure would begin to fall. And as he got closer to land, the dropping pressure would affect the wildlife in more obvious ways.

She had seen it in the behavior of her family's cats when Hurricane Cleo was approaching, the way the cats had hidden, burrowing into closets, clothes, into dark, enclosed spaces. She had heard it in the whimpering of neighborhood dogs, in the strange chatter of birds in their yard. Animals knew and it didn't matter if it was a hurricane, an earthquake, or the death of a loved one. They knew.

So now Albert was out there mulling things over, taking a good, long look at the Florida peninsula, and waiting for the tug of that magnetic attraction toward a particular spot where he would make landfall.

His choices, as she saw it, were divided. He could head for the Keys, which wouldn't slow him down and would keep him for the most part over water, where he would continue to gain strength. From there, he could charge into the Gulf and up the west coast of Florida, ending finally at some favored haunt along the Texas or Louisiana coast. Or he could barrel his way straight through the warm seas between Cuba and the Bahamian islands and slam into Miami with everything he had, sweep across the state, and head straight across the Gulf toward Mexico or veer north toward Texas or Louisiana.

The other possibility, which she believed was the least likely, was that Albert would tear a path across Eleuthera and Great Abaco and make landfall somewhere in the Carolinas. But the Carolinas weren't due and Miami was and Nature loved to balance the books. Besides, in terms of her theory about hurricanes and consciousness, she was betting that Miami would be the final target.

At roughly two miles, she stopped, drenched with sweat, a hand pressed to the stitch in her side. She usually did three miles at home, but she hadn't run since she'd gotten here and now she was paying for it. She made her way up Ocean Drive, and outside Mappy's Café she called Chique Cherries. The receptionist she'd spoken to yesterday had told her the best time to get Helga was after 6 A.M., as she was finishing her shift. A woman answered, her voice slightly accented.

"May I speak to Helga, please?"

"This is Helga."

"My name is Quin, Helga, and Tiffany suggested that I get in touch with you. She—"

"Give me your number," she said softly. "I'll call you right back."

Quin read off the number on the pay phone, hung up. Moments later, Helga called back. "This phone is safe," she said. "What did you say your name was?"

"Quin. I'm a private investigator and I'm looking into the death of a friend of mine. Tiffany thought you might be willing to talk to me about certain things going on at the factory."

"When did you talk to Tiffany?"

"Last week."

"Where?"

"Where she showers."

Helga laughed. "Even the big man himself doesn't know where she showers."

Then he must not have been trying too hard to find out. "Would you be willing to talk to me about the factory?"

"Who do you work for?"

"Myself. I think Mr. Crandall may be involved in my friend's death."

"What was your friend's name?"

"Charlie Potemkin. He—"

Softly: "Yes, I knew him. Look, there's a bar in Little Havana called Un Paso. I can meet you there tomorrow night around eight."

"What about tonight?"

"I can't."

"How will I know you?"

"Ask for Alfonso. Tell him who you are."

"Wait. How did you know Charlie?" *Were you the mystery lady in his life?*

"It's a long story. I'll see you tomorrow night."

She disconnected.

Quin went into Mappy's to order a coffee to go, but as soon as she saw the menu, she claimed one of the twirling stools at the counter and ordered breakfast. Three bucks for bacon, eggs, toast, and coffee. She couldn't afford *not* to eat here.

The walls were covered with sayings that kept the customers occupied while they waited. Among them were: *The South Florida*

Screenwriters' Guild was founded at Mappy's on May 30, 1990. Hemingway never ate at Mappy's, but he would have if the joint had been open. Then there was the inevitable reference to *Miami Vice: Philip Michael Thomas and Don Johnson shot up the joint while filming several* Miami Vice *scenes at Mappy's.*

Crandall's resort, if and when it happened, would be just two blocks down the street from here. He claimed the hotel association on the beach supported the resort, but it didn't surprise her to discover that the family who owned Mappy's did not.

According to the family *abuelita,* a dumpling of a woman with gray hair who ran the cash register, the resort would be the death of Mappy's as it existed now. "And the man, he know this," she said, her hands punctuating the air as she spoke. "Señor Crandall." She gave a disgusted snort. "He come here one morning, yes? He come here in his *guayabera* shirt and his big smile to talk to my son. He invites us to move Mappy's into the resort. My son tell him he not need to move Mappy's. We already have this space, this corner. No, no, the man say. Space on the lake. What lake? my son asks. Oh, just a small lake he be going to build in the resort. If my son sell him this Mappy, then he promise to give him space on the lake."

"Why would Mr. Crandall want this property? The resort is planned for the eleven-hundred block."

Her sparse white brows lifted, looping at odd angles over her eyes. "For now it be that block. But later it be the next block and then this block and then maybe more blocks. Yes? You understand?"

Perfectly. She could see Crandall planning exactly that. To own three entire blocks of Ocean Drive. Not tomorrow, not next month, but certainly within the next few years. And that meant that whatever he had going with the Iraqi would have to pay off in a mighty big way.

Drugs were the first thing that came to mind, but not the street favorites, not coke or crack or even heroin. Crandall, the primo control freak, the man whose dining requirements could drive a waiter or waitress into paroxysms of frenzy within five minutes, wouldn't mess with third parties. Too risky. Especially when the third parties were Colombians or Peruvians with a fondness for terrorist tactics. It would have to be something that could be produced synthetically—in his factory?—and over which he had control. Since one facet of Haddan's vast business interests included the construction of a pharmaceutical company, then maybe pharmaceutical drugs were involved.

If the drugs in question were recreational it seemed likely that Haddan would buy the stuff to be sold somewhere other than Iraq. He was, as Kiara had pointed out, a Muslim who apparently followed Islamic law: no alcohol, no pork, no recreational drugs. He had homes in Paris and New York, places where a market for such drugs certainly existed. He also had the money to buy.

But the pharmaceutical industry was certainly as lucrative as its darker sister, the illicit drug trade. Her own limited exposure, for instance, involved nothing more than antibiotics for her daughter, who was prone to ear infections. A ten-day dose of a penicillin derivative for which a generic drug existed cost as little as ten bucks. At the other end of the scale was Ceclor, for which no generic yet existed, which cost nearly sixty bucks. The big offenders—AZT, certain drugs for cancer, high blood pressure, and so on—could cost in the hundreds for a single dose.

But.

That would require experts on his staff, chemists, physicians, people who had an army of initials after their names. Benson's contact in the company had run a check on all of Crandall's employees and no one with those kinds of credentials showed up. She would have remembered. Rau, though, owned the actual warehouse, so perhaps the business was in his name, which would make it more difficult to get information.

Difficult, but not impossible.

On the walk back to her apartment, she called Benson at home. He was rushed, she heard it in his voice when he snapped hello, and guessed she had caught him on his way out the door. "It's not even eight yet, Tim, it can't be a bad morning already."

"Quin. Hi."

"Got a minute?"

"About that. What's up?"

"Does the name Haisar Haddan ring any bells for you?"

"No. Should it?"

"I don't know. But I think you should check it out." She explained briefly, without incriminating Kiara or the hotel. "Also, we need a list of employees who work at that cherry-flavoring factory."

"That's already in the works. I just got off the phone with Mac. Have you talked to him since yesterday?"

"No. Why?"

He gave her a quick rundown on what had happened to McCleary and Boone last night. They were okay, but the Miata wasn't. "Mac estimates it's got between two and three grand worth of damage."

She saw their insurance rates leaping for the stars.

"The department's going to take care of it," Benson assured her. "I was just on my way out to meet him at the garage."

"Is the factory under surveillance now?"

"It will be by noon."

"We need that list of employees, Tim."

"I'll try to have it by this evening."

"Any word from your federal source about Steve Heckler?"

"Yeah, I just told Mac. Steve Heckler disappeared in February, on a job in southern Colombia. He's presumed dead."

She wondered what Will Boone, the great conspiracist, would say about that. "You trust this source of yours?"

"I don't have any reason not to. But on the other hand, his loyalty is to his employer. Quin, look, we're coming up for budget renewal on July first. The mayor's really riding my ass about hiring two free-lancers for a job he thinks can be done by one. The bill for the Miata isn't going to help matters any."

"So what're you saying?"

"I don't know. I just want you to know where things stand."

"I'm making headway, Tim." She told him about her meeting with Helga tomorrow night.

"Tape the conversation, Quin, and urge her to talk to me. Tell her it's between us."

"I'll see what I can do."

"I need evidence that's going to get a search warrant for the factory and indictments that will stick."

"Give us another forty-eight hours."

"I can probably stall until the end of the week. Beyond that, I can't promise anything."

Today was Tuesday. Not much time, but it was better than the forty-eight hours she'd asked for.

When she got back to the apartment building, a cable-television truck was parked in the lot. She'd noticed it in the neighborhood several times in the past week and, in fact, had seen it as she'd left on her run. Since when did any cable company start making rounds before eight in the morning?

The various meters and power boxes for the building were in a room off the courtyard. The door was open, so she walked over and poked her head inside. Both men had their backs to her and were wearing jumpsuits with UNITED CABLE stitched between their shoulderblades. One appeared to be reading the meters; the other was fiddling with a power box that she knew belonged to Southern Bell.

"I think you've got the wrong box there," she said.

Their heads snapped around simultaneously, as though they were controlled by the same brain, the same set of reflexes. It was like seeing double, like running into Tweedledum and Tweedledee. They had identical chubby faces, identical short, plump bodies, identical expressions. The man on the right—Zeek, according to the name stitched on his pocket—spoke first. "Begging your pardon, ma'am, but we've got some crossed wires." Big smile from Zeek.

"All this rain we've been having," said his twin, Zicky, offering an identical big smile. "Got two complaints from this building."

"You boys have ID?"

"Sure thing, ma'am," said Zeek. "You the building super?"

"Right."

He stepped toward her and she stepped back through the doorway, into the courtyard. Zeek flashed a laminated photo that didn't prove shit, but she wasn't about to press the point. "Well, just checking. You know how it is here in Miami."

Chuckles from Zeek and Zicky. "Sure do, ma'am. You have a nice day now."

She felt their eyes on her as she walked across the courtyard toward her apartment and decided to play it safe. She went around to the back of the building and entered her place through the rear porch. She didn't have a key to the sliding glass door that led to the kitchen, but the pass-through window was unlocked, so she opened it and climbed in.

Wall phone. She picked up the receiver, not sure what she expected to hear. A buzzing like insects, perhaps, or clicking noises or a dead line. But there was only a dial tone. She replaced the receiver, jerked open the kitchen drawer and pulled out the yellow pages. She flipped the directory open to cable companies: no listing for UNITED CABLE.

She dropped the directory on the counter and marched out the front door, speculating about who they worked for. Crandall? The feds? Some other player she didn't know about?

Zeek and Zicky were just leaving the room, tool boxes in hand. "Hey, guys," she said, "maybe you can tell me something."

Zeek's smile was a flash of stained, crooked teeth. "We can sure try, ma'am."

"You work for United Cable, right?"

Zicky spun, offering the name on the back of his jumpsuit. "That's what it says."

"Located in Dade?"

The twins exchanged a glance that telegraphed a message she couldn't decipher. "We're new," Zeek said, then tapped the face of his watch. "If you'll excuse us, ma'am, we've got to shove off."

They hurried away and Quin stood there in the morning heat until she heard the truck pull into the street. Then she walked back to the meter room, wasn't surprised to find the door unlocked, and stepped inside. The box Zeek had been working on was clearly labeled PROPERTY OF SOUTHERN BELL. She popped it open. According to the blueprint on the inside of the lid, the wires to Apartment 6, her place, were yellow and red.

The labyrinth of wires covered half a dozen panels of microchips. She followed the red ones with her fingertip until she located two that had been recently soldered to the panel. Using the tip of a stick she found in the courtyard, she tore them out and tucked them around some other wires so they wouldn't show.

"Pound sand, boys."

• • •

The Miata sputtered and coughed when he cranked her up and sounded like a giant with laryngitis. But at least she started, McCleary thought.

As he pulled away from the curb in front of Boone's place, he saw the Explorer headed toward him. It stopped directly in front of him and Quin swung out, Quin in her running clothes. My wife, not Liz Purcell, he thought as he got out of the car.

"Tim wasn't exaggerating," she said, shaking her head as she walked over, eyes pinned on the Miata.

"When did you talk to him?"

"A few minutes ago." She reiterated their conversation as she walked around the Miata, touching the fender that hung by a single bolt, the broken taillight, the gouges in the sides. He followed, but kept glancing around uneasily, wondering if they were being observed. They stopped at the front of the car and she folded her arms at her waist and asked who was driving the Lincoln last night.

"Your buddy Cindy."

"Was Dave Petrovsky there?"

"Sure. And Rau was in the car." He told her what had happened, an abbreviated version, then said, "I don't think we should be standing out in the open like this. Let's get in the car."

They did and sat there in the bucket seats, at the curb, each of them waiting, he knew, for the other to say something. When he started to speak, so did she, then they both stopped, laughed, and said, "You first," at exactly the same moment.

"You'll need backup tomorrow night," he said.

"For what? We're just meeting in some bar in Little Havana. If anyone needs backup, Mac, it's you for tonight."

"I'll have Bean."

"That's not what I mean."

Mimicking her earlier tone, he said, "It's just some paddlewheel boat on the Intracoastal."

"I hate it when you do that."

He grinned. "Yeah, I know."

She poked him in the shoulder and swung her long legs away from the seat as she opened the door. "Call me in the morning before eight, okay? Or better yet, drop by so I can ravage your bod."

Then she was gone and the faint scent of her skin lingered in the car. McCleary watched her through the windshield, astonished that she had begun to move like Liz Purcell again, to hold herself like Liz. He sat there until the Explorer was nothing more than a wink of aluminum in the bright morning sunlight.

■ ■ ■

The clerk on duty at Mango's was the same young man who had been there the day Tark had checked in. He looked tanner, a deep George Hamilton tan, fit for a poster. Tark wondered if he rushed out to the beach during his lunch hour.

In the old days, he'd known people like that, both men and women who worked on their tans the way other people worked on their investment portfolios. They knew which lotions to slather on before and after, how to maximize the sun's ray with aluminum foil and reflectors, how many minutes each side of their bodies required for an even tan, a perfect tan. Now these fanatics were probably lining the pockets of dermatologists all over South Florida. What the hell, we all have our poisons, he thought.

"I'd like to settle my bill." Tark eyed his room slot for messages and was relieved to see that it was empty.

"Cash or credit, Mr. Gabriel?"

"Cash."

The clerk played the computer keyboard. "Did your friend locate you?"

"My friend?"

"There was a man here earlier this morning who insisted he was a friend of yours and wanted to know what room you were in. I told him it's against our policy to give out room numbers and that I'd ring your room or leave you a message. Then he demanded to see our manager, and when I explained he was on vacation, the guy left in a huff."

"What'd he look like?"

"Short fellow, brown hair." He limned a snout in the air with his fingers. "Sort of a pointed face, like a rodent."

Lamadero. Back from the swamp where Tark had left him and probably looking to get even. "Nope, doesn't sound like anyone I know. But thanks for not giving out my room number." The man handed Tark his bill and he paid it. "Tell me something. Who made the reservation for my room and left the package I picked up the day I checked in?"

"I don't know, Mr. Gabriel. My manager took care of it."

"Is there anything on the computer?"

The clerk checked, shook his head. "Nope. No contact number, no name."

"Is that normal?"

"For here, sure. We're small."

Tark scanned the road as he stepped back outside, but he didn't know what he was looking for: a waiting car, someone watching from a nearby café, something out of place. But it was business as usual along Ocean Drive, traffic and sun and women in string bikinis. No sign that Albert was churning off the coast somewhere, no sign except a hefty breeze.

Lamadero probably had more pressing business at the track. Lamadero, the loose end he should have taken care of when he'd had the chance.

He ran some errands, then drove over to Little Havana. The streets didn't conspire to deceive him this time and he found Un Paso without any problem. The peak of the lunch rush had ended, Julio still crooned love songs from the jukebox, and Alfie was seated in his usual spot under the stained-glass windows, a pitcher of beer in front of him.

Things change and yet never change, Tark thought, and slid in across from him. Alfie looked as if he'd been drinking since sunrise. "Don't ever do that to me again, you son of a bitch."

"What'd I do now?"

"I didn't know how the hell to get in touch with you." His fleshy jowls trembled; sweat glistened on his forehead. "You call me in the middle of the goddamn night with questions and then you don't even leave me a phone number."

"I forgot. I apologize."

Alfie made a huffy sound, then shrugged and poured Tark a glass from the pitcher. A peace offering. All was forgiven. "*Salud*, Gabby."

They clicked glasses. Tark sipped at his beer, watched Alfie chug his, and thought of his dream. He wished for a glimmer, an impression, something that would hint at Alfie's future. But the voice within was silent now.

The old man saluted the stained-glass window above them. "Once more I tempt God. I think it may be the thing that I do best, Gabby. Tempting God."

"He was here?"

Alfie laughed. "God? I hope not."

"Lamadero."

"Oh." He flicked his hand through the air, dismissing Lamadero. "That *pendejo*. I don't want to talk about him." More softly now: "Carmen came to me last night."

Her name became a magical incantation when it fell from Alfie's mouth, the quick roll of the "r" that seemed to gather momentum until it almost overtook the "m." It was the perfect name for the woman who had enriched Tark's own life beyond imagining, but it terrified him to hear his dead wife's name spoken beneath the stained-glass window.

"She came to me while I slept, Gabby." Alfie's hands cupped his glass of beer. His eyes were fixed on a point just to the right of Tark's shoulder. " 'Papa,' she says. 'Papa, wake up.' And I saw her, Gabby, I opened my eyes and saw her standing at the foot of my bed. Teresita was with her. It's the first time she's ever brought Teresita."

Tark didn't say anything.

Alfie's eyes slipped back to Tark's face, smiled slightly. "I know, I know. I drink too much."

"You said it, *amigo*, I didn't."

"Well, it's true." He refilled his glass, all business now. "The *pendejo* struts in here like he owns the place and wants to know where you are, how he can get in touch with you, and when I tell him I don't know, he starts threatening me. *Me*, Gabby, the *pendejo* actually threatened me. I told him not to show his ugly face in here again and tossed him out."

"Was Lamadero alone?"

"He came in alone. What the hell did you do to him, anyway? His face and arms were scratched to shit. He was covered with bites."

"Got some answers and left him in the swamp."

Alfie exploded with laughter. "Good place for a *pendejo*." Another gulp of beer, then: "What I wanted to tell you, Gabby, was that yesterday I saw my friend who wired the cherry-flavoring factory. When he was doing the job, he got friendly with a German woman who works there, Helga Bucholtz. Turns out she's working on an expired green card and she's afraid to go to the cops with something she knows or suspects about the factory. She wants help and my friend was wondering if I had any suggestions. I talked to her early this morning and she's going to drop by here tomorrow night at eight. You interested?"

"Definitely."

"Then be here by seven-thirty."

A normal man, Tark thought, would be sleeping it off by sundown of any day when he'd been drinking since breakfast. But Alfie had never been a normal man. "You got it."

"Someone else will be here, too, a woman named Quin."

"Who is she?"

"Helga says she's a private detective who's investigating the professor's murder."

Liz Purcell? If so, then things were going to get real interesting very fast.

"I figure the four of us can have a nice chat, eh, *amigo?* We find out what she knows, then I send her to my good friend in the immigration office."

"I'll be here."

Alfie's eyes followed Tark as he stood. "Tell me, Gabby. How do you sleep at night? How do you sleep without hearing the explosion? Without seeing the glass as it shatters? How do you fall asleep without all that?"

Tark started to tell him that Sunday night was the first night in years that he hadn't dreamed. But the old man would question him and Tark didn't want to mention Estelle. He knew Alfie would see another woman as a betrayal of Carmen's memory. Perhaps, in some dimly lit pocket of himself, that was how he also perceived it. So he simply said, "I don't, Alfie."

He turned his glass of beer slowly in his hands and gazed into it as though the pattern of foam against the sides could tell him the future. A gypsy with his tea leaves.

"Last night when she came, Gabby, she promised it wouldn't be long. Not long at all."

"Not long for what?"

Alfie didn't answer, didn't look up. He'd slipped into the dark place where booze took him. The early-afternoon light streamed through the stained-glass window overhead and fell around him in designs of blue and gold and crimson. Tark squeezed his shoulder and left the bar with the past tightening like rubber bands around his heart.

17

Voices, Heckler thought. He heard the distinct murmur of voices. But coming from where?

He got up from his bed, lowered the volume on the TV, tiptoed to the door. Ear pressed to the wood, he listened. No voices on the stairs. No one headed this way.

Frowning, he turned slowly and realized the voices were coming from the AC vent he'd opened a few minutes ago. It was one of three in the room and he usually kept it shut except in the late afternoon, when the sun beat against this side of the house. It was on the north wall, about a foot up from the floor. He crouched in front of it, straining to make out what was being said, and realized he needed something to amplify the voices. He hurried into the bathroom for the Styrofoam cup he kept on the back of the sink. Then he sat on the floor again, placed the top of the cup to the metal grate and pressed his ear to the bottom. Summer camp. That's how old this trick was.

He moved the cup around, a physician with his stethoscope, seeking the spot where he could hear their voices most clearly. He heard Pisco first, fresh from Miami with his report on Lamadero and the tracker. Initially, he talked about how difficult it had been to locate Lamadero in Miami, the trouble he'd gone to, each step detailed as though he hoped to impress Kilner with his cleverness, his dedication. Then he got to the specifics.

". . . Gabriel nabbed him at the track, hauled him out to the Everglades, and started shooting at him and demanding answers. Lamadero swears he didn't say anything, but I have my doubts."

"Just what does Lamadero know about you?" Kilner asked.

"Next to nothing."

"That's too goddamn vague, Dan. Does he know who you work for?"

"No."

"Where you live?"

"No, nothing like that. We've always met at the track."

"I don't like it."

The air conditioner clicked on, muffling their voices. Heckler shifted positions and pressed his other ear to the glass, waiting for the AC to click off. When it did, he still couldn't hear well and guessed they had moved to the other side of the room. Finally, he heard Kilner's voice again. "How'd he react when you told him to get rid of Gabriel?"

"Hell, you kidding? He was stuck in the Glades for six hours and had to thumb a ride home. And there I was telling him he'd get paid for knocking the guy off. He said it'd be taken care of within the next forty-eight hours."

Heckler's hand slipped and the cup dropped to the floor. He swore, snatched it up, repositioned it. Their voices were barely audible now; they had moved again. *Back this way, guys, c'mon, c'mon, please.*

The phone rang and Kilner picked up before the third peal. Heckler couldn't make out what was said. But when his muffled conversation with Pisco didn't resume, he guessed Pisco had left the office. He moved quickly away from the grate and was sitting at the foot of his bed, staring at the tube, when there was a knock at his door and Pisco let himself into the room.

The late-afternoon light struck his face in such a way that he seemed younger somehow, a teenager in a man's body. "Figured you'd be outside fishing, Steve."

"Your substitute isn't much of a fisherman. I asked for my pills and he brought me back here."

Pisco jammed his hands into his pockets and shuffled over to the chair near the bed. He didn't sit; he slouched in it like a man with a guilty conscience.

"Who'd you get stuck with?"

Heckler told him and they talked for a few minutes about some of the employees and other patients. The narc from the DEA who was strung out on coke and had blown a sting in Manhattan; the woman from the FBI who had been putting away a quart of rum a day; the colonel from Air Force Intelligence with the valium habit.

Then Heckler asked how the trip to Miami had turned out, and Pisco, eyes on the TV, just shrugged. "Okay." He pulled his right hand from his windbreaker pocket and tossed a rusted pocketknife on the bed. "It's old, but the blades are sharp. Stash it someplace safe. Kilner's on the phone now with LeFrank and I got a feeling you're the main topic. If the order's come down, I don't think I'm going to be the guy Kilner picks to carry it out."

Heckler didn't reach for the knife but could barely wrench his gaze away from it. *Setup,* whispered a voice at the back of his mind. "So I'm supposed to take the knife and then come clean about what I know out of some sense of obligation or loyalty to you? Then you run back to Kilner with the information. Isn't that the agenda, Dan?"

But the expression on Pisco's face said otherwise. He looked like a man who had glimpsed what lay ahead of him on this particular route to the future and had decided he didn't want any part of it. "Think what you want." He pressed his hands to the arms of the chair and pushed himself to his feet. "I don't even know what the game is anymore."

"Sure you do, Dan. The game never changes. You take orders and carry them out."

"Then I guess I'm just tired of taking orders."

He was nearly to the door when Heckler spoke.

"Does LeFrank know Gabriel is going to be knocked off?"

Pisco turned, his eyes narrowed, the blue one pinned on Heckler's face, its brown partner drifting slightly to the right of center. "How—"

"Because I've been in this business since before you were out of diapers, that's how. Does LeFrank know?"

"No."

"Does he know about this Lamadero fellow?"

Pisco shook his head and moved away from the door. "No. He leaves the details to Kilner."

"Sit down, Dan. And listen good."

Pisco glanced at the door, then at Heckler, hesitating, then he sat down. He was either a consummate actor, Heckler thought, or dumb as dog shit when it came to this business. He hoped to hell it was the latter.

. . .

"Want to take a ride?"

Quin glanced up from the papers on her desk. Betty O'Toole stood there in a demure shirtwaist. Her hair had drooped from the humidity, her makeup looked damp. Odd, Quin thought, that a woman could have such an attractive face and yet look so frumpy.

"A ride where?" Quin asked.

"To pick up Mr. Rau."

Betty in the mood to talk? To confide? Maybe to confess to something? "Sure." She plucked her purse out of a desk drawer and slung it over her shoulder as she got up. "How come Cindy's not driving?"

"She's picking up Mr. Haddan. They're all going out tonight."

The Jungle Queen.

"We're taking Larry's car," she said on their way downstairs.

"I thought the Lincoln was his."

Betty gave her a small, secretive smile that hinted at the chest of wonders in Crandall's world to which she'd been privy. "That's the company car. The Beamer's his and happens to be my personal favorite."

And what a fine car it was, at least sixty grand worth of leather and comfort. The quadriphonic sound miraculously transformed music, any kind of music, into an epiphany. The sunroof whispered open at the touch of a button. With the flick of a switch under the dashboard, a panel slid back on what Quin had mistaken for the glove compartment and a computer screen appeared. It was as round as a lozenge, glowing like a full moon. Betty punched a three-digit code on the panel next to it and a black grid materialized. A tiny bright ball blinked across the grid.

"That's us," Betty said. "We're in Zone Two, which covers everything west of the causeway to the interstate."

"I thought these things were experimental."

"They are. This cost Larry almost as much as the car." She giggled, actually *giggled*. "Makes you feel like you're in *The Terminator*, doesn't it?"

"Is it just his toy or what?"

"His toy?" She laughed. "Hardly. Larry's gizmos always have a purpose. He drives this car when he's got someone with him he wants to impress. Let's say he wants to check out something he owns in Zone Four, okay?" She punched a four-digit code on the panel, the screen cleared, another grid appeared. "Zone Four is everything between the university and the Everglades."

"Which university?"

"Florida International. See that pulsating black dot? That's one of his buildings." She hit another button and the address printed out in sharp black letters across the bottom. The address for the factory. It had an asterisk next to it.

"It's pretty far west of the action. What is it?"

"Oh, just an old warehouse." She quickly punched two more buttons, clearing the screen, then pressed another number. A new grid lit up. "Zone One. South Beach. How it looks now, okay? The Neon Flamingo is the blip closest to the left; the eleven-hundred block is off to the right." Everything but the Sea Witch. The old Tuttle Inn had an asterisk next to it, just like the factory.

"What's the asterisk mean?"

"A connection between two or more pieces of property. They might be priced in the same range or on sale simultaneously or completely paid for or under mortgage by the same bank. It varies."

"What's it mean in this case?"

"I don't know."

She knew everything else about the program, but not this? Quin wasn't about to call her on it; things were getting too interesting. "Does it just cover Dade?"

"For now. But I guess it could be programmed for virtually anywhere. What's really neat is that it's impossible to get lost in Dade if you're in this car. Using the keyboard under the dash, you enter the address you're looking for, the computer locates it on a map of Dade, then shows you the easiest route."

"Seems like Cindy should have taken this car. Mr. Haddan would probably be impressed by this."

"He's the one who turned Larry on to it. In New York and Paris he's got cars that are equipped with this system."

"You've seen them?"

"Yeah. Larry took me on a couple of trips."

"How'd Haddan make his money?"

"Originally in oil, then he expanded."

"Is he one of Larry's private investors for the resort?"

Betty looked over at Quin. "You really ask a lot of questions."

"It's a bad habit I developed when my marriage fell apart and I realized I hadn't asked enough questions."

Betty turned off the computer and changed the subject. "Look, I'm really sorry about the way I acted on Saturday, Liz. It's just that Larry and I, well, on weekends, we, uh . . ."

"Usually work alone," Quin finished for her.

"Yes."

"How long have you two been having an affair?"

She hesitated, apparently uncertain about how candid she should be. "Off and on since before his divorce. He's had other flings, but he always comes back to me."

Quin just nodded.

"I guess Cindy told you all about Tiffany, huh."

"She mentioned her. But I heard more from a clerk in a lingerie store in Marathon than I did from Cindy."

"Eve's Delights?"

"Yes."

"He ought to just press charges against her for grand theft or something. She's put something like eight or ten grand on his store accounts since the divorce."

"Maybe he's afraid to press charges."

"Afraid? Why would he be afraid?"

Quin shrugged, playing it close. "Maybe Tiffany knows something that Larry doesn't want to come out in court."

"Like what?"

"No telling."

"That he's involved in something crooked, right? Isn't that what you're saying?"

"I'm just speculating, Betty."

They stopped for a light in Coral Gables. "Well, you're wrong."

And love is blind. Or perhaps Betty really didn't know anything. Or maybe she did and the suspicions that had grown from that knowledge now terrified her.

"I hope so. I just think it looks a little strange that the old man who was causing Larry headaches and delays over the Sea Witch got murdered."

"Professor Potemkin? You think Larry *killed* him?"

"I'm just telling you how it probably looks to people. Stop putting words in my mouth, Betty."

She gave a small, nervous laugh. "Larry's no killer."

Horns blared; the light had turned green. Betty sped through the intersection and didn't slow down. She whipped in and out of turns, raced through two yellow lights, ran a red one, and charged through a stop sign. The BMW clung to the road like a spider, its speedometer needle springing toward seventy.

"You'd, uh, better slow down, Betty."

She didn't. She was leaning into the steering wheel, gripping it so hard her knuckles were white. Tears coursed down her cheeks and her entire body seemed to shake in an effort to hold them back.

"What is it?" Quin asked gently. "What's wrong?"

She just shook her head, unable or unwilling to speak, and suddenly pulled into the right lane and swung into a gas station. She stopped next to an air hose, dug Kleenex out of her purse, blew her nose.

"I'm . . . I'm okay. I must be getting my period or something."

Or something. Yeah, tell me about it, Quin thought.

"Everything seems so . . . so screwed up."

"With Larry?"

"I think he's screwing Cynthia."

"I doubt it. She told me he wasn't her type."

Betty looked at Quin, hope bright in her damp eyes. "She said that?"

"Yes."

"Then how come she's the one who goes everywhere with him? He didn't ask *me* to go on the Jungle Queen with them tonight. He didn't ask *me* to go up to Palm Beach with them to meet Mr. Haddan."

But, according to Benson, Betty had accompanied Crandall and Rau to the factory last night.

"Cindy's his chauffeur."

"But what's she ever done for him, Liz?" The naked pleading in her voice bordered on hysteria. "Has she ever covered his ass? Has she ever lied for him? Has she ever put him first? Has she? Huh?"

Would you kill for him, Betty? "Trust me. She's not screwing him."

It was as if she hadn't spoken. "I know how it is with him, Liz. He gets rid of women when he's tired of them. That's why he's gone through so many secretaries and personal assistants. But he'd better not try to get rid of me. He just better not try." She started the car, revving the motor. "He better not," she finished softly.

Because you know too much, don't you, Betty?

■ ■ ■

The boat stood at the Fort Lauderdale dock, a carnival of lights against the cloudy evening sky. The Jungle Queen: a misnomer if there ever was one, McCleary thought. Jungle had never existed here, only swamp that had vanished decades ago. But there was something majestic about the boat, a double-decker paddlewheel that would be more at home plying the Mississippi than these polluted Intracoastal waters.

He and Bean waited in the dock's parking lot, inside the beige Chrysler the department had provided when his car had gone into the shop this morning. Bean was squirming in his seat, worse than a five-year-old on a car trip. "No Crandall, m'man, and we were the first ones here. Maybe he's not boarding in Lauderdale."

"The dinner cruise doesn't make any other stops, Joe. It goes straight south, turns around just past the Dade line, and heads back."

"Then I say we get on board and wait."

"Let's give it a few more minutes."

Four more cars drove into the lot. One of them was the blue Camaro that had slammed into the Miata. Crandall's bodyguard stepped out, Dave Petrovsky, the Schwarzenegger clone. He walked over to the passenger side as his partner emerged. He was shorter, with a body as compact as a brick, and blond hair pulled back into a ponytail.

A white Cadillac appeared moments later and pulled alongside the Camaro. Cindy Youngston was at the wheel and was the first to exit. Gone was the casual attire; the lady looked as if she'd stepped off the pages of *Vogue* and was ready to boogie. Next came Rau, then Haddan. The last person out—from the front passenger seat—was a woman in a red-and-white dress with a black lace shawl around her shoulders. Her white hair was swept up off her shoulders and gathered at the back of her head in a way that set off her long neck and dangling earrings. Despite the clothes, the hairstyle, and McCleary's shock at seeing her here, he recognized her: Clara Villa, the *santera*.

■ ■ ■

Quin followed Betty's dark Buick through evening traffic, west off the beach, then south on the interstate to Coconut Grove. Although she didn't appear to be in any particular hurry, she didn't linger at intersections, didn't stray from the main road, and didn't stop until she swung into a public parking lot. Quin drove past, found a metered space two blocks later, then hoofed it back to the street where Betty had parked.

She spotted her hurrying north past the shops and cafés, a woman with a definite destination in mind. Quin tailed her at a discreet distance, grateful that it was dark. But Betty was oblivious; she seemed so swept up in her own thoughts she probably wouldn't have noticed Kevin Costner if they had bumped into each other. In front of the Coconut Grove Playhouse, she slowed, then paused at the curb and glanced up and down the street, as though waiting for someone.

Quin ducked into the doorway of a café and watched through the glass. Within five minutes, a navy-blue Mercedes double-parked across the street and a man with salt-and-pepper hair got out. Betty hurried toward him, then both of them stood there in the spill of the streetlights, arguing. He was lean, under six feet tall, and casually but expensively dressed. He kept his hands in the pockets of his slacks, nodding or shaking his head to whatever she was saying, then they got into the Mercedes and drove off before she could see the license plate.

Quin hurried back to the lot where Betty had left her Buick, pulled out the set of keys Charlie had given her way back when, and found one that fit the lock. Seconds later, she slid behind the Buick's steering wheel, shut the door, and turned on the overhead light.

The mess inside appalled even Quin, whose own vehicle was certainly no paragon of neatness. There were wrappers, empty soda cans, crumpled cigarette packs, cassette tapes strewn across the dashboard, coffee stains on the passenger seat, a trash bag jammed to overflowing. Her nail file opened the locked glove compartment, which wasn't much better than the rest of the car. Tattered maps, a set of keys, a few letters dated more than a year ago from Aunt Ethel, who was so proud of Betty for "making something of herself." Whatever that meant.

At the bottom of the heap of papers was a wallet that contained some rather interesting items: a thousand bucks in hundreds, a scrap of paper with a phone number scrawled on it with a 301 area code, and a photo of Betty with the man with the salt-and-pepper hair. They were standing side by side, the man's arm loose around her shoulders, both of them smiling, posing for the camera. They didn't resemble each other in the least, but there was something about the picture that suggested a father-daughter relationship.

Quin jotted down the phone number, then returned everything to the way she'd found it and quickly left the car. Before she went, she checked the trunk. It had been used so infrequently it looked almost new and contained only a spare tire, a flashlight, a jack, and several flares. Not much to go on, she thought as she hastened out of the lot and headed back to where she'd parked the Explorer. For all she knew, the guy with the salt-and-pepper hair was actually Betty's father and right about now they were sitting in some fancy restaurant having a steak dinner.

But the longer she thought about it the more wrong it seemed. There had been a furtiveness to their meeting, the way the Mercedes had driven up, the way Betty had ducked inside, the way they'd driven off. She discounted the possibility that they were lovers; Betty was hardly the type who could juggle simultaneous sexual relation-

ships. And by the time Quin reached her apartment building, she
didn't believe they were father and daughter, either.

She stopped at the pay phone in the courtyard and opened the
phone book to the map of the U.S. where the area codes were listed.
Betty had once told her she was originally from Arizona, but 301 was
an area code for Maryland. She called the number on her credit card
and on the third ring a woman answered.

"Good evening. LeFrank residence."

LeFrank, LeFrank, who the hell was LeFrank? "Uh, is Mr. Le-
Frank home?"

"No, he isn't. May I take a message?"

"When do you expect him back?"

"I'm not sure. He's away on business."

"Oh. I was supposed to call and . . . well, do you have a forwarding
number?"

"Your name?"

What the hell. "Betty. This is Betty."

"Ms. O'Toole. I didn't recognize your voice."

"My allergies are acting up."

"I know how that is. I don't have a number for him, but he'll be
phoning in for his messages, so I'll tell him you called."

"No, that's all right. Don't bother him. He'll probably get in touch
with me. Thanks again."

She hung up before the woman could say anything else, debated
about calling Benson with the information, then decided to wait until
tomorrow. When she turned around, Tark was striding toward her
through the courtyard. He was wearing jeans and a windbreaker, the
collar turned up against a breeze that smelled of rain. He smiled as
he greeted her, a quick, mercurial smile that could snag a woman's
heart in seconds flat.

"You were right," he said.

"About what?"

"Jerboa's a word."

"O ye of little faith."

"You won't believe what the J stands for. I finally asked her."

"Jezebel?"

"Nope."

"Jewel?"

"Nope."

"Not this again."

"Jazz."

Quin laughed. "No wonder she's strange." But in all fairness to Jazz Link, she thought, *Quin* wasn't much better.

"You free for a rematch tonight?"

She wondered, suddenly, what it would be like, the two of them in her apartment or his, matching wits, eating dinner, loosening up, maybe even walking on the beach, holding hands, touching. She'd sometimes imagined herself with another man, but he'd never had a face, a body, any sort of reality beyond what her imagination conjured. Now he did.

Now he was standing in front of her, in front of Liz Purcell, who was divorced and available, and she thought: What if? What if she nodded and said sure? What if they went inside, had dinner, and discovered they had a million things in common? What if they ended up in bed? What sort of lover would he be? Would she be different with him than she was with McCleary? *What if?*

She realized she was staring at his hands, at those long fingers that she could almost feel against her own skin, stroking, burning, igniting a kind of teenage lust in the center of her. Tark, a juncture, she thought, and quickly raised her eyes. "I'm so bushed tonight I'm brain dead. Maybe tomorrow."

"Sounds good."

His disturbing hazel eyes never strayed from her face, and for a moment, she had the distinct impression that he *knew* Liz Purcell was a fraud and was about to say as much. "Got to run," she said. "See you tomorrow."

It started to sprinkle as she stepped into her apartment and shut the door. She had intended to call her sister tonight, to check on Ellie before they headed out for Disney World tomorrow. But she didn't want to go back outside and run into Tark again. She was afraid he had guessed Liz was a fraud, afraid that he saw right through her, afraid that she might change her mind and invite him in.

She decided to call her sister in the morning, early, before Tark or anyone else would be up, before Ellen and the crew left for Disney World. She would spend the evening listening to the latest storm advisories, tracking Albert's progress on her hurricane map, trying to fit the pieces together, and she would not, she absolutely would not, think about what-ifs that she would never act on.

18

The paddlewheel churned her way south beneath a quarter moon
and stars that shimmered like sequins against the black cloth of the
sky. But in the distance, lightning flashed through mounting thunderheads, signaling the approach of a storm that was sure to squelch the
evening's festivities, McCleary thought.

With seventy-five to a hundred people on board, it wouldn't be too
difficult for him to stay clear of Clara Villa, the only member of
Crandall's entourage who could recognize him. She was at a table at
the front of the ship. Although she was sitting with Cindy and Haddan, she seemed to be quite separate from them, as though she didn't
want to be here. And yet her presence implied more than a passing
acquaintance with Crandall.

McCleary and Bean stood at the railing on the east side, away from the band and the huge buffet table that had been set up on the open deck. "The noise is going to be a problem," Bean said.

"Maybe not." McCleary tilted his head toward the glass-enclosed bar and the tables inside. Crandall and Rau were at the end of the bar. "It should be quieter in there. Let's try it."

Bean strode off and McCleary turned to the railing again to fit the receiver's earphone in his ear. Within a few minutes, he heard static and glanced around. Bean was at the bar inside, his body angled toward Crandall and the German so the mike could pick up their voices more clearly. McCleary rolled his thumb across the volume knob on the receiver. Noises reached him with surprising clarity, ice tinkling in glasses, laughter, chairs and stools scraping across the floor, voices.

Bean was now about ten yards from Crandall and Rau. McCleary recognized the German's voice by his slight accent, and for several minutes listened to the two men discussing stocks, that was all. Stocks. Then Rau told Crandall it was a mistake for him to invite Clara Villa.

—*The woman makes him uncomfortable, Larry. You know how these people are. Their religion forbids fortune telling.*

—*C'mon, Ebo, he doesn't have any idea who she is.*

—*He suspects. One only has to look at her to suspect she isn't like the rest of us.*

—*He doesn't have to like her. He doesn't even have to talk to her. She's here because I . . .*

—*I know, I know. You trust her. You want her impressions. That's fine, my friend. That's fine. All I'm saying is that this eccentricity of yours could cost us.*

—*It's your job to make sure it doesn't, Ebo.*

—*How the hell do you expect me to do my job when you don't inform me about your plans? Tell me, Larry. Tell me that. I'm not a goddamn mindreader like Clara.*

—*Give it a rest. She's here. She'll do her job and you do yours. You fix things. You smooth it over. I don't care how you do it, just do it.*

—*A small sample might make amends.*

—*Your memory's damn short. He's already gotten a rather large sample and we've yet to see any money for it.*

—*That was merely a courtesy.*

—*Fuck the courtesy. I . . .*

—Shut up and listen to me, Larry. That courtesy sample was enough to convince Haisar that he wants to do business with us. He would like to buy everything we have and whatever we can produce over the next four years. But after tonight he may change his mind, he may decide you're not the man with whom he should do business. Forty to fifty million, my friend, over the next four years. Okay? Are you convinced now? I don't care how you deal with Clara. Tell Cindy to bring her in here, tell her to go away, I don't care. Just do it. Haisar is serious. He's already opened an account at our bank in the Caymans. A phone call tomorrow morning will transfer three million into our account as a courtesy. A courtesy, Larry. The other seven will be in cash upon delivery. So do what—

Part of the conversation was lost here as the two men turned away from the bar. They headed toward the door at the other end of the room that led to the open part of the deck. Bean hurried along after them. Crandall was saying something about the terms yet to be discussed. Then they pushed through the doors and music blasted in the earphone. McCleary removed it from his ear and watched Bean do an aboutface, a black arrow headed this way.

■ ■ ■

Heckler knew something was up when he heard the jingle of keys outside his door and Kilner walked in without knocking. How quickly the rewards for good behavior were snatched away, he thought, when the head man figured he'd gotten all he was going to get. He wondered what would be next. Freedom of movement? Meals? Bathroom privileges? Or maybe this time Kilner would really get down and dirty and use some of the tricks he'd undoubtedly learned during his long career in the spy biz. Cattle prods, water torture, slivers of wood jammed under his nails and set afire. Heckler put nothing past the man.

"Your manners suck, Jerry. LeFrank would be disappointed. You know how meticulous he is about manners."

"LeFrank's the only reason you're still alive, Steve."

How right you are. "He owed me a few. Not that you can count on what he owes you." Then, more softly, he said: "So what's he offered you, Jerry? An appointment as his campaign manager when he runs for the Senate again? Or maybe his sights are higher now, like the White House. But it doesn't really matter, you know, because he'll dump you before it happens and find some other lackey to take your place."

"I doubt it." Kilner was smiling as he strolled over to the window and gazed out into the rainy dark. "Elliot usually honors his obligations, particularly if he's prodded."

Heckler laughed. "And you're going to do the prodding? With what? He's Mr. Clean."

"Not quite."

The first flutters of fear brushed across Heckler's heart, but it didn't leak into his voice. "Fascinating. Dissension in the ranks. He must've pushed all your buttons, huh, Jerry. And I bet one of those buttons had to do with your operation here on Long Key. It's going to be shut down due to budget cutbacks. Something like that."

Kilner didn't say anything; he didn't have to. The look in his eyes told Heckler everything he needed to know about the things that Kilner feared.

"Well, no great loss, Jerry. As far as I can tell, your rehab center here doesn't do all that much rehabilitating. In fact, I'd venture a guess that what you do best here is silence security risks. You give the order, Pisco or someone else carries it out, and bingo, a burned-out case from the CIA or the FBI or the AFI disappears and then you clean it up on the computers and who ever suspects? The family's told their beloved died in the line of duty and of course they're taken care of with pensions and life insurance and whatnot. Am I warm yet, Jerry?"

Kilner's smile was a shark's, all teeth. "Like Charlie once said, someone's got to do the dirty work. And just for your information, you're listed on the computer as missing in action and presumed dead. So I'll make a deal with you, Steve. Tell me who helped you obtain the information you passed to Charlie and you walk with a new identity within twenty-four hours after Crandall's business deal is done."

Sure I do, Jerry. Heckler thought of the pocketknife under his pillow, of how easy it would be to just slide it out and sink the blade into Kilner's neck. Nothing, he thought, would give him greater pleasure. But he knew he wouldn't get very far after that. If he was going to escape, it would be due to decisions Kilner would make when he left this room. Decisions, he thought, which he could influence by what he said now.

"Okay, Jerry, let's go through it a step at a time, just like Charlie used to talk about way back when. Remember those days, Jerry? Remember how Charlie used to stand up there and talk about the steps? *Ask the right questions:* that was step one. So let's look at the questions, Jerry. How did I get access to highly classified information?" He paused, giving Kilner a chance to respond. When he didn't say anything, Heckler went on. "You don't want to take a guess on that one, Jerry? Okay, let's look at it another way.

"Elliot LeFrank knew Charlie and I had been in contact. He knew I had access to certain sensitive material because he'd given me that access. He also knew where I'd most likely head with the information and assigned one of his young goons to tail me. And that goon could've nailed me at any point along the way. He could've nailed me when I was meeting with Charlie. But he didn't do it until *afterward.*"

Color had leaked out of Kilner's face, he was rolling his lips, his hands were clenched, and he seemed incapable of speech. Heckler ventured into pure speculation now, but Kilner didn't know it. He was beyond the point where he could make such a distinction. "Don't you see it yet, Jerry? If LeFrank's going to be running for public office again, he's going to have to clean house very thoroughly. He set you up, Jerry, by having Charlie knocked off. You."

A beat passed. "Since you've got it all figured out, who killed Charlie?"

"Interesting question, Jerry, and that's the bottom line, isn't it? But you can be damn sure Elliot didn't do the dirty deed himself."

"You don't know."

"Remember Charlie's primary axiom? If you can't find the answer, it's because you haven't figured out the question. So I'll give you the question. Where're you most vulnerable?"

Kilner drew back as though Heckler had struck him. "You don't—"

"Are you absolutely sure that the not-so-sweet young thing you've planted in Crandall's office is working for you and not for Le-Frank?"

Astonishment burned in Kilner's eyes with the power of a living thing. "You're bluffing, you don't know anything."

"You hope."

"You bore me, Steve."

Kilner marched out of the room, slamming the door behind him. When Heckler heard the soft click of the lock, he slid his hand under the pillow and brought out the pocketknife. He flicked open the longest blade and touched his finger lightly against the edge. It was sharp, all right, just as Pisco had said. And when the time came, it would serve him very, very well.

■ ■ ■

While Joe Bean made his way through the buffet line, McCleary stood at the back of the railing, well out of the *santera's* view. Now and then, his thoughts seemed to rise toward something significant, something he could seize, tear apart, analyze, fit with other pieces. But the moment always passed and he was left with a few facts, a great many suspicions, and nothing solid to connect them.

In any investigation, it always came back to an individual's connections with other people, to the intimacy of those connections. Links in a chain. Charlie and Clara, Charlie and Boone, Charlie and R.D., Charlie and Crandall, Charlie and Helga and Tiffany. And of course, Charlie and Heckler, where it had begun.

But there was another layer, too, Crandall and *his* connections, his links, his secrets. Crandall and the information about him that Heckler had given to Charlie. Heckler, he thought. Find Heckler and he would have the missing link. He might as well undertake a quest to prove that God was alive and well on South Beach. Heckler, after all, was presumed dead.

The sagging sky suddenly tore open and rain poured down. McCleary moved back under the awning and watched the mad scramble for cover on the open deck. In the confusion, he lost sight of Bean and of Crandall and his crew. The narrow awning under which he stood was now crowded with people. He felt someone brush up behind him, and when he looked around, the *santera* pressed something into his hand, then quickly lost herself in the crowd.

McCleary opened his hand. The note was scrawled on a cocktail napkin:

> *Meet me inside Salgado's Market tomorrow at three.*
>
> *Clara*

It rained off and on throughout the night, a noise that initially lulled Quin into a soft, velvety sleep. She dreamed about McCleary and Tark, surreal dreams in which both men were aliens whose faces and bodies, whose very identities, were interchangeable.

But it was a dream about Charlie that woke her, Charlie weeping as he lay dying on her linoleum floor. She came to with her cheeks wet with tears and an ache in her chest for the friend and mentor she had lost. Charlie, who symbolized everything that was old and traditional on Miami Beach, and Crandall, the visionary who would destroy it all.

She tossed and turned for a while, dozed fitfully, but the thunder and rain kept waking her. She finally got out of bed and turned on the TV in the living room for an update on Albert. He was a hurricane now, all right, with winds of eighty-five and a tight, well-defined eye. He was also moving forward again, finally, pushing slowly westward at a meager five miles an hour. He was expected to pick up speed and would probably change directions; it was rare that a hurricane traveled in a straight line. But in the event that his direction didn't change, he would make landfall somewhere around Biscayne Bay by late Friday night or early Saturday morning. Three or four days from now: that was an eternity in the life of a hurricane. Wait and see, that was the name of this part of the game.

Wait. She had never been much good at that.

As she showered and fixed breakfast, she made mental lists of things either she or McCleary should do if and when a hurricane watch was posted for the coast. According to the experts, a watch was the time you were supposed to pay close attention to the advisories and simply check supplies like flashlights and propane stoves.

But to Quin the watch was as good as a warning. It meant fill the car with gas (the pumps probably wouldn't be working afterward because of power failures), stock enough water and food to last a week, buy flashlights, batteries, plywood, check the hurricane shutters, turn the fridge up as high as it would go, learn the evacuation routes. McCleary, naturally, would accuse her of being an alarmist and would remind her that a watch simply meant a hurricane was threatening land, not that it would strike. But by doing all these things during a watch, you had a jump on the panic buying if the watch became a warning; even McCleary couldn't argue with that, could he?

It was still drizzling when she stepped out into the courtyard at five to call her sister. Ellen was up and preparing breakfast, just as Quin had expected. She said all the right things, naturally, to assure her that Michelle would be fine. The fact remained, though, that Michelle didn't seem as far away when Quin could imagine her in her surroundings. All she had to do was close her eyes and conjure her in her cousins' playroom. But on the highway, in Fantasyland, in a hotel Quin had never seen, it wouldn't be the same. The distance would loom, a continent of asphalt she would be unable to cross. That frightened her.

"We'll keep an eye on the hurricane advisories," Ellen said. "If it threatens South Florida, we'll just stay in Orlando with Hank's aunt. Hey, there's a little girl here who wants to say hi, Quin."

Michelle sounded so small at first, that soft voice, the uncertain words. Then Quin told her that Flats missed her almost as much as Mommy did. She laughed with delight and apparently clapped her hands, because the phone clattered to the floor. Ellen got back on and gave her the number where they'd be staying. Quin didn't want to hang up, didn't want to break the connection, but she heard one of the kids wailing in the background.

"Got to run, Quin. Talk to you tomorrow."

Quin hung up and immediately called Boone's place. When McCleary answered, he sounded like he was six hundred feet underwater, his voice weighted with sleep. He'd gotten back late last night and not too much had happened. Could she call him later? No, she thought, talk to me now, talk to me this second, please.

"I'll call you this evening after work. By then we should know more about what the storm's going to do," she said.

"The storm?"

As if this was the first he'd heard about it. *Pay attention, Mac.* "Yeah, you know, Hurricane Albert."

"Oh, right." Yawning. "I wouldn't worry too much about it. He isn't doing much of anything. Look, I've got to get some sleep, Quin. I'll talk to you later."

"Ellie's leaving today. Maybe you should call and say goodbye."

"I called last night."

Well, then. "Flats okay?"

"She's fine, really. Is something wrong?"

Wrong? Whatever made you think that? No, no, of course nothing was wrong. Her daughter was going to Disney World without her, a scourge was churning somewhere off the South Florida coast, she had been tempted to invite Tark in last night, but no, nothing was wrong, nothing at all. "Talk to you later," she said, and hung up with her throat tightening and her eyes burning.

Behind her, a voice said, "I'd like to talk to you a minute."

A figure rose from the wooden bench in front of the trees. Not until the person neared did Quin realize it was Tiffany Crandall, the collar of her raincoat high against her neck, a man's wide-brim hat pulled low over her forehead, the spill of the courtyard's dim lights painting her face a nicotine color.

"Tiffany."

"I trusted you." She marched over, arms swinging, hands balled into fists. "I gave you a lead and you fucked me over."

"What're you talking about?"

Her eyes floated in their shadowed sockets like black olives in oil. She wasn't just pissed, she was a fruitcake on overload. "The cops," she spat. "I'm talking about the cops. You told them where I was, didn't you? They were crawling all over the marina today, five, six, seven of them. That's who you're working for, the cops. If I'd wanted to talk to the cops, I would have."

"Look, I told you—"

"You're a lying bitch!" The words flew out in a spray of spittle and she lurched toward Quin like a drunk. Her arm jerked up, a fingernail file hooked like a talon in her hand. It tore down the inside of Quin's left arm as she blocked the blow and let her right fist fly. It struck Tiffany in the jaw, snapped her head back, knocked her hat off. She stumbled, tripped, and went down.

Quin walked over to her, rubbing her hand, wondering if she'd broken it, blood streaming down her other arm. "Let's get something straight, asshole. I'm interested in who killed Charlie. For all I know, you may have set me up with this Helga lead."

Tiffany, sprawled on her buttocks in the dry leaves, blinked against the drizzle, and wiped blood from her lips with the back of her hand. "You don't know what you're up against."

"So you've said."

"I didn't file for divorce, Larry did. I confronted him with something and he gave me a choice. A settlement of fifty thousand or my body would end up in the canal."

"In your first version, it was seventy-five grand and he was knocking you around. So pardon me if I find your credibility somewhat questionable, Tiffany. Come back when you've run out of bullshit."

Quin left her chasing her hat and went into her own apartment. She locked the door and hurried down the hall to the bathroom to tend to her arm. Benson, she thought. This was Benson's fault. She'd told him about Tiffany and he'd gotten right on it. She was tempted to call him and chew him out, but the mere thought exhausted her.

The rain was coming down harder when the doorbell rang fifteen minutes later. Quin figured it was Tiffany with a postscript, with one more fiction to deliver before she went on her way. She threw open the dead bolt and yanked the door open, prepared to let the ex-Mrs. Crandall have it. But the twins stood there, Zeek and Zicky in their drenched, identical jumpsuits, water rolling down their noses, their cherubic faces smiling, smiling.

An alarm shrieked at the back of her head. She tried to slam the door, but one of them stopped it with his foot. Then they were on her faster than she thought possible, moving in flawless synchronism as one grabbed her by the arms and the other slapped something wet and cold over her mouth.

Chloroform. Don't breathe don't breathe don't . . .
She sank.

19

"I think this is a big mistake," Boone said. "You can't just go barging in there at eight in the morning, Mike."

"Watch me."

They were in the loaner from the department, cruising down Washington toward the *santera's* place. Boone, who had forgotten his sunglasses, was hunched over the steering wheel and squinting against the intermittent but bright morning light. Flats was in the backseat, her snout poking through the open window and lifted into the wind. As they approached the *botánica*, splashing through puddles from last night's rain, Boone slowed.

"Look at that. No cars out front. I told you it was too early."

"Go around the block," McCleary said. He wanted to be absolutely sure that Clara Villa wasn't under surveillance.

Boone hung a left at the light, circled, and started down Washington again. There were cars, but they were parked and empty and probably belonged to the residents of the buildings along the street. Satisfied, McCleary asked Boone to pull over and let him out. "Park around the corner and wait."

"For how long?"

"As long as it takes. If you see anyone arrive, send Flats through that gate and into the courtyard." He pointed at the driveway, where the iron gate stood open.

"How's she going to know where to go?"

Flats, aware that they were talking about her, stuck her nose between the seats and whimpered. McCleary stroked her head and smiled as he pulled a handkerchief out of his back pocket. "Give her this, tell her to find Mac, and point her in the right direction."

"Right."

He took the hanky and held Flats's collar as McCleary opened the door and got out. The Chrysler whispered away and McCleary headed for the front door of the *botánica*, then changed his mind and walked through the iron gate. He shut it until there was a space wide enough for Flats to squeeze through, and walked on into the courtyard. It was deserted—no people, no goats, no chickens, no caged doves, nothing at all but a heavy, weighted stillness broken by the cough of the air conditioner in the aluminum shack.

He glanced toward the back door of the shop, at the windows above it, then walked over to the shack. He pressed his ear to the metal, hearing nothing. You, he thought at the *santera*. You're the connection, the center of it, the focus, the heart. He turned the knob and opened the door.

The small wooden table was filled with candles, all of them lit, flickering and hissing in the cool air. The statues were arranged in a circle, with Margarita Ordóñez and her grandmother seated inside of it on low wooden chairs. Both were dressed completely in red and white. Both were barefoot and puffing on cigars.

Margarita's head snapped toward him, but before she could rise or speak he stepped into the room and shut the door. Clara Villa seemed oblivious of his arrival, his presence, of everything except the soft click of her tongue against her teeth as she leaned forward and snapped her fingers close to the floor.

"You have no business here," Margarita said softly but with authority.

He couldn't wrench his gaze from the old woman, from the flowing white of her hair, the spread of her legs, her bare feet flat against the floor. She looked like some sort of mythological being that had taken on flesh, bones, reality.

"This is private, Mr. McCleary. I'm asking you to leave," Margarita said.

"Your grandmother has answers that I need."

She blew a cloud of smoke toward him, her head tilted back, contempt bright in her eyes. "If she had any answers, we wouldn't be in here. Now I want you to—"

"What's she doing?"

A resigned sigh. "Calling Fernando."

"Who's Fernando?" He leaned against the wall, watching, fascinated by the sight of the old woman puffing on the cigar, blowing smoke, tapping a wooden staff against the floor.

"Her guide. Two hundred years ago, he was a slave in Cuba. His creature was a snake; she calls the snake by snapping her fingers, and if the snake hears her call, then Fernando comes through. He's the sentry at the gate and decides which *orishas* may speak through her." She set the cigar at the edge of the table, picked up a bottle of Florida water, poured some into her palm, and flicked it at her grandmother and at the floor where the staff tapped and tapped. "Watch her left leg, Mr. McCleary. Fernando had a wooden leg. His left leg."

He watched, watched as Clara's left leg began to move, to stretch out, watched as she dropped the cigar to the floor, stood, and hobbled over to the table like a cripple, leaning heavily on the staff. She picked up a fifth of gin, spun the top, and tilted it to her mouth, drinking deeply. Then she threw her head back and began to laugh, a man's laugh, deep and crude.

"You," she said in a harsh, guttural Spanish, in a voice that was nothing like a woman's. The staff lifted from the floor, pointing straight at him. Her glassy eyes were fixed on his face. "You want to believe, but you find it difficult. You need proof, you always need proof." She hurled the bottle of gin to the floor. It knocked over one of the wooden statues and shattered. Shards of glass twinkled in the lambent light and the stink of gin suffused the air. "I, Fernando, will give you proof, *señor*."

She walked barefoot across the bits of glass, her eyes pinned on him. He heard the broken glass crunch under her feet, but if she felt it she gave no indication. She snapped her fingers at Margarita, who held out her own cigar. Clara took it, puffed on it as she moved toward McCleary, then ground the glowing end against the skin on her inner forearm. He smelled the burning flesh, was nauseated by it, and nearly lurched toward her and knocked the cigar out of her hand. But her eyes had paralyzed him. She stopped less than a foot from him and held out her forearm.

"Touch," she said in that same voice, that masculine voice.

He brushed away the ashes; the skin beneath was soft, white, uninjured. Now she lifted her right foot. Slivers of glass protruded from the sole, but there was no blood. She snapped her fingers at her granddaughter again and Margarita leaned forward and removed a piece of glass with her fingernails. It was as if she'd pulled it from a slab of rubber. He could see the hole where it had been, could see it clearly, a hole large enough to accommodate his thumbnail, but again there was no blood, and as he watched, the hole began to close.

"I protect her," said the voice. "She is my consort, my love, my chosen. No harm comes to her when we share this body. Ask your questions and go."

He opened his mouth but nothing came out. Clara, Fernando, whoever the hell she was, started to laugh again, threw her head back and laughed until the sound of it filled the shack and pounded against the walls of his skull. She turned away, dismissing him, then stopped when he asked, "Who killed Charlie? Tell me that. Who? Was it you, Clara?"

She spun around, her body lean and powerful, no longer old. Her lips pulled away from her teeth in a grin that was mocking, savage, frightening. "You know nothing, *gringo*." She spat the words. "Nothing." Then suddenly her face contorted, seized up, and she doubled over, whimpering, and sank into the low wooden chair. She groaned, clutched her arms to her waist as if consumed by a terrible pain, and whispered something he couldn't hear. He moved closer, awkwardly, as though his own legs were wooden. The odors, the light, the weirdness, his own eagerness: it all made him dizzy, lightheaded. His eyes flicked from Clara to Margarita.

"What is it?" he whispered hoarsely. "What's she saying?"

"Shut up!" Margarita snapped, blowing smoke at her grandmother, flicking Florida water at her, then murmuring words in a language McCleary had never heard, but which he knew was Yoruba.

He dropped to his knees in front of her, dropped into the shards of glass, and grabbed her by the arms. "What?"

Her head snapped up, her eyes blazed, and his hands dropped to his sides. Her mouth fell open, and when she spoke, it was in English, in a pained but familiar voice that would haunt him the rest of his life. "Christ, Mac, be careful, be careful, you've got no idea . . ."

Charlie's voice. Sweet Christ, this was Charlie's voice, the same tone, the same inflection, the same soft hoarseness. Charlie. Tears sprang into his eyes and something tore open inside of him and through it seeped a million questions, contradictions, pains. If Charlie could speak through this woman, then so could his dead sister, of course of course, Cat's voice, please, that was all he wanted to hear, just once, now, immediately.

He didn't realize his fingers were digging into Clara's arms, that he was shaking her, begging, pleading to hear his sister. Margarita swept over him, jerking him back. His hands fell away from the *santera*'s arms and she emitted a soft, choked sound and slumped off the wooden chair, melted off of it like some sort of alien creature.

"What have you done?" Margarita shrieked and dropped to her knees in front of him, blocking his view. "Get out of here, go, just get out!"

He scooted back on his knees, through the glass, through the stink of smoke and gin and the putrid odor of his own confusion, back, back toward the door, away from the old woman, her granddaughter, away from the fixed, cold eyes of the statues.

The door swung open and he lurched outside and nearly stumbled over Flats. The sheepdog barked and leaped at him, his handkerchief hanging wetly from her mouth, then trotted toward the iron gate, stopped, barked at him again. He stood there stupidly, blinking beneath a sky that had clouded, then hurried after Flats. As they emerged from the courtyard, he saw Crandall's mocha-colored Lincoln at the curb and the man himself walking toward the front door of the *botánica*. Crandall, alone. Crandall, who had also come for answers. He glanced at McCleary and for the instant that their eyes connected he was sure Crandall recognized him but couldn't place his face.

Last night, asshole. The Jungle Queen. McCleary averted his eyes and followed Flats to the right, away from Crandall and the *botánica.*

■ ■ ■

Quin was cold. She couldn't move, her bladder ached, and there was a needle in her arm. She couldn't see the needle, something blocked her view, but she felt it, the sharp discomfort, the cold seepage into her vein. And she could see the IV line to which it was connected, a rubber snake that blurred as it climbed into the twilight above her head.

Quin heard something to her right, footsteps, voices, and quickly shut her eyes. *Where am I?* Dreaming. Yes, that was it, she had awakened inside a dream. She willed herself into someplace more pleasant, the mountains, a beach, a lake in the woods, but the landscape didn't change. The voices were closer.

Something nagged at her, but she couldn't bring it into focus. Her head felt as if it had been stuffed with mildewed rags, the back of her throat ached with dryness, her stomach was cramped with hunger. *Remember, remember.*

Why couldn't she move?

Open your eyes.

No. The voices were too close. The voices frightened her. She didn't want to see.

The pressure against her ribs, chest, and arms grew worse and her eyes flew open. She was tied down. She saw a face. A man's face. Blurred at the edges. When she tried to speak, nothing came out. Her tongue felt thick, heavy, swollen like a bloated corpse.

Then, the voice: "I think she has something to say, Dan. Give her a sip of water through the straw."

Her head lifting. Something sliding between her lips. Water, Christ, water that was cool, silky, a balm that eased the ache at the back of her throat. "Please," she croaked, and wondered what she was asking for. More water? Answers? Release? All of the above, take your pick, please, please.

Now the face leaned closer to her. The man. She saw his bald head. His strange dark eyes. His constipated mouth. "You're probably feeling quite relaxed right now," he said. "And that's how it should be. I'm going to ask you a few questions and I'd like you to answer them to the best of your ability. The drip will impair your speech a little, but don't worry about that."

She sounded inebriated when she spoke, vowels and consonants sliding together as though they were interchangeable. "Who'reyou?"

"Kilner, the name's Kilner."

Kilner Kilner Kilner. The name bounced like a Ping-Pong ball against the walls of her skull. And on one of those bounces, this name snagged another. Zeek. Then Zicky. And with that, it all came back to her, Zeek and Zicky, the fat twins.

Guess what, Quin. You're in deep shit.

"What's your name?" he asked in that same soft, even voice.

Liz Purcell. The name was right there, trundling down her tongue like a semi, but that wasn't what she said. "Quin St. James."

Wrong wrong wrong.

"And you also go by the name Liz Purcell, isn't that right?"

Nope. "Yes." Dear God, what was wrong with her? What had happened to the connection between her brain and her mouth? What?

"And besides Larry Crandall, who're you working for, Ms. St. James?"

"F-f-f . . ."

"What was that?"

"Fo-for myself."

"Yourself." A chuckle from Kilner. "Speed up that drip, Dan." Then: "Let me rephrase the question, Ms. St. James. Who hired you to investigate Crandall?"

Pentothal, that's what the drip was. Sodium pentothal. She'd had pentothal once before, she remembered this clearly, remembered sitting in a dentist's office with pentothal rushing through her veins while an impacted wisdom tooth was dug out of her lower jaw. When the procedure was over, the dentist had asked her a simple question, an innocent question about how she felt. And she'd told him, yes, indeed, she'd really told him, *You're a butcher.* No small courtesy, no punches pulled, just the unvarnished truth as she'd seen it right then.

As she saw it now.

Kilner repeated the question.

"Tim Benson."

"And what's his position?"

"Chief of Metro-Dade police department."

"And what are you supposed to find out about Mr. Crandall?"

She told him.

More questions followed and she answered them, answered them all. But she seemed to be outside of herself by then, like a ghost observing a loved one from the life she'd left. Yes, it was a little like that, like death, like sliding into and out of darkness, the landscape slipping past in a blissful blur. Then the pressure against her ribs and chest was eased and she moved away again, deeper into the darkness, where she stayed.

She came to in a puddle of warm sunlight, in the stink of her own urine. Her eyes darted around the room, taking inventory. A chair, a table, both bolted to the floor. Concrete walls paneled in wood. A metal door. Two windows that were covered with black metal-mesh gratings, with heavy blackout curtains pushed to one side. Bottom line: no way out.

Those were the broad strokes. But the finer details were worse. There was a straitjacket lying on the floor against the baseboard. A pair of handcuffs hung from either side of the brass headboard, and her left wrist was locked into one of them.

Quin could maneuver it enough so she could sit or stretch out on her back, that was it. She was still in the same clothes she'd been wearing when Zeek and Zicky had grabbed her, soiled clothes that smelled. She was also minus her belt. Her panty hose had been removed, her shoes were nowhere in sight, her bladder had already let loose, her stomach was cramped with hunger. The inside of her mouth felt like she'd been eating sand. A thick sourness coated the back of her throat. She had a vague memory of a needle, of a man with a bald head, of her own voice talking, talking, talking. She thought it had happened this morning sometime, but she wasn't sure. Maybe a day had already passed.

By shifting positions on the bed, Quin could see the adjoining bathroom: no door, a sink, the corner of a tub but no curtain, a towel on the rack, the toilet, lid shut. On top of it were folded clothes, objects that looked to be toiletries, a small black bottle that was probably shampoo, a hairbrush, a bar of soap. For the guests, she thought. As if this were a hotel.

A hotel with handcuffs on the headboard for those guests who were into bondage. She started to laugh, but it sounded so frantic, so close to collapse, she shut up.

Deep breaths. Close your eyes. Flex your fingers, your toes, think about nothing.

But the light pressed against her eyes and she opened them and stared into it. Afternoon light. Yes, okay. And she could hear the wind outside and the hiss of the air-conditioning as it poured out of an overhead vent, and now footsteps. The bald man?

No, no, she remembered his footsteps were quick, purposeful, those of a man in charge. There had been another man, too, Dan Someone, but it was Kilner she remembered most clearly and the footsteps she heard now weren't his. These were a shuffle, those of a fat person. A very fat person.

The black woman who entered the room was definitely fat. Fat trembled when she smiled, shook when she moved, fat swung back and forth under her arms as she set a tray of food and clean sheets on the table.

"Bet you're anxious to get out of those nasty cuffs, aren't you, hon? They always are, yes siree, they always are. But I'm 'sposed to make sure you understand the rules before we do anything else."

"I think the rules are pretty clear."

She waddled over to the foot of the bed; her plump fingers curled around the brass bar. "No shouting. No temper fits. No throwing food. When you're asked a question, you answer. If you break the rules, it's back in the cuffs and they sedate you. There's a right way and a wrong way to go through detox."

"Detox?"

"Doesn't matter what your demon is, this detox works."

"I'll take your word for it."

"You understand the rules?"

"Perfectly."

"Good, that warms Gracie's soul, it does." She pulled a key from a pocket in her voluminous housedress and unlocked the handcuff. She helped Quin to her feet and over to the table as though she were handicapped. "It's long past breakfast, but I figure breakfast is always the best place to start. And this is one of Gracie's personal favorites, it is. Pancakes, slices of that good Canadian bacon, homemade muffins, hash browns, grits, cin'mon coffee, fresh orange juice. We'll put some meat on those bones of yours, hon, we sure will. You eat and Gracie will strip this bed and put clean sheets on. I can see no one thought about your bladder." She clicked her tongue against her teeth. "I'll have to talk to Mr. K. about that."

Quin's hunger was so extreme she wolfed the food down. Nothing in her life had ever tasted so good. Nothing.

"Best not eat so fast, hon. Seen grown men in detox get mighty sick on a meal like this.'

"Where am I?" she asked in between bites.

"Long Key."

South of Marathon, south of Miami, south of just about everything except Key West and Cuba. "Who's the bald man?"

"Mr. Kilner. Dr. Kilner, actually, but no one calls him that. He's in charge of our little facility here." She stood nearby, beaming as Quin ate. "Knows whatever there's to know about detox treatment."

"Treatment for what?"

Gracie got a good chuckle over that one. "They all say that. 'Treatment for what, Gracie? What drug problem, Gracie?' Got to tell you, though, hon, you look better than most who come through here, yes siree, you do. What agency you with?"

"Agency?"

"You know, CIA, FBI, NSA, CID, DEA. There're so many."

Fourth rule: when you're asked a question, you answer. Even if you don't know the goddamn answer. Yeah, she was getting the hang of it. "None of those."

"Well, it's a good sign you're not suffering from a wicked temper like some of the cases I've seen."

"You know all the patients here?"

"Sure do. I cook their meals."

"How many patients are there?"

"We've had as many as twenty at one time, but in my opinion that's pushing the limit. Can't tend to them the way they should be with that many."

That didn't answer her question, so she pushed on. "How many now?"

"Oh, I'm not 'sposed to say." She was now changing the sheets on the bed. "But it's a good sign you're asking so many questions. That shows a healthy interest in your environment. Got one man who never asks questions, just watches TV all the time or goes fishing with Mr. Dan."

Mr. Dan: the spook equivalent of Mr. Green Jeans. Christ. She took a stab in the dark. "You ever heard of Mr. Heckler? He and I worked together for a while."

Gracie raised her head, astonishment scrawled all over her face. Then she quickly went back to what she was doing. "No, no, I don't recall a patient by that name."

"Is he okay, Gracie? Please tell me if he's okay. He's really a good friend."

Silence. She snapped a clean sheet as she unfolded it and didn't look at Quin.

"Please," she whispered in the most despairing voice she could muster. "It would really help me to know."

Gracie smoothed the top sheet over the mattress and tucked it in at the bottom.

"We . . . we were working together on this job." *Make it good.* "We got separated, it was my fault, I made the wrong choice, and I never saw him again. I thought he . . . he was dead. He's not dead, is he, Gracie?"

Silence, then: "No. But there's probably times he wished he was."

"Is he all right now?"

She sighed and let her bulk sink onto the edge of the mattress. "I can't talk about this. Not right that I should talk about it." She shook her head and kept right on talking. "But that Mr. H., he's been a tough one, all right. When he first came here, he gave me an awful time, throwing his food around, shouting like the devil himself had him."

Goddamn, keep her going. "And now?"

"He's better. Stronger. And he's learned the rules. He's outside, swimming and fishing with Mr. Dan." She brightened. "That's how it is here. You follow the rules, you get privileges."

"Has he been discharged yet?"

"No, no, he's still got a ways to go."

Heckler, here.

"Now don't go asking me to pass any messages or anything like that. Can't do it. Just can't." She pressed her palms to her huge thighs and pushed up from the bed. "I've said enough already. Mr. K. will be around sometime to talk to you and it's best if you don't mention our little conversation. I'll be back later with your supper. Maybe tomorrow you and I will go out for a walk around the compound. It's a real pretty place. You'll see."

"Do you know what the latest is on the hurricane?"

"That's Mr. K.'s department."

"You haven't heard anything?"

"I'm not allowed to say, hon. When you get to a certain point in the program, then you get TV and newspapers and whatnot. But you just arrived. You have to work your way like everyone else."

"Right. I understand. And thanks, Gracie. You've really put my mind at ease."

"Guess so, just look at that plate, ate every last crumb, drank every last drop." She pulled a white plastic garbage bag out of a pocket, picked up the paper cup, the paper plate, the plastic spoon, then deposited them inside the bag, and slung the bag over her shoulder. "You'll be wanting to take a shower. There's plenty of hot water and I left you some clean clothes. They should fit. I'm washing the clothes you were wearing. You won't find shoes, Mr. K. doesn't allow them until you've come along a ways. You'll find everything you need."

Everything, it turned out, except a razor and a hair dryer and a belt for the jeans. Everything, in fact, that might be a potential weapon was absent.

Once her physical discomforts were relieved and she had showered and dressed, she began a detailed inspection of the room. The door appeared to be steel and was as smooth as a newborn's skin except at the spot where Gracie had placed her hand to open it. When Quin touched her own palm to the depression, nothing happened. Computer-controlled. There were no loose floorboards, the AC vent was large but not large enough to squeeze through even if she could reach it. A single bare bulb graced the ceiling. The table was almost directly under it and she could probably reach it if she stood on the table. But exactly what the hell would she do with it? Break it and threaten to slit the throat of the next person who walked in here?

Too risky. She suspected that even Gracie was armed. If she did anything at all with the bulb, it would be toward evening, when the blackout curtains would block the fading light. She tested the light switch, climbed onto the table, and discovered that yes, she could reach the bulb. She stripped the covers from the bed, inspected the mattress, the box springs, and measured the distance between it and the floor. She learned everything there was tᴏ learn about the two rooms to which she was confined.

But what bothered her most was that, for all she knew, the meal she'd just consumed might have been her last before execution.

■ ■ ■

Kilner stood in front of the TV in his office, listening to a meteorologist deliver the latest hurricane advisory. He turned the volume up and rubbed absently at the hard knot in the center of his chest.

". . . Albert continues on a westward course with top winds at a hundred and twenty-five miles an hour. His forward speed is slightly higher, six miles an hour. The slower the storm moves, the greater the possibility of a storm surge if the hurricane makes landfall along the South Florida coast. There's still a chance, however, that the high-pressure system to the north will intensify and push Albert farther to the south so he would miss the coast entirely. A hurricane watch is now in effect for the Bahamas. South Florida residents are advised to stay tuned to their local channel for further developments."

Kilner jotted down the latest coordinates on his own map, then sat back, studying the progress of the storm since its birth as a tropical depression several weeks ago. Evacuate now or wait?

Wait, he thought. Wait until a watch was posted for the Florida coast.

"Mr. Kilner?"

He glanced toward the door, where Pisco was standing. "Yeah, Dan, what is it?"

"Gracie wants to know what you'd like her to do about the woman's dinner."

The woman, Heckler, the other patients, Crandall, Haddan, so many details to keep track of, to make decisions about. "Dinner at six, a hypo at eight."

"Of pentothal?"

"No. Something to make sure she sleeps through the night. I don't want any trouble."

Pisco nodded, he always agreed, and yet Kilner saw something in the man's strange eyes that he couldn't pinpoint, couldn't define. Something that disturbed him.

"What about the cops?" Pisco asked.

"What cops?"

"She said she was working undercover for the cops, sir. Now she's missing, that could create problems."

"I doubt it. Besides, that's my problem, not yours."

"Yes, sir."

Pisco turned away and Kilner went back to his map, the coordinates, the storm, and tried not to think about cops, about problems, about any of it.

20

"You sure it was Charlie's voice?" Boone asked for the umpteenth time.

"Positive," McCleary replied.

"Hey, she's a *santera*," R.D. said. "That's what they do—they talk to the dead, the dead talk through them."

The three of them were in Boone's kitchen fixing dinner, the animals hovering nearby for handouts. "I say she faked it," Boone opined. "She'd been around him enough to fake it."

"Shit, General. She's the real thing. Take my word for it. You don't stay in business as long as she has if you're a phony. Not around here."

Boone smiled and shook his head. "Kid, I don't believe in ghosts and that's what we're talking about here. A ghost that possesses some woman's body and speaks through her. Uh-uh, sorry."

McCleary didn't bother joining the discussion. There was nothing to be gained by trying to convert Boone. He was as adamant in his beliefs as people on both sides of the abortion issue were in theirs. Besides, McCleary was no longer entirely certain what he had heard or whose voice had said it, and in the end what difference did it make? The point was that Clara Villa knew a great deal about all this which she hadn't told anyone and he wanted the information.

The peal of the phone interrupted R.D. and Boone. "You want to grab that, Mike?" the old man asked. "It's probably for you, anyway."

McCleary expected to hear Quin's voice when he picked up the receiver; she'd said this morning that she would call after work and he still hadn't heard from her. But it wasn't Quin. It was Clara Villa, speaking softly, hesitantly.

"I apologize for what happened this morning, Mr. McCleary."

He walked out into the hallway, stretching the cord as far as it would go, and addressed her in Spanish. "Save the apology. I want answers."

"I understand. Can you meet me tomorrow at two? At Salgado's?"

"I went by there today and you didn't show." He had waited, in fact, for thirty minutes, hoping she would appear but knowing, somehow, that she wouldn't. "Why should I waste my time again, Mrs. Villa?"

"Because I have what you need. Because Don Carlos wants it this way. Because I can no longer carry the burden alone. Because I am being watched."

"I'll be there."

She hung up and for seconds he stood there with the receiver tight against his ear, listening to the voice in his memory, Charlie's voice saying, *Christ, Mac, be careful, be careful, you've got no idea . . .*

■   ■   ■

Tark thought she looked as German as her name. Helga Bucholtz was tall, large-boned, with bold facial features and short auburn hair. She wore black Levi's, a striped cotton shirt, and black canvas shoes that squeaked as she paced.

They were in a back room off the kitchen in Un Paso and she kept pausing at the door to glance at the wall clock in the hall. She finally shrugged and settled at the table. "We might as well get started, yes? I don't think that woman is coming."

He'd apparently been wrong in his assumption that Liz Purcell was "that woman," as Helga put it. Otherwise she would have been here. But before he shut the door to the room, he poked his head out into the hall and scanned the dining room. Affluent Latinos, affluent gringos, affluent tourists. No Liz Purcell.

He shut the door, turned on the ceiling fan, and opened the pair of windows that overlooked the alley behind the building. The AC vents in here weren't working right and it was oppressively warm.

He sat across from Helga. Alfie claimed his spot at the head of the table, tore a sheet off the legal pad in front of him, and gave it to Helga. "That's the name of the man you should see at the immigration office, Ms. Bucholtz. I've already spoken to him and he'll expedite matters with your green card."

She seemed surprised that he upheld his end of the bargain before she'd told them anything. "You're a man of your word, Mr. Ruiz. Thank you. Thank you very much." She folded the sheet of paper and slipped it into her purse. Then she looked at Tark with open curiosity. "I know you're Mr. Ruiz's son-in-law, but what is your interest in all this? Were you a friend of the professor's?"

"No. I'm just trying to piece together the facts about his murder."

This apparently satisfied her and she began to talk. More than two years ago, she'd been working in an import-export store in Berlin for a man named Ebo Rau. He knew that she wanted to come to the States to work and said he had a job for her at a cherry-flavoring factory in Miami. The pay was excellent, he would take care of the paperwork, and was she interested? Three months later, she was an employee of Chique Cherries.

"My first day, Mr. Crandall spent a couple of hours with me. He showed me around the factory and explained that I would be cleaning the building six nights a week. *Cleaning.* He showed me exactly what he wanted done, how it should be done, and what areas were restricted. I was not to talk about my job or the factory to anyone.

"I was most insulted and told him Mr. Rau had promised me a job, not menial labor. He seemed disappointed by my attitude and asked if there was anything he could do to change my mind. He said Mr.

Rau had spoken so highly of me that he believed I would be an asset. So I told him that if the pay was high enough, I might be prompted to stay. He offered me fifty thousand a year with many benefits and a cash bonus of five thousand at the end of each year. So here I am.

"And six nights a week for the last two years, I have swept and mopped floors, cleaned vats, scrubbed sinks, and emptied trash cans while wearing special clothes and a face mask. I was told the clothing and mask were to protect me from the chemicals used in the extraction process."

"Extraction from what?" Tark asked. "What's the flavoring made from?"

"Peach and apricot pits and the kernels of bitter almonds."

"What about cherries?" asked Alfie. "Aren't they used?"

"Yes. They're brought in from Mr. Crandall's cherry farms. My understanding is that the type of pit or kernel used depends on the byproducts they need at the time."

"What kind of byproducts?" Tark asked.

"A compound that is used in inks, carbon papers, copier ribbons, things like that."

"And they sell these things?"

"So Mr. Rau has told me."

"How much cherry flavoring has been produced since the factory opened?"

"Four hundred pounds."

"You've actually seen the stuff?"

"Yes, certainly."

"Who was it sold to?" Alfie asked.

"I don't know."

Tark had a sudden impression of a sealed room, a mental image so lucid and detailed he could see the sheen of the metal door. "What about this area that Crandall said was off limits? Did you ever go in there?"

"Twice. It was at the back of the factory. In the front room were dozens of metal drums and empty wooden crates with labels on them that said, PRODUCE. KEEP REFRIGERATED. I thought they were the crates the cherries had come in from Mr. Crandall's farms, but they were too new. There was another room beyond this one but I couldn't get into it. It had a steel door and a computerized security system."

"Did you ask anyone what was inside?"

"Naturally. But no one knew. Or if they did, they weren't saying. Then a month ago, after a day off, I came in to work and found the restricted area empty, the steel door standing open. It's been open ever since. I have no idea what happened to whatever was inside."

Alfie asked how she had met the professor and she smiled. "Quite by accident. I've been taking courses at the University of Miami to improve my knowledge of this country, yes? We were studying the Kennedy assassination and I was at the public library one day looking for material for a term paper. The librarian told me about an old man who lives on the beach who used to work with Jim Garrison. So I went to see him. William Boone."

The old gumshoe, Tark thought. The professor's chess buddy.

"Professor Potemkin was there that day. They were playing chess. It's a game I enjoy, yes? So I challenged the winner. The professor won, then he and I played. We became friends, good friends once he discovered that I worked at Chique Cherries. I eventually found out that he believed the factory was a, how do you say—"

"A front?" Tark offered.

"Yes, yes, that's it. A front for the production of illegal drugs. About this same time, the professor had tracked down Mr. Crandall's ex-wife. She also believed he and Mr. Rau were producing drugs and was supposed to get copies of papers or something that would support this. But she disappeared. I guess she was scared. The first I'd heard of her in months was when this woman Quin called me. She said she was a private detective who was investigating the professor's murder."

"When did your green card expire?" Alfie asked.

"Last Friday. Mr. Rau had been promising me all along that he was taking care of the renewal. But when I saw him on Monday, he handed me a check for three months' wages and a ticket back to Germany. He said the factory was closing because the money has run out and that my old job is waiting for me. Today was my last day."

"You didn't have any hint that they were closing the factory?" Alfie asked.

"None. But I don't think it's being permanently shut down. My feeling is that they're going to replace the staff and begin production again, perhaps in the fall."

Someone knocked on the door and one of the waitresses stepped into the room holding a briefcase. "Excuse me, Señor Ruiz. But a busboy found this briefcase in a booth. There isn't any name tag on it. What do you want me to do with it?"

"I'll put it in the safe." He heaved himself to his feet. "I'll be right back. Helga, Gabby, do you want anything to eat or drink?"

They both declined. Helga asked where the bathroom was and Tark walked over to one of the windows. A handful of customers were headed to their cars. Most of them looked to be YUCCAs—Young Up and Coming Cuban Americans—who were decked out in gold and the latest fashions. He was aware of a hard, tight pressure at the back of his head and suddenly realized what it was. The window. Wasn't this the window in his dream? But in the dream Liz Purcell had been standing here with him, his hand had been touching her arm, and—

As he spun around, Alfie's name at the tip of his tongue, an explosion tore through the room. A wall crumbled, part of the ceiling collapsed, Tark was hurled back. He heard screams, cries, shouts, then a second explosion shuddered through the building, plunged the room and the hallway into darkness, and knocked him to the floor. His head struck something. Dazed, fighting to remain conscious, he struggled to his feet, shouting Alfie's name, stumbling over debris. Then he smelled smoke, fire, and gas, Jesus, *gas*, and knew the building was going to blow.

He hurled himself against the screen that covered the open window, struck the ground, leaped up and charged toward his Honda on the other side of the alley. The place blew before he reached the car, four or five rapid explosions that flung greasy plumes of smoke and flames into the sky and belched out chunks of concrete, wood, metal.

Tark dived between the two buildings, where the Honda was parked, curled up in a tight ball, and covered his head with his arms to protect himself from the flying debris. Something crashed into the Honda's roof, crushing it like a tin can and shattering the windshield. He rolled, jumped up, and raced away from the car, the smoke, the shrieks, away from the last vestige of his past.

He kept to the alleys, running when he could, his fear and grief growing inside him like an accelerated cancer. He heard sirens, cops, fire trucks, ambulances, the sounds pressing in on every side of him until they seemed to penetrate his flesh and bones and converge at some point deep within him, obliterating everything but the need to escape, to flee, to get away.

He would later have no recollection of how he reached the bus station. One moment he was running and the next he was moving along the wall of lockers: the transition seemed to be that quick. A blink of the eye. The magic of perception. He had come here early this morning, one of the errands he'd run on his way over to Un Paso to see Alfie, and had stashed his canvas bag inside Locker 8. He unlocked it, slung the bag over his shoulder, ducked into the men's room.

Tark's hands shook as he splashed water on his face, as he drank water from his cupped palms. The smell of smoke clung to the inside of his nostrils, to his hair, his clothes. The lump of sorrow in his throat wouldn't dissolve.

Where to go.

What to do.

How to do it.

He went into a stall, locked it, changed clothes. He rolled the soiled jeans and shirt into a ball to dump in the garbage on his way out. Then he removed five hundred bucks in cash from the bag, stuck it in his pocket. He combed his fingers through his hair, thinking of Lamadero, of the briefcase Alfie had been holding, of the order he was sure had come from some anonymous fuck on Long Key.

He walked out into the lobby and up to a ticket window. "When's the next bus to the Keys?"

"Ten minutes," yawned the clerk.

"One way to Marathon."

"Just for one?"

"Yes."

"Fifteen-fifty."

Twenty minutes later, the bus was trundling south through the darkness. Tark sat at the back, clutching the bag against him, his head turned toward the window. His eyes drifted in the glass, dark, haunted, smoldering.

■ ■ ■

The phone. The phone is ringing and McCleary can't find it. He hurls aside clothes, dishes, old food, newspapers, digging through a seemingly inexhaustible heap of junk until he locates it, snatches it up. "Yes? Hello?"

"It's Cat, bro, and I want you to pay attention. Ask Benson about his source. . . ."

"You're dead," he whispers.

". . . trust no one . . ."

"Dead."

He slams the receiver down but it peals immediately, quick, shrill sounds that poke through his ears like nails. He grabs it and her voice is there again, his sister's voice, exactly as he remembers it, the irreverence, the quickness like light.

"Wake up, Mike, wake up . . .

"Tim Benson's on the line. It's urgent."

Boone, leaning over him, shaking him. The bedside lamp was on, light spilling into McCleary's face. "Okay, I'm awake, Will. I'm awake." McCleary knocked the old man's arms away, sat up, dropped his legs over the side of the bed, rubbed his face with his hands.

"Take it in the kitchen," Boone said.

"What time is it?"

"Seven."

Seven? Apprehension fluttered through him as he got out of bed, pulled on his jeans. Elvis, curled on the old chair near the window, a paw covering his bandit eyes, didn't stir. But Flats jumped down from the foot of the bed and padded after him as he headed toward the kitchen.

His sister, he knew he'd been dreaming about his dead sister, but he couldn't recall specifics. He picked up the phone and heard Boone hang up in his bedroom.

"What is it, Tim?"

"I'm in Little Havana." He ticked off an address. "Place called Un Paso."

"That's where Quin was last night."

"Yeah. How soon can you get here?"

"What's happened, Tim?"

"Just get down here." The line went dead.

21

Heckler bolted upright in bed, straining to hear the noise that had awakened him. But there was nothing, just the soft moan of a wind that was stronger than it had been last night when he'd turned in.

Pale light seeped through the venetian blinds. As he got up to open them, he heard the noise again, a faint rustling, and glanced down at the chair where he'd left his clothes. He saw a pair of garden lizards, one about five inches long, the other maybe seven inches. The longer one, the male, stood utterly still on the arm of the chair as a flap of skin at its throat billowed out, an iridescent blue like a peacock's tail. The shorter lizard, the female, seemed attracted by it and drew closer. As she did, the male suddenly rushed her, mounted her, and they copulated furiously there on his jeans.

Heckler laughed, then suddenly realized what it meant. The storm.

This was about the storm, about a drop in the barometric pressure. He moved quickly to the TV, switched it on, tuned in to a Miami station. He sat at the foot of the bed, the remote control clicker in his hand, and stared at the screen.

There: the familiar shape of the peninsula, the white swirl to the east that was Albert, the bright red rim that bordered the northern Bahamian islands and signified a hurricane warning. Now, as he watched, a bright yellow line traveled up the eastern coast of Florida from Key West to Titusville. A hurricane watch. A kind of giddiness bubbled up like soda water inside of him.

A watch, a fucking hurricane watch.

The storm's coordinates materialized on the screen, followed by white words and numbers: the forward speed (10 –11 mph), wind velocity (130 mph), and the storm's distance from Miami: 420 miles.

Kilner was going to be forced to make some decisions, and the shit, Heckler thought, was about to hit the fan.

■ ■ ■

The air around Un Paso smelled as if a giant iron had been pressed against the air, scorching a hole straight down to hell. In the gloomy morning light, the building itself was a blackened husk littered with rubble and charred shapes that had once been tables, chairs, booths, the bar. Men picked through it all, filling evidence bags. Rain dripped through holes in the ceiling. Benson said that Quin had been here to talk with someone named Helga who worked at the factory. But the Explorer was still parked in the lot of her apartment building. McCleary knew because Benson had told him. So how had she arrived? By cab? Why would she take a cab when she had the Explorer? Why, Tim? Why would she do that? She didn't do it, that's what. He said as much and Benson rolled his eyes, exasperated.

"Then where is she, Mac? I spoke with her yesterday morning and she said she was going to meet with this woman last night."

"I'm telling you she didn't make it."

"Then where the hell is she?"

"I don't know."

Benson poked at his wire rims. Boone cleared his throat but didn't butt in. People stepped around them, Benson's people, firemen, forensics, someone from the mayor's office, all of them apparently oblivious of the drizzle that had been falling off and on since last night. They were standing somewhere in the back of the building now, near what had once been the kitchen. McCleary could see the remnants of a floor freezer, a sink, exposed pipes. Part of the ceiling here had collapsed and wooden beams had fallen across the ruin like pickup sticks.

"We think there were two explosives and that the first one detonated back here somewhere," Benson said finally. He jammed his hands into his pockets and kicked at a pile of debris. "One of the explosions hit the gas main and took care of the rest of the place."

"What kind of explosives?" Boone asked.

"We don't know for sure yet."

"Bullshit," Boone snapped. "You've had people here since eleven last night."

"We couldn't even get in here until after three this morning because of the fire, Will," Benson said sharply.

"But you've got a theory," McCleary said.

"We've got a million theories, Mac."

"So let's hear at least one of them."

"Timed explosives, sophisticated, but something you can buy on the streets if you know the right people."

"Two briefcases?"

"Yeah, it looks that way."

"Having something to do with Helga?"

"Maybe, maybe not. The guy who owned this place was Alfonso Ruiz. His body was one of the first that was identified. He was an icon in the Cuban community, with more friends in high places than the three of us are likely to see in a lifetime. Eleven years ago, his wife, daughter, and granddaughter were killed in an explosion here."

Boone snapped his fingers. "I knew there was something familiar about this neighborhood. That explosion back then was drug-related, right?"

Benson nodded. "Most likely. A cartel kingpin was one of the fourteen people killed that night. He was having dinner here. Nothing was ever proven, though. Vice got the case and it's still open. I drew a complete blank on it, so I checked the records. It happened when

you and I took that long fishing trip to Wyoming, Mac. By the time
we got back, it was old news."

Which explained why he couldn't remember anything about it,
McCleary thought. "Are you saying the explosion was directed at
him?"

"There aren't any conclusions yet, Mac. I'm just telling you what
we know."

They were outside now, in the wet, blustery alley behind Un Paso,
where Benson's cruiser was parked. He reached inside for a large
umbrella, which he passed to McCleary, and a thermos of iced tea.
McCleary opened the umbrella and the three of them huddled under
it, passing the thermos around. "Twelve people were killed last night,
sixteen were critically injured, and another three dozen or so got out
with minor injuries. Eight bodies, including Alfonso and Helga, have
been identified.

"According to one of the waitresses, a woman matching Helga's
description came in shortly before eight looking for Alfonso. She
joined him and Alfonso's son-in-law in the booth where they were
sitting at the front of the restaurant. The three of them moved to
another room, she wasn't sure where."

"Was Quin seen here by anyone?"

"So far, no. We ran makes on the cars that were here in the lot and
parked out front." He gestured toward the two buildings on the other
side of the alley. "A Honda was parked over there. Roof smashed in,
windshield shattered. It turned out to be a Hertz rented to a guy
named Fernando Gabriel. He originally rented a Cherokee on June
seventeenth. A black Cherokee, the same type of car that tailed Quin
two days after Gabriel landed in Miami.

"On the day Quin was tailed, Gabriel traded the Cherokee for the
Honda. We found his passport in the glove compartment, so I ran the
number through customs. He arrived on a flight from Lima on June
seventeenth, gave Un Paso as his address. I ran his name through the
computer. Nothing turned up. But the prints we lifted from the car
belong to Alfonso's son-in-law, John Gabriel Tark."

The air suddenly hissed out of the space where McCleary stood.
Tark. Sweet Christ. Tark, the friendly neighbor.

"He used to own a chartering business at Opa-locka airport. His
prints were on file because for a while he was a suspect in the first

explosion, due to a quarter-million-dollar insurance policy on his wife and kid. He gave the money to the old man and split less than a year later."

"How do you know that?" Boone asked.

"It was in the file," Benson replied. "And a relative confirmed it." Benson stabbed his thumb toward a cruiser that blocked one end of the alley. A cop and a kid of perhaps eighteen stood next to it, talking. "Second cousin. Works out at the track. He said Tark showed up at the track on Sunday, looking for a guy named Ramón Lamadero. Not a total stranger to the department. He's a two-bit bookie with fingers in a hundred pies.

"Anyway, he and Tark left the track together. Yesterday morning, the kid heard that Lamadero was looking to get even with the man who'd dropped him in the Glades. There's an APB out on him now. Explosives aren't his style, but he's obviously got some answers that we need. We've also got an APB out on Tiffany Crandall, since she's the one who gave Quin the lead on Helga."

McCleary found his voice; it sounded weak, insubstantial, scared. Yes, that most of all. "Tark lived next door to Quin."

"I know. The building manager mentioned him when one of my men spoke to her. It didn't mean anything until we got the make on the prints." He paused, rubbed his stubbled chin. "If you or Quin had said something about him earlier, Mac, I could have checked him out."

"I thought he was just a goddamn neighbor."

Color blazed in Benson's cheeks. "I told you both from the start to report any and everything to me, no matter how trivial it seemed."

"Knock it off, Tim," snapped McCleary. "It just didn't seem that important."

No, that wasn't quite true. Tark had been important from the very beginning, since the moment Quin mentioned him. The only reason McCleary hadn't said anything to Benson was because Tark had inadvertently become the focus of an argument about infidelity. Because his own jealousy embarrassed and shamed him.

"I may be speaking out of turn here." Boone jammed his fingers in his back pockets. "But to me this whole thing reeks of CIA."

Boone the conspiracist. Boone the loon. Don't, Will, McCleary thought. Don't start. But Boone was hyped up, and now that he'd given his opinion he expanded on it. Charlie here. Crandall and his game, whatever it was, over there. Heckler here. Tark there. He would have continued on if Benson hadn't exploded.

"Fuck your theory, Will. Heckler's been presumed dead for months."

"A couple weeks before Charlie died, he told his son that Heckler was in town. How do you explain that?"

"Charlie was eighty-five years old. He probably got confused."

"Confused?" Boone laughed. "Charlie was more lucid than all of us put together. I'm telling you the CIA is involved."

"We don't even know for sure that Heckler worked for the CIA. I haven't been able to confirm that."

"He worked for some intelligence outfit," Boone persisted. "That's what Charlie's son said, right, Mac?"

But Benson replied before McCleary had a chance to. "I don't think the feds have anything to do with it."

Boone, unruffled, just crossed his arms at his chest. "And I suppose you believe everything you read in the newspaper, too, don't you, Tim?"

Benson rolled onto the balls of his feet and leaned into Boone's personal space. When he spoke, his voice was very, very soft. "Let's get something straight, Will. You're here only because you and Charlie were good friends. That's it, got it? And just for the goddamn record, I'm not particularly fond of feds and it doesn't matter whether they're CIA, FBI, or whatever. But I've got no reason to doubt what my source tells me. He's nearly as high in the intelligence community as you can go and—"

"He's lying. I don't care who he is or how high up he is. He's lying. That's what they do best. The bunch of them."

McCleary was sure that Benson was going to drive his fist into Boone's face. He could see it in Benson's eyes, in the bright pink of his cheeks, in the posture of his body. So he grabbed Benson by the arm and walked him away from the old man.

"Keep that idiot out of this, Mac." He shook his arm free.

"Is there an APB on Tark?"

"Of course there is. And I've got a tail on Crandall."

"Did you get a search warrant for the factory?"

"Look, don't tell me how to do my fucking job. I—"

"Yes or no, Tim. Just give me a simple yes or no."

"No, damnit, not yet. I don't intend to tip Crandall off."

Certainty, proof, evidence. Benson was struggling against the gravitational pull of the system, sinking into the black hole of rules, regulations, politics. He had become its mouthpiece, its indentured servant, and McCleary should have seen it coming.

"And while we're on the subject, I would have appreciated a call from you about what happened on the Jungle Queen. I left half a dozen messages on Will's machine yesterday."

Yeah, McCleary thought. And he hadn't returned the call because he didn't know what he could possibly say about his visit to the *santera*. "Nothing happened."

"Nothing? C'mon."

"Zip, nada, zero. Catch you later."

McCleary turned away, but Benson hurried after him and fell into step alongside him. "Don't do this, Mac."

"Do what? I'm going to look for my wife. Give me a call if you hear anything." He gestured at Boone, who was leaning against the cruiser, and they headed for the front of the building, where they'd parked. Benson didn't follow.

■ ■ ■

Around eleven that morning, a chopper landed on the seldom-used helipad just outside the compound's gate. Kilner knew who it was as soon as he saw the craft hovering.

Elliot LeFrank blew in with Albert's wind a few minutes later, just as Kilner and Pisco had sat down for an early lunch. Kilner didn't rise from the table. "You're just in time for Gracie's excellent pasta, Elliot. Pull up a chair."

"I've eaten." LeFrank glanced at Gracie, who was hovering in the kitchen doorway. "We'll take coffee in Mr. Kilner's office."

She didn't move, making it clear that she didn't work for LeFrank. Her dark eyes slipped to Kilner, waiting, patient. He nodded slightly and only then did she walk over to the coffeepot. Kilner dabbed at his mouth, set his napkin down, rose. "Delicious, Gracie."

"Thanks, Mr. K. I'll make a fresh pot of coffee and bring it around in a few minutes."

As soon as they were in Kilner's office, LeFrank said, "There was an explosion last night in a restaurant in Little Havana."

"I hadn't heard."

"It was owned by a Cuban fellow, Alfonso Ruiz. You know the name, Jerry?"

"No." Kilner stared at the pulse that beat at LeFrank's temple. He had a sudden inkling that he was about to be led into a place he would rather not go. "Should I?"

LeFrank ignored the question. "He has—had—a son-in-law named John Tark. Metro-Dade now has an APB out on him."

"He's a suspect in the explosion?"

"No. He may have been killed in the explosion, but for now that's unconfirmed. I think the police just want some answers from him in the event that he's alive. His alias is Fernando Gabriel. Isn't that a fucking hoot?"

Kilner's head began to pound. Lamadero, he thought. Lamadero had taken care of things, all right. "Are you sure?"

"Bet your ass I'm sure. If we're lucky, Tark got killed last night or has since left the country. But I abhor predicating the future on luck, Jerry. So as of right now, we're out of this game."

He set you up by having the professor knocked off: Heckler's words, Heckler's theories. Maybe, maybe not.

Either way, getting out was looking better by the second.

"I agree completely. I was never that crazy about this project to begin with."

"Steve will have to be taken care of."

Kilner nodded. "That should have happened weeks ago."

"And this facility will be closed next month."

He thought of the photographs locked in his safe.

"And notify Zeek and Zicky that they're off surveillance as of this afternoon."

"We just let Crandall's deal go through?" Kilner asked.

"Our men in Germany will take care of it when Haddan's plane lands in Berlin to refuel."

In Germany, of course. Well away from anyone who knew anything. And when the whole deal went down, LeFrank would get the credit and look like a goddamn hero.

"Any questions?"

"Just one." Kilner got up and walked over to the closet where the floor safe was. He dialed in the combination, removed the envelope, returned to the desk. "You wouldn't be planning on fucking me over, would you, Elliot?"

LeFrank flashed one of his famous smiles. "Funny, Jerry, I was just about to ask you the same thing." Old buddy, old friend. "And we've known each other what? Fifteen years?"

"Sixteen." Kilner removed the photos inside. "But you know what they say, Elliot. Even in longstanding friendships there're secrets. And sometimes they aren't very pretty, are they, Elliot?" Old buddy, old friend.

He turned the photos over and pushed them toward LeFrank. Four photographs in living color of LeFrank, pedophile. Kilner hadn't asked for details, but suspected the kids, all boys who looked younger than fifteen, were runaways. Only LeFrank knew the truth, though, and he sure as hell wasn't talking. At the moment, in fact, he didn't seem to be capable of doing much of anything but remain standing, and even that was debatable.

"In the event that I die suddenly, Elliot, the negatives are with a friend who has orders to release them to the press. Nothing personal, you understand. I just felt it was a necessary step. Politics, you know."

LeFrank raised his head slowly, as though the muscles in his neck had rusted. His face was the color of Elmer's glue, but he managed a thin, weak smile. "It's a nasty business we're in, isn't it, Jerry."

"It does have its bleak moments." He gathered up the photos, tapping them against the surface of the desk as he straightened them. He slipped them into the bottom drawer. "Oh, one other thing, Elliot. What was it you said about this facility closing?"

Contempt seeped from a dark cellar inside LeFrank; it smelled of mold, fungus, dead things. "You must have misunderstood me." He pushed to his feet and, in a feeble pretense of power, said, "Take care of Heckler."

Heckler was probably the only point they agreed upon. "No problem."

"And the compound should be evacuated by this evening."

"We're making preparations already." Kilner opened the door for him and there was Gracie with a tray.

"Coffee, Mr. K."

"Mr. LeFrank won't be staying, Gracie."

She barely stifled a smile. "Would you like your coffee in a cup to go?"

"No, thank you," LeFrank murmured, and brushed past her.

Neither of them spoke as they walked outside. LeFrank trotted down the steps and hurried up the walk toward the gate and the waiting helicopter. Kilner stood on the balcony, listening to the branches shake like castanets in the blustery air. Leaves blew across the compound. The rain had picked up again. Kilner could hear waves crashing against the beach. Albert, he thought, rushing in to fill the vacuum of LeFrank's departure.

He thought of the evacuation. The traffic jams. The opening of shelters. School closings. Panic buying. Eight million people scrambling to protect themselves and their property.

Kilner went back inside, into his office, shut the door and locked it. He punched out a Miami number, reached a beeper service, left his own number. Less than five minutes later, the phone rang.

"You read my mind, babe," she said as soon as he answered. "I was just about to call you."

"Where do we stand?"

"There've been a few developments. Larry's spooked. He wants to culminate the deal before the storm hits. He's planning on moving the stuff late this afternoon."

"He's pushing his luck."

"Not really. The National Hurricane Center hasn't posted a warning yet. Even once they do, that gives him a minimum of twelve hours. The deal will be over and done with and Haddan will be on his happy way by then and we, babe, will be ten million richer. How soon can you get here?"

How soon? For ten million? For a new life? Immediately. But. If Crandall changed his mind, if Haddan wasn't amenable to the arrangement, if, but, suppose . . . "Call me back in a few hours. I'll know by then."

She laughed softly. "Still playing it safe?"

"Just being careful." He hung up, his face bright with sweat.

■ ■ ■

She waited, waited in the terrible solitude of her spacious prison, waited and listened to the wind, the rain, the intermittent periods of near-calm. Gracie arrived and departed with breakfast, with lunch. In between, Quin paced, thought, stared out the window.

Charlie Charlie Charlie. You knew, didn't you? You knew about this little compound here before you and Heckler got together that day. You knew, of course you did, you were privy to thirty years of secrets. But he hadn't known the full truth until Heckler had given him the photographs. And now she was here where Heckler was and she didn't have to be a spy to know they were going to end up in the same place. Six feet under, buried, gone, *adiós.*

Unless she could get out of here.

Unless.

She turned, facing the metal door, then she began to roam through the room again, searching for a weakness, a way out, an idea, anything. Anything at all.

22

McCleary let himself into her apartment with his spare key. The quiet possessed a terrible, waiting quality that made every sound, however small, seem louder than it was. The whisper of his shoes against the floor, the tick of the clock in the kitchen, the hum of the refrigerator, the click of Flats's claws as she trotted down the hall, leading the way to Quin's bedroom.

Clothes were heaped on chairs, the bed was unmade, covers were puddled on the floor, shoes without mates spilled from the closet, an empty bowl and two empty glasses sat on the nightstand—a reminder of Quin reading and munching in bed. His wife's love affair with food sometimes appalled him nearly as much as the chaos that grew up around her when she remained anywhere for a length of time. If this had been anyone else's room, he would have concluded that it had been trashed.

He could peel away the chaos in layers, an archaeologist at a dig, and each level of stuff would tell him something about the state of her life on a given day. But there was a comforting familiarity about it that even Flats felt. The sheepdog curled up on the fallen covers and shut her eyes.

Given the chaos in the room, it was difficult to tell from her dresser drawers whether any clothes were missing. But since her suitcase was still on the closet shelf, he didn't think her disappearance had been planned. He opened the little wooden box where she kept her jewelry and found her wedding ring.

He pocketed it.

McCleary hit the message button on the answering machine. Betty O'Toole had called twice, asking if she would please call in; Mr. Crandall wanted to know if she would be at work tomorrow. But those calls had been placed *yesterday*, the first around 11 A.M. and the second just after 3 P.M. yesterday. He had spoken to her shortly after five, so sometime between then and eleven, when Betty had first called, she had—what? Pursued a lead she hadn't mentioned? Even so, she would have gone in to work afterward, but she apparently hadn't shown up at all. He didn't know what it meant or implied, but it gave him a modicum of hope that she hadn't been at Un Paso last night.

The next message was from Tiffany Crandall and it had come in last night at nine. "Okay, I believe you and I apologize for that little scene in the courtyard yesterday morning. I liked Charlie. He was good to me. So I'm going to return the favor. Check your mailbox."

He'd looked in the mailbox on his way in and it was empty. So much for Tiffany's favor.

He punched Rewind, erasing the messages, then called Benson at the station. His voice, when he finally came to the phone, was cool, cautious, and thick with fatigue. No word yet on Tark or Tiffany Crandall. McCleary considered telling him about the messages, but quickly dismissed the notion.

"What about Lamadero?"

"His body was found two hours ago, slumped in the front seat of his car. Looks like suicide. The gun was still in his hand and he'd been shot through the mouth."

"Where was the car?"

"Behind a bar where he did business."

"A bar? And you're calling it suicide?" McCleary laughed. "C'mon, Tim."

Testy now: "I'm not *calling* it anything until the doc does the autopsy. I'm just telling you what it looks like. Listen, I've got the mayor and the entire Cuban community banging on my door for answers. I think it'd be best if you just backed off for a while."

Back off. Get lost. Disappear. "Get real, Tim."

"The mayor nearly hit the roof when he heard what the Miata's going to cost. I just can't justify the expense, Mike."

Mike. Something in the way Benson said it struck McCleary. "You're not alone?"

"That's right."

"The mayor?"

"No, definitely not."

"Someone higher up?"

"Yes."

No one was higher than the mayor in city politics. That meant it was someone within the state's hierarchy, the governor or one of his emissaries. Or a fed. "Your source, Tim? Is that who's there?"

"Yeah, right. Just stay out of it, Mike. When I have anything on Quin, anything at all, I'll call you."

Benson hung up. The hollowness that echoed along the dead line bumped up against the baggage of McCleary's regrets and he replaced the receiver. He listened hard to the silence, hoping it would speak to him, hoping to feel the burn of a hunch, hoping the phone would ring and Quin would be on the other end. But there was only the silence.

Whistling for Flats, he left the apartment and stopped by the manager's apartment. A woman answered the door with the chain on. He saw one thinly plucked brow, one small, suspicious eye, one plump, pink cheek.

"Are you the manager?" he asked.

"That's right." The eye dropped to Flats, sitting quietly at his feet. "We don't allow pets."

"I don't need an apartment. I'm looking for Liz Purcell."

"Who're you?"

"Her husband."

The eye rolled as she sighed. "Just a second." She shut the door and unfastened the chain. Then she opened the door wide and leaned against the jamb, rubbing her back against it like a cat with an itch she couldn't reach. "Her husband, huh? Didn't know she was married."

"We're, uh, separated. When was the last time you saw her?"

"Night before last to talk to her. But early yesterday morning, before the sun was up, she was out here in the courtyard arguing with some woman. Figured it was none of my business. Then the cops come by this morning and they've got all kinds of questions. And later they show up again with a search warrant for Mr. Tark's apartment. So hey, I figure I've got two tenants who're in trouble and that's grounds for eviction in my book. Tomorrow their stuff is getting hauled off. Not that Mr. Tark had so much stuff. But your wife does, Mr. Purcell."

"I'd appreciate it if you'd just leave her things in the apartment. I'll be glad to pay you a week's rent or whatever you require."

"I'll keep the deposit and we'll call it even. Another week."

"Thanks. I appreciate it."

"You mind telling me what kinda trouble she's in?"

"I wish I knew. Did you happen to pick up her mail?"

"Oh, yeah, I did. Hold on a second and I'll get it for you." She returned with a small white plastic garbage bag. "It's all in here."

"I sure appreciate this—" he glanced at the name on the door— "Mrs. Link."

"Jazz." She smiled. "That's what the J. stands for."

He left her Boone's number and asked her to call him if she saw Liz or if anyone else came around asking questions.

As soon as he and Flats were in the car, he dug the mail out of the garbage bag. Besides the usual junk-mail flyers was an unopened manila envelope with nothing written on it. He tore it open. Inside was a second, smaller envelope addressed to Tiffany Crandall at a post office box here on the beach. McCleary recognized Charlie's scrawl and noted it had been mailed the day after his murder.

The third packet. The lady had returned the favor, all right.

It contained three photographs. The first was of the Chique Cherries factory, a long shot at dusk, with a truck in the foreground. The second photo was a closeup of the same shot. The vehicle was a moving van, not a truck, and was clearly marked with the name of the company. In the third photo, the van was parked behind the factory, its rear doors were thrown open, and two men were loading a metal drum into the back. The boys from the blue Camaro.

He now had three of the four packets, but what did they tell him that he didn't already know? Suppose Charlie had divided the original material into fifths and kept one part for himself? And what if that was the part the killer had?

Flats pawed at his arm, asking for some attention, please. McCleary patted her. "I've got to make a couple of calls, girl, then we'll go back to Boone's until we meet with Clara."

And then what? Wait for Quin to call? Evacuate Boone's apartment? What? He didn't know.

■ ■ ■

Tark recognized the photograph of himself as soon as it appeared on the TV screen. It had once graced the front of his pilot's license and was the same photo that had been published in the *Miami Herald* after that explosion nearly eleven years ago. He looked secure, smug, young, naïve.

That cocky smile. The slant of his baseball cap. The fixed levity of the eyes. *Fool, you goddamn fool.* "You look like an ex-con," Estelle said, strolling into the living room with a bowl of chips and a container of dip. She folded herself onto the cushions of the couch, nodding as the picture on the screen was enlarged for the viewer. "Yeah, definitely like a con."

He laughed. "Thanks. Your car packed?" he asked.

"As much as it'll ever be. We should probably shove off in an hour or so. If we wait much longer, the roads are going to be a mess. I'm betting everyone on the Keys will head for Orlando." She scooped a chip through the cheese dip, popped it into her mouth, and crunched noisily.

"You have access to a boat?"

"Just the Zodiac."

"Could I borrow it?"

"Now?"

"In a few hours."

Silence.

Tark glanced at her. "Is that a yes or a no or a maybe?"

"You can't take on the whole fucking compound, Gabby."

"I don't intend to. I'll wait in the mangrove."

"Wait? Wait for what? For the wind to start howling? For the waves to swallow the beach? How do you expect to ride out a hurricane in a Zodiac raft?"

"I won't."

She rolled her black olive eyes and dropped her feet to the floor. "Yeah, you won't. Great answer."

"Yes or no, Estelle? That's all I'm asking."

"I'll go in with you."

Tark shook his head.

"Then I'll drop you and the raft off."

"And head out for your sister's."

She didn't like that part of it. "I figured I'd wait here for you to finish whatever it is you're going to do."

"No."

"Just how the hell are you going to get out of the Keys without a car?"

"There're probably enough cars on that compound for me to borrow one without too much of a problem." He grinned but she didn't.

"I think you're nuts."

"Probably." But he was fairly sure that someone on the compound—Pisco? Kilner?—was ultimately responsible for the explosion at Un Paso, for Alfie's death. Lamadero was just a hired hand, carrying out orders that happened to fit his own agenda. Either way, settling the score would be his last act as Fernando Gabriel. "Where's the raft?"

"Out back, with the engine."

"Will you drive me over to the mangrove?"

She untangled her legs from the cushion, dropped her bare feet to the floor. "Yeah, yeah, I'll drive you."

Tark caught her hand as she stood and pulled her against him, his gratitude so extreme it bordered on pathos.

■ ■ ■

McCleary had called the other investigator in their office, who assured him he would put up the hurricane shutters, bring in the patio furniture, and take the cats with him when he left. He had not been so fortunate, however, in contacting Quin's sister, and tried the Orlando number once more before he left Boone's apartment. She picked up on the first ring this time, speaking in a whispery voice that meant the kids were taking naps. He didn't mention Quin and Ellen didn't ask; she merely assumed it was McCleary's turn to check on their daughter. They were planning on staying in Orlando until the storm had blown itself out, she said, but what about himself and Quin? Where were they going to ride out the storm?

"Not on the beach. We'll call you, don't worry."

"Is everything okay? I didn't hear from Quin last night or this morning and I was afraid something had happened."

"Everything's fine." How easily the lie came out. "She was putting in some extra hours at Crandall's."

"Well, take care and we'll talk to you tomorrow or something."

"Right."

As he hung up, Boone and R.D. came through the door with their arms laden with bags of groceries and hurricane supplies. "Never seen nothing like it, Mike. There're so many people in Woolley's it was almost impossible to move in there. All the bottled water's gone, the shelves of canned foods are nearly bare. You start talking about winds of one-forty-five and people don't mess around."

R.D. set his bags on the counter and brushed his hands together. "Got to split, General. Concha and I are taking *abuelita* up north a ways. I want to get out of here before traffic gets real bad." He glanced at McCleary. "Any word from your wife?"

"Not yet."

A frown creased his forehead. "Hey, I'm sure she's okay, Mr. McCleary. You guys aren't staying here, are you?"

"No."

"We aren't?" Boone asked.

"I talked to Joe. He thinks the office in North Miami is pretty secure, and suggested we ride out the storm there with him, animals and all."

"Whatever you do, don't stick around on the beach," R.D. said. "They're predicting a storm surge of at least ten feet. Got to split, guys. Good luck."

As if luck had anything to do with any of it, McCleary thought.

He helped Boone transfer the groceries to cardboard boxes and suggested he head over to the North Miami office with the animals and the supplies, then they'd meet back here.

"Where're you going to be?"

"Talking to Clara."

Boone snorted. "Waste of time. She probably won't show."

"I think she will."

"You give people too many chances, Mike. Charlie used to do that and look what happened to him."

The remark irritated McCleary but he let it pass and wondered if Boone's particular brand of crotchety cynicism rode tandem with old age. He hoped not. They loaded up Boone's '57 Chevy, then brought down the animals. All three of them were acting weird. Elvis kept her paws over her eyes, Fox burrowed her way under the front seat, and Flats whined as the door shut and leaped into the backseat. As Boone pulled away, the sheepdog's face was in the rear window, gazing longingly at McCleary.

Thirty minutes later, McCleary turned onto Ocean Drive at Fifteenth Street. The Atlantic loomed to his left, gray and angry, churning with whitecaps and waves that crashed against the beach. Wind whipped off it, hurling sand across the sidewalk and into the road. Palm trees were beginning to bend like straws. Their dry fronds shook loose and scuttled away, as quick and frantic as roaches.

Up and down Ocean Drive, crews were boarding up hotels and businesses. Everything that wasn't nailed down had been brought inside—sidewalk tables and chairs, trash cans, umbrellas. In most of the hotels, the upper-story windows weren't protected by anything more than giant Xs of masking tape to prevent glass from shattering. Farther inland, of course, the usual skeptics would wait until the watch was upgraded to a warning before they acted, but apparently no one on the beach was taking chances.

Although Salgado's was still open for business, two young men were nailing plywood across the windows. McCleary parked at the curb on Collins and went inside. The place looked as if it had been plundered. The shelves were nearly empty, there were no bags of ice left in the freezer, the deli case had been cleaned out. But customers still moved up and down the aisles, picking through what remained.

In the café at the back of the store, he ordered an expresso for himself and waited. Clara Villa arrived forty minutes late. Her white hair was swept up off her neck and covered with a blue silk scarf. Sunglasses hung from a chain around her neck. She wore khaki slacks, a T-shirt, sandals. She looked so normal, so incredibly *ordinary,* he found it difficult to reconcile this woman with his memory of the *santera* in red and white who had puffed on a cigar, guzzled straight from a bottle of rum, and had spoken to him in Charlie's voice.

As she sat down next to him at the counter, he addressed her in Spanish. "I wouldn't recognize you on the street, *Señora* Villa."

"That's the idea. Let us hope that Mr. Crandall is too preoccupied with the storm to worry about me. I'm sorry I'm so late. It was impossible to get away before."

She ordered a coffee for herself, he asked for a refill, then she said, "Margarita said Carlos came through."

"You don't remember?"

"No. Trances are like fugue states. I usually have a sense of myself standing to one side, watching what happens, but I rarely remember the details. What did he say?"

McCleary told her.

"Did it sound like him?"

"Yes."

She nodded thoughtfully. "Before I forget, I have something to give you." From her straw bag on the floor, she brought out a small wooden box, which she set down and opened. It was a portable chess set with magnetized chess pieces exquisitely carved from wood and already set up. The sixteen major chessmen bore striking resemblances to some of the *orishas* he'd seen in her shack. He picked up the white king.

"Obatalá?"

"Very good, *señor*. Do you know his role within the hierarchy?"

"He's the father of the *orishas,* the patron of peace."

"He's also in charge of the human mind. He is how I think of Carlos."

"Then this would be you." McCleary pointed at the black queen, who held an infant at her breast. "Oddudúa. Wife of Obatalá and mother of fourteen of the most important *orishas.*"

She laughed. "A flattering comparison, though flawed. It is how

Carlos thought of me, but it is not what I am. The difference is important. He gave me this chess set and was trying to teach me the game, but the nuances are beyond me." She turned the set on its side, slid open a panel at the bottom, and withdrew a small white drawstring bag.

"A talisman, *señor*. It contains several herbs, garlic, a small bit of camphor, and the bark of a palm tree. It has been dipped in holy water from seven different churches. The bark represents my *orisha*, Changó. He has a certain fondness for palm trees. I urge you to keep it on you at all times. It will dispel negative influences and protect you." She handed it to him. "I made it for Carlos, but he was killed before I could give it to him."

"Frankly, I'm more interested in Larry Crandall."

"Larry." She made a soft, aggrieved sound, as though the very name caused her pain. "Eight years ago he came to me on the recommendation of another client. He had very specific questions about a redevelopment project he was about to become involved in on Ocean Drive. I gave him my impressions about which hotels he should buy, which he should stay away from, how he should proceed in his negotiations. He followed my advice, Miami Beach eventually became a paradise again, and he became a very rich man. So he kept coming back and now he rarely commits to a project without consulting with me first."

"That's a lot of power to hold over one individual's life."

"Carlos said exactly the same thing." She smiled sadly. "And the money has brought me a few comforts I would not have had otherwise; Carlos noted that, too. But I never intentionally abused the power until Carlos and I became close."

"You must've known about Crandall's interest in the Sea Witch long before the county decided to put it up for sale."

She nodded and sipped at her coffee. "And I told him then to forget the Sea Witch and this resort he wants to build. Do you know about that?"

"Yes."

"For the past four years, it seems that almost everything he has done has been to further his dream about the resort. But from the beginning I have felt it would never exist. I don't know why; I just never saw it. That isn't what Larry wanted to hear, but he kept seeking my advice. Whenever he was considering property on the eleven-hundred block, he would come to me first. He no longer wanted to know whether he should *buy* the land because he knew what I would say, so he asked about the details of the negotiation. How he should proceed, what I could tell him about the present owner, things like that."

Crandall, closet mystic or fruitcake, visionary or the Machiavelli whose greed would result in the new subsuming the old: take your pick. The man apparently had as many faces as Eve and how you perceived him seemed to depend on where you stood in your own life, McCleary thought.

"Is that what you were doing on the Jungle Queen the other night?"

"Yes. I had never met Mr. Haddan before and Larry wanted my impressions."

"Your impression on Haddan as a person or as a business partner or what?"

"He wanted to know if he could trust Haddan to fulfill his promises."

"And?"

"I believe he can. Whatever agreement they have made will be honored by Mr. Haddan. I don't know what the agreement entails," she went on, her voice softer now, "but it has such darkness around it, *Señor* McCleary, that I found it intolerable to be in Mr. Haddan's presence for more than a few minutes at a time."

"How did Charlie fit?"

She brought her hands together and touched them to her chin in an attitude of prayer. "Eighteen months ago, he came to me for a consultation. In the shack. That was about the time the county began to publicly consider the sale of the Sea Witch, so I realize now that his initial interest in me was because of Larry."

"He knew Crandall was one of your clients?"

"I believe so. I think he found out through Larry's ex-wife." She paused, her smile soft, secretive. "Can you imagine, Mr. McCleary? A former professor from Princeton, American to his very heart, and a Cuban woman whose life began on a sugar plantation? We seduced each other's minds. We were quite proper about it, though. To my granddaughter he was just Don Carlos, a client, and as far as his son was concerned, I didn't exist. Even his friend William Boone didn't know. There's a certain beauty in such secrecy."

"Not when it's about murder."

"Oh, I'm afraid it's about much more than that. From the beginning, Carlos was looking for something that would convince Larry he shouldn't buy the Sea Witch. And once he and I became close, I helped him any way I could, passing along dates, information, and urging Larry to forget the Sea Witch. But Larry wasn't listening and he's been very secretive about his dealing with Mr. Haddan. It entails a great deal of money, whatever it is, and I think he hopes to use the funds to finance his resort."

"Why haven't you gone to the police?"

"For what? What purpose would it serve? Larry would discover my relationship with Carlos and would sever all connections with me. The police would consider me a suspect. I knew that sooner or later someone would find me and ask the right questions. I knew he would be a son of Changó with dark hair and a beard and that I was to give him what I have. You are that man. I realized that after Margarita told me Charlie had spoken. I have given you the talisman and now I will give you the rest."

Her hand dipped into her straw bag again and reappeared with an envelope addressed to Clara in Charlie's scrawl. "I received this two days after he was murdered."

There was only one item, a copy of what appeared to be a CIA memo, dated more than two years ago:

> To: Jerome Kilner
> From: Elliot LeFrank
>
> *This is just to confirm our conversation the other day, Jerry. As you know, the February raid on the pharmaceutical factory in the Libyan desert was a complete success, which has boosted the agency's image in the circles where it counts. I don't think there will be any problem procuring funds for the project we discussed, but a few fine details still have to be hammered out.*
>
> *The word has been dropped in the right places*

*and it looks like Haddan will bite. As you know,
we've already got our lady in the company. She'll
report directly to you.*

*This is the one we've been waiting for, Jerry.
Let's do it right.*

Elliot

A plant in Crandall's company. A woman. Either Betty or Cindy.

"Did you know about Charlie's connection with the CIA?"

She nodded. "But Carlos told me only recently and because he wanted to know if I'd ever had any impressions about Larry's employees at the Neon Flamingo. Whether any of them were working for the government."

"What did you pick up?"

"The only ones I've met are his bodyguards, his chauffeur, and the woman who is now his personal assistant. I don't like any of them. They are all duplicitous in one way or another, just as Larry is."

"Did Charlie ever mention a man named Heckler?"

"Yes. Steve Heckler. I'm almost certain this memo came from him."

"Does Crandall suspect something? Is that why he's having you watched?"

"I don't think it's his doing. My guess is that Mr. Rau initiated it, as a concession to Mr. Haddan, who believes I'm the devil." She smiled, amused by the thought. "But I don't think I was followed here. My housekeeper and I exchanged clothes. She went in one direction and I went in another."

"Sounds like you took a few lessons from Charlie."

"A few."

"May I keep this memo?"

"That's why I gave it to you. There's one more thing I wish to share with you, then I'd better leave. I'm certain the threat of the hurricane is going to alter their plans somewhat. Mr. Rau, in particular, is uneasy about it. When they were at my house yesterday, I overheard him say to Larry that they need to move from the Tuttle Inn."

"Move? The inn's been boarded up since Crandall bought it."

"I know. I'm only passing along what I overheard. I believe that once we know the riddle of the inn, we will know all of it."

No, not quite all of it. "My wife had gone undercover in Crandall's company. Now she's missing and . . ."

"Say nothing," she interrupted. "The less you tell me the better. Do you have anything of hers? Something she wore or handled frequently?"

He shook his head, then remembered the wedding ring and dug it out of his pocket. "Just this."

She pressed it between her hands. In the subsequent silence, McCleary realized there was no natural light left in the room because the market was sealed beneath planks of plywood. The only illumination came from a light over the stove, where the Cuban woman who had waited on them was stirring something in a pot. The air seemed tight, cramped, claustrophobic, swollen with the odor of food and coffee. The wind shrieked as it prowled the edges of the plywood, seeking a way in.

The hiss of the flame on the stove, the heat in the room, the noise of the wind, himself and the old woman: they possessed the quality of a dream. He suddenly felt as though they were enacting a tribal drama so ancient its origin had been lost in time. She was the shaman, he was the seeker who had come for answers.

When she finally spoke, her voice startled him. Her eyes were shut, and beneath her pale, translucent lids her eyeballs rolled rapidly from one side to another, as if in REM sleep. "Your wife. Is she tall? Thin? Dark-haired?"

"Yes."

Silence, then: "Her name?"

"Quin."

"Quin," she repeated softly. "I want to be Quin, Quin, I want to be Quin." Her fingers flexed over the ring. She rubbed it between her palms, shut her eyes, kept rubbing, a genie with her lamp. When she spoke again, her voice was different, changed. The tempo was faster, the expressions were American, even the diction was not hers but Quin's.

"My shoulder bothers me, my left shoulder. . . ."

Where Quin had been shot several years ago.

"And I don't like being cooped up in here, I don't like being hungry, I don't like not knowing, I don't like any of this. The bulb, something about the bulb up there, think, think, what is it about the bulb? See it, shut your eyes and look at it. The bulb there, the door there, the table in front of me, the . . ."

And just like that, she fell silent.

McCleary almost expected her to twitch, to gasp, to topple from the stool and flail against the floor like an epileptic. But she didn't. Whatever current she'd been swept up in had simply run dry. She released the ring as though it had burned her and rubbed her palms against her slacks.

"She exhausts me," Clara murmured.

"Could you tell where she is?"

"No." She touched the back of his hand. "She's in danger, but for now she is alive and uninjured. She has more resources than you realize."

He pocketed the ring, paid the bill, and they walked back through the shop in silence. When they reached the door, McCleary thanked her, started to extend his hand, then put his arms around her and hugged her hard. She patted him as though he were a small child in need of comfort. The backs of his eyes burned and ached from lack of sleep and he felt an absurd urge to bury his face in her neck and pray.

She stepped back, her hands gripping his forearms. "When you leave here, get in your car and drive off Miami Beach. Do not stay."

Then she turned and walked outside and he stood there feeling small, stupid, and scared. Yes, that most of all.

23

Ole Albert was on his way. Quin, standing at the window, could see it in the churning waters, the violent whipping motions of the trees. She was betting a hurricane warning had been posted since the twins had grabbed her yesterday.

She turned away from the window, wondering what time it was. Three, maybe four o'clock; it was hard to tell with the rain. When would Gracie arrive with dinner? Would the compound be evacuated? And when? She knew, courtesy of Gracie, that there were currently nine patients here, including Heckler. If the compound was evacuated, where would they be sent? But more to the point, would she and Heckler be included among the evacuees?

Sure, Quin. One of you was kidnapped and the other is presumed dead. Do you really think Kilner can risk taking you out of here?

Footsteps. She sat quickly at the table and opened one of the magazines Gracie had brought her. The door whispered open and a short, muscular man strolled in. His eyes seemed to be all pupil, utterly cold and dark, as opaque as a pair of eight balls. He wore jeans and a navy blue windbreaker beaded with water. Kilner: she recognized that bald head, those eyes.

"Quin St. James," he said without preface. "Teacher turned private investigator, now in business in Palm Beach. Your partner and husband, Michael McCleary, is a former homicide detective with Metro-Dade."

"Tell me something I don't know," she said.

He laughed. The fucker actually laughed. "That you do well under pentothal. Not everyone does. Heckler didn't. But he'd been trained not to. How long did you know Charlie?"

"You don't know? You missed a question yesterday?"

"I'm just making conversation, Ms. St. James. Or do you go by Mrs. McCleary? You never know these days."

Yeah, Jerry, you never do.

"So how long did you know him?" he asked again.

"Nearly thirteen years."

He moved away from the open door and she tried not to appear too interested in it. But a part of her was already calculating the distance, estimating whether she could make it past him and get the door shut before he reacted. Probably not. Physically, Kilner looked to be in good shape and it wouldn't surprise her if he'd left the door open intentionally just to see what she'd do.

"Charlie was a brilliant guy," he was saying, "the best speaker they've ever had at Langley." He turned then, walked back toward the door, touched the depression in it. As it shut, he walked over to the table where she sat. "So who do you think killed him?"

"Any of your boys seem like good candidates."

His eyes crinkled with amusement. "Not really. Not if you think about how many problems Charlie's murder has caused us. Personally, I believe someone in Crandall's outfit killed him. Crandall had the most to gain."

"I don't think so. The murder delayed the sale of the Sea Witch and put Crandall under scrutiny."

"Well, it's a moot point right now." He smoothed a hand over his head, patted his midriff, emitted a sigh as phony as the smile on his face. "Here's the situation, Quin. May I call you Quin?"

"Whatever." *Jerry.*

"Whatever." His mouth puckered in a constipated smile. "You sound like my son."

Hey, this guy has a son. Terrific. Mafia dons have sons. Jack the Ripper probably had a son.

"The situation is Albert. As I'm sure you've guessed, warnings have been posted for the southeast coast from Key West to Titusville. He's headed straight for us, toward a point just to the south. I think the high-pressure system to the north is going to push him farther south so that he'll miss the Keys entirely. He's a relatively small storm, just a little over two hundred miles in diameter. But he's packing winds of one-fifty and has a storm surge of six to ten feet."

She felt the blood rush out of her face. A category-four storm. Stronger than Cleo. Nearly as strong as the Labor Day storm way back before they started naming hurricanes.

"So I can't take the risk," Kilner went on. "We have too much sensitive equipment here. We're going to be evacuating everything and everyone to Homestead Air Force Base and from there north to Patrick Air Force Base."

Uh-huh.

"Any questions?"

"No."

"Funny, I'd pegged you for the sort who would have plenty to say about constitutional rights and all that."

"I get the impression that constitutional rights aren't a real high priority around here."

"Quite the contrary, really. Constitutional rights are what we're all about, Quin. We work to conserve those rights, and if it requires doing things which seem contrary to that end, well, so be it."

The end justifies the means. That story was nearly as old as the planet and it was coming from a man who probably ran his life like the Republican Party platform. A guy, she thought, who believed that everyone should be white, heterosexual, and Christian. But the fact remained that he had broken a few laws. Quite a few.

"Once Crandall's business deal is tied up, you'll be released within twenty-four hours."

Right. "And when do you expect Crandall to tie up business?"

"Let me put it this way, Quin. You'll probably be released by Friday, the day after tomorrow."

"And when will Heckler be released?"

Kilner looked as if he'd just swallowed his tongue; under other circumstances, it would have been funny. But to Kilner's credit, he didn't act as if he'd never heard the name. "Steve Heckler disappeared in South America last February. Whatever gave you the idea he's here?"

Whoever, pal, get the pronoun right. "It seemed logical. I get the impression this place is the end of the line."

This elicited a chuckle from Kilner. "That's sometimes how our center is perceived, but actually it proves to be a new beginning for many of our patients."

Nothing infuriated her more than a man who believed she was stupid. "Let's get the semantics straight, Mr. Kilner. I'm not a patient. I'm not an employee of the federal government. I'm not addicted to anything. Two of *your* boys chloroformed and kidnapped me. I was subjected to interrogation under pentothal that was administered without my permission and without a court order and I'm being held here against my will. Unless the laws in this country have changed appreciably since yesterday, you've broken at least four of them. So don't stand there giving me a line that we both know is bullshit."

"You obviously don't know what Crandall's business deal involves."

"Drugs."

"*Drugs?*" He laughed. "We aren't the DEA. We don't spend two years investigating drug cases."

"Then what's involved?"

"The future of the free world."

He uttered this with a perfectly straight face and Quin burst out laughing. "Oh, c'mon, you can come up with something better than a line from John LeCarré, Mr. Kilner."

He didn't crack a smile. "Gracie will be along shortly with an early dinner. I suggest you eat well because once we evacuate it'll be some time before you eat again." And with that, he walked out, the door whispering shut behind him.

The future of the free world. Sure.

Right now she was more concerned with her own future and freedom. And she had the feeling it would be no larger than this room, that Kilner intended to leave her here, a sacrificial lamb for Albert. Even if it was low tide when the hurricane made landfall, a six-to-ten-foot storm surge would be enough to sink the Keys like stones. She got the picture, all right.

Her dinner would probably be drugged; that's what the "eat well" remark was about. While she was conked out, she would be handcuffed to the bed, sound asleep when the big bad wolf really started blowing, asleep when this place collapsed like the little pig's house of sticks. Or maybe he intended to haul her up the road a piece when the convoy moved out and dump her body in the mangrove. A tidy death and who would ever know?

Sink or swim, Quin.

She got up, walked over to the window. The rain was coming down hard, but she'd seen summer showers doing more than this. The sky, though, promised an eventual deluge; it sagged like wet sacks of flour. Quin pulled the blackout curtains across the windows, and pressed them in at the sides of the metal grating so light wouldn't seep through. There would be some illumination from the hallway outside when the door opened, enough for whoever entered to see a shape in the bed.

Quin opened one of the curtains again, climbed up onto the table, loosened the light bulb. She tested it, flicking the wall switch off and on. Nothing. Next, she stripped the top sheet off the bed and bunched it and the two pillows under the quilt. A ruse so hokey it just might work. She walked over to the door, surveyed the room, decided the shape in the bed looked like the real thing.

She noted that she could see the bathroom sink from where she stood, but not the tub or the toilet. She went into the bathroom, put the plug in the tub, turned on the faucets. The pipes in the wall clattered and clanked. While the tub was filling, she soaked her towel, wrung it out, then held it at either end and twirled it until it was as tight as a rope. She snapped it a couple of times, practicing, wondering if she could snap it accurately enough to strike someone's eyes. Then she set it aside and experimented with the bathroom light. She decided to leave it on; no one ran water for a bath in the dark.

She wet the towel again and twirled it as she hurried into the other room. The bathroom was to the right as you came in the door. The light, the overflowing bathtub would be the first things Kilner—or someone—saw. In theory, anyway.

She pulled the curtain shut, then took up a position on the left side of the door.

■   ■   ■

Heckler knew he was looking at the final mile. Whatever happened from this point forward would most likely determine the rest of his life. Assuming, of course, that he survived.

He was standing at the window in his room, watching the evacuation of the compound. Vans were being loaded; Kilner's employees were scurrying around in yellow slickers, carting equipment from the communications shack; and an ambulance had just pulled up to one of the cottages, the vehicle in which patients would eventually be transported.

Eight patients besides himself.

But no one was being brought from the cottages yet, which led him to believe they would be dealt with last. After an early supper. After the evening allotment of medication and sleeping pills. Sure. Drug them up to avoid problems later. Either way, he doubted he would be included.

He fingered the knife that Pisco had given him, slipped it into a pocket in his jeans. He turned the mattress over and dug into the slit in the fabric until his fingers touched the chubby notebook and the pen. He removed them, adjusted the mattress again, made a few notes.

Charlie wouldn't have approved of the notes. He could almost hear the old man admonishing him about the risk, the danger, the threat of discovery. *Never put it in writing, Steve. Never. There're no exceptions to that rule.* But Charlie, he thought, had never been where he was now.

He stuck the notebook down inside his sock, so the cuff of his jeans covered the bulge, and returned to the window. Watching, thinking, planning. He was still there when Pisco arrived a few minutes later with a dinner tray. He shut the door, listened at it, set the tray down on the table.

"All your favorites, including pecan pie," he announced in a voice that was a shade too loud, then touched a finger to his mouth, indicating a need for caution.

Heckler nodded that he understood. "Looks like an evacuation is in progress."

"Yeah. Gracie split for her place to get a jump on traffic, which is why I'm delivering meals." Pisco moved over to where Heckler stood, whispering now. "Kilner got a call and has left for Homestead, supposedly to meet LeFrank. But it wasn't LeFrank on the phone. It was a woman."

"How do you know?"

"I listened on the extension."

"What'd she say?"

"That it was time to move because Crandall's going to do his deal before the hurricane hits. I'm supposed to take you and another patient in my own car and get rid of you. I'm going to stall until nearly everyone's off the compound, just to minimize the chance that someone will want to ride with me, and I'll drop you and the woman at a shelter near Homestead."

"Who's the woman?"

"A friend of Charlie's who was working undercover in Crandall's outfit for the local cops. The Miami surveillance team grabbed her yesterday and brought her here. Kilner put her under pentothal, emptied her head, and wants her out of the picture."

"How do you know she was a friend of Charlie's?"

"I put the needle in her vein and listened to her, that's how. You still got the knife?"

Heckler patted his pocket.

"Keep it handy. I'll be back when it's safe and I'll knock twice at the door, like this." He rapped his knuckles against the wall, two quick, two slow. "If you don't hear the knock, it's not me. It'd be just like Kilner to tell someone else to take care of you and do me in at the same time."

"Is the food safe to eat?"

Pisco's strange eyes slipped toward the table. "I don't know. Don't risk it, just in case. I'll be back."

He started to move away, but Heckler caught his arm, then couldn't speak around the lump in his throat. Pisco squeezed his hand and smiled briefly. "We'll get you out of this, man; one way or another, we'll do it."

Then he was gone and Heckler was alone again, alone with the sound of the rain, the wind, and the oppressive weight of his own uncertainty.

■ ■ ■

The boat putted through the mangroves just off the coast of Long Key. Tark was pretty sure the wind and the steady rain covered the noise of the outboard motor. He just hoped the activity he'd been observing in the compound for the last hour would keep everyone so busy that he wouldn't be noticed.

He cut back on the throttle as the boat chugged out from under the protective canopy of trees and headed east, into the wind. This was, he knew, one of the outermost bands of squalls that preceded Albert and which had been drumming the coast for the last few hours. It would be followed by a period of less wind and a drizzle as irritating as a postnasal drip. Then it would start up again, with the periods in between squalls growing progressively shorter until the hurricane was on them.

Waves washed over the sides of the Zodiac. Even though his canvas bag was waterproof, there were a few things inside that weren't, so he moved it into his lap and under his poncho. He could almost hear Alfie chiding him for his decision to come here, shaking a finger at him. *You're a crazy man, Gabby. You don't need to do this for me.* But it wasn't just for Alfie; he needed to do this for himself. To be released, he thought. Released from the past, from the man he had become in the years since his wife and daughter had died.

When he was within three feet of shore, he killed the motor, slid into water up to his knees, and pulled the raft to the beach that probably wouldn't be here by sunrise tomorrow. He tied the raft to a palm tree, grabbed his canvas bag, and dug inside for the gun he'd taken from Lamadero. He slipped it into the right pocket of his poncho and moved quickly along the brush that paralleled the fence. When the brush ended, he stopped, and scanned the compound.

He counted a dozen people, six vans, two Jeeps, and two regular cars. And an ambulance. No question that an evacuation was underway. Two men in ponchos were loading things into a pair of vans parked under the blue house. It was closest to the guardhouse at the front of the compound and the most distant from where he was. Windows on the various houses were, for the most part, already covered by shutters.

He pulled a hammer from his bag, waited for an opportune moment, then darted out from the protection of the bushes. Two quick blows took care of the padlock on the gate the jogger had come through three days ago. The wind hurled it open.

He dropped to his knees, watching, then decided it was as safe as it would ever be. He sprinted for the closest house, ducked behind one of the concrete pillars that raised the building seven feet into the air. In the space beneath the house were a workbench, tools, storage room, and another set of steps leading up into the house. He removed his shoes, socks, and poncho, and stuck them in the canvas bag. Then he brought out Lamadero's gun, disengaged the safety, and crept up the stairs.

The door at the top was shut. He listened, opened it, stepped inside, shut it quickly. A pantry. He'd emerged in a pantry.

It was a long, linear room and its accordion door was open enough for him to see a man shuffle into the kitchen and lean against the counter, his back to Tark. He was built like Humpty-Dumpty and wore a yellow windbreaker that strained across the shoulders and spine, rendering his weapon in excruciating detail: the angle at which its muzzle was stuck into the back of his pants, the lines on its grip, even the width of its barrel. Tark crept forward, then stopped when someone else entered the room. "Hey, Zeek, you going to check on Rapunzel or what?"

"Yeah, in a minute. Take a look at this."

The second man stepped into Tark's line of vision; he was as fat as the first. They had a good chuckle over whatever they were looking at. "Guess Gracie forget to take the mail with her," said Zeek, laughing.

"I kind of figured things were pretty sour between Jerry and Elliot, but I didn't know they were *this* bad."

"Maybe we should show these to Dan."

"Fuck Dan. We'll keep it."

"I'll keep it," said the first guy. "Find Dan and ask him what we're supposed to move out of here. I'm going to bring the van around front."

They left. Tark moved closer to the door, waiting for one of them to return. It didn't matter which one, either would do.

■ ■ ■

By the time Quin finally heard someone in the hall, water had been pounding full blast into the tub for the better part of an hour, and spilling over the sides. Although she couldn't see anything in the room—she'd turned out the bathroom light a while ago—she guessed the water on the bathroom floor was now calf deep. The excess poured over the wedge of wood on the floor that separated the two rooms and streamed into the bedroom.

She didn't think any of it had seeped under the metal door. It created an effective barrier against which the water rose and rose, lapping at her ankles.

Okay, Kilner, let's do it, let's get this over with.

Quin tightened her grip on the towel and pressed up hard against the wall. The door slid open and a man hurried in, stopped, looked down. "What the fuck." He held a dinner tray in one hand and patted the wall with the other, looking for the light switch. Quin snapped the wet towel at his head, neck, then lurched toward him.

Her body slammed into his just as he was turning. Although he outweighed her by at least fifty pounds, she caught him by surprise and the floor was more slippery than a truckload of banana peels. His legs flew out from under him, the dinner tray flew up, and she stumbled back but not fast enough. He grabbed her ankle, jerking her off her feet, and when she struck the floor on her buttocks, he was still holding on, twisting her foot as she struggled, as she kicked, as she tried to wrench free.

Both of his hands were around her ankle now and climbed her leg as though it were a rope, yanking her toward him through the water as she kicked with her right leg, her free leg. She knew she landed several hard blows to his chest, but it was like striking cement.

She snapped forward and clawed at his face, his eyes, forcing him to use one of his hands to protect himself. She felt it the second he let go, felt the sudden release of pressure on her leg, felt his fingers tighten around her arm. He began to twist it, to twist her arm as though he intended to twist it right out of the socket. She shrieked with pain and panic overtook her, transformed her into some wild, primitive beast for whom anything was fair. Her head whipped left and she sank her teeth into his forearm and held on until she tasted blood. He made a terrible noise deep in his throat, a noise that was barely human, and hurled her away from him.

Quin leaped up, but so did he. He tackled her at the waist before she reached the door, the *open* door—she could see the dim light, the hall, the wooden floor tracked with mud—and they both went down. She wasn't sure what happened then, whether one of them twisted or kept moving forward as they were falling. But suddenly he smashed into the wall, smashed headfirst, and slumped to the floor.

For seconds, Quin lay there beneath the weight of his arms, her mind pushed into a white, blank space, her cheek squashed against her own hand, water trickling into her nose. Then she reared up, coughing, sputtering for air, and scrambled away from him on her hands and knees. When she had caught her breath, when she was sure he was actually out cold and not faking, she went over to him. Crouched beside him.

Dan. This was Dan Someone.

She searched his pockets and kept his automatic, his keys, his wallet. Then she stripped him of his rain slicker and put it on. She grabbed him by the hands and dragged him across the room to the bed. She propped him up against the side near the headboard, lifted his right arm as far as it would go, and snapped the cuff around his wrist.

"Sorry, guy. Hate to do this and run. But you'll probably figure out something." His type always did.

She turned off the bathtub faucets and hurried into the hall. Now. The door. How to get the door shut.

The panel on the wall glowed with half a dozen buttons that weren't labeled. Below them were two buttons, a red and a green. She punched the green and the door whispered shut. Then she punched the red button, the one labeled POWER, and heard the door as it died. As a manual lock clicked into place.

She was still barefoot and the raincoat hung on her, but she and Dan were about the same size, so perhaps in the rain, in the gloomy light, no one would know the difference. She slipped past black, silent rooms. Empty, this house was empty. Where was Kilner keeping Heckler?

She peered through the glass oval in the front door. She could see two vans parked under the house on the other side of the walk, a car and a van moving up the driveway toward the guardhouse. Two men emerged from the house, carrying boxes that they loaded into the vans.

They were evacuating.

She backed up to the wall, disengaged the safety on the automatic, took another look. They were still there. Wait, she thought. Wait, watch, and then take your chances.

■   ■   ■

Fat man was back, peering into the fridge. Tark touched the edge of the pantry door, opening it wider, and stepped into the kitchen. The man lifted a container of orange juice to his mouth and guzzled it. When Tark was within three feet of him, the guy suddenly straightened up, apparently sensing something. He set the orange juice back inside the fridge and Tark knew he was going for his weapon. "Don't," Tark said very, very softly. "Or I'll blow away a kidney."

Fat man froze.

"Lock your hands on top of your head."

He did.

Tark moved up behind him, pressed his weapon to the back of the man's neck, kicked the refrigerator door shut, and relieved the fat man of his gun. He stuck it in the waistband of his jeans. "Where's Kilner?"

"U-upstairs."

"Yeah? Then maybe you'd better shout for him."

Silence.

"Go on, call him."

"Hey, Mr. K-k-kilner," he shouted, his voice echoing in the shuttered rooms.

"I think you lied to me." Tark cocked his gun. "So let's start over again, fat man. Where's Kilner?"

"M-m-miami," he stuttered. "He ha-had to go to Miami."

"And Pisco?"

"H-he's serving dinners to the patients."

"Who else is around?"

"That's it."

"Sure it is."

"I swear."

"What about the other fat guy?"

"He's getting the van."

"What's your name, fat man?"

"Z-zeek."

"What's your job, Zeek?"

"Miami su-surveillance."

"Then how come you're not in Miami?"

"I ha-had to come down here."

"Why's Kilner in Miami?"

"Elliot Le-LeFrank called him."

"Who's LeFrank?"

"K-kilner's boss."

"And what's his job, Zeek?"

"T-top dog."

"In what?"

"Here."

"I thought Kilner was top dog."

"Of the compound. But LeFrank oversees everything. He's the money man, the guy who makes the major decisions."

"Who's he work for?"

"CIA. H-he's third-highest in the agency."

"Got anything else you want to say, Zeek?"

"You're . . . you're m-making a b-big mistake, pal."

"Uh-huh. Sweet dreams, Zeek." Tark slammed the gun over his head and he melted to the floor, fat quivering. Tark patted him down, found a set of keys, pocketed them, and pulled a manila envelope from inside Zeek's windbreaker. He set it on the counter, then dug a pair of handcuffs from his bag and snapped one cuff on Zeek's left wrist and pulled him over to the sink. He opened the cabinet door beneath it and snapped the other cuff around the pipe inside. He stuffed a dish towel in Zeek's mouth, then opened the manila envelope.

There were four photos of a white-haired man in various lewd activities with a boy of perhaps fourteen. The accompanying note, unsigned and handwritten, was addressed to a reporter at the *Miami Herald* and read:

> *The man in the photos is Elliot LeFrank, a shoo-in for the number-one slot in the CIA when the present director retires.*

Nasty little secrets as stepping stones to power. But if Kilner had left to meet with LeFrank, why hadn't he taken the photos with him? Blackmail wasn't blackmail unless the person with the secret knew you held the cards.

It was just one more question begging for an answer.

Tark put the photos in the envelope, slipped it into his canvas bag, and crept to the kitchen doorway, listening. Wind, rain, and, more distant, the soft drone of a television somewhere.

He followed the sound through the gloom of a dark hallway, across a living room, and stopped at the foot of the stairs that led to the second floor. The TV was louder now.

Tark ascended the stairs at an angle, his back to the wall. Only one door up here and it was locked. Tark rapped once, waited, rapped once again. Then he removed Zeek's keys from his pocket. The second one did the trick. He nudged the door open with his foot, his gun moving as he turned slowly, surveying the room.

It smelled like an attic that had been shut up for years. The flickering light of the TV, tuned to an old western, provided the only illumination, and it cast long, blurred shadows against the walls. "Anyone here?" Tark said softly, opening the door wider with his foot.

It creaked, touched the wall, and he continued past the bed and moved toward the bathroom. Then he heard it, heard it when his back was to the bed, a small, almost nonexistent sound, like the rustling of leaves.

Or clothes.

He spun and saw *something* moving toward him, something with long white hair that floated around its bony head like ectoplasm. Its lips were drawn back from its gleaming wet teeth, its arm was raised, it was hissing, and it was charging toward him through the flickering light from the TV. He didn't know if it was man, beast, ghost, and he didn't care, it didn't matter, the thing was gripping a knife.

He squeezed the trigger, squeezed without thinking, squeezed because it was either him or it. The explosion hurled it back, the knife clattered to the floor, and when Tark reached the shape on the floor, blood was seeping across the front of its shirt.

Not an it, a man. A man who had been a bag of bones with white hair.

Tark touched his fingers to the man's neck, checking for a pulse despite what his senses told him. There was none. He stared for a moment at the man's vapid eyes, then shut them gently, his own heart swelling with regret.

You going to check on Rapunzel or what?

"You're Rapunzel." A man imprisoned in a room like a tower; suddenly he knew this guy was Heckler. "Aw, Christ." He rubbed his eyes, touched Heckler's neck again, hoping to feel a pulse, praying that he would. But dead was dead. Whatever secrets Heckler had possessed had died with him.

Tark got up, shut the door, then returned to the body. He patted Heckler down. Wedged inside his right sock was a small notebook with a dinosaur on it, the kind a kid would buy at the local drugstore for less than a buck. He moved up close to the TV so he could read.

The first entry was dated five days after Charlie Potemkin's murder. It was obvious that Heckler had been trying to conserve space, because it was written in print so small Tark figured he would need a magnifying glass to read most of it. But he was able to make out enough to realize that it probably contained the key, the key to everything.

24

". . . Albert's forward speed is now twenty miles an hour and his leading edge is slightly more than two hundred miles west of Miami. Top winds are a hundred and fifty miles an hour and the barometric pressure has fallen to 28.01. The storm surge is expected to be eight to ten feet.

"If the storm continues on its present course, it will make landfall between three and four tomorrow morning. All coastal areas between Key West and Fort Lauderdale are under an evacuation order, as are all mobile-home parks, islands in Biscayne Bay, and low-lying flood areas inland. If you're in an evacuation area, proceed to the shelter nearest you. If you don't know where the nearest shelter is, call the Red Cross at 555-HELP or stay tuned for the list of shelters that will follow this broadcast. Do not call 911 for anything other than emergencies. . . ."

Boone turned down the volume. "I knew we should've stayed at the office. I knew it."

McCleary swung into the municipal parking garage on Eleventh Street and Collins. "No one twisted your arm, Will."

"It could have waited, that's all I'm saying."

"No, what you're saying is that *I* shouldn't have come back to the beach because *you* didn't want to. And what I'm saying is that you didn't have to come."

He uttered this more sharply than he'd intended, but Boone finally shut up. He'd been griping since they'd left his place twenty minutes ago, a drive that usually took a fraction of that on a normal day in rush-hour traffic. But this wasn't a normal day. The evacuation had created mass confusion; it was as if gasoline had been poured into a massive anthill and someone nearby had struck the match that would ignite all of it.

McCleary paid the attendant four bucks; she handed him a short form that released the city from all liability and asked him to sign it. "The storm, you know. No one's going to be on duty here past six-thirty."

"Right." He scribbled his name at the bottom, handed it back to her, and started up the ramp. The garage was one of the tallest on the beach, four stories, and it was jammed with cars, a sure sign that not everyone intended to evacuate.

In and out of the Tuttle Inn, he thought. Thirty minutes, tops. That would give them more than enough time to make it back to the office in North Miami before the rain and wind worsened. Enough time even with eighty thousand people pouring out of the Keys and choking the roads and Christ knew how many other thousands fleeing Dade for points farther north. Orlando. Gainesville. Tallahassee. Inland.

McCleary finally found a space at the very top of the parking garage. He grabbed ponchos and a backpack from the rear seat and they got out. He pulled the poncho over his head and slung the strap of the backpack over his shoulder.

They took the stairs to the main level and walked up Eleventh Street toward Ocean Drive, into the rain and wind. Traffic moved at a crawl under streetlights that had blinked on several hours early. He supposed some of the drivers were gawkers, that peculiar breed of homo sapiens who also frequent homicide scenes, disaster sites, and fires, and who fill the bleachers at high-risk spectacles like the Grand Prix. They were drawn by the blood, the violence, the titillation. They were the ultimate spectators, virtuosos of vicarious thrills.

Before they reached Ocean, they ducked down an alley that ran behind most of the now-shuttered buildings on Ocean Drive. A part of him kept circling the puzzle of Quin's disappearance. He tried to reach that place within himself where he could seize one of the invisible connections between them, pluck at it and feel the welcome resistance at the other end that would tell him she was still alive. But the route to this secret inner place eluded him.

Two blocks later, they turned up a second alley that stood between the old Tuttle Inn and the half-renovated restaurant next to it, which Crandall owned. They scrambled under the construction fence to the side of the building. Wind gusted around them. His poncho flapped at his legs like a wet tent. Boone held on to his checkered cap and leaned into the wind, sufficiently pissed to prove he could be a trooper.

The inn was sealed like a mummy's tomb. So much plywood covered the structure it looked as if it were made of the stuff. McCleary wedged his fingers under the edge of a piece of plywood and pulled. It held fast.

He walked to the back of the alley to try the rear doors and passed several pieces of heavy construction equipment. It seemed unlikely that the wind would cart these suckers off, but they should have been removed when the watch had gone into effect. He jerked on the rear doors, but they were locked. When he returned to the side of the building, Boone was pacing, as edgy as an expectant father.

"How the fuck we going to get in there, Mike?"

McCleary ignored him and unbuckled the backpack.

"How, Mike?"

"Go keep watch or something."

"I don't like your attitude."

"Then quit being a pain in the ass."

Stony silence again. After all this, McCleary hoped to hell there was something in here, that the *santera* hadn't misunderstood what she had overheard.

From the backpack, McCleary removed the three pieces of the

most useful tool he owned. He snapped them together, and plugged the wire into the battery pack clipped to his belt. He pressed the switch and regulated the thin beam of light that shot out of the end.

"Looks like a Star Trek gizmo," Boone remarked.

"Same principle, I guess."

The apparatus had been custom-made in Zurich and had been given to him by a woman he'd met the summer he'd suffered temporary amnesia. Powered by the battery pack, it emitted a thin, high-powered laser similar to what was being used on coronary patients with clogged arteries. In the medical procedure, lasers were shot through a catheter fed into the heart and burned out fat in the arteries. Adapted, this little beauty cut through virtually anything except lead.

It took twenty seconds for it to cut a hole through two layers of plywood and another minute for the beam to enlarge the hole enough so that he could squeeze through. He broke down the tool as he waited for Boone to climb in. He moved like a snail and was as clumsy as a kid learning to scale a tree.

C'mon, move, old man, move.

■ ■ ■

Quin was huddled under the front steps of the cottage, watching a pair of men, one tall, the other short and fat, lift objects into the back of a van. Off to her left, she saw another man jogging away from the house that was most distant from her, coming this way, his raincoat flapping at his legs.

Stay put, she thought. She wasn't about to take on three men and risk alerting the guards at the gate, the guys who were probably armed with automatic weapons and wouldn't hesitate to fire at anyone they didn't recognize. She didn't intend to be carted out of here in a body bag.

She waited. The tall man who had been loading things into the van now headed back up the steps and into the cottage. His fat partner hurried into the space under the house, where he started going through several boxes. He apparently hadn't seen the jogger, who was almost directly across from her now, slowing to a walk, approaching the van with the stealth of a guy up to no good.

An intruder? A wayward patient? *Maybe Heckler?*

The jogger slipped carefully around the front of the van, which faced Quin, and moved like lightning on the fat man, knocking him flat. As Quin watched, the jogger began to roll the fat man through the veil of rain and under the house. He obviously didn't know about the guy who now stood in the open doorway of the cottage, his arms laden with boxes. Whoever the jogger was—wayward patient, Heckler, renegade on a mission—she decided she would be better off with him on her side.

Quin swung out from under the steps, the hood of the slicker tight over her hair, her head bowed slightly, and darted through the fading light toward the stairs of the cottage. She waved as the tall man descended and he, mistaking her for one of his own, shouted something she didn't hear. She kept her head down and charged up the stairs, one hand on the railing, and crashed into him. He fell back with a grunt, boxes tumbling down around him, spilling reams of paper and boxes of computer discs, and bounced down the stairs on his back, his head banging like a volleyball against each step.

Then he lay motionless at the bottom, rain pouring over him, computer paper fluttering like giant wet leaves in the air around him. *Don't be dead.* Quin trotted down the steps and dropped to a crouch beside him to check for a pulse. Faint but steady. He'd probably have a bitch of a headache and a sore ass when he came to, but he definitely wasn't going to check out.

She stood. Turned. And there, his face in shadow, was the jogger, his gun aimed at her chest.

"That's far enough," he snapped, and stepped into full view.

Her astonishment rendered her utterly speechless and she just stood there staring, blinking rain out of her eyes, trying to piece it all together and failing miserably. It was Tark. Here. Tark, lowering his gun and looking at her as though she were some curious species of bug that had crawled out of his shoe.

■ ■ ■

The beams of their flashlights skipped across debris from the fire that had gutted the Tuttle Inn several years ago. Nature had invaded despite the barriers of plywood: swarms of ants, roaches, droppings from small animals, even weeds that had pushed up through the cracks in the floor. They passed a burned-out staircase that ascended into nowhere, pieces of charred furniture, and the crumbling remains of walls that had once divided rooms and were now blackened by smoke.

The area near the doors at the rear of the building was littered with things left by man: crumpled cigarette packs, cellophane, discarded beer cans, a stained tarp, yellowed newspapers. But the metal doors weren't stained by smoke; they looked new. And the ceiling was spotless. McCleary guessed that Crandall's reconstruction efforts had included a new roof, new rear doors, new exterior walls.

"Nothing here," Boone whispered. "You satisfied now?"

"No." McCleary made his way into what had once been the inn's kitchen. The wind whistled past the boarded windows like a noisy animal on the prowl. The counter was still standing, a solid block of concrete that ran from one end of the room to the other, its sides blackened, the terrazzo on the surface chipped, broken, filthy. Pipes jutted from the walls where appliances had once been. On one side was a tremendous pantry and beside it a pair of metal doors.

The inn's walk-in freezer, McCleary guessed. From the looks of it, these metal doors were as new as those at the rear of the building. They were secured with a thick chain and padlock. "Can your gizmo take care of the lock?" Boone whispered.

"Unless it's lead."

Fifteen seconds later, the padlock popped free. Boone pulled the chain through the handles and McCleary pressed down on one of them and pulled. The door creaked and scraped against the concrete floor.

Inside, the walls were also metal and were lined with several rows of metal cylinders. At first, McCleary mistook them for dive tanks. But he realized they were slimmer, lacked the hardware on top, and appeared to be as smooth and seamless as an egg. Upon closer scrutiny, he discovered a flip top at the upper end of each tank that revealed a high-pressure nozzle.

"I say we hoof it back to the garage, call Tim, and let the cops take care of it," Boone said.

"He won't be able to move without a search warrant and he's not going to be able to get a warrant tonight. Besides, if this is the stuff worth forty million bucks, Will, Crandall isn't going to just let it sit here, not with Albert on the way. These cylinders are going to be moved tonight. I'm sure of it."

"So what're you saying? That we should wait? That's what you're saying, isn't it? We should hide in here and wait for something that may or may not happen."

The glow from their flashlights threw Boone's face out of whack, smoothing some creases, deepening others, changing angles and planes until he resembled the man he had been nearly twelve years ago, the man whose life had come apart at the seams and whose mind had plunged into a black, spinning abyss. McCleary suddenly understood that if he pushed Boone he was going to have a total flake on his hands. That prospect was worse than Boone the pouting teenager or Boone the crotchety old man.

"C'mon. We're leaving. I'm going to call Tim and you're going to take the car and drive to the office where Joe is."

"Then you're coming back here to wait?"

"Yeah." McCleary pressed the car keys into Boone's sweaty hand. He looked at them as an alien might, as though he'd never seen a key in his life.

"I can't just leave you here."

Like it was abandonment and not a favor. "Don't worry about it. I'll meet you back at the office."

Boone fell into step beside him as they crossed the freezer to the door. "Maybe we should flag down one of those cops out there on Ocean Drive."

"And tell him what?"

"That, uh, well . . ."

"Exactly."

Boone caught his arm, stopping him in the center of the freezer. "Listen, Mike. I just want you to know that I appreciate everything you've done. I know I've been an asshole, but I . . . I . . ." His voice swelled with emotion, his mouth began to twitch and quiver, and McCleary realized he was going to break down and weep.

"Hey, come on." He gave the old man's shoulder a quick squeeze. "We've known each other too long for bullshit. Besides, I'm getting paid for this and you're not."

Boone smiled in spite of himself. "I don't know if you can understand this, but something happens to you when you get old. You can't remember who you were at thirty or forty or fifty. Sometimes you can't even remember who you were yesterday. Time gets all mixed up. You do things to people you love, say things that . . ."

A bright light suddenly impaled them, eclipsing Boone's sentence and momentarily blinding McCleary. A man's voice radiated from inside the light. "Hands up where I can see them and back up nice and slow to the wall. Good, that's fine. Follow directions and you'll live longer. Check them, babe."

The beam skipped to a point just above McCleary's head, where the ceiling diffused the light. Now he could see the bald man who'd spoken, and the woman, Crandall's chauffeur, Cindy Youngston.

"Hi, Mr. Boone. Imagine running into you here," she said cheerfully, frisking him with practiced hands and pulling things out of his pockets. "Hey, suntan lotion." She held up a squeeze bottle, laughed, shoved it back into his pocket, patted some more. "He's clean." She looked at McCleary and those baby blues smiled. "But I bet you're not. What's your name, doll?"

"Mike."

She frisked him. "Oops, what's this?" She held up the battery pack, shrugged, tossed it over her shoulder, continued to pat and probe. "Well, well, Mr. Mike's carrying. A Magnum. Big gun, Mr. Mike." She stepped back, the Magnum aimed at the ceiling. "Slide the backpack off, Mike, drop it on the floor, and don't try to be a hero. Oh, look at this, Jerry. Look how well Mike follows directions."

"Shut up," Jerry snapped. "Check the pack."

She glared at him and tossed the pack at his feet. "Check it yourself. I'll cover them."

He gave her a look that could melt asphalt in seconds, crouched, and went through the backpack as he talked. "What's your last name, Mike?"

"Griffin."

"Griffin." He removed a screwdriver from the pack, extra ammo, a small canteen of water, and several other objects before he brought out the three separate parts of the laser. His small eyes met McCleary's. "Now how come I don't believe that, Mike?"

McCleary didn't say anything; he watched the man fumbling with the three parts, trying to fit them together. He was certain he would fail; the apparatus was a Rubik's cube unless you'd seen it assembled a few times.

"Jerry asked you a question, Mike," said Cindy. "I think you'd better answer it." She cocked the Magnum. The sound echoed sharply in the metal room and drew a quick warning glance from Jerry. McCleary recognized something in his dark eyes—fear, anxiety, a spurt of panic—and realized it had to do with the cylinders. That he was telling her not to fire the gun in here, not to risk puncturing one of the cylinders.

Jerry didn't impress him as the kind of man who spooked easily, but he was clearly spooked now. Beads of sweat erupted on his forehead. His eyes were fixed on the gun. And yet his voice was soft, cool, soothing, mountain water slipping over mossy rocks. "It's not that important, babe. I already know who he is. Mike McCleary."

McCleary's head began to pound; he watched the woman's finger ease up on the trigger. Watched the cocking mechanism close. Watched the way her long, lovely neck swiveled slowly as she looked at Jerry. "Quin's hubby."

"Right." Jerry smiled. "She does well under pentothal, Mike. Real well." He set the pieces of the tool on the floor, gathered up the other objects, and shoved them back into the pack. "Talks a blue streak. She should've left my boys well enough alone when they were messing around with the phone line, but no, she had to show how clever she was. She was so clever we decided to pick her up."

He raised the parts again and his fingers worked with them until two of the three snapped together. "You have a sixteen-month-old daughter who's staying with your sister-in-law somewhere around Disney World. Her name's Michelle, Ellie for short. Your dog, Flats, belonged to your sister, who was murdered in November in Gainesville." Those malignant eyes met McCleary's again. "Want me to go on, Mike?"

The woman grinned. "Goddamn, Jerry, I'm impressed."

"Ready to hear more, Mike?"

A dozen questions scrambled around in his head. But to voice them would give this guy more power than he already had. "No."

Jerry stood, snapped the third piece onto the tool, aimed it at the floor, and pressed the switch. The beam of light shot out, burned briefly against the concrete. He shut it off and pressed the toe of his running shoe into the indentation. "Most impressive, Mike. Where did you get it?"

A bit of technical banter before the shit flew. "It was custom-made in Zurich."

"Fascinating." The way he stroked it was almost sexual. "Did it make the hole in the plywood out there?"

McCleary nodded.

He turned it on again, moving the beam in a small, tight circle against the concrete floor. "What won't it cut through?"

"Metal," McCleary lied.

"Oh?" His arm came up, the beam aimed at the wall just to the right of McCleary's shoulder. "Looks like it'll cut through metal just fine. I detest liars, Mike. I really do."

And suddenly the beam struck McCleary's shoulder. It felt like a long, white-hot nail was being hammered straight through him, through skin, muscle, bone. He gasped, his knees buckled, and he went down with a soft, pathetic whimper.

"Jesus, Jesus," Boone sputtered. "You can't . . ."

"I can't what, Mr. Boone?" Jerry said, laughing. "Do tell me. I'm eager to know just what it is I can't do."

Cindy giggled. "Oh-oh, Jerry. Mr. Boone's pissed on himself."

"On the floor, Mr. Boone, facedown, hands behind your back."

McCleary sucked air in through clenched teeth. His shoulder throbbed, burned, stank of charred flesh. When he took his hand away from the spot, there was a perfectly round black hole half the size of a dime in his windbreaker. No blood: the beam had cauterized the vessels. But he knew if he poked his finger into the hole it would slide past tissue and muscle as spongy and damp as a soft-boiled egg and strike bone.

"C'mon, Jerry, we've got to move," Cindy said.

But Jerry wasn't finished. "Smarts, doesn't it, Mike?"

McCleary raised his head. He would remember this bastard's face the rest of his life, those sadistic eyes, the sweep of bald head, the mocking mouth.

"Doesn't it?" he snapped.

"Yes."

"Flatten out on your stomach, Mike."

McCleary did and the hot throb in his shoulder bubbled up and exploded in a new wave of pain. The stink, the horrible stink of his own seared flesh, nauseated him. Bile swelled in his throat; he swallowed it back and tried to focus on breathing. On nothing more than the act of drawing air in and letting it out. Next to him, Boone was weeping, his cheek flat against the floor, his eyes squeezed shut.

"Poor Mr. Boone," said Jerry. "I sympathize, I really do, but there's nothing worse than a sniveling old man." He turned the laser on again and aimed it at the floor just an inch from the tip of Boone's nose. "If you don't shut up, I'll burn off your fucking nose."

Boone stifled his cries.

"I want you to think very carefully before you answer this question, Mr. Boone. Is your pal Mike working for the cops like his wife?"

"Ye-yes."

"And what're you two doing here?"

Boone spilled what he knew, spilled it as he stuttered and sniffled and struggled not to weep. He didn't know everything that McCleary did, but he knew enough. Jerry glanced at McCleary when Boone was finished.

"Let me put it this way, Mike. Right about now, your wife and Steve Heckler are mired in muck at the bottom of the mangrove in the lower Keys. They got in the way, just like you and Mr. Boone. Too bad about your wife. Of the four of you, I liked her the best."

McCleary didn't move, didn't breathe too deeply, didn't give the fucker any excuse to use the laser. The words clattered around inside him as he and Boone were cuffed to each other and Boone's other hand was cuffed to a metal grating in the wall. As Jerry and the woman wheeled a metal cart into the freezer and proceeded to load the cylinders onto it, specific images moved through McCleary with the heavy slowness of a toxic liquid. Quin at the bottom of a swamp, stuck in the silt like an old shoe. Quin's body rising, arms floating at her sides, part of her face chewed away.

A part of him knew these images were precisely what Jerry had intended to produce. But worse than the images was the horror of not knowing whether they were true. Clara Villa had said she was alive, but that wasn't enough. He tried to reach the private, inviolate place within himself where the images couldn't follow, that sacred site of his inner world. But it was like swimming through black syrup. He couldn't find the place, couldn't find the connection, couldn't find anything but more blackness and a deeper horror. He was distracted by the hot, persistent ache in his shoulder, the movements around him, the noise of the carts, the cylinders, and finally, the sound of Boone's voice, asking what the cylinders contained. The question wasn't addressed to anyone in particular, but the woman laughed in response.

"Cherry flavoring."

Cindy patted one of the cylinders. "Cherry flavoring or, more to the point, benzaldehyde, the stuff that makes almond extract smell and taste like cherries."

Jerry picked up the explanation. "There's a byproduct in the production of cherry flavoring that's called ferric ferrocyanide, a nontoxic compound that's used in inks and carbon paper. It can be transformed into sodium cyanide liquid or hydrogen cyanide gas. What you're looking at here is about four hundred pounds of cyanide gas."

He let that sink in a moment and smiled at McCleary. "You're an ex-cop, Mike. You know about gas chambers. A pellet of this kills a man in just a matter of seconds. Actually, it doesn't take more than a hundred to two hundred milligrams of gas to kill a full-grown man."

"And it doesn't matter whether you inhale it," Cindy went on, "or whether it gets into your body through the skin. Either way, the end result's the same. It prevents the cells from using oxygen."

"If all that's true," Boone said, "you wouldn't be carting the stuff away in cylinders."

"Oh, these are quite safe, Mr. Boone. The cylinders are based on the same premise as binary artillery shells, which were developed to improve the safe handling and storage of a variety of toxic agents. In the shells, two nontoxic and intermediate forms of a particular agent are stored in separate compartments. When fired, the components are mixed within the shell and the toxic gas is released when the shell explodes. In other words, these cylinders would have to be dropped from a twenty-story building or be in an explosion before the substances would mix and the cyanide would be released."

Jerry set the flashlight on the floor, the beam aimed at the ceiling. "The most important thing is that Haisar Haddan is willing to pay ten million just for this load and most of it will be in cash."

"Which Crandall will never see." Cindy flashed a triumphant

smile, which made it abundantly clear that she and Jerry were certainly going to have a terrific time with their millions.

"Wait," Boone said softly. "Was this . . . the two of you . . . a setup from the beginning?"

The question wasn't addressed to either of them, but Cindy answered, first with a laugh, then with a sly look at her companion. "For me it was, but not for Jerry. I don't think it became a serious possibility for him until the money entered into it and LeFrank got to be a real pain in the ass. Wouldn't you say that's right, Jerry?"

He looked pissed, McCleary thought, and didn't even glance at her. "I'm afraid we're out of time, Mr. Boone. We really have to make tracks. And just in case your next question is who killed Charlie, I don't know who.

"C'mon, babe."

Jerry dropped the backpack on the cart and pushed it out of the freezer. Then he turned, Cindy at his side. "We'll leave you the flashlight. By the time you get out of here—if you do—it won't make any difference to us. I do wish we could stick around and see how this is going to turn out, but we have to press on, gentlemen. And oh, Mike." He held up the laser. "I'll think of you every time I use this."

Cindy grinned and waggled her fingers. "And I hope you boys think of Jerry and me on a Caribbean beach somewhere."

Then they pushed the metal door shut. McCleary heard the chain being pulled through the handle again.

■ ■ ■

He was doing it, he was actually doing it. He, Jerry Kilner, ex-operative, ex-husband, ex-father, was driving a moving van loaded with chemical weapons, driving it into an uncharted future. No more late-night calls from the total fuckup who had been his son, no more Elliot LeFranks casting a pall of gloom over his life, no more Hecklers, no more Piscos, no more, no more. He had never felt such exhilaration.

Now the van was rising over the bridge that led to the mainland. Now it was pulling onto the interstate, sliding into the heavy traffic.

Now it was cruising at fifty miles an hour, the wipers whipping across the windshield. And now, he, Jerry Kilner, threw his head back and laughed, laughed until his ribs ached and tears coursed down his cheeks.

Bye-bye, Jerry Kilner, and hello to whoever he would become.

25

McCleary stood slowly, his knees creaking like rusted hinges, his shoulder throbbing. Thanks to the flashlight Jerry had left on the floor some distance away, he could see. The five-inch chain that connected his cuff to Boone's rattled as he moved; the old man's eyes followed him up. "Jesus, how're we going to get out of here?"

Ask Houdini. Ask anyone but me. McCleary ran his fingers along the periphery of the metal grating. It was about two feet square and appeared to be an opening to some sort of air duct. He couldn't tell how it was held in place; there were no visible screws or bolts. He dug his fingers under the lower edge, pulled, and a metal strip popped loose, revealing umpteen tiny screws. Rusted screws, the kind of screws whose threading had probably worn smooth. But even rusted screws could be removed with time, patience, and a little luck.

"You still carry that penlight inside your sock, Will?"

The old man grinned, reached down toward his shoe, and pulled McCleary's arm with him. "Shit, this is going to take some getting used to."

Yeah, McCleary thought. They were Siamese twins joined at the wrist.

Out came the penlight. Boone set it on the floor, then they began emptying their pockets, taking inventory. During their years on the streets, they had both developed the same habit of hiding certain potentially useful items in their clothes, their socks, their shoes, in places that a routine frisk for weapons couldn't detect. Between them they had an impressive stash: five packs of matches, a metal nail file, a butane lighter, a needle and thread, a length of fishing line, a small hook, kerchiefs, a pack of Kleenex, three iodine tablets for purifying water, two triple-A batteries for the penlight, a pocket knife, the talisman Clara Villa had given him, and the squeeze bottle of suntan lotion that Cindy had found so amusing.

"Suntan lotion, Will?"

The old man shrugged and grinned a little sheepishly. "That got in there by mistake. I never even go to the beach. Can't swim."

They wouldn't be doing much sunbathing, but what the hell. "Maybe we can use it for grease or something."

"I think the first thing we should do is try to conserve the big flashlight," Boone said. "Can you reach it?"

"I'll give it a try."

It was near the door, much too far for McCleary to reach even when Boone strained against the cuff that locked him to the grating. McCleary rigged up the fishing line and hook and cast. He snagged the flashlight on the fourth try and reeled it in. Boone switched the penlight on, McCleary turned the big flashlight off, and strung it on his belt.

They focused on the grate next. The wire mesh was too thick to see what lay on the other side—the opening to a pipe, an old AC duct, or some sort of exhaust system. But the grate and the drain in the middle of the floor were the only possible escape hatches. Also, Boone's right hand was connected to it, so they tackled the grate first.

They concentrated on the rusted area in the mesh, which lay about a third of the way down from the top. While Boone held the penlight,

McCleary used the butane lighter like a welder's torch and heated the rusted wires to either side of the handcuff until they glowed red. Then he paused and took the nail file to them, working it back and forth. He fell into a mesmerizing rhythm, the flame, the file, the flame, the file, over and over again.

Minutes melted away. The pain in his shoulder subsided to a dull, distant ache. His awareness shrank until it was nothing more than the flame, the file, the squares of wire mesh. When he paused and glanced at his watch, he was shocked to see that three hours had passed. He could hear the wind now, a distant, muted noise, like a sound effect in a movie.

He resumed and the flame on the butane lighter grew shorter and the smaller pieces of wire began to weaken, to bend, to break. When the flame finally sputtered, he resorted to matches, lighting three and four at a time. The flame wasn't as hot as the one the lighter had produced, but the mesh was already sufficiently weakened so that when Boone gave several hard jerks on the cuff it popped free.

They whooped and laughed and Boone's tired voice held something McCleary hadn't heard in it for years: hope, optimism. The air in the room was now uncomfortably warm. They couldn't strip off their windbreakers or shirts because of the handcuff that joined them, so they unzipped and unbuttoned. For the first time, McCleary got a good look at the wound in his shoulder. It was very small, as round as a dime, blackened at the edges. There was no blood, but a clear fluid leaked from it.

"Is it deep?" Boone asked, holding the penlight up as McCleary touched the skin around the wound.

"Yeah, I think so. But it's pretty clean. The skin around it is barely warm."

"Now you know what kind of fucks work for the feds. Especially for the CIA." The bitterness in his voice was reflected in his face. "Charlie never believed me when I talked about the things Garrison and I uncovered about the agency and JFK's assassination. He didn't want to hear it."

Because it was old news, Will.

"That memo the *santera* gave you got me thinking. Suppose the pharmaceutical factory they destroyed in the Libyan desert was a chemical-weapons factory, Mike?"

"Could be."

"If it was, I figure that once they realized how destruction boosted their standing in the political community, they decided to set up a sting and spread the word in certain circles that there were chemical weapons for sale."

"And Haddan bit."

"Yeah. And they must've already known through Cindy that Crandall was manufacturing the stuff."

". . . and Charlie got in the way," McCleary finished softly.

He thought of the rain, the wind, the slippery roads, the traffic. And chugging through it all was a moving van with enough cyanide in it to create a disaster that, regardless of what Jerry had said about the safety of the cylinders, would make Hurricane Albert look like a game of Tiddlywinks.

"C'mon, let's get back to work."

Instead of attempting to remove the screws that held the grate in place, they worked on enlarging the hole in the mesh. They went after it as though it were a wild, primitive beast that they intended to subdue, to conquer, to kill. They hammered at it with their shoes, pounded it with their fists, used up another two packs of matches to weaken the parts of it that resisted their assault.

They were hampered by the handcuff that joined them; sometimes Boone's hand was moving right as McCleary's was moving left. But after a while, they got the hang of it, and gradually, the entire middle section of the grating began to cave in.

When the hole was large enough to squeeze through, McCleary turned on the large flashlight and shone it around inside. He guessed it was an exhaust duct of some kind. It was big enough to crawl through—barely big enough, though. But any kind of movement was going to be a problem as long as he and Boone were connected by the handcuff.

"Lemme look," Boone said, and McCleary stepped to the side as Boone stuck his head inside the hole, then quickly pulled it out. "It's hardly big enough for one man, much less two."

"It's not like we've got a whole lot of choices. The duct or the drain, take your pick."

McCleary aimed the beam of his flashlight at the drain; his heart plunged through the cavern of his chest. Water, mud, and silt bubbled up through the drain and with it came a quivering tide of insects pushing up like something out of a Japanese horror movie. Roaches, ants, beetles, spiders, centipedes, dozens of other bugs he couldn't name, some no larger than a fingernail, others as big as his hand. They scrambled frantically in every direction, then continued to pour out in suppurating waves, in surges, a mass exodus from whatever subterranean place they had inhabited. And behind them were other kinds of creatures, frogs, toads, lizards, snakes that slithered and whipped their way through and over the living tide.

In the minutes it took McCleary and Boone to scoop their supplies off the floor and stuff things in their pockets, the area within two feet of the drain was an undulating dark body. They scrambled into the duct, into the noise of the storm. McCleary could hear it clearly now, the shriek of the wind, the rain hammering the building. They fell over each other, slammed their heads against the top of the duct, struggled to arrange their bodies in a way that would accommodate the cuff.

Once they were squatted side by side, with their backs against the right wall of the duct, they rolled pieces of Kleenex into long strips, set them on fire, and dropped them to the floor under the duct to discourage the insects from coming up the wall.

Then, with Boone in the lead, they moved awkwardly forward, into a suffocating blackness that even the beam of the large flashlight barely penetrated. McCleary could feel the walls trembling around them. He didn't know if this was the way out or the route to something worse. The only thing that mattered was movement, putting distance between them and the undulating wave below as quickly as possible, and climbing high enough into the walls to escape what he suddenly knew was happening outside.

The only explanation for the panicked bugs and wildlife was that Ocean Drive was flooding.

Flooding.

■ ■ ■

Quin felt as if she were sealed up in a space capsule that hurtled through time at luminal speeds. Landmarks flashed by and were forgotten. County lines appeared and disappeared. The rain and wind diminished in severity the farther north they went, until they encountered only periodic squalls. Depending on where they were, traffic swelled, stopped, thinned, and began to crest again.

The main north-south arteries were jammed with cars pouring out of the Keys, so Tark had driven farther west to the Sawgrass Expressway. It was the most westerly route on this side of the state, and although the traffic was heavy, it wasn't as bad as the interstate. Here they made up for the time they'd lost getting off the Keys.

Throughout the drive, they had exchanged information in much the same way she and McCleary did, in a kind of vocal shorthand. Each possessed pieces of information that the other did not, and although it wasn't a complete picture, Heckler's notebook had helped fill in the gaps.

In his strange syntax and often shaky printing, Heckler had recorded the background and the facts on how the CIA, working in conjunction with Kilner's outfit—the Hereafter, as Heckler referred to it—had used Crandall to set up Haddan. It was exactly the kind of proof Benson would need to get Crandall and his business partners indicted; her testimony and Tark's would take care of Kilner and LeFrank. At the very least, Kilner would be charged with kidnapping and Tark would emerge as the renegade hero.

Some of Heckler's information—about the explosion at Un Paso, for instance—had come to him secondhand through Dan Pisco, who was fed up with Kilner and his games, and some of it was merely speculation. Lamadero was responsible, acting on Pisco's orders, which had come from Kilner. In his final entry, recorded shortly after dinner this evening, Heckler had surmised that, owing to the threat of the hurricane, Crandall might consummate the deal before the storm struck. Given Kilner's unexpected departure for Miami, supposedly to meet with the man whom he intended to blackmail, she believed he was right.

She could think of several places where the exchange—the cyanide for the cash—might be made, but the most logical spot was the Boca Raton airport, where Haddan kept his Lear. Boca was far enough north of Albert so that the Lear could probably leave within the next several hours, head in the direction opposite to the storm's approach, and be clear of any turbulence within minutes.

It was possible, of course, that the exchange had already been made and the Lear was now somewhere over the Gulf with its lethal cargo. In that case, she and Tark would head to West Palm and ride out the storm at her house.

The problem was that she had been unable to get through to Benson or to McCleary. Since they'd gotten off the Keys, they had stopped twice so she could place calls, but the lines were tied up. She even got busy signals when she tried the operator and 911, a clear indication of the kind of chaos the storm had created. Tark was reluctant to stop again. He had a score to settle with Kilner, the man who he believed was ultimately responsible for the death of his father-in-law.

The marker for Palm Beach County flashed by on the right. Tark took the next exit and they headed east to State Road 441, then north for a quarter of a mile to Yamato Road. Traffic got heavier. They passed state police cars, power-company vehicles, ambulances. Another squall had moved inland and rain blew across the road in horizontal sheets.

Quin turned on the radio for the latest advisory. The high-pressure system that was moving down from the Carolinas was pushing Albert farther south than anticipated. He was now expected to make landfall somewhere between Key Largo and Cutler Ridge. He remained a category-four hurricane with a barometric pressure equal to that of the second-lowest on record. He was preceded by an eight-foot storm surge that was at least thirty miles long. Tides were dangerously high and severe flooding had already been reported throughout the Keys, along Miami Beach, and in low-lying inland areas in Dade County.

"All roads onto Miami Beach are now closed to eastbound traffic. If you need assistance in evacuating, please call 555-HELP. . . ." She turned the radio off, dread balled inside her like a lead weight.

"Do you have any idea where your husband is?" Tark asked, as if reading her mind.

"No."

"He'd evacuate, wouldn't he?"

"I'd like to think so. It would depend on what he was involved in. And he always thinks he has more time than he actually does."

Tark nodded. His profile was illuminated briefly by a street lamp, that long, straight nose, the curve of his chin, the expressive mouth.

And yet, pass him in a crowd and the only thing you would notice about him was his height.

But she felt, as she had several times since she'd gotten into the van, that he was wired differently. Although most investigators had hunches from time to time, the capacity in Tark seemed to be sharper, more refined, an actual sixth sense. "Why did you ask?"

He glanced at her. "I could tell you're worried."

"C'mon, Tark, it's more than that."

He shrugged, braked for a streetlight that swung in the wind like a pendulum. "Just for a second, I glimpsed an image of you and me headed over the bridge to Miami Beach. I figured the best reason we'd be going anywhere near the beach was if your husband was still over there." Then he hastily added: "But it doesn't necessarily mean anything. I had a dream before that meeting with Helga that you and I were blown through a window in Un Paso. In reality, you weren't even there."

The light turned green and he drove cautiously through the intersection. "But I was supposed to have been there that night and you *were* blown through a window."

"Look, all I'm saying, Quin, is that just because I have an impression about something doesn't mean it's happening or is going to happen, especially when it concerns other people. And when it does happen, it frequently happens differently than what I've seen."

But.

"Airport dead ahead," he announced, and killed the headlights as he turned in.

It had been five hours since they'd left Long Key.

A few lights glowed in the empty parking lot, but the runways weren't lit, the terminal building was boarded up, the tie-down area was devoid of small planes, and the hangars loomed in the wet darkness, sentinels of some lost race. The place looked abandoned. Tark swung through the lot and back onto the road.

"What's wrong?" she asked.

"I don't like it. I don't like how it feels. Let's ditch the van and go in on foot."

And she was still barefoot. "Make a U-turn and drive into the trees on the other side of the road."

A few minutes later, armed and draped in ponchos, they darted across the road to the terminal building. For a second or two, she thought she saw a flicker of light in the shuttered building. But it was probably nothing more than a reflection against the shimmering rain. After all, neither Crandall nor Haddan had access to the terminal.

They huddled under the outcropping of roof at the back of the building. The wind moaned through the line of trees that separated the airport property from the road, shaking branches until the leaves rattled. Her heart raced, blood pounded in her ears, and the longer they stood here, the more uneasy she felt.

As though they were being watched.

She wiped her hands over her face, glanced around nervously. Tark leaned close to her. "Which hangar is it?"

Quin thought back to the day she'd played chauffeur. Hadn't Cindy or someone else mentioned that Haddan kept his Lear in Hangar 12? Or was it 13? No, Hangar 10. That was what Kiara had told her. "Ten. Hangar ten. I don't know which one it is."

"I can figure it out. I used to do business up here."

In his other life, she thought.

"I'm going to have a look. Meanwhile, you get inside the terminal and go to the flight-safety office. There should be a switchboard inside that controls all the exterior lights—for the parking lot, the runway, the hangars, everything. If I'm not back in thirty minutes, start turning on lights. There's obviously still power, otherwise the parking lot would be completely dark." He unzipped the canvas bag he was carrying, removed something that he slipped into a pocket of his poncho, and handed the bag to her. "You'll find a hammer and some other tools in there to loosen the plywood on the front door so you can get in."

"Right."

Then, just like that, the darkness swallowed him.

Quin moved to the other end of the building with her back to the wall. She gripped Pisco's gun in one hand and Tark's bag in another. She was still wearing Pisco's poncho and the clothes Gracie had left her, and she was barefoot. Her daughter was somewhere in Orlando with her sister, she didn't know where McCleary was, where Flats was, if her cats were safe, if her house was safe, if the Explorer was safe. She had no ID, no money, no food. Her life was scattered across the state, and she was standing outside an airport terminal that was boarded up like a UPS crate, here because someone had killed Charlie.

This, she thought, was not the path to enlightenment.

She peered around the corner of the building. Nothing out there. She side-stepped along the front wall, the wind whipping the poncho against her legs and burning her eyes until they teared. At the door, she set the canvas bag on the ground, unzipped it, put the gun inside, and took out the hammer and a chisel. She worked the chisel under the edge of a piece of plywood and slammed it three times with the hammer. She dug her fingers under the edge to pull it off and the door suddenly swung open. It happened so fast her hands were still gripping the edge of the plywood and she stumbled into blackness, tripped over something, and sprawled on a cold floor.

The light, she thought. The light she had mistaken for a reflection.

"Get that fucking door shut," someone whispered.

A moment later, soft, dim lights came on overhead. Boots moved into her vision. She pushed up, her eyes sliding from the boots to the army fatigues to the face of the man in front of her.

That slick smile, that white hair. It was him, the perv in the blackmail photos, Elliot LeFrank. And next to him was Betty O'Toole.

■ ■ ■

Another dead end.

McCleary had lost count of the number of dead ends they had encountered. He told Boone to slide back, and minutes later they entered another duct—and encountered the bugs again. They were everywhere. They scampered over his feet, legs, chest, arms, hands, face. They were in his hair, on the back of his neck, inside his clothes. McCleary knocked them off, squashed them, crushed them, but always there were more, more. On the floor, the walls, the roof of the duct.

He set one of the handkerchiefs on fire, which held the insects at bay long enough for him and Boone to swipe at the bugs on each other and make some headway. But as soon as the flames had gone out, the goddamn things had surged forward again.

"Jesus, man," Boone shouted. "We got to do something."

McCleary rolled the last handkerchief into a long, thin sausage, handed it to Boone, and set it on fire. "Wave it around and burn away the little fuckers. I've got an idea."

"Hurry, Christ, just hurry."

McCleary pulled out the bottle of suntan lotion, squeezed a glob onto his palm and slathered it in his hair, on his face and arms and hands and neck, anywhere that skin showed. Then he slapped it on Boone as the old man kept waving the hissing torch and shouting at him to hurry up, please please. McCleary jerked back, pulling Boone with him, and squirted the lotion at the floor, the walls, the ceiling, around and around until it covered the duct in their immediate area in a thick, oozing blanket.

Goo to slide in. Goo to drown in. And drown they did, hundreds of them stuck in the stuff like black glitter in glue. Boone laughed and sobbed and scratched at his rapidly swelling hand where something had bitten him. *He's losing it fast*, McCleary thought, and yanked on the cuff. "C'mon, Will, up this way. It can't be much farther."

"*Can't* be?" His voice rolled toward the upper reaches of the musical scale. "We've been stumbling around in here for hours, Mike. Up one duct, down another, into dead ends, this fucking building has more ducts than it ever did hallways, I can tell you that. And stop jerking on this goddamn handcuff, okay? My wrist is scraped to shit, my hand hurts like a son of a bitch, my . . ."

"Shut up and move. The duct veers just ahead and it looks like it slopes upward. With any luck, we'll come out on the roof."

"The roof, oh yeah, that's great. We'll get blown off the fucking roof."

McCleary didn't reply and Boone seemed to have exhausted himself. They began inching forward again, waddling like a couple of ducks, their backs to the trembling wall. The air was hot, thick, oppressive. The stink of McCleary's own fear leaked from his pores. His mouth was parched. His muscles and bones ached from being in the same position for so long, and suddenly, all he wanted to do was stand up. Stretch. Lift his hands above his head. Feel space around him. A wave of claustrophobia swept over him, and for seconds he could barely catch his breath. Then the large flashlight in his hand started to dim and the thought of being trapped in utter blackness spurred him on.

Faster.

Faster.

The duct sloped gently upward now for a few minutes, then steeply down, then quickly up again, a little roller-coaster. But at the crest of the second rise, McCleary felt air. *Fresh air.* And the wind was much louder now, screeching, howling like a beast in pain.

He scrambled, Boone hurrying along behind him, the duct widening enough so they could raise up on their knees. The duct ended at an exhaust fan. Years of muck and dust coated the rusted grate that stood between them and the fan. But its blades spun in the whistling wind, cooling them, hurling rain in their faces. They huddled next to it, sucking at the air, licking their lips, then McCleary shifted around and slammed his feet against the edges of the grate. In seconds, the entire unit just fell away, bits of rust flying around them as the wind and rain roared in, a force so powerful it tore at his shirt and literally took his breath away.

"Hold on to my hand, Will," he shouted.

He sidled at an angle toward the opening, gripping the flashlight, Boone clutching his cuffed hand, and peered down. Five feet below was water. *Water,* for Christ's sakes. Not just a few puddles, but a rising river with debris bobbing on its surface. He couldn't tell how deep it was, but the pieces of construction equipment he'd seen earlier were still above it. Given his druthers, he would rather risk riding out the storm in a tractor than in the husk of a building that was probably going to collapse.

He tugged on the cuff and Boone crept up alongside him. McCleary leaned close to him, hand cupped around his mouth. "We're going to jump."

"Jump?" Boone scuttled back like a bug, shaking his head violently. "No way, no fucking way I'm jumping!"

McCleary grabbed him by the shoulders and shouted into his face. "Our best chance is down there!"

Boone's eyes bulged in their sockets like ripe grapes about to pop from their skins. He shouted, spittle flying from his mouth. *"Your* best chance, *your* ideas, *your* agenda, *your your your.* I'm sick of it, you hear me? Sick of it. You're just like Charlie, worse than Charlie, you got that? I can't *swim,* okay? I don't know how to swim. I'm not jumping."

And his arm flew up, the fist balled, the fist aimed. McCleary blocked the blow and did what he should have done hours ago. Punched him. Then he strung the flashlight onto his belt and heaved himself and Boone to the lip of the opening. McCleary hugged the old man tightly as he groaned and struggled, and then he jumped.

He landed hard on his right side, Boone shrieking above the roar of the wind, Boone fighting, completely panicked. They sank, McCleary released him, and the old man leaped up, sputtering for air, jerking on the cuff. McCleary grabbed him around the waist, trapping his arms against him, and lifted him out of the knee-high water. He stumbled blindly forward, unable to see anything. Too dark, too much rain, too much wind, too much of everything. It was as if all the excess in the world had been dumped here at once, here in a back alley on South Beach.

Things bumped up against his legs, pieces of furniture, cardboard boxes, a trash can, plywood, debris. He tripped and they pitched sideways, into something solid, and he lost his hold on Boone. The old man slipped, went down, and nearly took McCleary with him. He yanked on his right arm and gripped Boone's shirt with his left hand and he surfaced, coughing, sobbing, spitting water.

McCleary somehow managed to scramble inside whatever piece of equipment he'd fallen against, a tractor, a bulldozer, he couldn't tell what it was, and sprawled across the seat, levers, gears, Boone on top of him. The wind slammed the door and they lay there, too exhausted to move, to speak, the storm howling around them.

26

Tark found Hangar 10 easily enough; the years hadn't dimmed his memory of Boca airport.

The building had no windows and an ordinary-sized door on the far side. If the layout was the same as other hangars, then the door would open into an office or a tool-storage area. He hoped so, at any rate, because unless there was a wall to buffer the sound of the wind, his arrival would be anything but clandestine.

He picked the lock, gripped Lamadero's gun with one hand, turned the knob with the other. He opened the door just enough to slip inside, into a silent darkness that smelled of the past. Oil, metal, planes, lazy Saturday afternoons talking shop with other pilots. Definitely a tool-storage room.

He shut the door quickly, dropped to a crouch. The storm sounded distant, muted, like a storm on a television somewhere in the building. He saw a crack of light on the other side of the dark that marked the door that opened into the hangar. He could just make out the tools to his left.

Tark moved in a straight line to the hangar door, listened. A radio. Voices. Someone laughed. Good, keep laughing. He slipped along the wall for several feet, making sure there were no windows that faced the interior of the hangar, then he lit several matches at once and held them up. It was a tool room, all right, but lining the wall to his right and left were slim metal cylinders.

Just as Heckler had described in his notebook.

Thirty of them. Filled with cyanide.

Tark blew out the matches. He could still hear the radio, but not the voices. Now, he thought, now.

He turned the knob, cracked the door, peered inside. Subdued light. The back of the moving van was in front of him and the Lear was on the other side of it, nose to the hangar doors. He couldn't see the radio but two dark-haired men were clearly visible. They were unloading wooden crates from the Lear's cargo hold. One of them had the musculature of a professional bodybuilder, thighs like tree trunks. Someone's bodyguard, Tark ventured. The other man was foreign, probably an Iraqi. An older man as bald as a radish walked over to them with a roll of labels that they proceeded to slap onto the crates.

Tark recognized him: the jogger from the beach on Long Key. The guy he now knew was Kilner.

Hi, shithead. Lights out time. For Alfie.

Tark darted to the moving van. He moved to its left corner and now he could see parts of two other cars parked in front of the van. And he could see the series of glassed-in office cubicles along the left wall, all of them dark except for one near the front. There sat Larry Crandall, the blonde who was his chauffeur, and two men. Tark guessed one of them was Haddan and the other was Rau. Considering what was in the back room, things looked pretty friendly and laid back, the men casually dressed, yukking it up and drinking from plastic-foam cups. Like it was just another business transaction.

Then the blonde got up and walked over to the door of the office, and stepped out. "Hey, Jerry," she called. "You and Ihsan can start packing up those crates."

The radio went off.

Tark ducked back inside the storage room.

． ． ．

Kilner detested the tone of her voice. It suggested that he was her employee, her lackey, her minion. Never mind that she played the role so convincingly no one had questioned his presence. Crandall's implicit trust in her hadn't given Rau or Haddan any reason to suspect he was anything other than what he appeared to be, a hired hand. Never mind that. Once they were out of here, he would set her straight.

So for now Kilner stacked wooden crates, pausing now and then to smooth down the labels that said: FRESH PRODUCE, KEEP REFRIGERATED, CRANDALL CHERRY FARMS. Then he and Ihsan, the Lear's pilot, began to line the crates with Styrofoam so the cylinders could be sealed inside. He didn't allow himself to think beyond the next few minutes. He knew the routine by heart, what he would do, what she would do. Once Haddan had flown off, Crandall and Rau would supposedly stick around to lock up the place and divide the cash. And that was when he and Cindy would make their move.

She had everything figured out, he thought, except what to do in the event that something went wrong.

． ． ．

War games, Quin thought. That's what this was. They had converted the terminal building into a regular command post with radios, computers, weapons, and Christ knew what else. There were half a dozen men in fatigues, all of them armed, prepared to move on the hangar, she guessed, as soon as the signal came down from Elliot LeFrank.

LeFrank, who talked as if she were a tourist in a government facility. He said a lot but told her nothing as he and Betty walked her deeper into the building. Betty hadn't said a goddamn thing, but she kept looking at Quin with haunted, liquid eyes, quick, furtive glances, as if she expected her to suddenly turn into something else, a frog, a witch on a broomstick.

Quin finally interrupted LeFrank's monologue. "Excuse my bluntness, but you don't have any right to hold me here."

"Hold you here?" His smile widened and he laughed. "No one's holding you, Ms. St. James. You're in here for your own protection."

"Why's she here?" Quin stabbed her thumb at Betty. "For her protection or yours?"

"Betty works for me." As though Betty weren't present. "And fortunately she remembered that we'd still be paying her bills if and when Crandall fired her." He flashed that same broad, irritating smile, that politician's smile, and glanced at Betty. "Right, Betty?"

Her eyes flashed with anger. "It would've been a lot easier if you'd told me Cindy was a plant, Elliot."

"We've already been over all that." He waved her objection away, started to say something else, but Quin butted in.

"Where's Kilner?"

LeFrank's smile shrank and she suddenly understood he didn't have anything to do with her confinement at the compound, that Kilner had acted alone, and began to perceive the connections among these people. Betty: LeFrank's personal mole in Crandall's organization, who had been screwing the Buddha himself and had gotten in a bit too deep; Cindy, the agency's plant in Crandall's outfit, who had teamed up with Kilner for Christ knew what reason; the power struggle between Kilner and LeFrank, the blackmail photos; Heckler, the wild card who had passed Charlie the information; Tark, hired by the agency to retrieve the stolen information. Then there were Crandall and his schemes, Charlie and his secrets, Benson and his agenda, and herself and McCleary.

She started to laugh, she couldn't help herself. LeFrank and Betty exchanged a look that made it clear they believed she had lost her mind. "Kilner's here," LeFrank said. "What do you know about him?"

"Nothing." Her laughter bubbled away. "Nothing. He's just a name." One of many. "How did you know the deal was going down tonight?"

"I told him," Betty replied. Then, with an indignant lilt to her voice, she added, "That's my job."

It had more to do with who Betty thought Crandall was screwing, Quin mused, but didn't bother saying it aloud.

"I'd, uh, like to get a statement from you on your involvement in all this, Ms. St. James," said LeFrank.

"I don't have anything to say."

"On the contrary, I suspect you have a great deal to say. But you don't have to give the statement to me." He stopped at the door of the flight service office, where eight men were monitoring radios, computers, and surveillance equipment. At the moment, they were all listening to voices coming over a radio. Voices she recognized as Crandall's, Rau's, and Haddan's. "Where do we stand?" LeFrank asked no one in particular.

"They're loading up," replied one man.

"Then radio the men in hangars to either side of ten and move out." LeFrank hooked his thumbs in his belt and hoisted his slacks. "Let's make this clean and quick. And, Captain, notify your boys to move in as well. Lights but no sirens."

"Already done."

The Captain turned. It was Benson, eyes widening with disbelief, Benson who shouldn't have been here. He was as shocked to see her as she was to see him and hurried over, hugged her, held her at arm's length and shook his head as though he couldn't quite grasp that she was here, that she was alive.

"We thought," he began, then shook his head again. "I don't know what the hell we thought."

"You can give your statement to Captain Benson," said LeFrank.

Benson moved her out into the hall, away from LeFrank and Betty, away from everyone. He started to say something, but she interrupted him. "That asshole in there is behind the whole setup, Tim. And right now one of your main witnesses to that setup is inside the hangar."

He frowned, blinking as if to clear his vision. "What're you talking about?"

"Tark." She pulled Heckler's notebook from the pocket of her poncho and thrust it into Benson's hands. "Heckler's journal. Written while he was imprisoned at Kilner's compound. Ask LeFrank about the compound, Tim. Ask him about Haddan's pharmaceutical factory in the Libyan desert, destroyed by the CIA in 1990. The factory that was producing chemical weapons, not drugs."

Benson moved down the hall, paging through the notebook, then pocketed it. "Will you give me a statement?"

"Of course I will."

"LeFrank claims Kilner went off the deep end, started calling the shots on his own, that he was ruling a little kingdom down there on Long Key."

"I have some photos in a van outside that'll make it pretty clear who went off the deep end."

Benson rubbed his chin. "I can't stop what's going to happen in the hangar, Quin. But I can sure as hell open an investigation when this part of it's over."

"You're not going to have an investigation if Tark gets killed."

Benson blanched, told her to stay put, and started to turn away, but she caught his arm. "Where's Mac? Have you heard anything from him?"

The stricken expression in his eyes frightened her. "He and Will were supposed to be with Bean at the North Miami office. But I talked to Bean a while ago and he said they never returned from the beach. He started down there to look for them, then heard the beach was closed off, so he turned around and gave me a call. He couldn't get through for a while and by the time he did and the call was patched through, there was nothing I could do about it."

"He's still on Miami Beach? Is that what you're saying?"

"He might be, I don't know for sure."

"Where on the beach, Tim? Where the hell were they going?"

"Bean didn't know." He gave her hand a quick squeeze and moved quickly into the flight service office. She stood there alone, in the twilit hall, thinking of McCleary on the beach, somewhere on Miami Beach, in 150-mile-an-hour winds.

■ ■ ■

Tark was behind the door when it opened. The light came on and two men entered the room. He waited until they stopped, then he slipped out, slammed the door, and smiled as they spun around.

The Iraqi's hand went to his jacket and Tark shot him through the head. As he was falling, the old familiar exhilaration swept through Tark, that sweet darkness, his constant companion for the last decade, the power of life and death. And then it was gone, gone in a flash when Kilner's arm moved, going for a weapon.

"Don't even think about it, Kilner. Lock your hands on your head."
He backed up to the door, threw the dead bolt, and gestured with the
gun. "Out the side door. You and I are going for a walk."

"Look here, I don't know who you are, but that shot you fired just
blew a two-year . . ."

"Yeah, yeah, a two-year surveillance by the CIA and the Hereafter. That is what your little outfit's called, right? The Hereafter?"
He laughed. "Nice name."

"Fernando Gabriel," Kilner breathed. "That's who you are."

"Tark. John Tark. And that bar you ordered blown up belonged to
my father-in-law, Alfonso Ruiz. Is the picture clearer now, Kilner?
Move your ass before I blow off your fucking kneecaps."

He moved, talking fast. "Listen, you've got it all wrong. I didn't
give the order to blow up the restaurant. That was Lamadero's doing.
Elliot LeFrank is the man you want. This was his project from the
beginning. He conceived it. He set Haddan up. He . . ."

"And I suppose that's why you blackmailed him."

He stopped a foot from the door and turned slowly, very slowly,
hands still locked on top of his bald head. His face was the color of old
bread and his small eyes had narrowed to dark points. "Blackmail?"
Oh, so innocent. "What're you talking about?"

"Open the door."

"I'd like an answer."

Tark fired at his feet and he leaped back. "Open the goddamn
door."

He did. The wind slammed it against the wall and Kilner suddenly
lurched through and charged left, toward the runways. As Tark
sighted down the barrel, aiming for his back, for that magic spot
between his shoulderblades that would blow his heart to smithereens,
blue lights flashed against the side of the next hangar. A voice boomed
from a mike, competing with the howl of the wind: "Lay down your
weapons and come out. . . ."

Do it, whispered the voice of darkness. *He deserves it, he killed
Alfie, do it do it. . . .*

Tark's eyes burned with emotion for Alfie, his wife, his daughter,
for the family he had lost. But the man he had become in the years
since, the man known as Fernando Gabriel, was as dead as they were,
and it was time to bury them all.

He dropped the gun, jammed his hands into the pockets of his windbreaker, and walked through the wet wind toward the flashing blue lights.

■ ■ ■

McCleary knew he was supposed to be doing something, but he couldn't remember what it was. He didn't want to remember. He wanted to sink back into sleep, deeper into the darkness, the silence, into the softness of this other place where his sister was speaking to him. Saying something he couldn't understand. The noise, that was the problem. What was the noise? Where was it coming from? Like static. That was it. Cat was on the radio and the reception was bad. Turn the dial, change the station, c'mon, Cat, talk, say something, please . . .

Rise and shine, bro
Can't hear you
Trust no one
Please

Then there was another voice, Charlie's voice coming from the old woman, *Christ, Mac, be careful, be careful, you've got no idea . . .*

"Wake up, Mike, Jesus, I'm sorry, I didn't mean to . . ."

Boone. Shaking him. Pleading with him. Boone's voice crackling. He lifted his head and the pain in his body woke up, a litany of sharp stabs, dull aches, throbs, stings, sprains, itches. His mouth was a sewer. His clothes were stuck to him like gauze. He knuckled his eyes and his joints screeched, the noise of metal grinding against metal. Bugs. Duct. Jump. Water. Bulldozer. Bingo.

Bulldozer. He was in the cab of a bulldozer. His legs seemed to be tangled in something, branches, sticks, no, levers, they were tangled in levers. He and Boone were squashed into a seat meant for one, handcuffed together, and the old man's breath was hot and damp and fetid against his face.

"Christ, Will." McCleary shoved him to the side and grabbed the pathetic penlight from Boone's left hand, his free hand, and flashed it around in front of him.

The beam weaved, a drunk making his way home.

McCleary steadied his hand and tried to make sense of the instrument panel in front of him. But Boone was shifting around, alternately laughing and weeping and babbling about the rising water, the screaming wind, the insects, Charlie, and he couldn't concentrate, couldn't focus. "Shut up!" McCleary shouted at him.

Boone wrenched back as though McCleary had struck him. His hair was plastered against his head, distorting its size and shape, blood had crusted in the corner of his mouth, his lip was swelling, his eyes were wild, his face was drenched in sweat. "Water's rising, Mac." Hissing. He was hissing like a fucking snake. "Get us outta here, okay? Can you do that? Can you figure out how this thing works? Please, okay? Please? I'll do anything you say. I don't want to drown."

"Get out of my face." Shoving him. "Stay put."

Light on the instrument panel. Bad light, puny light, too small, too small. Shine here, shine there, ignition button no key needed, punch that button, jerk that lever, go motherfucker go. It sputtered. It kicked. It died. Again. Again. Hear that wind? Hear that rain? Hear that water rising? Hear this old man weeping, raging, telling?

Telling: listen to what he's telling.

". . . Charlie knew the truth, Mike, at least I think he did, yeah, I think he knew most of the truth about Crandall, the feds and their setup, the cyanide, but he didn't want to share what he knew with me. Uh-uh, no way, the only thing he gave a shit about was the Sea Witch, that's it, just the Witch with a bunch of old farts living there who half the time don't know their names, you've seen them, you know what they're like, and so what, Mike? So what?

"We both know that if Crandall didn't get the place someone else like him would've sooner or later, but no, Charlie wouldn't budge, Mike. He told me he'd contacted a guy he knew who was going to get him proof, proof he could use against Crandall. That must've been Heckler. But he wouldn't tell me the whole thing, Mike, he wouldn't. I knew some of it from Helga, but after a while even she wouldn't tell me anything. And . . . and Charlie wouldn't go public the way I wanted him to, the way he should have, the way he should have. And then when I knew he was going to meet with Heckler, I mean, what could I do? What choice did I have?

"He was so relentless, Mike, you don't have any idea how relentless Charlie could be. I met Helga first, that should have entitled me to something, to some say in how the information would be used, but no, uh-uh, Charlie just took over."

Boone's voice rang in McCleary's skull as the bulldozer shuddered to life again. McCleary slammed the heel of his hand against a lever, any lever would do, push it forward, pull it back, forward and back, again and again.

"Mike? Mike? Did you hear me?" Boone grabbed his arm, shook it like a kid demanding attention, shook it like the desperate old man that he was.

"I heard you, Will." So calm, so utterly calm, the calmness of revulsion. The bulldozer groaned backward. McCleary slammed his hand against the lever again and the bulldozer shuddered off the mound on which it had been resting. Lights. Where were the lights?

"You see, don't you? I needed the information he had on Crandall's operation, on the CIA's involvement. He kept a memo for himself but that didn't spell out all of it, so I needed the photos, too, Mike, I knew you'd help me find them. The photos and the memo were the proof I needed. I mean, it was the whole Garrison thing all over again. It was. That people won't believe you, that they'll laugh at you, think you're nuts, but you've got the truth, the truth, Mike, that's what Charlie didn't understand. That's what Charlie didn't care about, about the truth."

Vindication, McCleary thought. That's what it was about for Boone. Vindication of his past. "He cared enough about the truth to die for it, Will." Gas, give it a little gas. "He cared enough to mail what he had to people who wouldn't fuck him over." Into the alley now, the bulldozer's blade raised up out of the water. "He cared enough to let you pull the fucking trigger, Will."

Boone, who owned a .38.

Who had shot it the night they were chased on the university campus.

Who had found Charlie.

Who had the perfect alibi.

"Let me go, Mike." He grabbed McCleary's arm. "You don't have to tell anyone. You can let me go. You can. I'm too old to go to prison. I'll die there. Let Crandall take the rap. Let . . ."

McCleary shook his hand away. "Christ, Will, Charlie thought you were his friend."

Boone's hands suddenly closed around McCleary's throat, thumbs squeezing as he shouted, his body angled over McCleary's, his knees digging into his groin. The old man's panic had imbued him with astonishing strength, and the cab was too cramped for McCleary to get the leverage he needed. Stars exploded in the backs of his eyes, his lungs screamed for air. He shifted, trying to rise up, to throw Boone off, and his hip hit the engine-speed control lever. The bulldozer lurched forward abruptly and Boone's grip briefly loosened, giving McCleary the respite he needed.

He grabbed Boone by the hair, wrenching his head back, and shoved him to the side. His body slammed against the door, knocking it open, and Boone tumbled back, pulling McCleary with him.

The old man dangled legs first, screaming, over the bulldozer's tracks, the water swallowed him to the ankles, and the wind whipped him back and forth, a metronome ticking at a speed too fast to count. McCleary tightened his grip on Boone's forearms, but the wind exerted a force like gravity on his body and McCleary began to slip. He shouted at Boone to get his feet on the tracks, to push up with his feet, but the old man was beyond hearing anything.

The bulldozer swung left and McCleary slid closer to the door, the wind blinding him, rushing over him, the door swinging. Then the door slammed shut against his hands, swung open again, and suddenly the weight wasn't there anymore. The chain between the cuffs had snapped or the door had hit it just right, he didn't know. He scrambled back away from the door, shot upright, grabbed the levers, and stopped the bulldozer. Then, gripping the edge of the door, he swung outside, shouting for Boone.

Debris bobbed through the wash of the machine's headlights. A table, a living-room chair, a filing cabinet, a playground slide. He shouted again for Boone, saw nothing. He started the bulldozer and turned it around so the lights shone east, where he had fallen. But there was no sign of him and the water was rising fast, churning, rushing south.

McCleary slammed the door, turned the bulldozer northward. He fixed his hands to the levers and his eyes on the beams of the headlights. "Get me out of here," he whispered. "Just get me out of here."

■ ■ ■

The preliminary damage reports began rolling in early the next morning to the local TV channels. Quin and Tark watched on a tiny television in the terminal building, where they had spent what remained of the night.

The news was sketchy at first, reported by broadcasters who looked as haggard and old as Quin felt. Flooding on Miami Beach, many areas without power, downed trees, downed electrical wires, roof damage to some buildings, windows blown out. All the things you expected to hear. But the consensus of opinion was that Albert hadn't been The Big One, he was moving too rapidly to cause the massive damage everyone had expected.

But then she saw it from the air, from inside a chopper Benson had procured from the Palm Beach County Sheriff's Department. She saw it as Tark piloted the chopper south, Benson in the passenger seat, herself crammed in the back, saw it with her face pressed against the window. First, the power lines that crisscrossed roads and neighborhoods; the fallen trees, hundred-year-old banyans uprooted and flung aside; then a neighborhood just north of Miami that had been leveled, flattened to a rubble of concrete, wood, glass, as if a bomb had been dropped in the center of it.

No one spoke. The radio crackled. Tark swung in over downtown Miami, where the once-seductive skyline was now irreparably changed. The tops of some of the tall glass buildings were gone, lopped off as if by some huge and voracious creature. Others, yet standing, looked like checkerboards, their windows blown out here and there in a pattern that seemed anything but random. And still others were completely destroyed, wiped out from top to bottom, leaving yawning gaps in the skyline.

Major thoroughfares were blocked by fallen trees, abandoned vehicles, power lines that swung in the blustery air. In some neighborhoods, people were outside, clustered together, as though their nearness to each other would somehow mitigate the shock of what surrounded them. But on other blocks there were no people, no animals, nothing moved.

Along U.S.1, a half-mile section of the MetroRail had simply caved in, collapsed like a house of cards, and yet to either side of it the rail was intact. The old Sears building was still standing, but everything around it was rubble. Bay Front, a ritzy shopping area that overlooked Biscayne Bay, looked as if it had been bulldozed. These were just the things she noticed immediately, the details that leaped out at her because she knew the landmarks. But everywhere her gaze paused, at every corner, every intersection, at every block, the unimagined breathed and pulsed in living color, the aftermath of a violence that seemed to be sentient, cunning, and ruthless.

The chopper's shadow glided over the ruin, and with every block they passed, her dread grew. Kilner and Cindy Youngston had left McCleary and Boone in the freezer of the Tuttle Inn. They had laughed when they had told Benson, *laughed,* and of course it wouldn't be standing, how could it? How?

They passed over the bridge. Damage was bad, but not as bad as it was on the mainland. Most of it seemed to be from water rather than wind, islands of sand and shells left on porches and steps and streets when the sea had receded; blocks filled with debris that the storm surge had swept from one place and deposited in another; and a low-lying area two blocks square that included Washington Avenue, which was still under three feet of water.

Ocean Drive resembled a long, discolored river, from which buildings rose like a child's sand castles, proud but scarred. The Carlyle, the Edison, the Neon Flamingo, the hotels that had survived four decades of hurricanes, were damaged but still standing. Mappy's Café had made it. Mango's Café had made it. And around the corner, Salgado's Market appeared to be intact but damaged.

Farther north, on the eleven-hundred block, Crandall's block, the Sea Witch stood alone, a watchful sentinel encompassed by the ruin of Crandall's vision. The Tuttle Inn was buried beneath timber, metal, concrete, and water lapped at its remains. Nothing moved down there but the water as the breeze skipped over it, rippling the surface like aluminum.

Since most of the beach had been washed away, Tark landed the chopper in the wet sand of what had formerly been a children's playground, two blocks south of the Tuttle Inn. As Quin climbed out of the chopper, she was struck by the absence of human noise, a vast quiet that seemed to stretch like a thin, frail net for miles. There was only the sound of the wind, the crash of waves. They made their way on foot, weaving through an obstacle course of debris that littered the ocean side of the street. Fallen palms, plywood, glass, clothes, a rocking chair, a mattress, a child's rubber ball, wooden boxes, pillows, chunks of concrete.

They waded across Ocean Drive, the water thigh-deep and filled with fish that bumped up against Quin's legs. The loafers she wore, which had been given to her by a cop early this morning, were too big and filled quickly with sand and seaweed. But they protected her feet from nails and glass so she kept them on. They made soft, sucking sounds as she emerged from the water and hurried over a mound of sand and shells.

She stopped at the edge of the lake that had filled the emptiness around the Tuttle Inn and shouted for McCleary. Her voice skipped like a stone along the surface of the quiet. She stepped into the water and shouted again, her hands cupped to her mouth, her eyes darting around, her ears straining for his answering call. But she heard Benson, then Tark, then nothing but the wild, frantic beat of her own heart, telling her what she already suspected, that McCleary wasn't here.

Quin headed to the left of the ruin, where the water wasn't as deep. She kept glancing at the Sea Witch, as if a part of her expected to see McCleary's face peering from one of the upstairs windows. She desperately needed sleep, her eyes burned, her throat ached with dryness, with fear. She would go as far as the next street, she thought, then turn back. She imagined herself repeating this day after day, flying into a neighborhood, landing, searching, leaving again when it got too dark to see.

Had he and Boone gotten off the beach? Been caught somewhere else? Or were they somewhere under the rubble, crushed and dead?

She stopped on the next street, the water cutting her off at the calves, and shouted his name. She heard the echo of her own voice and then the chatter of an approaching helicopter. It swooped into view, black and yellow like a bumblebee, CHANNEL 4 NEWS bright and shimmering against its side. It hovered four or five hundred feet above her, and when Tark and Benson reached her, it lifted and flew on. In the wake of its noise, she heard a deep rumbling.

"What the hell," Benson muttered.

Tark pointed at the end of the street. "There!"

It crawled around the corner, a yellow metal beast splattered with mud, its glass-enclosed cab rising from it like a crab's eye, its blade shoving water and debris along in front of it. People were clinging to its open doors, four, five, maybe as many as half a dozen, all of them shouting, waving, whooping with delight. Even before it stopped, Quin knew, she knew and stumbled toward it laughing, sobbing, everything else blurring at the edges like an old photo. She forgot about Tark, Benson, about where she was. There was only the bulldozer as it pulled up short and McCleary, jumping into the street with the people he'd rescued, McCleary splashing toward her through knee-high water, and then the reality of his arms, his chest, his beard rough against her face, his voice whispering her name, whispering, "Let's go home."

Epilogue

July 16

Dear friends,

    *St. James & McCleary Investigations is proud to
announce that John G. Tark has joined the firm as
an associate investigator. He brings eleven years
of international experience in the recovery of lost
and stolen property and locating missing persons.*

    *Also joining us for the remainder of the summer,
as John Tark's assistant, is Roger Darren (R.D.)
Aikens.*

                All the best,
                Quin St. James
                Mike McCleary